T0305021

# FIREFIGHT

*By Tom Wood*

The Hunter
The Enemy
The Game
Better Off Dead
The Darkest Day
A Time to Die
The Final Hour
Kill For Me
A Knock at the Door
A Quiet Man
Traitor
Blood Debt

*Ebook short stories*
Bad Luck in Berlin
Gone By Dawn

# FIREFIGHT

## One hitman in the
## battle of his life

# TOM WOOD

SPHERE

SPHERE

First published in Great Britain in 2024 by Sphere

1 3 5 7 9 10 8 6 4 2

A CIP catalogue record for this book
is available from the British Library.

Hardback ISBN 978-0-7515-8490-5
Trade paperback ISBN 978-0-7515-8491-2

Typeset in Sabon by M Rules
Printed and bound in Great Britain by
Clays Ltd, Elcograf S.p.A.

Papers used by Sphere are from well-managed forests
and other responsible sources.

Sphere
An imprint of
Little, Brown Book Group
Carmelite House
50 Victoria Embankment
London EC4Y 0DZ

An Hachette UK Company
www.hachette.co.uk

www.littlebrown.co.uk

For Sonya

# PART ONE

PART ONE

# ONE

A bar in Rotterdam that met Victor's requirements was hard to find. Too busy and it would be difficult to keep track of who was coming and going. Too quiet and an enemy might be tempted to use it as a strike point, striding through the entrance to fire an automatic weapon or spraying rounds through a window in a drive-by. This bar hit the sweet spot between those extremes. Located near a theatre, two-thirds of the establishment was a brasserie specialising in both pre- and after-show dinners. The remaining third was a separate cocktail bar, busiest early in the evening with after-work drinkers. Approaching closing time, the brasserie was still loud with diners eating late and the many waiting staff serving them, while the bar had plenty of tables and booths unoccupied. Victor sat at the bar, which was perpendicular to the entrance. He could not see it from his position, with interior walls separating the bar from the brasserie. Yet, from the mirror behind the bar itself, he could watch the gap in the wall that fed the hallway separating the two halves of the business.

He nursed a gin and tonic, sipping with enough infrequency for its alcoholic content to be metabolised by the enzymes secreted by his liver before it could have any impact on his cognitive abilities. And though he had only ever consumed to excess in the protective environment of one of his secure abodes, it was essential to maintain his tolerance. An assassin who could not handle his liquor was a dead man walking.

On many occasions he gave off enough subtle cues in his body language that most people left him alone. Sometimes those signals were not strong enough, and he found himself being talked at by a person who was too unselfconscious or too drunk to realise he wanted no part of the conversation.

Every so often he found himself wanting company, and adjusted his manner to encourage it.

Victor saw her draw near because no one ever came within his personal space without him noticing.

Maybe thirty. In bars with flattering lighting and due to the prevalence of non-invasive cosmetic procedures, it was getting harder and harder for him to determine someone's age. This woman could have been anywhere between twenty-five and thirty-five. Like him, she wore a suit, hers with a subtle pinstripe of pale grey. Her blouse was sky blue, which accentuated her eyes. She had hair of a mid-brown colour, parted at the centre and hanging straight before it curled a little at the ends just above her clavicles. In the heart of the city, with its many offices and financial institutions, she seemed like any number of businesswomen. Maybe a banker. Perhaps a human resources manager. She appeared relaxed and confident, and it was no surprise when she initiated conversation.

'My friends will only drink rosé,' she said with a tone of disdain but not malice. A Dane by her accent. She wasn't yet looking his way, merely letting out her thoughts in words for him to hear. 'But I need something a little more grown-up.'

Even when politeness did not help his disguise of normalcy, Victor liked to be polite, so he humoured her with a response.

'I recommend a gin and tonic.'

Manners cost nothing, he had been told over and over again a long time ago, and although long ago he had heeded the lesson only to avoid the punishment for rudeness, it was a sentiment he did his best to abide by still.

She threw him a glance. 'Not a bad idea. Any particular gin?'

'How's your constitution?'

'Iron.'

'Then ask for the Botanist.'

Turning to meet his eyes for the first time, she said, 'I will, thank you.'

When a bartender took her order, she asked for a light tonic to go with it.

The bartender was a big, heavyset guy who would have looked too young to work in such an establishment without the thin, neat goatee beard. He wore a black shirt buttoned up at the collar, black trousers and shoes. The waiting staff serving in the brasserie were distinguished by their white half-aprons. A hostess in a tailored black suit stood behind a high, brass-topped desk and directed visitors to either the bar or the brasserie, depending on their desires and reservations.

'I'm Emilie,' the Danish woman said, offering a hand to Victor once the bartender had left to prepare her drink.

Victor took a light grip of her hand and shook it. 'I'm Ken.'

'Very nice to meet you, Ken.'

'Likewise. How's your evening?'

She glanced back over her shoulder and gestured to the entranceway. 'Our late supper has gone on long enough. Everyone needs to get the last train home and try to convince their partners they only intended to have one drink, but the boss *insisted* they stay for another.'

'Nice work if you can get it, I suppose.'

'That's banking for you. And what do you do for a living, Ken?'

He had a range of dull occupations he could lay claim to, if he was following protocol. Sometimes, however, Victor enjoyed breaking his own rules.

He said, 'I'm a professional assassin.'

She hesitated for a moment, eyebrows pinched closer, then smiled as she settled into what had to be an obvious joke. 'Ooo, exciting. I figured you for some typical city worker like me, so this is most definitely an upgrade. Are you on a mission right now?'

'We call them contracts. But no, I'm cooling my heels between jobs.'

'Fascinating. How many people have you killed?'

'I'd tell you, but I wouldn't want it to come off as boastful.'

'So you're prolific then,' she said, still smiling. 'Killed anyone famous?'

'Define fame.'

'I don't know – celebrities, movie stars ... royals.'

'Then, no,' he told her. 'I generally don't accept jobs with high-profile targets.'

'How come?'

'The less exposure my work has, the longer I'll stay alive.'

'Very shrewd,' she said. 'Is it your main employment, or do you have another job? Like a double life? Pharmacist by day, killer by night?'

'This is all I do,' he answered. 'There's no room for anything else in this line of work.'

The bartender returned with her gin and tonic. The gin was served in a cut-glass highball with lots of ice and a thick wedge of lime. She thanked him, took a small sip, considered the flavour for a moment, and then looked Victor's way. 'Not bad,' she said. 'Not bad at all.'

'Glad you like it.'

'Come to think of it,' she began, 'I'm not sure which is actually the more morally corrupt profession: a banker or a hitman.'

'I'm not a fan of that term.'

'How come?'

'I don't like euphemisms when it comes to my line of work,' he said. 'It all seems a little immature. I kill, I don't hit. I'm a killer.'

'How much would you charge to kill me?'

'It's more a case of whether your enemies are offering enough for me to consider killing you.'

'That's what it comes down to, then? Money?'

'What else is there?'

She shrugged. 'You could just kill bad people and not the good ones.'

'Who decides who is bad and who is good in that scenario? Me?'

She thought for a moment. 'I guess so.'

'But I'm a killer,' he said. 'Who am I to judge anyone else?'

'If you only kill bad people, then you're actually doing some good.'

'If I'm the arbiter of morality here but also committing immoral acts, then I'm not sure that passes muster.'

She laughed. 'I'm trying, okay? This is the first time I've hit on an assassin.'

'You're hitting on me?'

The smile became something more self-deprecating and shyer. 'That was my intention, but you threw me off my game with this whole joke of yours.'

'Then I apologise profusely. Please continue to hit on me, and I'll try not to put you off again.'

'Oh, I think it's too late now. I think you've blown your chance.' She picked up her drink from the bar and raised it his way. 'Nice chatting to you.'

'And to you too.'

'I think you're onto something there, sir,' the bartender said after she had gone.

Victor asked, 'What makes you say that?'

'You weren't watching, but she looked back before she left. That's always a sign.'

'Too late now,' Victor said.

The bartender pursed his lips. 'She'll be back, guaranteed.'

Victor went to reply but felt the vibration from his latest burner phone. Only one person had the number, so he knew the unknown number meant Lambert was calling.

'Excuse me,' Victor said to the bartender and then answered the phone.

'Roman, my boy,' his broker began. 'I hope this is a good time to talk.'

'It'll do.'

'Great,' Lambert continued, 'because the details of your next assignment have come through. The client needs you in Bucharest, which I hear is lovely at this time of year.'

'You heard right. Give me the highlights.'

'Will do, but first, are you okay? You sound a little tired.'

There seemed to be genuine concern in Lambert's voice, which made Victor uncomfortable, so he said, 'I'm fine.'

Although they had not known one another for long, Lambert could tell a deflection when he heard one.

'What happened in Belgium?'

# TWO

*Last night*

The assassin attacked with rapid, downward stabs of his knife to the head or neck, followed by sweeping slashes aimed below the ribs. Victor used his forearms to parry the incoming stabbing blows, hitting up at his opponent's elbow or laterally into the wrist to prevent the knife's point from reaching its target. Backward steps created distance, so the subsequent slashes fell short, but his enemy was so fast, his transition from the downward stabs to the horizontal slashes was so fluid that the blade cut Victor's suit jacket and dress shirt several times.

Sensing imminent blood being drawn, the assassin pressed his assault, forcing Victor into a continuous retreat. With his enemy facing him side-on, left hand trailing behind and out of reach, Victor had limited options for countering until he had mastered timing the knifeman.

'Who sent you?' The assassin was confused, unable to comprehend why someone was trying to kill him – why he was now on the receiving end of a contract instead of the one executing it. 'Tell me, and maybe I'll let you live.'

Victor remained silent. There was nothing to be gained from conversing with his target. He was here to complete a job, not to chit-chat.

His disarmed pistol – an FN Five-seveN – lay somewhere nearby, unseen in the darkness. Even if he knew where it had ended up, scooping it off the floor would only result in six inches of steel through the top of his skull.

Light from streetlamps seeped through the whitewashed windowpanes in diffused swathes of orange, and in thin intense beams where the paint had scratched or peeled. Half-buried underground, the windows of the closed-down bakery were high on one wall, near the ceiling. Where the light did not reach, the rest of the space was almost black.

In a small town twenty miles outside Brussels, the bakery was tucked out of the way in a commercial neighbourhood. A good spot to lie low after a job, Victor thought. Had their roles been reversed, he could imagine himself selecting such a place.

'Who sent you?'

They moved in and out of the darkness, some attacks catching the light on the knife's blade in sharp glints of orange, some just a blur in the shadows.

Although the establishment's electricity and gas supply had been cut off, Victor could hear a dripping tap between the scrape of footsteps and the *swoosh* of the assassin's weapon.

He backtracked through the baking trays, dishes and pans scattered across the flooring from when he had wrestled with the assassin, each disarming the other's gun in the close confines before either weapon could be brought to bear. Among the kitchen items, Victor had sent the assassin's weapon – a 9mm SIG Sauer P226 – spinning and clattering on the hexagonal tiles. He risked a glance, noting where it ended up, but could not go for it with the assassin staying so near to him. The anti-slip coating of the floor's ceramic tiles – meant to reduce spills and workplace accidents – helped Victor remain vertical while backtracking blind.

'Why are you protecting your employer?' the assassin asked, stalking forwards through the path Victor had cleared.

On the wall opposite the windows were three equidistant ovens and a sturdy, porcelain washbasin, with a large metal island in front of them in the centre of the space. Victor circled the island, his enemy pursuing him with his inexorable knife attacks.

For the moment, Victor was content to let the man do his thing. As much as Victor liked to strike first with decisive violence, there were benefits in defending. For one, it was less taxing on his endurance, but, more than that, it provided him the opportunity to test his opponent's speed and skills while also giving him an insight into that enemy's mindset.

'The only chance you have,' the assassin said, confident and in control, 'is telling me what I want to know.'

This assassin, aware his primary advantage was his speed, exploited this trait by not relenting in his deadly rhythm.

And he was right to do just that.

Victor had no time to formulate a counter-attack. He used every iota of his own speed and experience to avoid a blade through the skull or his intestines spilling out of a rupture in his abdominal wall.

The blocks were taking their toll on his opponent, however, even if he was yet to realise it.

'You're tiring,' the assassin told him. 'You're running out of time.'

Victor's forearms were conditioned from a lifetime of physical activity, his bone density increased with every climb of frozen waterfalls and mountainsides in the Alps, with every intense workout, with every hand-to-hand confrontation. Joints were always weak spots, and the assassin's elbow and wrist were never going to hold up when pummelled by the combined force of Victor's powerful blocks and his own downward strikes.

'Last chance,' the assassin said. 'Tell me.'

Maybe he had a high pain tolerance, or the adrenaline coursing through him was dampening the sensation. The damage was being done, nonetheless. With his unfaltering reliance on his speed, he only made Victor's life easier.

First, hairline fractures in bone, forming stress risers.

Then, a break.

The only question was where the bones would fail first: the wrist or the elbow.

When the assassin grimaced as Victor's next block connected with his elbow – the inevitable hairline fracture or fractures – the question was answered.

To ensure his enemy did not change tactics to protect his elbow, Victor let the follow-up sweeping slash connect with his abdomen enough to split the skin.

Invigorated by the sight of blood staining Victor's white shirt and his genuine grimace, the assassin maintained his rhythm and repeated his attacks, bringing the knife up and then down in a stab at Victor's skull.

In return, Victor struck the incoming elbow from beneath with the edge of his forearm.

*Crack.*

# THREE

*Last night*

Finally, the assassin stopped talking.

The impact broke his ulna at the radial notch, and that sudden release of energy split the collateral tendon attaching the ulna to the humerus.

The downward stab lost all acceleration, and the follow-up sweeping slash never materialised as the sudden pain of injury drained him of coordination.

Sidestepping to avoid the assassin toppling into him, Victor kicked the back of the trailing knee to collapse the leg, causing the disorientated man to slam straight into the stainless-steel doors of a wall-sunk refrigerator next to the entrance to the pantry and storerooms.

The metal dented as he rebounded from it, using the momentum to assist a fast one-eighty as he switched the knife from the grip of his injured right arm into his left hand.

Victor was ready for the inevitable backhanded slash that

accompanied the spin, batting the blade away with a cast-iron skillet he'd grabbed from the nearby island.

The weight of the improvised weapon meant it had too much inertia to bring back to parry the assassin's counter-strike, so Victor released the skillet, caught the attacking wrist in both hands, pivoted into his enemy's torso, and hurled the man over his shoulder and onto and across the island. The knife flew from his grip as he slid over the smooth metal surface before tumbling off the far side.

Using only his single, uninjured arm to break his fall, the assassin could not recover before Victor had circled the island and leapt onto his back, snaking his right forearm in front of the man's throat until it was pincered between biceps and forearm, and locking it off by clutching his right hand in his left.

With one arm useless, there was no way he was escaping the chokehold before brain death unless Victor elected to release him.

Which Victor did when he heard the telltale *click* of a switchblade opening.

He scrambled away before the assassin's second knife could plunge into his exposed arms or legs.

Maybe drawn from a pocket or a concealed sheath, it made no difference. The difference, however, was that the assassin was nowhere near as accurate using his offhand, and his right arm was unusable, hanging down at his side.

Which gave Victor the time to scoop a baking tray from the floor as he hopped to his feet, holding it lengthwise in both hands to use a shield, deflecting his enemy's increasingly desperate stabs and slashes once he was on his feet too.

Timing his enemy, Victor thrust out the baking tray in the

exact opposite trajectory to an incoming stab, the switchblade penetrating in a grating, high-pitched whine straight through the tray, all the way to the knife's small guard.

With the weapon momentarily jammed, Victor spun the tray ninety degrees, twisting the knife with it along with the assassin's outstretched arm until the elbow was facing upwards and the limb was locked out at the shoulder joint.

Wrenching him closer so he lost his balance, Victor swung the assassin face first into the heavy washbasin.

Blood smeared on the porcelain, and teeth clattered on the ceramic floor tiles.

Dazed, his grip on the switchblade failed and Victor tossed the impaled tray aside to grab hold of the assassin's hair in one hand as he turned on a tap with the other.

Slotting the plug into place, Victor pressed the semi-conscious man's head down into the sink as it filled up, holding him submerged beneath the reddening water until well after he had ceased thrashing and the last bubble of air popped at the surface.

# FOUR

*Last night*

Twisting the tap to shut off the water, Victor released the fistful of hair and stepped backwards. With nothing to hold him in place, the dead assassin's head and shoulders slid out of the sink, and his whole body slumped into a pile on the floor.

A suit drenched with cold water was far from ideal, but Victor considered it a far preferable inconvenience than drowning. He was sure the corpse would agree.

In the quiet once more, Victor listened.

The dead assassin on the floor had been part of a team of three using the bakery as a place in which to lie low after their most recent contract in nearby Brussels. Instead of taking them all on at the same time, Victor had planned to catch the first guy unawares while the other two ventured out to restock their supplies, and then ambush them upon their return. The drowned assassin at his feet had been more perceptive than he had anticipated, as the overflowing sink,

Victor's sliced abdomen and the many scattered items on the bakery floor could testify.

Still, Marcus Lambert had not brought Victor into his organisation to fulfil straightforward contracts. Professionals like him were not disposed to die easily.

Hearing nothing, he retrieved the assassin's nearby SIG and would have looked for his own Five-seveN too, if not for a gentle *creak* of wood that interrupted the silence.

From the front entrance, a set of old steps led down into the bakery's storefront, where the many varieties of bread, pastries and cakes had once been sold. Victor aimed the SIG at the set of swing doors that connected the kitchen to the other space; these had no windows through which to see, and there was not enough light in the storefront to give away shadows through the gap between the bottom of the doors and the floor.

Victor had come via the back entrance on the opposite wall, picking the lock to enter through the storerooms and pantry behind the kitchen that opened out to a small courtyard behind the building.

Another creak confirmed that at least one of the other two team members had returned and was descending the entrance steps at a slow, cautious pace.

The fact that they were being so cautious told him they knew for sure something was wrong. Either they had heard the last stages of Victor drowning the first assassin or they might have sent a message to their now-dead companion to notify him of their imminent arrival, and his lack of response had been correctly interpreted.

No reason to assume only one had returned, so Victor pictured two men with guns drawn, crossing the open space of the storefront between the steps and the L-shaped counter that ran the length of two perpendicular walls. Then, they would pass through the gap in the counter to approach the swing doors.

Had the layout been different, he might have charged out to catch them unawares, but it was too much of a gamble without knowing their exact positions. Even in the best-case scenario, he would trap himself behind the counter while they had the mobility to outflank him if he failed to drop them both with his initial shots.

Assuming the remaining two were no less competent than the dead guy on the floor, Victor did not fancy his chances in a straight two-on-one gunfight.

Instead, they could come to him.

If both assassins breached together, fast and decisive, Victor was certain he could drop one of them, but would he be fast enough to shift his aim, shoot and score another lethal hit before the second drew a bead on him first?

Maybe. Maybe not.

To rebalance the odds, he lifted himself up and onto the kitchen's central island, climbing at a slow, deliberate pace, to remain silent.

Lowering himself onto his stomach, the cut to his abdomen sent a stinging jolt of pain as he stretched himself out on the metal surface, feet protruding off the far end and both arms out in front, P226 aimed at the middle of the swing doors.

At an unusual height, with most of his person concealed by the angle from a typical person's line of sight and out of the swathes of the streetlights, Victor waited.

He heard no footsteps, so they were keeping their movements slow and silent until they were in position.

His pulse elevated from the fight, Victor breathed in a slow, controlled manner to bring his heart rate back down and, in doing so, improve his fine motor skills.

The swing doors provided enough room for wide trays and whatever else a baker might carry between the kitchen and shopfront. Both remaining assassins could exploit that, each shoving or kicking open a separate door to breach together at the same moment. If they did, aiming at the centre point would mean missing both, so Victor adjusted his aim a little to the right. That half of the doors was closest to the gap between the counters on the other side. Should only one assassin have returned, that would be the one they pushed open. And if both breached at the same time, there would still be an enemy who came through it.

A double-tap, Victor thought, before he would shift his aim to the left to do the same again. Headshots following.

The front of his suit soaked with cold water, and lying on a metal surface, Victor felt the chill seeping deeper into him. The ambient temperature was already single digits so if they waited much longer, he was going to start shivering. Pressed against the steel island, the inevitable rattling of his knees and elbows, not to mention his belt buckle, against the stainless steel could not fail to give his position away.

Seconds passed.

They had to be in place by now.

They were cautious and noiseless because they knew an ambush awaited them on the other side of the swing doors.

He imagined them communicating with hand signals and gestures.

*You go left, I'll go right. Ready?*

*Ready.*

But how long before they . . .?

The door to Victor's right exploded inwards from a mighty kick, swinging in a fast arc and slamming into the adjacent wall as a dark silhouette charged through the opening.

Squeezing the trigger twice in a quick double-tap, Victor put two 9mm rounds at centre mass, not seeing in the semi-darkness the exact points the bullets struck.

The left-hand side of the door did not swing open at the same time, so Victor had no need to switch his aim in that direction, instead angling the SIG up a fraction to put a third bullet to the head.

Maybe only one of the remaining assassins had returned . . .

Or the other had entered the building via the same way as Victor . . .

And was coming up behind him.

# FIVE

*Last night*

Performing a fast, lateral roll, Victor flipped over onto his back, whipping his hands around to aim at the entrance on the opposite wall and continuing the momentum of the roll to fall off the island as a burst of sub-machine gun fire raked it with bullets.

Subsonic rounds shot through a suppressor dulled the muzzle report but could do nothing to dampen the loud *thunk-thunk-thunk-thunk* of the bullets punching holes in the stainless-steel surface of the island where Victor had been a split second beforehand.

He returned fire – first as he rolled, then as he fell – squeezing the SIG's trigger several times in rapid succession at another silhouette in a doorway before striking the floor on his back and rolling to absorb the energy of the impact.

Some of his shots hit their mark, but the gunman was still standing, if staggering, shifting his aim as the SMG continued to spit out rounds, blasting more holes into the island

and then around the kitchen as Victor's bullets interrupted his accuracy.

Metal pinged and brickwork fragmented as Victor finished his roll on his back once more, bringing the SIG back into line at the silhouette in the doorway as he, in turn, tracked Victor's movements, the bullets now cracking and shattering the floor tiles around him.

As ceramic fragments peppered his face, Victor emptied the pistol's remaining bullets, the air now thick with dust and turning the darkness into blackness.

The clatter of a released magazine hitting the floor told him the assassin had also run out of ammunition at the exact same moment.

With the P226 now spent, Victor flipped to his feet to charge down the gunman before he could slam in more rounds, but as Victor emerged out of the cloud of tile dust, he watched the silhouette drop his SMG.

The figure remained stationary for a moment more before collapsing backwards through the open pantry doorway.

Now seeing where his Five-seveN had ended up, Victor retrieved it from the floor and checked the two new arrivals to see if they were dead or merely wounded. He found the first guy twitching on the floor of the shopfront on the other side of the swing doors, the bullets from the double-tap glinting in a strip of light from the outside streetlamps. They were embedded in an armoured vest that would have saved the assassin's life had Victor's subsequent headshot not removed a significant portion of the skull as it exited.

The third man was still alive, lying on his back. Half of him was still inside the kitchen and the other half in the pantry, a nasty cut to his scalp from a glancing hit painting one side of his face red, and clusters of holes in the abdomen and chest of his armoured vest, all but one with a stopped bullet protruding out.

Victor found it interesting that these two wore body armour but the first had not. They must have anticipated an attack was imminent, whereas the first of the trio had been more complacent.

Not that an armoured vest would have done much to protect him from a lungful of water, of course.

'Who sent you?' the prostrate man wheezed, blood bubbling from his mouth.

An American. The youngest of the trio, and yet no less competent as a result. They had an impressive track record as a team, but all good things had to come to an end.

One of his arms was outstretched, trying to reach the SMG that had fallen out of his hands before he tipped over. He would not give up the fight even when the situation was hopeless.

Victor respected that.

Again, the American said, 'Who?'

'Why do you guys care so much?' Victor asked in return, kicking the dropped weapon clear. 'It won't make any difference.'

Sudden pain caused Victor to wince and rub at his lower back, now feeling the effects of having rolled off the island to land on one of the scattered baking dishes on the floor. He knew he would have a fierce bruise come the morning.

The American said, 'I need to know, man.'

'You have a punctured lung,' Victor explained to him, 'but the vest slowed the bullet enough so that it didn't reach your heart. Your head wound isn't fatal either. So you can live through this if you're smart. Tell me who hired you and I'll call you an ambulance. They are my ultimate target, so there's no need for you to follow your teammates into the next life unless you really want to.'

He watched the young man thinking for a few seconds before he said, 'Trade. Tell me who sent you, and I'll tell you ... who sent me.'

'Deal,' Victor agreed. 'But you first.'

'An Australian named Ken Harvey ... works out of London ... One of the other guys knows him from way back.'

'You gave him up very easily,' Victor noted.

'SOB's been trying to worm out of paying us for the job,' the American said before coughing up more blood. 'I knew this side hustle was a bad idea from the start. I knew it ... I *told* them ...'

Victor used his current burner phone to put the client's name and occupation into a search engine. He showed the prostrate man the results.

'Is this Harvey?'

'That's the arrogant Aussie snake.' He grimaced again. 'Come on, man ... keep your end of the deal. Who sent you? It was Marcus Lambert ... wasn't it?'

There was no harm in answering, so Victor said, 'That's right.'

'Then you're a chump,' the American told him in response. 'We work for him too.'

'I know you did,' Victor replied. 'But your moonlighting job for Harvey didn't go too well. You left a mess in Brussels. Not only did you shoot up a café, you left a trail. It was only a matter of time before the authorities tracked you down.

Given you're all registered contractors for Lambert's legitimate business, that would be very bad for his reputation.'

'So much for loyalty.'

'You made a mistake,' Victor reminded him. 'And I'm afraid you're in the wrong profession if you expect your employer never to turn on you. Take it from me; it's a given. Even with a perfect track record, it's only ever a question of when.'

'I meant *you*,' the man hissed, disgusted. 'We both work for Lambert, so we're on the same side here. What happened to unity, man? What happened to brotherhood?'

'You must have me mistaken for someone else.'

Victor angled up his Five-seveN.

The American eyed the pistol. 'I see that ambulance you mentioned is . . . delayed.'

'You changed the terms of our deal, remember?'

The grimace became a grin. Bitter. Defiant. 'Go to hell.'

'All in good time,' Victor said before squeezing the trigger.

# SIX

Another reason Victor had selected this particular bar in Rotterdam was due to the relaxing lounge music that played. Loud enough to give the place an atmosphere without stifling conversation, and – even though he chose his words with professional care – to let Victor speak on the phone without being overheard.

'I can get you a doctor,' Lambert said after Victor had finished his recap of the previous night's events. 'Any time you need one. Drop of a hat, you can be stitched up by someone who knows what they're doing.'

'I know what I'm doing,' Victor told him.

He rubbed at his stomach where the assassin's knife had sliced him. It was a superficial injury as far as Victor was concerned. The blade had split his skin and the minuscule layer of subcutaneous fat, and yet the fascia beneath was intact and the abdominal wall unscathed. A medical staple gun, gauze and antiseptic had been simple enough to apply and nothing he hadn't done a hundred times before. The wound was healing well. Aside from the constant pain, he was unimpeded. The bruise to his lower back caused more discomfort.

'But I appreciate the offer,' he added.

'Did you happen to find out who those traitors were working for?'

'Ken Harvey.'

Lambert huffed. 'Figures.'

'You know him?'

'Oh yeah, he used to work for me too. He's managed illicit monies for a lot of people in the trade ... other PMCs and mercenary outfits, arms manufacturers, you name it. Anyway, good work getting a name. The client will be very happy we've helped identify another rat in their sewer. Funny thing is, I heard Harvey was going legit, so this is something of a surprise. But I guess it makes sense that when he needed shooters, he would know my organisation could supply them. He should have given me a call, not gone behind my back to save a few pennies.'

'Then I take it you would like me to pay him a visit as much as the client?'

'Harvey can wait for the time being,' Lambert began. 'The Romania assignment is more pressing. Although the client is still trying to work out who stole the plans for their special new HEL systems from them in the first place, they know their plans are being purchased by a private intelligence operative named Marion Ysiv in Bucharest. We don't know who is selling to her just yet beyond that they're in the same business as Ysiv, but now we can tell the client that Ken Harvey is a part of the chain handling it, I'm sure they'll put two and two together in no time. Whoever this seller is, the client wants us to ensure neither they nor Ysiv walks away from that rendezvous.'

'The more customers in one place, the more complicated the pitch.'

'I appreciate that,' Lambert conceded, understanding Victor was speaking in a public space and translating the information provided in the same way he had when Victor had described what happened in the bakery. 'But spies-for-hire are savvy; apparently they've been in communication for a while. You kill one on their own and the second will take the hint and vanish before you can get to them too. The client is adamant both have to go, and go together. An example needs to be made. HEL systems are the future and for once the UK is leading the field.' He chuckled. 'And you just know that whoever came up with that anacronym is more a marketer than a scientist. Aren't all lasers high energy by default?'

'When are they meeting?'

'In about a week's time,' Lambert answered. 'I know you'd prefer more of a lead, but spies, private or otherwise, try not to advertise their schedules. The client is paying a premium for the rush, and they're not the kind of people I want to turn down since they're a bigwig in the Ministry of Defence. A fat payday is nice, naturally, but this series of assignments is all about favours. If I want a five-year licence renewal to supply security staff to embassies in Africa, I need to keep the power brokers happy. The MOD will look bad if it gets out someone has leaked the plans to their shiny new toys before they've even been put into service, which means Downing Street will look bad. We do this and we not only reinforce existing friendships, we make new ones too.'

'When I told you in Tunisia that I don't care about the why,' Victor responded, 'I meant it.'

'You should care,' Lambert was quick to reply. 'Your last job for those Russian mafia bozos was a messy affair.'

One of the reasons he had decided to work for Lambert in the first place was because of the circumstances immediately before the start of their agreement. Lambert was a well-connected man with an extensive network. And though Victor had always preferred to work alone, with as much distance between himself and his employers as possible, doing so over an extended period created problems of its own, and he had found such isolation inevitably meant his work, and the associated activities, left an ever-increasing trail behind he could do little about without help.

'It wasn't a job.'

'Regardless, just because you could walk away and leave the dirty dishes in the sink doesn't negate the fact that someone had to come along and scrub them clean. We do these contracts and someone else will volunteer to put those dishes back inside the cupboard.'

'I'm lost,' Victor said. 'Are the Russians the sink in this metaphor, or are they the cupboard?'

Lambert hesitated. 'Uhum ... Well, I suppose what I'm saying is—'

'It was a joke.'

'God, you're deadpan.'

'No blasphemy.'

'Sorry, sorry, habit. Speaking of which, does HEL offend you?'

'It's an acronym, so no.'

'Interesting,' Lambert said. 'Anyway, the job is a good

move for both of us. If you want the Russians off your back, this is the best way to do it. The more friends we have, the safer you'll be.'

'Noted,' Victor agreed. 'I can be in Bucharest in a few days.'

'The meeting is next week. Don't you want to head there now? Arrive nice and early to be ready?'

'There's somewhere I need to be first.'

Lambert said, 'I don't like the sound of that. Whatever it is can wait until after you've delivered.'

'Not this,' Victor said in return, then repeated, 'I'll be in Bucharest in a few days or not at all. Your choice.'

A moment of silence, in which Victor pictured Lambert rolling his eyes before he conceded with, 'Fine. If that's what it takes for you to agree.'

'It does. Where will I be making the pitch?'

'A hotel. They have a room booked for the meeting.'

'In my experience, hotels do not make good sites to host a presentation.'

'If I could convince them to meet in a bunker in the middle of nowhere, I would.'

'In such a location, the pitch is likely to garner a lot of attention.'

'The client would like it to,' Lambert explained. 'They want everyone to know what happens when someone steals from them, so make as much noise and as much mess as you want.'

'I don't like sending someone else's message,' Victor countered. 'I'm not a courier.'

'You are whoever the client wants you to be.'

'The client wants me to deliver their pitch and send a

message at the same time, whereas I want to walk away after the client gets what they want. I don't want that message to interfere with my gait.'

'Pardon me?'

'I want to walk away from the pitch,' Victor clarified. 'I don't want to have to run.'

'I never took you as a man scared of breaking a sweat.'

'You know exactly what I mean.'

'I do,' Lambert admitted. 'But I find it helpful to inject a little levity into this business whenever possible. I recommend you do the same for the sake of your own sanity.'

'You want me to tell jokes to my customers before pitching to them?'

'Well,' Lambert began, 'waiting until after you've killed them is probably leaving it a little late.'

# SEVEN

When the call disconnected, Victor removed the SIM card and battery from the phone before placing the components back in his pocket.

'Another?' the bartender asked, seeing Victor's glass was little more than melted ice cubes.

He nodded. 'Why not?'

'I do enjoy being right,' the bartender whispered as he looked over Victor's shoulder.

He saw Emilie return in the reflection behind the bar but acted unawares, pretending only to notice her when she was standing alongside him. She ordered a second gin and tonic.

'One is not enough,' she told him. Then, after the barman had delivered her drink, she added, 'Don't think I'm coming back to hit on you again.'

He nodded. 'I wouldn't dream of it. I'm well aware I already blew my chance.'

'I'm glad we're clear on that.' She smiled. 'I returned to

speak with you again because I have a question to ask you that I didn't think of earlier, and it's been on my mind ever since.'

'Shoot,' Victor said.

'You're a hit— a *killer*, sorry, as we've established. You don't take high-profile missions – I mean contracts – because they put you at too much risk . . . am I correct so far?'

'Two for two.'

She smiled wider, still enjoying the game. 'So why did you admit it to me? Isn't that also putting you at risk?'

He nodded again. 'I suppose we could say I'm going through a period of self-reflection. There are aspects of my life that I've been putting off addressing for a long time. Being more honest about who I am and who I was in the past are parts of that process.'

'So even assassins go through a midlife crisis?'

He raised an eyebrow.

She laughed at his reaction. '*Early* midlife crisis then.'

'Chance would be a fine thing,' he said in return, thinking there was no way on Earth he would live to double his current age.

From her expression, he realised he had revealed too much of himself, but she did not understand the subtext, only his sudden detour into seriousness and away from the game they were playing.

'So, aside from cooling your heels between jobs,' Emilie said after a moment, refusing to give up on her fun, 'what else do you like to do when you're not killing people for money?'

'I enjoy fishing.'

'I . . . definitely wasn't expecting that answer. So, what appeals about fishing?'

'I find it relaxing. I try to squeeze in a fishing trip whenever I have the time. Which is why I'm here now as it happens.'

She gave him a look of puzzlement. 'In a city? In Rotterdam?'

'Cities offer some of the best locations for a fishing trip.'

'You cannot be serious.'

'If we get to know one another better, you'll find out.'

'If,' she echoed, then asked, 'What's the best way to fish?'

'Probably with dynamite, but that's generally frowned upon.'

'I can imagine.'

'But the way I prefer to fish is the simple, classic way. I use a lure and see what bites.'

'What kind of a lure? Like a worm?'

'If you want a small fish, use a worm, yes. If you're looking for a bigger catch, you need to use the kind of bait your intended catch finds irresistible.'

'So,' she said, leaning closer in interest. 'What kind of catch are you looking for on this particular trip?'

'The most dangerous kind.'

'Like a shark?'

'In a way, yes,' he answered, thinking of an old acquaintance from Bologna.

'Pray tell, what kind of bait do you use when you want to catch a shark?'

Her smile was playful, and her eyes were wide with expectation.

'Isn't that obvious?' he said. 'To catch a shark, you need to use a lure that the shark is after.'

After a moment's pause she said, 'Don't keep me in suspense here. I'm dying to know.'

'Funny turn of phrase,' he said, then, 'To catch a shark, I use the only thing that will satiate its hunger. Myself.'

She burst out laughing. 'Do you smear yourself in garlic butter, too?'

'Almost,' he said. 'But I find a gin and tonic works better.'

Her smile faltered in confusion as she waited for him to elaborate. When he said nothing, her gaze dropped to look at the highball glass in front of him, at her own and then back to his, before her eyes met his again.

'Fishing,' she said.

He nodded.

'Using yourself as bait.'

He nodded again.

She took a much-needed sip of her drink. Then another. She looked at him, and he saw the workings of her mind in her expression. The only thing he was not sure about was how she would react to what she now realised. He figured there were two options. Maybe she would walk away without a word. Perhaps she would try to pretend this wasn't exactly what they both now knew it to be.

'You made me shadowing you, right?' she asked, taking a third option he had not considered. 'That's why you did the whole schtick about *pretending* to be a hitman. I should have realised sooner.'

He shook his head. 'The *schtick* was just that – a little levity, as my broker would call it. And the first time I saw you was when you approached the bar. You're very good.'

She stared into her glass. 'Not good enough.'

'Don't beat yourself up. It would have worked on anyone else.' He gestured. 'Why don't you take a seat?'

'Is that another joke?'

He shook his head. 'No reason why we can't be professional about our differences. You're simply doing your job and doubtless here now because of my own work. I find this line of work a lot more palatable if I don't take these inevitable situations personally. I recommend you do the same.'

She looked at him, surprised and confused, before shaking her head and perching on the barstool next to him. 'You are, without a doubt, the most unusual mark I've ever had.'

'I'll take that as a compliment.'

'Please do,' she said. She sipped her gin. 'I never ask why … I find it's simpler not to know, you know? But now, having met you, I'm curious. What did you do to them that ended with me picking up the phone?'

'Who is "them" in this instance?' Victor asked. 'I'm afraid you'll have to be a little more specific.'

'Oh, I see,' she replied. 'You're a popular man then. They're Russian organised crime, I think. I mean, I know they are; I couldn't give you any names, however. Can you tell me why they want you dead? If you don't mind, that is. If it's not too intrusive an ask.'

Victor shook his head to say he did not mind at all. 'Let's just say I used to work for them, albeit briefly, and not everyone in that organisation was fond of me or the manner in which we parted terms.'

Emilie stared into her glass. 'That must make me the severance package.'

'I'll drink to that.'

She smiled at him as she regarded him with more surprise and confusion. 'Like I said, my most unusual mark yet.' She paused, looked away for a second, then back again. 'It's occurred to me that I could tell them I didn't catch up to you.

They would never know any different. It's payment on delivery, so there's no blowback if I walk away. I'm only down a little on expenses and my time. Not enough to really feel it, so how about we both finish our drinks and part on friendly terms?'

'Why would you do that?'

'Call it a professional courtesy. As you said, it's not personal. It's no skin off my nose if you carry on your merry way.'

'This is not how I predicted this conversation going.'

'I know, right?' she said, amusement in her tone. 'Up until five minutes ago, I was all set to have a couple more drinks with you and then lead you off somewhere quiet where we could be alone and ...' She made a quick check to be sure no one was watching and ran a finger across her throat. 'But here we are anyway, a couple of jaded pros bonding over gin and tonic. I didn't read that in my horoscope earlier.'

'I'll bet.'

'So,' she said, leaning closer so he could smell the lime on her breath. 'What do you say? Bygones?'

'I appreciate the offer, but it's not necessary.'

His reply caught her off guard, and for a moment she did not know what to say in return, until: 'You're telling me you would prefer it if I don't walk away? You're telling me you'd rather I kill you?'

'That's not exactly what I said.' He explained: 'I've been here for the last few days, so if anyone is currently shadowing me, they'd have the chance to make a move. That way, I can end the threat because I'm taking a trip – part of that self-reflection we discussed a moment ago – and I can't risk even the slightest chance of bringing a tail along with me.

You, in turn, are here to fulfil a contract. What I'm saying is let's stick to our respective plans.'

'I see,' she said, unable to control the disappointment in her tone. 'I don't understand, but it's your call. At least tell me what I did wrong. You said my approach would have worked on anyone else, so why didn't it work on you?'

A reasonable question, Victor thought, and no downside to answering.

He said, 'Unlike any other killer out there who is on the lookout for threats, I took you for a professional the moment you approached, because I assume everyone wants to kill me until they prove to me that they don't.'

'Interesting philosophy. And why didn't I prove to you that I don't?'

'You came back.'

'That can't be it,' she said. 'Not on its own.'

'You asked me questions and listened to the answers.'

A groove formed between her eyebrows. 'People wanting to talk with you is proof they mean you harm? Perhaps they really like you.'

'It's not impossible for someone to like me,' he admitted. 'But no one ever really likes me. I'm not that interesting.'

'What if you're wrong and you just never gave them the chance?' She leaned even closer, her eyes mere centimetres from his own. 'What if this could be the single time your whole life could swivel on a dime if only you let it?'

'Change is overrated,' Victor told her. 'I prefer routine.'

'This is routine?'

'Not *this*,' he said, referring to their conversation. 'But what happens after we leave here together will be about as routine for me as it gets.'

# EIGHT

The road's surface was a slick reflection of lights blurring into one another from the windows, signs and streetlamps. Any moonlight was lost into the haze of the city at night, but it watched them regardless. High above, its silver shape broken by wisps of drifting cloud, the moon saw all.

A chilly night. Emilie fastened the belt of her overcoat on the top steps of the short set that led up to the brasserie's entrance. Behind them, the door swung shut, and behind that, a couple complained to the hostess that they should still be seated despite being half an hour late for their booking.

'How do you want to do this?' Emilie asked, finished with her belt and looking at Victor alongside her.

'Not here,' he answered, looking out at the busy city-centre street with its many pedestrians, bars and restaurants, and CCTV cameras.

'Then what are we doing?' Her tone was curt, harried.

'Don't be so impatient. Tell me, what would your next move be if this all worked out the way you had planned?'

'I told you inside. Take you somewhere quiet where you would lower your guard.'

'And how were you planning on doing that exactly?'

She gave him a look of disgust. 'Get your kicks elsewhere.'

'That's not what I meant,' he clarified. 'Where were you going to take me? A hotel room? A dark alleyway?'

'Rented apartment. I have a nice bottle of champagne on ice if you fancy a nightcap.'

'Cute,' he said, then, 'Who else is there?'

She frowned. Confusion and surprise, or a good impression. 'I'm alone.'

He raised an eyebrow.

'When we get there, you'll see there is nowhere for anyone to hide. It's a bohemian studio, one big room, all bare brick and floor-to-ceiling windows. Kitchen at one end, bed at the other.'

He said, 'Okay.'

She smiled a little. 'Does that surprise you?'

'A bit,' he admitted.

'You think a weak woman like me would be too scared to be with such a scary man as yourself all on her lonesome?'

'That's not what I meant,' he clarified. 'I'm surprised my former Russian friends trusted you and you alone with my demise. That's not their style.'

'If it soothes your bruised ego, they wanted me to have backup. A whole team of Slovakian mercs, in fact. I told them no. That's not how I operate. I'm not a brute; I'm an artist. I work alone. I'm better alone.'

'I bet you wish you had a team right now.'

She said nothing to that.

'Where are you parked?' he asked.

'Why?'

'Because you're going to take me to that rented bohemian studio of yours.'

'What if I say no?'

'You won't.'

'What if I scream for help and run?'

'You won't,' he said again. 'You still have a chance to complete your contract, don't forget. As you said, you're an artist. You're already thinking of ways to get the drop on me when we reach our destination. There's no point pretending otherwise, so let's get on with it, shall we?'

He watched her consider for a moment, then nod. Point. 'This way.'

A short walk side by side brought them to her vehicle, a black Suzuki Vitara, parked in a bay of a multistorey garage. He gestured for her to stop and had her stand alongside the bodywork while he patted her down.

'Is this necessary?'

He didn't answer. When he was sure she was unarmed, he motioned for her to climb behind the wheel.

She asked, 'Do I get to check you for weapons too?'

'No need,' he said. 'I have an FN Five-seveN under my left armpit.'

He tapped the weapon through his suit jacket. It hung there courtesy of webbing, which he rarely wore unless he expected trouble. The pistol made a distinctive noise as he tapped it, dull and rigid, nothing like clothing with mere flesh beneath would make.

'Why am I driving?' she asked.

'Because it's your car.'

She used a key fob to unlock the vehicle and opened the

door. At the same time, Victor climbed into the back seat, sitting directly behind Emilie in the driver's seat.

'You're making me uncomfortable,' she said.

'I'm not going to kill you here,' he told her. 'Too many cameras, too many people saw us walking together.'

'Reassuring.'

She pushed the power button with her thumb, and the dashboard came to life. Then, she reached for the seatbelt.

'Keep it off,' Victor told her. 'That way, you won't be tempted to crash the car.'

'I've been drinking.'

'Then you'll drive carefully.'

He kept his seatbelt off as well, not wanting to be trapped by the belt and unable to react to whatever Emilie might try during the drive.

After checking her mirrors, she reversed out of the bay and followed the one-way system to the exit, inserting her ticket into the machine to open the barriers.

'How far?' Victor asked.

'Ten, fifteen minutes. Depending on traffic, of course.'

Meeting her gaze in the rear-view mirror, he nodded at her.

'Still time to change your mind,' Emilie said.

'Why would I want to do that?'

'I was being genuine back there,' she continued. 'In the bar, when I said I could walk away and tell them I didn't find you, I meant it.'

'I know.'

'When I told you I liked you, that wasn't a lie.'

'Right now, you'll say anything,' Victor said.

'If you kill me,' she began, undeterred, 'they'll just use

the Slovakians. They're a serious crew. Not like me, I mean. They wouldn't track you down and try to catch you off guard in a bar. Oh, no. Instead, they'd rely on someone else to pinpoint your location, and then they'd be bringing down the entire building with C4 or RPGs and bury you in the rubble. They're on standby right now, but they're good to go at the drop of a hat.'

'I don't wear a hat.'

'I'll tell my employer I never found you. I can say I saw you board a plane for Antigua. Get them off your back for a long time. Those mercs will waste months looking on the wrong continent. By then, you'll be long gone and as good as untouchable. That sounds like a pretty sweet deal from where I'm sitting. I know you said you're taking a trip and can't afford anyone knowing about it and, my way, no one ever will.'

'Often,' he said, 'I find it can be useful to everyone concerned to simply remain silent.'

She took his advice then, he found. She kept her gaze on the road and her hands on the wheel. Although he sat behind her, he was a little closer to the centre of the back seat than in a direct line behind. This enabled him to see more of her and her actions than he could have otherwise.

He noticed her gaze would flick to the rear-view mirror every minute or so, no doubt in anticipation of a sudden, violent attack and trying to pre-empt it. No surprise to find she did not trust his word. Why would she?

Within a few minutes, they had left the inner city behind. Within a few more, they were outside the city proper. Here, the streets were quieter – no neon lights of bars. No businesses at all were open at this hour. No pedestrians on the street. Little traffic.

Victor heard the panel van's approach only a moment before he saw it.

The headlights had been killed, so the dark vehicle was all but invisible in the night. Within a few seconds, the innocuous rumble of a nearby exhaust swelled into a roar.

He had just enough time to grab the seatbelt and shove the clasp into the connector.

Only when it was mere metres away did Emilie see it emerging from the darkness and understand it was about to crash straight into them.

Which was far too late.

# NINE

The Vitara was hit on the driver's side just in front of Victor, the impact crumpling bodywork and sending the car into a horizontal flip.

Victor's view of the world was sent into a chaotic spiral as the seatbelt pinned him in place and pebbles of glass pattered against his face. The roof collided with the road for a brief moment before the vehicle continued to roll through a cloud of its own exhaust fumes and brake dust.

While upside down, he caught a glimpse of the van out of control, the collision sending it swerving erratically along the road.

And Emilie – not quick enough to strap herself in – tossed out of her seat and slammed into the roof, then back down with every roll, hurled from the driver's side to the passenger's and back again.

The Vitara clattered and banged as metal dented and distorted, landing back on all four tyres in a shower of glittering shards from broken headlights, and scattering fragments from the windscreen's safety glass, before the momentum of the roll bounced it back up on its suspension and turned it over once more.

Rubber screeched against the asphalt as the tyres struck the road at the end of the roll, the car sliding sideways before the leftover energy rocked it back and forth while the stench of burnt tyres and rubber smoke further darkened the darkness.

One headlight had smashed, while the other gleamed off the broken glass scattered across the asphalt before fading to a tiny, short-lived glow. Then, only night remained.

The rear bumper landed from a high arc, thrown off during the roll, and skidded along the pavement.

It took a few seconds for Victor to shake off the discombobulation and dizziness.

He peered through the cracked and pitted windscreen, his eyes not yet focusing, to see the panel van had crashed itself after the collision, hitting a line of parked cars and setting off a chorus of alarms he could not hear at first. Instead, a piercing whine was the only sound.

Her mid-spine snapped in the crash, Emilie lay in a broken tumble of limbs across the front two seats. Her eyelids, strobe-like, flickered as she stared back at him.

When she spoke, he could not hear her words with the shrill whine in his ears. And although his vision was still blurry, he did not need to focus to make out the short, obvious words of her plea to him:

*Help me.*

Through the windscreen, he saw the nearside sliding door of the panel van opening and men jumping out of the vehicle, pistols already in hand or drawn from belt or underarm holster.

Even without the threat of nearby gunmen, he could do nothing for Emilie had he wanted to try.

Which, of course, he did not.

When the door wouldn't open, Victor unclasped the seatbelt and leant across to work the opposite door handle on the passenger's side. Nothing happened. The chassis was collapsed in several places, and the resulting deformity of the shell had wedged the doors shut and unable to open. The windows remained up when he pressed the buttons to lower them. The dashboard instruments were all dark. When he leaned over Emilie to push the power button next to the steering wheel, the engine did not come back to life.

He heard her whimper beneath him.

Swivelling onto his back, Victor held onto the seat for purchase and stability, and used his heel to kick at the door window on the driver's side. Already cracked from the crash, it broke apart enough on the second impact so that he could clear away the remaining glass with his elbow before pulling himself through the opening.

More dazed than he had realised, he fell to the road surface, scraping his palms on the asphalt and debris.

As the piercing whine inside his head faded little by little, Victor heard the nearby van's engine rev and hum from behind him. It was a pitiful, stretched noise that meant whoever was left in the vehicle would have no choice but to join the others on foot.

*Get up*, Victor told himself.

# TEN

No shots came at Victor yet – the Suzuki was a shield between them – but the respite would be short-lived. In seconds, they would round the vehicle and draw clear lines of sight to his back.

Despite the disorientation making his balance unreliable and his footing unfirm, Victor forced himself to his feet and into a run.

He glanced back as the last of five men dropped out from the back of the van, who, along with one from the passenger seat and the driver, comprised what had to be the Slovakian mercenaries Emilie had mentioned. Her Russian client wanted her to use them as backup; although she had declined, they were here anyway. Her employer may have professed to agree with her reasoning as a lone operator – an artist, as she had put it – but they'd had other ideas. They had sent out the team of seven anyway, having them keep tabs on her not as insurance should she require the backup but as a different kind of contingency altogether.

She had even told Victor the mercenaries were not the kind of people to track a target down, opting instead to have someone else do it for them.

Emilie had failed to realise they had used her for that exact purpose.

Victor zigzagged away, his gait becoming straighter and more sure-footed with each step, and his strides longer and faster as his eyes focused again.

He was already sprinting before the first gunshots drowned out the wailing chorus of car alarms.

With twenty metres between them now, the bullets whistled past him on either side. However good the Slovakians were as shooters, he was a fast-moving target at a distance.

Hard to know without looking back whether they had stopped to shoot or were running at the same time, but either worked for him. If they stopped to increase their accuracy, he improved his lead. If they fired as they moved, the odds of hitting a mobile target from an unstable shooting stance were dire.

No civilians on the streets at this time of night, which was both a blessing and a curse. It would help to have more obstacles to put between him and his pursuers, but in Victor's extensive experience, civilians seemed to do their very best to get in his way at the worst possible moments.

In the quiet outskirts of the city, there were no passing vehicles so long after the close of business either. At least, not where Victor chose to run. However, he was heading towards the ambient noise of traffic. If he could acquire – steal – a car while they remained on foot, he could escape without any other effort. And even if a passing motorist did not helpfully stop their car directly in front of him and open their driver-side door, moving vehicles meant other obstacles he could use to his advantage.

Victor veered off the road and onto the pavement, snaking between parked cars to put them between himself and the Slovakians chasing him and, more importantly, between himself and their bullets.

Some made a hard *thunk* as they punched into steel bodywork. Others blasted through safety glass.

With some cover and his sensibilities returned, he risked swivelling as he ran, to put some fire at the chasing gunmen.

Even with significant numerical superiority and his fleeing, they had still spread themselves out to avoid making a cluster of targets. He had no choice but to aim at the closest Slovakian. Trying to shoot at them all would slow him down too much.

His shots were no more accurate than their own, with the distance, with them running fast and him running faster, and he achieved nothing except to cause his target to flinch and duck for a moment.

Still, maybe that would be enough.

In their return fire, muzzle flashes brightened the night in bursts of bright yellow light.

Sparks flared from a security grille behind him, and an exploded cloud of brick dust peppered his suit jacket as he passed.

The night became an orchestra of overlapping, inharmonious noise: loud, tinny gunshots; sharp snaps of passing rounds; dings as those bullets ricocheted and thumps as they buried into concrete paving or brickwork.

A storefront window shattered ahead of him into a storm

cloud of shimmering shards, and more sparks brightened the night in front of his face as a round clipped a lamp post.

He felt a tiny spot of heat on his forehead as he charged through the haze of glass dust and super-heated metal particles.

Instinctively shutting his eyes to protect them from the debris, Victor lost his footing, tripping on the uneven pavement, falling sideways into one of the parked cars before recoiling, then flailing forwards to maintain his balance but losing speed and precious distance in the process.

When his eyes opened again, he saw the line of vehicles shielding him was coming to an end, and a glance over his shoulder told him his pursuers had closed much of the distance between them.

No helpful turnings ahead for him to take and leave the street.

At least on his side of the road.

On the opposite side, an alleyway between storefronts offered sanctuary.

But to reach it, there was an empty killing field of asphalt to cross first.

# ELEVEN

Their pace was frantic, although not urgent. The Slovakian mercenaries were hungry to kill their target and make their escape before the sirens came. They had not been expecting their vehicle to become disabled in the crash, but shit happens.

Besides, there was a thrill to such chases, fun to be had in pursuit, a feeling of power and expectation. Each second their target ran, the Slovakians became evermore emboldened, more assured in their higher status as warriors, as predators. This kind of exhilaration was almost non-existent in the regular, civilian world in which even the most battle-hardened of soldiers spent the vast majority of their time. And yet, these true warriors spent their remaining time longing to feel that exhilaration once again. When it returned, it was intoxicating. It was the kind of high that pushed people to the absolute limits of their potential.

The cacophony of their gunshots and the resulting impacts filled the night air.

Muzzle reports, bullets snapping by at close range, thumping into metal, cracking brickwork, shattering glass.

Accompanying these man-made noises were the intertwined sounds of deep breathing and quick footsteps, both solid and scraping, and the rustling of clothes as limbs worked harder and faster.

And most of all, there was one that a few heard coming from within: frenzied, thumping heartbeats.

Slowing at the last in the line of parked cars, Victor ducked low as he veered off the kerb, using the vehicle as a complete shield to block line of sight and slow and deflect the path of any incoming rounds.

As soon as he reached the far corner of the bonnet, he swivelled out his right arm, along with his shoulder and head, and shot at the pursuing mercenaries. In the cold night air, he saw their breath clouding silver in the moonlight, like a pack of wolves on the hunt.

Still spread across the street, two of the Slovakians were sprinting along the centre of the road straight ahead of him, focusing on speed to close the distance instead of defending themselves against counter-attacks.

Without a single slice of cover to interrupt the path of his bullets, Victor put a double-tap at each before switching his aim to the others, either further back or running along the pavements, partially obscured or unseen from his low-down point of view. Nothing he could do about the latter, but he sent rounds at those he could see even a little of, encouraging them to duck or slow as sparks flared and glass cracked.

One of the two Slovakians in the middle of the road dropped – too dark and too far to get an idea of the lethality of the hits – while the other scrambled for the cover. Whether hit or not, that man's tactics had now switched from pursuit to survival, not wanting to risk future shots coming his way that would drop him like the other man.

Either way, it gave Victor a window of time in which to dash out from behind the car's bonnet and sprint across the road towards the mouth of the opposite alleyway.

Asphalt exploded behind and in front of him. He felt fragments pelting his legs.

A bullet came so close to his head that he not only heard the snap but also felt the disturbance as it cut through the air.

Rounds struck the mouth of the alleyway, crumbling brick and cracking concrete at head height, as one or more realised his ultimate destination and organised a welcoming party at which he was the reluctant guest of honour.

He dropped and slid the last metre to avoid running face first into the flight path of the bullets.

The act of him fleeing and them pursuing had been built over the last few minutes into a solid narrative that took little thought to understand and required no improvisational thinking to maintain. So Victor waited in the safety of the alleyway for a count of three, switched the gun to his left hand, and popped back out into the street from which he had just fled.

Dashing along the adjoining pavement, previously unseen behind parked vehicles, a mercenary in a black leather jacket and black beanie hat went wide-eyed when the prey he was pursuing suddenly reappeared in front of him.

In the darkness, the wide eyes with their unmistakable white sclera made the perfect target to aim between.

No exit wound and too dark to see the impact, Victor knew his shot had landed as the Slovakian's momentum sent him flying head first into the pavement, his gun gliding out of his hand, rebounding on a parked box van and clattering along the ground as the corpse slid to a stop at the end of a glistening smear of cranial blood.

The parked vehicles blocked Victor's line of sight to the road itself, so anyone there was spared more bullets. On the opposite side of the street, however, another gunman, this one with a shaved head and an APC9 sub-machine gun, emerged in a half-crouch from behind the line of cars against that kerb before he could stop himself.

Extending his arm, Victor fired three snapshots at this new arrival.

Two bullets hit the car – one smashing the nearest headlight, the other forming a hole in the bonnet – while the third caught the mercenary in the abdomen.

He fell backwards into the cover of the car, smart and fast enough to withdraw his trailing legs before Victor could shoot out his knees.

With no other targets visible, and knowing they were still closing the distance, Victor rushed along the alleyway, ducking behind a large, wheeled garbage bin almost as tall as himself, its stack of bulbous black bags rising high from an open lid.

Unless some of those bags contained rocks or blocks of steel, the bin would not stop any bullets, yet standing behind it obscured the entirety of Victor's person.

The car alarms were still blaring in the distance and muffling any other sound, so he could not hear their approaching footsteps, whether sprinting or edging closer, and they could not hear him in return.

For all they knew, he was fleeing along the alleyway as fast as he could run.

The alleyway was narrow, just wide enough for two people to stand side by side but not to walk along without knocking and bumping into one another. If the Slovakians followed him, they would have to traverse it in a single file to maintain tactical coherency.

Victor peeked out from behind the large garbage container, left hand cradling his right, holding the pistol close to his face, with his elbows tucked into his abdomen so only the weapon, his hands and his head were exposed. Outside the light from the moon and streetlamps, the alleyway was black, and its mouth was a bright glimpse of the street beyond. He pivoted back behind the container.

Would the mercenaries fall for what amounted to the same trick twice?

There had to be at least a measure of doubt in their minds, and yet if they hesitated for too long and let him gain even more of a lead, they would lose him altogether.

If they still wanted to fulfil their contract, they had no choice but to continue their pursuit.

And in doing so, would head straight into Victor's trap.

# TWELVE

The Slovakians were cautious and slow. The previous thrill of the chase they had felt had been shot out of them. The alleyway, being narrow, forced them into a single file. A young guy with a beard went first, not by design. He was neither the leader nor the bravest nor the most enthusiastic. He had simply reached the mouth of the alleyway before the next mercenary, who happened to be a lot taller. A trait that meant he could see over the shoulder of the one in front.

The young guy with the beard had been with the other mercenaries for a while now, completing several assignments, although this was his first experience of a target fighting back. His stress hormones and his heart rate were working in overdrive as a result. Bad shit happening was not only likely, it was expected, he reminded himself. The other team members had instructed him on these simple, immutable facts of the profession, of life in general. People died. Their targets died. Civilians died. Their teammates also died. Not that he had experienced the latter until tonight.

This was it.

This was what he was being paid for, not filling civilians full of lead. Because anybody could do that. It did not require a team. It did not necessitate the individual components of that team to have military experience, combat experience and trigger time. They operated as a team for when things went wrong, for when targets did not accept their fate. Hire one man to do a one-man job, and that will be enough four times out of five.

But nothing ever went to plan.

The universe conspired against everyone sooner or later. Account for everything you can think of, and you will find you cannot think of everything. This was one of those nights. This was when everything that could go wrong did go wrong. The universe was not uncaring tonight; it was cruel.

The Slovakians had always known they had a hard target to kill. They had been well briefed. But they were finding out that there were hard targets and there were harder targets. This guy was the latter. This guy was not prey.

He was a predator just like them.

The corpses he had left behind were a testament to this particular predator's apex status.

Still, the young guy with the beard maintained his focus and resolve. He was ostensibly there for the money only – for the pay cheque. He told himself he was a professional. In a calmer, more rational moment, he might have thought better about what he was doing for his money, and if the payday was worth the risk.

As he shimmied down the alleyway, comforted by the presence of the taller man peering over his shoulder, he was no longer thinking about finishing a mere job. He was thinking about victory, about accomplishment.

He was breathing hard, his pulse 160 beats per minute, his face shimmering with sweat, and driven by an emotional need to succeed.

He had yet to learn just how detrimental emotion was to survivability.

'I can't wait to kill him,' he said in a whisper as two more of the team fell in behind him.

'Yeah,' one of them said in return, his own voice a little louder than a whisper because his response was said with so much enthusiasm.

He felt the same way as the younger guy in the lead. It was about more than just money.

They would not have slowed had they received word at that very moment that the job was cancelled, and they would still have been paid the full fee for completion. They would not withdraw. They were hunting the apex predator at this point, not because they were being paid to kill him but because they had to kill him. They needed to kill him. Nothing was going to change that. Nothing would interfere with this singular desire.

Only death could stop them now.

And, in this instance, Death himself was waiting.

# THIRTEEN

Victor remained in position as he heard the scrape of their heels on the ground of the alleyway despite the blaring of the car alarms, which meant they were close. As expected, they were moving with care now, knowing the risk of entering the alleyway and being forced into a single file that killed their advantage. They were both unwilling to give up the pursuit but operating with far more consideration than they had out on the street.

However, that only made the situation worse for them.

It let Victor hold his hidden position until the most opportune moment when the lead man was so close the scent of his cheap cologne was detectable.

Victor peeked out – fast and smooth – just his head and the gun.

The lead guy – young, with a beard – less than half a metre away, had only enough time to draw in a panicked breath before a double-tap tore a massive chunk out of the back of his skull and plastered the face of the next guy – immediately behind him – with hot blood and brain matter.

The shower of gore blinding him, the second gunman had no way to spot Victor and could do nothing to prevent the following two bullets from passing straight through his forehead.

The third and fourth guys were further back, scrambling and stumbling away with frantic speed as their teammates dropped in front of them, leaving behind two concentrated mists of pink.

Victor squeezed the trigger three more times as the two corpses cleared his line of sight. By which point, the second two men were dashing back out of the alley, both going in the same direction, and his bullets sailed through the mouth of the alleyway to pierce brickwork on the far side of the road.

In the darkness, it was impossible to tell if all of his bullets had missed their mark or whether a round or two had landed. He pictured the two gunmen, unsure of themselves, fleeing a few steps before slowing and checking to see if they had been wounded in their escape. The effects of adrenaline were so strong it was possible to take a bullet and not realise at first or even for a while afterwards.

Wounded or not, their heart rates had already been sky high from the chase, then pushed towards maximum by the sudden and surprising terror of seeing their teammates killed with them about to follow. It would take a few seconds to get their heads straight again, to assess what had just happened and how they should respond. During those few seconds, with their parasympathetic nervous systems overloaded, their gazes would be locked on the mouth of the alleyway and the danger posed by their target should they attempt to enter it again.

Which was a fatal mistake.

Because there was another, greater, danger that they, in their state of hyperstress, understood only when Victor burst out of the alleyway.

Entirely focused on how and when they would risk entering the alley again, they were not expecting their quarry to come to them instead.

Victor caught them both by surprise, double-tapping the first one his aim fell upon as he rounded the corner of the alleyway, then double-tapping the next guy, both centre mass, before adding a headshot to each in the split second of extra time he'd bought for himself with the double-taps.

Releasing the spent magazine, Victor inserted a fresh one and slipped the empty mag into a pocket – then dived to the ground when he caught a glimpse of movement across the street in his peripheral vision.

The mercenary he'd shot in the abdomen was now back on his feet.

The closest corpse cushioned Victor's fall as multiple bullets from the APC9 raked the wall next to where he'd been standing, exploding brick and sending fragments scattering down across his shoulders and the back of his head as clouds of dust expanded above him.

'*Son of a bitch*,' the gunman yelled after the burst of SMG fire and before a second, longer one slammed into the bodywork of the adjacent parked car and turned the windows into spiderwebs. Pebbles of glass joined the brick debris on top of Victor.

Rolling over onto his back, Victor slithered off the corpse

and onto the pavement, trying to ignore the hard little fragments of brick and glass that poked and prodded his shoulder blades. Despite the discomfort, even the sharper pieces were not going to pierce through his jacket and into his skin.

He swivelled his head to the side to peer beneath the undercarriage of the car riddled with bullet holes.

He saw a thin line of black road and a dark sliver of the tyres of the cars parked alongside the opposite kerb. No gunman's ankles to aim at, he was disappointed to discover – the guy shielded by a wheel through design or chance.

'*I have you now*,' the mercenary yelled. 'Where are you gonna go?'

Given the trajectory of the brick debris explosions, Victor judged the Slovakian had not shot from exactly opposite but a little further down the street from where they had pursued, which would put him approximately behind the next car along.

Victor called back, 'I'm quite content where I am as it happens.'

'You're gonna be content and dead soon.'

Equal odds that the mercenary was behind either far-side wheel, so Victor extended his arm beneath the adjacent car and shot five rounds at each.

From his position, he could see a portion of each wheel, although those on the near side obscured most of the other two.

No hits, but his shots were close enough that the gunman hiding behind the rearmost wheel sprang out to avoid the rounds punching through rims and deflating the tyres.

In doing so, Victor saw the man's shoes and the hems of his joggers.

The Slovakian yelled '*I have you now*' again, as he loosed another burst that pinged off metal and punched into brick-work – then he screamed and dropped as Victor's shots struck his feet and ankles.

Further bullets hit him in the hip and torso before Victor's pistol clicked dry.

The Slovakian slithered back into cover as Victor reloaded, but now there was no doubt behind which wheel he cowered.

Gun up and aiming where he looked, Victor crossed the street, seeing his own breath cloud in the light of the street-lamps and no such clouds from the prone figures on the pavement.

Always worth checking, he knew, because playing dead was an instinct engrained in almost every living creature. When attacked by a predator too fierce to fight and too re-lentless to flee, sometimes the only option remaining was to do nothing and pretend to have already fallen victim to it.

As he neared, he saw vapour rising from behind the vehi-cle, emerging in staccato clouds from the only member of the mercenary team still alive.

No noise, however, so Victor pictured the man with a hand over his mouth to stifle the inevitable expressions of agony.

Out of options, that mercenary had nothing left except pure hope. Maybe he was praying Victor had fled, unable to hear his footsteps on the road surface because the din of the car alarms drowned them out.

As Victor rounded the line of parked vehicles, he saw that not only had he been right in anticipating the Slovakian would have a hand over his mouth, but he had his eyes pinched closed too.

Blood seeped from the wounds to his torso and pumped from the lower extremities, flowing in a red waterfall over the kerb into the gutter.

One foot had been almost severed by multiple bullets striking the connecting ankle.

Pity was a concept that Victor understood, and sometimes could even feel if many contributing factors aligned at just the right time.

At this moment, there were none.

Sensing he was no longer alone, the Slovakian's eyes flickered opened. With the posterior tibial, peroneal and anterior tibial arteries of the ankle all ruptured, unconsciousness followed by death was mere seconds away.

'Do you still have me?' Victor asked him.

# PART TWO

PART TWO

# FOURTEEN

The building had a gravel drive that had become sparse over time. Grass and weeds grew up in intermittent patches. Tall Irish yew trees framed the property along with a low, iron fence. Though at least a couple of centuries old, the entrance had been modernised with a glass door and intercom that no one answered when Victor used a knuckle to push the call button.

Through the glass, he saw a long entrance hall with a blue carpet and a curved desk at the far end next to an opening that led into an even longer, if slimmer, hallway. He could hear a television playing from somewhere inside. There were open doorways leading off from the entrance hall, and he imagined one or more leading to a lounge or other reception room.

In the longer, slimmer hallway, he saw figures appear for brief moments as they went about their business. If he could see them, they could see him, yet no one looked his way. He could tell they were busy and wanted to avoid interrupting them so elected not to bang on the door or wave to attract their attention.

Of all his skills, patience was the first he had mastered.

The day he lost it, he knew, would be the same day he lost his life.

The entrance was set a few steps from ground level, so standing before the glass door, he was visible to passers-by if there had been any, but this property was along a country lane in a peaceful village in west County Clare. And though standing still in an elevated position was a blatant breach of protocol, he was as safe as he had ever been. Any shadow here could not hope to remain hidden. Everyone he had seen since stepping off the train and out of the station had looked at him with the unmistakable wary intrigue with which locals in such isolated communities viewed anyone they did not know. He had no need to look out for threats because any such threats would be signposted for him by suspicious villagers.

He turned around to look beyond the gravel drive and the short decorative fence of painted iron that had been set there before the invention of the internal combustion engine. On the other side the country lane was flanked by hedgerows, and from his elevated position he could see the fields and trees of rural Ireland extending far into the distance. This part of the country was beautiful in any season, whether the greens were enlivened by the summer sunshine or made deeper and richer in the haze of fog and rain.

This afternoon, sunlight streamed through patches of white clouds.

'I'm sorry,' a voice said behind him. 'Have you been waiting long?'

She wore a purple uniform that looked a bit like hospital scrubs. With one hand, she pulled open the glass door, while, with the other she tucked her magnetic key card and its accompanying chain back into a pocket.

It had been a few seconds over eight minutes. However, as Victor turned around, he said, 'Only a moment.'

'Mag's on her lunch,' the woman said in explanation, looking backwards at the desk at the far end of the entrance hall. 'I really am sorry.'

'Please, don't be. I can see you're busy today.'

'When are we not?' She gestured for him to enter, and he did so. 'Have you been here before?'

'No,' he told her.

'I didn't think so. I have a good memory for faces. Will I make you a cup of tea?'

'No, thank you.'

She pointed to a tablet computer on the desk. 'If you could sign in here, please.'

He nodded and examined the screen, where there was a dialogue box to input his details. No one had followed him, and no one would ever know he had been here, but he did not want to use his knuckle to tap the screen in case the woman mistook the action as mistrust in the levels of hygiene here. Instead, he looked away as if distracted, then reached into a pocket of his trousers.

'Pardon me,' he said. 'I need to take this call.'

'And I should get back to changing those sheets.' She pointed back to the glass door. 'You need a key card or a code to get out, so come find one of us when you want to be on your way, won't you?'

'I shall,' he answered. 'Thank you ... I didn't catch your name?'

'I'm Fran,' she told him. 'And you are?'

'Richard,' he said.

It was a name he had heard someone use on the train here.

'A pleasure to meet you, Richard. You have yourself a pleasant day now.'

In an increasingly interconnected world, acquiring truly clean identities that could cross borders was becoming increasingly complicated, and the expense of those legends had skyrocketed. For any typical contract, Victor would use a single new identity, and that alone would constitute the most significant individual expense.

Three separate identities he had never used before, which he had been keeping in reserve for this purpose, had accompanied him. Now only one remained, the first burned before he had taken the ferry from the UK across the Irish Sea, leaving out of Liverpool this time, since the last time he had made such a trip he had flown first into Belfast before the long journey south. The second identity he had cut to pieces in Dublin after checking out of his hotel prior to leaving the city to come here by train. The third, final one would see him back to the Isle of Man, and there he would await the arrival of an entirely new legend before returning to the mainland to ensure it was impossible for anyone, whether lone professional or intelligence agency, to know he had ever come to this little village in the middle of nowhere.

A woman with bone-white hair shorter than his own emerged from a connecting corridor. She pushed a small trolley that looked to him as if it had some specific purpose he could not decipher – it had been repurposed to carry an assortment of clothes and old shoes.

She asked, 'Do you have any dried timber?'

Her pale green cardigan was stained with spots of custard or some pudding.

'Not on me right now.'

He saw that she had no teeth, and she clutched a set of dentures in one hand.

'For furniture,' she explained. 'Janice said she would get some for me, but I can't find her.'

Victor looked both ways along the corridor. 'I'm sure she's just busy at the moment and will get back to you when she can.'

'I don't want to keep making excuses for her. Would you like the blue scarf?'

She rummaged in her trolley, pulling out a black sock from the pile and offering it to him.

'I already have two just like it, thank you.'

'Keep your neck warm in the winter.'

'I appreciate the offer, but I'm good.'

'This is what I'm looking for,' she said, dropping the sock back in her trolley and taking hold of a wooden handrail that ran the length of the corridor.

With both hands wrapped around the rail, she tried to heave it from the wall. Victor watched, unsure what to say or do.

'Ow,' she said, releasing the handrail after a moment of ineffective pulling on it. She looked at her palms. 'That hurt.'

'Maybe wait for Janice,' he told her. 'She'll be back soon.'

'Did you see her?'

'Oh, yes. I bumped into her on the way here. She told me to let you know she's bringing the dried timber shortly.'

The woman frowned, her forehead becoming a crinkled mass of deep lines. 'Why ever would I want dried timber?'

He had no answer to that.

'Silly boy,' she said, pushing her trolley away.

He stood for a moment, listening to the squeaks of the trolley wheels fade. He could hear wailing too. Far off and dulled by intervening walls and ambient sounds, it was unmistakable to his ear, which, like no other, knew all the melodies of suffering.

He could leave, Victor realised at that moment.

He could walk away right now and no one could stop him.

No one would even try to stop him.

He could turn around and walk straight back through the glass doors, and that would be it. No consequences, no fallout. The woman with the trolley had no doubt already forgotten he had ever existed. The woman who had let him in had mistaken him for someone he was not; if it occurred to her to wonder what became of his visit, she might conclude he had finished his business before leaving without her noticing. It wasn't as though she would think twice about him, let alone track him down to extract an explanation.

And it was better to go, he concluded.

Nothing good could come of what he was doing. It had been too long, anyway.

What was the point?

The glass-fronted entrance stood at the other end of the hallway. Beyond those doors was the gravel drive, along with the short fence, the hedges and fields across the street, all bathed in bright sunlight.

A lovely day to take a walk and enjoy nature's simple pleasures.

How many years had it been since he had been able to do just that? He had gone to the expense of three clean legends to come here and had first used himself as bait to give any potential enemies the opportunity to expose themselves.

Right now, he was as anonymous and safe as he might ever be in his entire life from this point onwards.

He could do it. He could take that walk without even needing to look over his shoulder, wander across the fields and see where it took him.

Maybe find a brook and take a nap in the shade of a tree, with the nearby water playing the kind of lullaby that he had never known before. If he did not experience it here and now, he knew for certain he would never get another chance.

He rocked his head from side to side to crack his neck.

Then he returned his attention to the tablet and used a knuckle to input his fake name before opting out of the optional details that included his email address and mode of transportation. The next box asked him for the resident's name, and he tapped out her details. The final box asked him to select his relationship to the resident from a list of four: healthcare provider, carer, friend or family.

Victor took a deep breath, then used his knuckle to tap the last of the four options.

# FIFTEEN

The tablet on the reception desk had not told him where to go, and he did not want to interrupt any of the busy staff. He was content to wander the corridors, glancing through open doorways as he went, to see who was inside, then moving on when he recognised none of the faces that looked back. He saw men and women with white hair or almost none playing cards or dominoes, or working at jigsaws in various stages of completion. Cups of tea, some in actual cups but most in plastic beakers, were ubiquitous wherever there were residents.

In the entranceway to a TV room at the back of the building, he stood to one side to let an old man shuffle by barefoot. His shoulders stooped and his head hung down low near his chest; the man walked backwards.

After passing Victor, the man stopped, and although his eyes could not be seen, it seemed as if he was regarding Victor. Maybe recognising him as a stranger, maybe wanting to say something but unable to find the words.

Then, the man continued on his way without colliding with anyone or any piece of furniture. It seemed almost an impossibility for him to do so, yet he glided through the space without trouble.

French doors led outside from the TV room, and Victor stepped into the garden at the rear of the building.

There, she was easy to spot even if she no longer wore the traditional full habit, retaining only the white cap and veil. Sitting in a wheelchair, a woollen blanket covered her legs and lap.

Not knowing how well she saw or heard, he made sure to circle around so he could approach her from the front, to give her as much time to notice him as possible. She had a book in her lap that was closed, her hands resting atop it as she gazed out at the garden. It was a neat, handsome space. Flower beds framed a long lawn, and a stone bird-bath lay at the centre point of the grass. Her wheelchair was parked on the edge of the paving stones that formed a patio between the building and the lawn. Other residents sat on nearby benches or under parasols at tables, drinking tea and nibbling on biscuits.

He noticed a change in her posture as he approached, her eyes shifting focus from whatever she had been looking at to him; then, when he was a few metres away, her posture became more upright in the chair as she stared at him with a puzzled expression.

That puzzlement continued until he stopped before her wheelchair and said, 'Good afternoon', after which she looked at him in a quizzical way as if he were a mystery to solve.

In a way, he was just that.

When he opened his mouth to say more, she raised a palm in the fast, sharp gesture he knew so well.

'It'll come to me,' she said. 'Give me a moment.'

'There's no rush.'

They had both changed a lot in the intervening decades: she had gone from middle-aged woman to old woman, and he from boy to man.

She had bright green eyes that had lost none of the lustre he remembered, only now they were ringed with creases and weariness. Those green eyes stared unblinking as she thought back years and decades, searching through all the faces floating in her memory, trying to match the one that looked down upon her. He had last seen her when he was a teenager, so the many surgeries that had altered his adult features made no difference to the face she remembered. Regardless, he was expecting her to give up and ask him his name.

He realised he would tell her if she should ask, although he had only uttered that name once in all the intervening years. He could only recall it now when he forced himself to remember who he had been so long ago. Now, that person seemed to be someone else entirely, someone he had only known in another existence, another reality.

Then it occurred to Victor that perhaps, like the woman with the trolley, she was suffering from dementia and would not know him even if he spelt out his name and detailed all he could recall from his days in the orphanage.

What would he do then?

What would he say to her?

The green eyes widened in sudden realisation, and her lips parted in surprise and disbelief.

'You were always so skinny,' she said eventually, her expression softening into a small smile before hardening again. 'I see my attempts to fatten you up failed.'

'Suits are slimming,' Victor assured.

She tutted, unconvinced. 'You're tall now.'

He nodded.

'You've lost your accent,' she told him.

'That happens when you travel a lot,' he said in return.

'I still have mine.'

When Mother Maria had joined the orphanage shortly after he had arrived himself, the boys had been told she had 'come all the way from Ireland to be with us', so in his youthful ignorance he had believed her accent was Irish. He had spent his life thinking she was Irish before hearing her speak again here and placing her as maybe Polish. Still, her way of speaking had been so influenced by her many travels, her missionary work, and her tenures in different nunneries and orphanages around the world, that even Victor could not be sure where she had been raised.

Now it seemed too impolite – and far too late – even to consider asking her for her nationality.

'What happened to your hands?' she asked, noticing his palms and the scabs and scratches he had acquired when falling out of Emilie's vehicle.

'I slipped on a banana skin.'

Her eyes narrowed in a way he knew well, and he found himself no longer a man making a joke but the boy who once quaked at her wrath.

'When you ran away,' she then said, 'I believed that was it and I would never see you again. I have to say I haven't thought about you in many years, but we looked for you back then. We really did.'

'I was always good at hiding myself from the world.'

'Do you still confess your sins?'

'Once every year.'

Another tut, this one of true condemnation. 'That is not enough.'

'Nowhere near enough,' he agreed. 'But if I went whenever I needed to, it would be unfair to the other sinners to take up so much time in the confessional.'

Her eyes narrowed to show her disapproval at his flippant tone. 'What are you doing here?'

'I came to see you.'

'Why?'

There was an accusation in the tone from which Victor did everything possible not to instinctively retreat.

'I wanted to come before now,' he said, and the guilt of not doing so was a crushing weight on his chest. 'But my work ... I'm always travelling, always busy.'

He could not say the truth, that for years he had done everything possible to ignore and forget his past, seeing it only as a distraction and, in that distraction, a vulnerability he was not prepared to accept. And, beyond that, a simple visit like this could be a death sentence to her if anyone managed to follow him. Only now, with the culmination of his skills and years of knowledge, and the incredible expense of three clean, unused legends, had he been able to ensure there was no risk to her at all.

Her mouth opened to speak, but no words emerged.

Instead, her eyes closed, and her head bowed, and she cried.

And Victor, who last shed tears as a small boy long before setting foot in the orphanage, felt a mist threatening to cross his own eyes.

She reached out her hands to him, and he held them while she sobbed.

# SIXTEEN

In time, Mother Maria pulled a handkerchief from a sleeve, dabbed her eyes dry and blew her nose. A member of staff saw her distress and approached, until Victor shook his head to tell them it was okay and help was not required.

After she had tucked the handkerchief away, she said, 'Go to confession more often, please.'

'I'll try.'

She showed a hint of a smile. 'You were never as naughty a boy as you were made out to be, I know.'

'Maybe I was worse, only I didn't let you see it.'

'You never once started a fight that I witnessed.'

'I should have done.'

'You were too quiet, yes. You kept to yourself too much. Boys will see that as a weakness and test it, especially when those boys, like you, have no family of their own. I'm sorry I wasn't always able to protect you.'

He did not tell her how valuable those early confrontations had been, how they had served him well in later life

84

because he had discovered back then that the pain of being hit was only ever temporary. He had never been scared of any pain since.

'Not that you really needed me to,' she added. 'Even smaller, you never complained, never cried. Your fault was only ever hitting them back with as much ferocity as they hit you, so by the time the staff arrived, it seemed that you were an equal troublemaker.'

He shrugged. 'I don't like to give up.'

'That's pride,' she said. 'We need humility. When we have too much belief in ourselves that goes unfulfilled, it only leads us to needless anger.'

'I'm not sure I can even remember the last time I was angry.'

As soon as he'd said the words, he realised they were incorrect. He could remember the exact last time he was angry, and why. It had been in Serbia, in a mansion outside Belgrade, the first loss of temper for several years. He could remember the two times before it too: in a café in southern Bulgaria and, in particular, in a bathroom in Nicosia, Cyprus, when the last sliver of humanity he had spent years burying had begun to claw its way out of the grave.

He corrected himself. 'It's very rare for me to lose my temper these days.'

'I'm pleased to hear this,' Mother Maria said. 'After you left, I worried you would only get yourself into more trouble.'

'I did,' he admitted, thinking of the time he had spent as a pickpocket, as a car thief, as a vagrant, before he ended up in the military. 'But I pulled myself together eventually.'

'Married?'

'No.'

'Children?'

'Not that I know of.'

She frowned.

'I'm joking.'

She tutted, not approving of his humour but not condemning him either.

She frowned. 'You should have a family by now. It does not befit a man to remain a bachelor too long. Eligible women seeking a partner will look at him and think there must be something wrong beneath the surface.'

'What do you know of marriage and what eligible women want?'

'You think because I devoted my life to God, I do not understand the needs and wants of His creations?'

He conceded the point. 'My work makes relationships difficult.'

'That's a poor excuse if ever I heard one.'

'You chose God; I chose a different path, yet one that is no less restrictive.'

Victor felt a prickle of heat in his armpits and the middle of his back because there was an inevitable question she would ask him, and of all the people in this world, she was the only one to whom he doubted his ability to effectively lie.

More than that, lying to her after all she had done for him felt like the ultimate betrayal.

When she asked, 'And what is it you do for a living that makes relationships so difficult?' the prickle of heat became an inferno.

She looked up at him with nothing except a genuine curiosity, and yet he had never felt so judged and had never been so woefully unprepared.

With his mind a blank, his lips parted as he willed himself

to think of something – anything – that would be convincing. 'I'm ... I'm a ...'

Her palm shot up like it had at the start of the conversation, as it had so many times all those years ago.

'Perhaps you should not say,' she said in a knowing tone. 'To save us both the ignominy of an untruth.'

There was no relief, only more judgement.

He consoled himself with the thought that although revealing the truth to her would bear no consequence to him – who could she tell who would even believe her, and what could they possibly do with that information? – he knew she would feel responsible for the choices he had made even outside her care. Mother Maria would spend her remaining time believing she had failed him, and he could not bear that thought.

Of all the occasions when he had survived adversity through sheer force of will, overcoming exhaustion, injury or certain death, none taxed his resolve as much as maintaining eye contact did now.

She lowered her palm and placed it back to the book in her lap.

'What time is it?'

Grateful to have the excuse to look anywhere else, he checked his watch, although he did not need to do so to know the time. He had also found that people tended to mistrust his accuracy until they had seen the assurance of a timepiece.

'Just gone two in the afternoon,' he said, neatening back up his sleeve.

'That will be why I'm tired,' she said. 'I always am after lunch these days.'

He imagined the food in such an establishment needed to be overcooked to ensure residents with impaired ability to chew or swallow would not choke. Soft food like that would be digested quicker, and with it, a rapid rise in blood glucose necessitating a spike of insulin to bring that level back down again. Such a sudden lowering of blood sugar would mean an inevitable tiredness. With metabolic diseases so common among the aged, he thought it evident that foods much lower on the glycaemic index should be served to residents to compensate. He considered sending them an email with a meal plan laid out to balance the needs of the residents while still being cost-effective to source and simple to prepare.

'Wheel me back inside, please.'

'Of course.'

He circled her and used a heel to release the brake. She felt so light it was almost like pushing an empty wheelchair. He imagined that, beneath the blanket, atrophy had shrunk her legs to little more than bones covered in skin.

'You haven't asked me why I'm in this chair.'

'That's none of my business.'

'Progressive multiple sclerosis,' she told him. 'Not merely old age.'

'I'm sorry.'

'Don't be,' she said. 'I was diagnosed late in life, later than most, so I've been more fortunate than many. It's my time, whether this or something else. I am ready for the embrace of our Lord.'

He manoeuvred her across the patio and between the tables. She waved at some of the other residents, and some waved back at her.

She motioned to him to stop pushing when they reached

an elevator midway down the long hallway. She reached to press the call button, and he watched how much that small action made her shake and tremble.

Inside her room, she asked him to fetch two staff members, explaining, 'I can no longer climb into bed unassisted.'

'I will do it,' he said and waited in case it was not polite to offer or should it compromise her nun's modesty.

'You?' Her tone was incredulous. 'I seem to recall you doing everything in your power to avoid exertion. The only boy in the home who reached for a book instead of a ball.'

'I changed,' he said, then thought about a lesson that had been drilled into him in his early days as a professional: that people like him did not change, they only adapted. They were words he had spent almost his entire adult life believing.

She accepted the offer with a nod, and gestured for him to proceed.

He removed the book and blanket from her lap and placed them on an armchair in one corner of her room. With gentle movements, he then manoeuvred one arm beneath her thighs and the other around her back.

'Are you certain you have me?' she asked. 'We can call the nurses if you prefer.'

She was trepidatious and unconvinced that he alone could do that which was typically done by two.

'I have you,' he assured.

With her safe in his arms, Victor lifted with his back and hamstrings, bringing her out of the chair at a slow, careful speed to ensure she had enough time to let him know if he held onto her with too much force or otherwise caused her unintentional discomfort.

Turning around on the spot, he lowered her down at the

same slow, gentle rate onto her bed, the covers of which he had already pulled back. Once lying down, she was able to manoeuvre herself into a comfortable position and drag back the bedclothes.

'Thank you,' she said.

'Any time.'

An inane thing to say, he realised, since the time she had left was so obviously finite, and he would never risk coming back here again. Even with the end near, there were still almost endless sufferings his enemies could inflict on her in the hopes of drawing him forth before her time had run out.

And it would work.

He would come back and show them the true meaning of suffering.

'I hope you still take your promises seriously.'

'Maybe too seriously,' he said, feeling a sudden itch on his left thigh.

'I'm glad I taught you at least one thing.'

'You taught me a lot more than simply that.'

'Maybe, and yet that is the most important because what makes us who we are is our word,' she told him. 'Never forget, though everything else can be taken from you, your money, your health, even your dignity ... it is only you who has the power to give away your honour.'

Victor elected not to tell Mother Maria this was one lesson of hers that was far too late for him to heed.

# SEVENTEEN

Bucharest was beautiful in the morning when the rising sun cast long, crooked shadows and before the air was saturated with traffic noise. Victor's rented apartment sat on the fourth floor of a building whose façade was still pockmarked with decades-old bullet holes left behind from the revolution. There were many such reminders across the city, whether unrepaired as a deliberate reminder of those days when communism fell or because there were better things to spend money on, Victor did not know.

The hotel across the street was a prestigious establishment with the flags of multiple countries rippling in the breeze above the awnings. No doormen, Victor noted, but from his reconnaissance, he knew many porters waited inside in the lobby, under the lead of a fiercely efficient concierge whose subtle gestures of direction to her staff carried the weight of a drill sergeant's bark. While sipping coffee and pretending to read a newspaper, Victor had been impressed by the concierge's almost inhuman level of poise and resourcefulness, no matter how many guests and members of staff demanded her attention. Assuming she had the same flexible attitude to morality as himself, Victor could imagine her as an exceptional professional should she decide on a change of career.

The concierge's dark hair and tanned skin made him think of a different woman, only one whose opposite sense of morality ensured she and Victor could never be more than allies of convenience, although any such convenience always ended with them as enemies. Sometimes, he felt as though Raven were here watching him. No matter how fast he moved or how long he acted as if ignorant, she was never there when he spun around. And if it was through a reticle of a rifle's sights that Raven watched him, she had not yet decided to squeeze the trigger.

This morning, Victor had no rifle to complete his contract. Because he was being paid to kill not one target but two, his weapon of choice was more suited to killing multiple people at once. For any typical job, a grenade launcher would never make Victor's list of appropriate weaponry. However, the client wanted him to deliver their message with as much noise, as much mess, as possible.

The FN40GL was primarily designed to operate as an underslung attachment for the SCAR assault rifle, also made by Fabrique Nationale. Victor was an enthusiast of the SCAR, but not only was he unable to procure one for this particular job, it wasn't helpful to its completion. His targets were meeting in a hotel suite, and every shred of information supplied to Victor indicated they were not the kind of people who would keep the blinds open for illicit liaisons. Since both targets were bringing security details – first-class security at that – Victor had no desire to enter such a hornets' nest at the kind of range that a SCAR would be necessary.

Far simpler to shoot a few grenades through the windows.

He had a tactical belt loaded with six 40mm frag grenades. The launcher was a single-shot weapon, meaning he would manually reload a fresh grenade after every shot. Still, the launcher automatically ejected the empty grenade case so he could place all six grenades into the hotel suite in around ten seconds. With a kill radius of five metres and the suite being twenty metres square, with both the main space and the separate bedroom, he deemed four would be more than enough to assassinate his targets and annihilate both security details wherever they were located. Should anyone be fortunate enough to be using the bathroom at the exact moment of the attack, they might live, but Victor would remain nearby to deal with that, assuming whoever survived was one of the targets. If a security guard happened to take a leak at the right time, then good for them.

Aside from the grenade launcher, he had his customary sidearm, a Five-seveN, also made by FN. Protocol stated that all weapons had a shelf life of a single contract, so this particular pistol was a separate weapon from the one he had used for the Brussels contract and then disposed of after his encounter with the Slovakian mercenaries in Rotterdam.

The Five-seveN was loaded with subsonic rounds to dampen the otherwise fierce crack of the 5.7mm ammunition breaking through the sound barrier. With a suppressor, the noise of the muzzle report was strangled down in decibels to the comparable slam of a car door. To a trained ear, a gunshot nonetheless, but one that could go ignored in the ambient rumble of a bustling city. In many ways, it was a waste of the Five-seveN to use it with subsonic ammunition since the primary benefit of that ammunition was its velocity that was more akin to a rifle than a sidearm. Combined with the small calibre, it rendered most kinds of personal body armour redundant and ensured the type of light cover that might otherwise block or divert the path of a bullet, such a car, would not save a target. None of which was true of subsonic rounds. Still, the pistol felt right in Victor's hand, whether because he had grown accustomed to using one for several years or via an accident of perfect ergonomics between the weapon's grip and his own, the result was the same. And the small calibre meant the gun could hold twenty bullets – if he could obtain the restricted magazine – which was otherwise unheard of with sidearms.

Victor checked both weapons one final time and waited for his targets to arrive.

In his extensive experience, targets fell into one of two broad categories: those who knew they were at risk of assassination and those naïve enough to believe no one could want them dead. Whether civilian or professional, everyone had enemies, and most had many more than they realised. Few, however, had the means to contact him and fewer still could afford his substantial fee. It was fortunate for those countless ignorant souls wandering around, unaware of how deeply they were hated or how inconvenient they were to another's ambitions.

On occasions, when faced with the inarguable reality of their mortality, some targets still refused to believe what was happening. In Victor's experience, denial was perhaps the most potent self-defence mechanism the human mind could conjure, sparing itself from temporary anguish even at the expense of its permanent existence. Not that acceptance would prove any more productive.

Understanding that Victor was about to kill them was not the same thing as being able to stop it.

# EIGHTEEN

Jan Schulz should have acted as though he knew he was a target. A private spy for the highest bidder, just doing his day job put him in the crosshairs of many influential individuals. He had to be aware that for every piece of illicit information he stole or traded, he added another enemy to an already expansive list. Victor's own roll call of adversaries was not dissimilar; only the manner in which he conducted himself could not be more different from that of the German he was hunting on behalf of Lambert's client.

Whereas Victor could take an hour making a ten-minute journey, thanks to the extensive countersurveillance measures he employed, Schulz finished that same trip in eight, not only taking the most direct route possible but moving at speed too. The man had a fast gait, as though he was always running late or as if the world itself rotated at too slow a speed. Such a pace meant he was never going to spot a shadow like Victor.

Schulz wore a grey Italian suit, his jacket open and showing the floral silk lining as the quarters flapped in the drag. He was unarmed – at least, he had no firearm on his person. The suit's cut left no room to hide even a compact sidearm. A knife could be concealed almost anywhere on his person, although any such weapon would have to be pocketknife sized not to give itself away.

The German had been an officer in the BKA – Germany's federal investigation organisation – before acting as a troubleshooter for politicians in various European countries. His extensive list of contacts supplied him with information that formed the core of his value to clients now, not any tradecraft or lack thereof. Nothing in the dossier suggested the German ever dirtied his manicured nails.

He had already been in the city a couple of days, during which Victor had taken the time to get to know him a little better prior to his meeting at the Marmorosch Hotel. At that meeting, Schulz was selling the intelligence stolen from Lambert's client in the Ministry of Defence. Although not the thief himself, Schulz was a conduit between the as-yet-unidentified thief and the ultimate buyer, Marion Ysiv.

Although they had not met in person before today, Schulz and Ysiv conducted business on a semi-regular basis, trading secrets back and forth. Sometimes Ysiv sold and Schulz bought. Other times, buyer and seller roles were reversed.

According to Lambert's information, neither target was known to carry weapons. However, for this first face to face, both were coming with protection. Schulz's two bodyguards were veterans of the German army while Marion

Ysiv, who was both former IDF and former Mossad, would be accompanied by three security personnel with the same background as herself. Given the disparity in numbers, Victor expected that Schulz had chosen the place and time and so Ysiv's extra protection was the parity to those choices.

From the rented apartment, Victor watched Schulz arrive at the Marmorosch twenty minutes before the meeting was due to start. The apartment had been let from a private host via a website for holiday rentals in Bucharest. Victor had never met the host, and communicated only via email and text messaging. One of Victor's Cayman Island bank accounts had paid the fee in full, in advance, on behalf of a shell company registered on the Isle of Man – an ever-revolving series of such accounts and companies handled his travel arrangements on behalf of people who didn't exist, existed only on paper, or were in fact real but were incapable of travelling themselves due to comas or similarly debilitating conditions.

Because Schulz and Ysiv were meeting in the morning, and like most hotels this particular one had a mid-afternoon check-in time, the suite had been booked from the previous day. The hotel suite was in Schulz's name, and yet fifteen minutes after entering the lobby, neither the German nor his security detail had stepped inside. Maybe this was a condition of the meeting between associates who didn't trust each other. Since Schulz booked the suite in advance, he had to wait in the lobby for Ysiv to arrive so she could witness him checking in, proving no one could be lying in wait to ambush her.

With Schulz and his bodyguards now inside the hotel,

and Ysiv due to arrive soon, Victor eased open the apartment's balcony door so there was nothing interrupting the arc of the grenades until they smashed through the windows of the suite and killed everyone inside.

# NINETEEN

Marion Ysiv arrived a few minutes later, her black Lexus SUV pulling up directly outside the hotel entrance and her security detail spilling out of the vehicle with quick, efficient movements. They did not hurry, but they understood the moment of vulnerability for both their client and themselves. As soon as the lead guy had given the heads-up that the lobby was clear of any threats, the other two ushered Ysiv from the Lexus and had her outside beneath the awning within a couple of seconds. The Lexus itself pulled away once Ysiv was inside the hotel proper.

Yes, Victor thought, he could have shot her within that small window of time had the contract not required he kill Schulz as well, although he would not have chosen this strike point. Far too public, far too loud, and far too amateurish for that increased exposure. More dangerous too, since the narrow street and steep angle meant he would struggle to keep a visual on the security detail. If they were so inclined, they could kick down the building's front door and ascend the internal stairs to assault his position without him realising. He had done similar himself once.

The efficiency of her security detail meant Victor caught no glimpse of Ysiv's face. Still, he had a better look at her bodyguards, who were a match for the photographs in the supplied dossier. That had no recent image of Ysiv, who had done such a fine job of operating in the shadows for several years that the only photographs of her were at least a decade out of date.

Even if Victor could see her face from this angle, it would be impossible to confirm it was her with the distance. If she was using a double, Victor would consider that a failure of Lambert's information, not himself. His broker was adamant the dossier was accurate, his sources reliable and his client inflexible. Victor was being paid to kill the woman and the man meeting together this morning. He wasn't being paid to ascertain their identities first. For one thing, he would have charged a lot more for the extra work.

With a high-end hotel like this, no one had to wait long to check in. Guests did it online before arriving, or in person at the front desk, where management ensured there were more than enough staff to avoid forcing their customers to queue up. For security's sake, Schulz would not check in remotely, and although this time of the morning would be one of the busiest periods for the front desk, with guests checking out, the plentiful, competent staff meant the entire process would take no more than ten minutes. Even at a leisurely pace, they would reach the suite within five minutes. Then, the security detail would take a few moments to check the suite and close the blinds, during which Ysiv and Schulz might be waiting outside, so Victor would give them a couple of minutes to get

101

comfortable. From the point when Ysiv arrived, they would be inside the suite within fifteen minutes, and all would be dead soon afterwards.

With the suite still empty as Victor's watch showed sixteen minutes had passed since Ysiv stepped inside the hotel, he wondered what had caused the delay. Based on the number of people coming and going from the entrance, it was no busier than usual, and nothing about their demeanours suggested anything was out of the ordinary. Perhaps Ysiv and Schulz had spent a few moments greeting one another in the lobby. How long did it take to say 'hello' and 'how have you been?'? Although he had become an expert at analysing behaviour and predicting actions, the intricacies of such simple interactions were so outside his own experiences that he had no frame of reference with which to understand them.

But when the blinds were still open at nineteen minutes, he knew something was wrong.

'They have another room,' Victor told Lambert when the line connected. 'The one you gave me is a decoy.'

'How can you be sure?'

'For the same reason you recruited me in the first place. I'm good at this.'

'Shit,' Lambert said.

'Don't curse,' Victor told him, then, 'Check for bookings made using different names, either Ysiv's entourage or Schulz's own.'

'I don't have time for this.'

'Then the job is over, and I'm walking.'

A few seconds of silence on the line while Lambert thought, then said, 'Hold on.'

Victor could hear Lambert breathing and tapping keys,

and he pictured him working on a computer, using illicit means to access the hotel's records in the same way he had done to establish the dossier in the first place.

'Nada,' Lambert said. 'None of them have booked into this hotel.'

'A fake name then.'

'Already looking at known aliases, and it's the same.'

'Then it's unknown.'

'And they could be anywhere in the hotel.'

'Not anywhere,' Victor said. 'Has anyone booked this hotel in the last fifteen minutes?'

'Seven separate bookings.'

'Bookings for today,' he continued. 'They would need to pay extra for early check-in, which'll be noted as an additional expense.'

'One booking.'

'That's them. Room number?'

'302 ... but it won't help you. They're foreign nationals on the booking, so they scanned their passports. It's a family of five from Dubai. And their nanny. I'm looking at their photographs right now.' Lambert sighed down the line. 'Schulz's people must have booked the suite at another time. Without knowing what name they used, we can't possibly know where they are right now.'

'This meeting was scheduled over a week ago, correct?'

'That's right.'

'It's important to both parties.'

'Absolutely.'

'Then they wouldn't have taken any chances with the hotel being booked up.'

'What are you saying?'

'They booked the decoy at the same time they booked the suite where the actual meeting is taking place. Accounting for the time it takes to actually fill in their details, there'll be a second booking made within five minutes of the first. That's where they are now.'

Lambert was tapping keys harder now, the plastic clicking louder and more urgent in Victor's ear. But no sounds of breathing this time. Lambert was holding his breath.

'There's two,' he said, sighing with disappointment and frustration. 'Both bookings with timestamps three and four minutes after the original, no passports scanned because they're both domestic bookings and so no way to tell which one we want.'

Victor said, 'The suite I'm overlooking has one separate bedroom. The hotel designates this kind of room as an executive suite. They also have junior suites, which do not have the separate bedroom and, therefore, less overall space. Schulz wants plenty of room to chat comfortably and, given their respective security details, a junior suite wouldn't cut it. If both of these bookings are for executive suites, then the job's over, but if only one is—'

'Four-sixteen,' Lambert said, voice loud with enthusiasm and triumph. 'It's on the same floor as the booking in Schulz's name, three doors along. We can still get this done.'

Raising the grenade launcher, Victor scanned the façade of the hotel across the street, searching for signs of life at nearby windows before remembering the hotel used the standard alternating numbering system for its rooms.

Lambert realised himself a moment later as Victor was already folding away the grenade launcher.

'It'll be an interior room overlooking the atrium.'

'I know,' Victor said. 'Can your people take care of the cameras?'

'The hotel server is about to become the unfortunate victim of a malicious hacker.'

'Then,' Victor said as he checked his Five-seveN, 'it's Plan B.'

# TWENTY

Jan Schulz opened up the suite and his pair of security guys stepped inside first. Two of Marion Ysiv's detail followed. At the same time, the third stayed outside in the hallway with his foot in the door to stop it from closing again. Ysiv and Schulz stood waiting, both patient and silent.

'*Alles klar*,' Schulz's most senior guy told him when he returned to the doorway after a minute.

One of Ysiv's security nodded his confirmation the suite was secure.

Schulz smiled Ysiv's way, who smiled back.

'Shall we?' he asked, gesturing for her to go first.

Their respective entourages made room for their clients to enter the room. Schulz headed straight for the chaise longue in the expansive lounge area of the suite. It lay against the far wall beneath a large window that looked out into the atrium that formed the hotel's core. The blinds were open, although a net curtain provided a degree of privacy from the many other rooms that overlooked the open space.

Marion Ysiv crossed the suite at a more conservative pace, her head swivelling to note the various features and fixtures. Her ex-Mossad heavies immediately took up sentry positions, while his own did the same. Schulz, already comfortable in the centre of the sofa, watched Ysiv with interest. She was more beautiful than he had expected, and he wondered how he could maintain his professionalism when conducting an illicit trade in stolen secrets with a former spy while angling to get her into bed at the same time. He adopted a power pose, arms stretched out along the back of the sofa, legs spread wide. Jan Schulz had a tall, lean build. At forty-five, he was well presented in a grey pinstripe suit and salmon shirt, open at the top button to reveal a patterned detailing around the inside of the collar. A thin, neat beard surrounded his mouth, and the dark blond hair swept into a side parting had lost much of its colour. His pale face was moisturised, and his eyebrows were dense rectangles that seemed to never stay still as he spoke and expressed. When he crossed his legs, she saw his socks were a paisley of baby blue and pink.

He made sure to smile, but not too much, and also to suck in his stomach. Though of a lifelong trim physique, a little belly had begun to appear these last few years since tipping over forty. Not that noticeable standing up or with a jacket buttoned. More pronounced when sitting down, however, the belt of his trousers acting as a shelf for his middle-aged spread to rest.

He carried a crocodile-skin briefcase that had been a lavish gift from a former employer as a little thank you for yet another job well done. Given his exemplary track record, Schulz bemoaned the fact he was not, in fact, buried under a vast pile of such rewards. Still, most businesses, and governments, were miserly and did everything possible to delay paying his fees while quibbling over every last billable expense.

That was one of the reasons he preferred to work for private clients. Not only did they have deeper pockets, but because they often had significant personal stakes in the outcome of his assignments, they were more likely to be grateful – and generous – when he delivered. His standard tactic was to overstate the difficulty of a given task, the time it would take to complete it, and the potential fallout of the means he took to achieve its success. Invariably, one of those factors would prove to be an understatement, such was the unpredictability of the private intelligence-gathering business, but all else being equal, the other overstatements would prove to be just that. And would therefore lead to gifts like the $5,000 briefcase.

Like Schulz, Marion Ysiv was a middleman – middle-*wo*man – so he was ignorant of her client's identity. Such ignorance was both a blessing and a curse. The latter was evident since it meant he could be dealing with all sorts of unsavoury organisations like terrorists and rogue states. Else, it could be helpful for him to know with whom he was ultimately dealing because they might prove to be a useful or profitable client to add to his list. The blessing was directly linked to this, since if he was passing secrets to jihadis or North Korea, then he would never know and could continue his life with a mostly clear conscience.

Both sets of security personnel finished their checks and passed wordless confirmations to their respective clients that it was safe to commence.

'I must say,' Schulz began, having carefully composed his words, 'despite our communications, you're really not what I was expecting.'

Settling into the sofa opposite, Ysiv replied, 'In what sense?'

Given that he had been so careful in engineering such a response, Schulz already had his follow-up prepared. 'What I mean is, you are a lot more glamorous in person than over email.'

He pursed his lips for a tiny sliver of flirtatiousness, which could also be construed as simple friendliness. It was a minefield just complimenting a woman in the twenty-first century without inviting puritanical wrath, so he could not simply say what he meant, that he found her highly attractive. Hence, an adjacent synonym like glamorous had to do in its place. If she seemed to like the compliment, he could walk the tightrope and try with something more forthright. If she showed even a hint of displeasure, he had plausible deniability.

At first, he thought he had overstepped to an irrecoverable degree as her face remained unchanged. She held his gaze with her unblinking eyes. His mind scrambled for some way to claw back the situation before she labelled him a misogynist on her way to the door, but, finally, she smiled.

Schulz smiled too with the rush of relief he had not ruined the deal before it could even be discussed.

Ysiv did not volley the ball back to his side of the court, he was sad to find, and she went straight into business.

'You have the plans?'

Though her ex-Mossad heavies were nearby, Schulz's two guys were by the door behind them, so there was no danger of a shakedown. One of Ysiv's heavies was in constant motion, checking and re-checking the bathroom and the bedroom, making it hard for Schulz to relax. Still, he reminded himself that Ysiv's reputation was paramount to her capacity to conduct business. Any rumour of deceit, let alone theft, would ruin her.

He nodded towards his briefcase. 'Hard copies, hundreds of pages. I'm sure we would both prefer digital files but there are far too many encryptions that cannot be broken needed to access such things. Thankfully, no password is required to read a printout. I find it funny that in today's world we forget how heavy data actually is.' He flexed his hand. 'I recommend you have one of your people carry the folder away.'

'I'm a lot stronger than I might appear.'

His masculinity challenged, Schulz smiled and ceased flexing his hand. 'Just a little joke between friends.'

'I'm afraid there's no such thing as a friend in this trade.'

'I disagree. I'm friends with most people with whom I do business.'

'Including this client? You assured me you've been dealing with them anonymously. If you know who they are then you're a liability to them. Which is not something you should want to be and it's not something that makes me comfortable dealing with you.'

'You have no need to worry,' he said. 'I see all my clients as friends, and as such they see me in return, even in situations like this when I don't know who they are.'

'Interesting strategy given you're stealing from them.'

He responded with a tight smile. 'They still get the plans for the lasers, so how can there be a theft?'

'Do they know you're selling to me on the side?'

The smile tightened even further. 'Why don't we skip the preamble and get on with it?'

'There's no rush,' she said. 'I want to make sure you've trod very carefully. Because if they find out what you're doing, they'll find out about me too.'

'I appreciate your concerns,' Schulz told her, 'but we're quite safe. No one knows we're here.'

# TWENTY-ONE

The morning air was cold and crisp, although the sky had few clouds, and the winter sun was intense and bright. Romanians referred to such weather as *soare cu dinţi*, sun with teeth, which was perhaps his favourite phrase in the entire language. Off the main thoroughfares, the street had little traffic as, aside from the hotel, there were few reasons to pass this way. There was a scattering of pedestrians, none of whom looked at him twice as he crossed the road with long, deliberate strides.

Victor had the option to walk away, of course, but killing Schulz and Ysiv was a necessary part of self-preservation as much as it was a day at the office. The reach of the Russian mafia was enormous, as they had shown in Rotterdam, and if Lambert's client could help ensure such an attack never happened again, it was worth the risk. And, given the difficulties and requirements of fulfilling the contract, Lambert would be pleased, even grateful. The more he was impressed with Victor's work, the better. Brokers and assassins had an uneasy symbiosis. The longer and closer they operated together, the greater the risk each became to the other. In Victor's experience, such a state could not endure indefinitely. Someone had to blink first, and when that time came he wanted to be the one that deemed their business relationship had come to an end, not Lambert.

*That's not true*, a previous broker had said to him after he had interrupted her while painting. *That's just the way you think.*

She had said other things to him too, words he had not understood at the time. Yet, he now knew they represented an uncannily accurate analysis of his psyche. He should have kept the painting, he now realised, and stored it in his safety deposit box alongside the vacuum-sealed bag containing an advert for a train set that was his most prized possession.

Although compact for such a weapon, the grenade launcher had been left behind. It was far too large to conceal beneath Victor's jacket and no good in a close-quarters battle environment.

As he pushed through the revolving doors, the dark-haired concierge gave him a passing glance, in an instant identifying him as someone she did not recognise and therefore not a paying guest, and then moved on to other duties.

The efficient concierge had already forgotten him in favour of servicing the pressing needs of the family from Dubai, who surrounded her with a barrage of requests and demands. Victor's gaze swept the space for threats. He was on the clock to complete the contract before too many unforeseen factors piled up on top of one another to create an insurmountable challenge. Still, protocol dictated that he could not do so blindly since he was entering a new space.

As well as members of staff, which included the concierge, porters, front-desk clerks and waiters, there were close to forty guests. Checking in or checking out, passing through, sitting in chairs enjoying a coffee or mimosa, or simply standing around. At any other time, Victor would be walking at a more relaxed pace and, in doing so, would have had a greater window to take an accurate count of those present and then make a proper assessment of who might require a second look. A reductive process, he did so by first eliminating those too young and too old to be professionals, then those of the wrong physical condition, before further whittling down by the manner of clothing and finally how they conducted themselves.

With two targets and their entourages upstairs in a strike point for which he had not prepared, and going in blind, he could not spend precious moments here in the lobby to ensure there were no fellow assassins, spies or members of law enforcement.

For a man whose entire life endured entirely because of his ability to assess and manage risk, this omission felt like signing his own death warrant.

But the reward was worth the risk.

Victor wanted Lambert to reinforce his existing friendships and make new ones. He wanted the favour Lambert would gain from a successful outcome here to fix some of the problems Victor had created that could not be repaired otherwise. He wanted those dirty dishes put back in the cupboard, squeaky clean.

He was prepared to take the risk of an improvised attack because he had already factored in a contingency plan as part of his routine preparations for this job, as he would for any other. For the most challenging assignments – such as assassinating the heavily guarded patron of a drug cartel in Guatemala – he preferred to have three separate strategies to complete the job. A single backup was adequate for a couple of private spies and their entourages.

From his preparatory work, he knew the layout of the hotel and so headed straight to where the bank of elevators was tucked out of the way around a corner to avoid ruining the lobby's grandeur with their functional ordinariness. Several guests waited before them for the lifts to arrive.

He glanced back over his shoulder as he passed through the hallway containing the elevators. It was the kind of motion he would never perform as a general rule, not wanting to draw attention to himself. Yet, because of the improper scan of the lobby, instinct compelled him to take one final look.

Movement in the lobby attracted his predator's gaze, and he saw a young woman with short brown hair dip her head while a glass mug of mint tea steamed in her hand. Maybe she had been looking his way and averted her eyes just in time as his head swivelled back.

He had no way of knowing.

Upstairs, his targets were waiting, and Victor never liked to be tardy.

# TWENTY-TWO

The stairwell did not have the same level of opulence as the rest of the hotel, with a plain metal banister and unadorned walls. However, a thick carpet covered the steps, so Victor increased his pace as he ascended, the sound of his rapid footfall dampened and unheard by anyone nearby.

Heart rate elevated a little by hurrying up eight flights of stairs, he breathed in a controlled manner to bring it back down again and slowed his pace he entered the fourth-floor hallway. With his prior knowledge of the hotel, there was no need to look at the signs to know in which direction to go, so he screwed the suppressor onto his Five-seveN and held it down by his right hip. At the same time, he withdrew his phone into his left hand.

As with the layout, he had committed many details of the hotel to memory, so he dialled the front desk within seconds.

Hotels like this did not let the phone ring for long, a man answering moments later in a polite voice.

'Please put me through to room four-sixteen,' Victor replied. 'It's Mister Limetree calling.'

'One moment, sir.'

Tapping mute, Victor slipped the handset back into his trouser pocket.

Standing outside four-sixteen's door, he raised his pistol and waited for the suite's phone to ring.

Kicking in a door was a simple process because, at its core, the door wasn't the target but the frame. More specifically, the attachment of the strike plate to the frame. Sufficient application of force focused on the point of the door where the locking mechanism existed transferred that energy through the deadbolt to the frame, where four tiny screws held the strike plate in place.

The instant the phone rang on the other side of the door – and all inside the room were momentarily distracted by its unexpected sound – Victor threw out a stomp-kick that struck the door just below and to the side of the handle, which caused the deadbolt to rip the screws from the frame, dislodging the strike plate and tearing a chunk of wood from the fame as the door swung inwards.

Inside the room – before the swinging door could even slam against the interior wall – Victor had the Five-seveN up to his eyeline, his elbows tucked against his torso to decrease the overall size of his presence in the confined space, and was acquiring his first target.

He saw Schulz sitting on the far side of the room, but there was no Ysiv.

Both targets had to wait because their respective security details – five threats in total – required Victor's immediate attention.

The average reaction time for a human is somewhere between two and three hundred milliseconds, but turning that reaction into action takes much longer.

Already distracted by the ringing phone, the explosion of sound from the door then flying open created the kind of sensory burden that only the most highly trained, experienced professionals could hope to overcome when their lives depended on it.

Which they did.

Two squeezes of the trigger meant two headshots for those closest to Victor and, therefore, the most significant threats.

The first hadn't even known what was happening – he was still looking at the ringing phone – Victor's bullet entering at the base of his head where the skull met the neck, missing the brain but severing the spinal column.

The second was turning Victor's way, reacting fast to the kicked-in door, but processing what he was witnessing and how to deal with it was eating up precious milliseconds he just didn't have to spare.

The 5.7mm round made a neat hole a centimetre above his left eyebrow and a far messier one on its way out behind his right ear.

Both parties of Schulz's entourage had been positioned near the door, presumably to secure it, and in doing so, had marked themselves to be the first to die.

They were still on their feet, still in the process of brain death and maintaining their instinctual balance, as Victor focused on the subsequent three threats.

Ysiv's security detail were faster to turn their reactions into action. Former Mossad, this was to be expected, but reaching for their holstered sidearms, drawing those weapons and raising them to an effective height took a lot longer than it took Victor to adjust his aim a few degrees.

More headshots, each to the centre of the forehead, thanks to the fact they had both helpfully turned to look his way.

Schulz's response was more muted. He had been sitting on the chaise longue beneath the room's window, which looked into the bright atrium that formed the hotel's core. He continued to sit as Victor executed the other four people in the room. Schulz remained sitting as each of the corpses collapsed to the floor one by one to leave behind four separate clouds of atomised blood drifting in swirling hazes.

Four.

Not five.

One of Marion Ysiv's security detail was not present in the room because he had been checking the separate bedroom, the open doorway of which was immediately perpendicular to Victor's right.

Fast, he pivoted in that direction as the ex-Mossad operative emerged through it.

# TWENTY-THREE

They saw one another at the same time: Victor glimpsing the bodyguard enter his peripheral vision as he began to pivot on the spot, the bodyguard having a visual as he rounded the doorframe.

Already within arm's reach and therefore too close to aim a shot, instead Victor used the FN as a club to bat the bodyguard's own weapon from his hand as he tried to snap it free from a shoulder holster.

Victor had his guard up in time, but the former Mossad operative's punches and elbow strikes were so fast and delivered with so much force that he still staggered from the impacts. With each enforced backward step, the bodyguard threw another elbow harder, generating more power with his whole body.

So Victor stopped blocking the elbows and released the FN to catch one of the attacking arms mid-punch and use the bodyguard's momentum to throw him to the carpeted floor.

Victor followed him down, jostling for position, trying to mount, then thrown away as the bodyguard bucked his hips and rolled out from underneath. The wall's proximity restricted Victor's room to manoeuvre, which meant he was slower to his feet. He blocked the elbows and punches aimed at his head, then winced as more found their mark below his guard.

He caught the next attack, pulling his enemy closer so he lost his balance and then exploiting that instability by shoving him to create distance.

Darting away from the wall, Victor launched a barrage of strikes – elbows to the face, punches to the ribs, knees to the groin – then looped his arms around the man's hips when he turtled to defend himself, and wrenched his legs out from under him.

Dazed, the bodyguard had no way to defend himself further.

Three pulverising stomps of Victor's heel cracked his skull before breaking his neck.

Victor retrieved his pistol from the floor to face Schulz.

'What is this?'

The German had impressive composure. The question came out in a calm, level voice. He had his hands raised to waist height. He hadn't tried to make a move. Although he could have attempted something, it had taken Victor only five seconds to deal with the bodyguard, so Schulz wouldn't have achieved much in that time. He knew when he was defeated.

Victor stepped closer.

'Whatever it is, we can work it out. Tell me what you need. Let's make a deal.'

He failed to understand he should already be dead, except for the fact that Ysiv was nowhere to be seen.

'Where is she?' Victor asked, his voice just as composed.

Schulz misread the question, believing this was Victor's sole purpose, and he was quick to gesture to the floor before him in front of the sofa opposite the German, an area currently in Victor's blind spot.

She must have hit the deck the moment the phone rang and been out of Victor's sight before the kicked-in door opened to reveal the room. If the German's composure was impressive, Ysiv's reaction speed was more so, even by the standards of a former Mossad operative.

Given that the dossier Lambert supplied stated she had been out of the spy business for at least a decade, Ysiv's processing of what the ringing phone meant, and her subsequent action to drop to the floor out of the line of fire, was not just impressive; it was extraordinary.

Unless she was not quite as out of the game as Lambert believed.

Something didn't add up.

Victor thought back to when he watched her arrive – only seeing the back of her head and identifying her only from her security detail.

Without moving any further into the room, he said, 'Stand up, or I'll shoot you through the furniture.'

Victor believed in instincts because he understood the brain performed thousands of independent processes for every conscious thought, and for every conscious conclusion the brain had already analysed thousands of separate pieces of information from every sense, every memory and every experience.

Consciousness was the end result of thought, not the beginning.

Therefore, when his instincts told him it wouldn't be Ysiv who rose from behind the sofa, he listened.

The woman who did rise did so with slow, obvious movements, her long, dark hair momentarily disguising her face, making him think of the concierge, before she reached her full height and said, 'Nice to see you again, Jonathan.'

# TWENTY-FOUR

In the lobby downstairs, the young woman with short brown hair continued to keep her head lowered even though the man in the suit had passed through almost a minute ago now. She had spent the time fiddling with her jacket as though analysing a stain or investigating loose stitching. Almost certainly overkill, but it was always better to be too careful than too dead.

Besides, she needed that almost minute to organise her thoughts, to process what – who – she had seen, what that meant now, and what it could mean going forward.

With an unsteady hand, she lowered her untouched tea back to the table, no longer thirsty. She leaned back against the dense padding of the armchair.

Around her, the life of the lobby continued uninterrupted. She could hear the man from the United Arab Emirates expressing his annoyance that his room was not on a high enough floor and complaining to the concierge. At the same time, both his wives and their children waited nearby.

No one else in the lobby but her knew he was a financier of fanatical terrorists across the Middle East. Not even his wives were aware.

From the table next to the young woman, a waiter collected used coffee cups and saucers left by a couple before they checked out. Though they had displayed little warmth towards one another, ostensibly business acquaintances on a work trip, she was sure they were having an affair. An unsatisfactory one too, judging by how well rested they both seemed.

Finally, confident enough to raise her head again, she checked that the man in the suit was gone. She had only ever seen him in photographs before and in the video – they had all seen *that* video – although his face had been covered by a mask when the hidden camera had recorded him. In Switzerland, in her guise as a student at the university, the old man she had been protecting had informed her what had happened and what needed to be done. Later, she had watched from nearby as arrangements had been made and she had waited with eagerness for the good news to be delivered.

Instead, more tears, more rage.

All because of the man in the video and the photographs.

Now, here he was in the flesh.

She'd heard a rumour he was dead, but they had not verified it themselves, and so most had not believed it. Most had not wanted to believe it.

She had seen him for only a few seconds, granted, but she needed no more time to identify him. Although his face wasn't quite the same – no doubt from cosmetic surgery – it was definitely him. There was only so much even the best surgeons could do, and the eyes could never be changed. Like everyone else, she had studied those photographs with unwavering focus until the point she could close her eyes and still see his features in her mind, with each detail in perfect clarity. She had read the many reports again and again and again, memorising every fact, every detail, every observation and supposition.

Although she had been in a protection detail in those days, she had begged to do more and to be sent out searching. Everyone who knew what had happened wanted in, and even those not privy to the events could feel it in the air that something unprecedented had taken place. But she had been too junior and inexperienced to jump the long line of volunteers whose better credentials ensured their pleas were louder than hers.

That was then.

Since that time, she had risen through the ranks, as tireless as she was determined, as ambitious as she was committed to the cause, and her talents had been rewarded with assignments of ever-increasing importance. There was now no challenge she deemed too great.

Still, she was alone, unarmed, here as an observer and a watcher.

She wasn't ready for this. None of them were.

They communicated via direct messaging on their phones. Slower than speaking, but no danger of being overheard or the connection being interrupted.

She found her palms were moist with sweat when she dug in her bag to withdraw her phone. Her fingertips left smudges of perspiration on the screen as she tapped in the code to unlock it.

What should she say? She had no idea ... and it wasn't like her to be lost for words. She was the kind of person who never shut up, yet nothing seemed adequate given the circumstances.

She was here to find out what the terrorist financier from Dubai was doing in Bucharest, a task of great importance she and the others needed to complete. Still, she knew the instant she sent the message, this essential duty of theirs would be abandoned because there would be no other priority.

All over Europe, critical operations that were just as vital would be put on hold, and those conducting them would be reassigned.

Almost giddy with anticipation, she set about typing her message.

They had been waiting years for this moment.

# TWENTY-FIVE

Raven looked much the same as Victor remembered her: just as tall, just as athletic. Her black hair was about the same length, and her eyes were large and dark, although not as dark as his own. Her arched eyebrows were a little thicker than before, to follow the current trends, and her lips were accentuated with a brighter red than he had ever seen her wear. She had always had the same rigorous devotion to physical conditioning as him, which was why she wore a smart pantsuit and overcoat to hide the breadth of her shoulders and so no one could see the strength in her arms. She was older now, of course, as he was older, but the years had been kind to her. An American by birth, her father had been Indian, and she had inherited a hint of his complexion. That hue was deeper now than it had been in Italy and Helsinki when they had last operated together, or in London when they had said their subsequent farewell.

He said, 'I've told you before, that's not my name.'

She said in reply, 'And I've told you before, you're Jonathan to me until you reveal your actual name.'

'What are you even doing here?'

She glanced at the corpses leaking blood and cerebrospinal fluid into the carpet. 'Perhaps we should save the catching up until later?'

Gesturing to Schulz, Victor asked, 'Is he with you?'

'Absolutely not.' Her tone was incredulous. 'Herr Schulz is my target too.'

His head swivelling between the two of them, the German was puzzled. 'Will someone please explain to me what is going on here?'

Victor spared him any further confusion with a bullet between the eyes.

To Raven, he said, 'Where's the real Marion Ysiv?'

'You're looking at her,' she answered. 'She's me. At least, I've been pretending to be her for the last few months.'

He glanced at Schulz's corpse, now slowly sliding from the couch and onto the floor, at the dead former Mossad security detail, 'How does that—?'

'Again,' she interrupted, 'perhaps it's prudent to save the specifics until we're no longer standing in the middle of the scene of a mass murder.'

'Good point.'

Noting his Five-seveN was still raised and pointing at her, she asked, 'You're not going to shoot me too, are you?'

For the first time since seeing her again, he asked himself the same question and then answered both of them, 'Not just yet.'

He lowered the gun, and she said, 'I guess I have no choice but to live with that.' She headed for the door. 'What did you say when we were stood in that square? Something like when next we meet, it will be as enemies?'

'Something like that. But I think you'll find that you, not I, made that statement.'

'And are we?' She held open the door for him. 'Are we here now as enemies?'

'We were always enemies, Constance. At times, however, our interests happen to align, and right now both of us want to walk out of here with our lives and our freedom. So, our past differences can wait for the moment.' He checked that no one was outside in the hallway, then nodded to her, letting her know it was clear. 'Come on, let's go.'

He saw a maid's cart without a maid and hoped for her sake she was turning down one of the rooms with its door closed and would not open it again until after Victor was done. He preferred to avoid killing anyone he hadn't been paid to kill. Still, eyewitnesses could not be left behind to provide investigators with details about him they would not have been privy to otherwise. No guests either, which was good for the same reason.

CCTV cameras peered at him from the vestibule ceiling leading to the elevators and stairwell, and again from the intersections where hallways met. Victor knew where to find the room containing the cameras' feeds and that a security guard was posted there, so Lambert had better be right when he said the hotel server was about to be hacked.

Anyone in nearby rooms would have heard a commotion, but would they call the front desk to complain or recognise the five loud whip-cracks in rapid succession for the suppressed gunshots they were and call the police? Unlikely, given it had all been over in a matter of seconds. Civilians did everything possible to convince themselves the world was as safe as they wanted it to be, Victor often found.

'So far, so good,' Raven whispered as they walked side by side to the stairwell.

A door opened somewhere behind them, but neither looked back. Better whoever it was did not see their faces.

Raven used a knuckle to hit the call button for the elevator.

'I always take the stairs.'

'I remember,' she said, not moving. 'You don't want to be boxed in. But this way is more natural. No one takes the stairs if they can help it, so neither should you. You want to blend in, you'd better take the lazy option like everyone else.'

He had no retort for that.

When the lift arrived and the doors opened, they stepped inside. Turning to face the doors again, she linked her arm with his own.

Before he could protest, she said, 'This is more natural.'

Again, he did not argue. She was right. He had entered as a lone man, and now he was leaving as one-half of a couple. Those who had noticed him alone before might not see him at all now. And alongside Raven, he might as well have been invisible.

The atmosphere of the lobby was the same as it had been a few minutes earlier. The events on the fourth floor had yet to affect the broader ecosystem of the hotel. The family from Dubai was still surrounding the concierge, although now the man was smiling, whatever his needs had been now fulfilled thanks to the efficient concierge's masterful handling of the situation.

With one elbow looped around his, Raven rested her free

hand against his upper arm too, settling into the guise of a happy couple with the kind of relaxed, instinctual closeness that Victor could never imitate himself. She smiled to deepen the role she played so well.

She said, 'Are you flexing?'

'Don't be ridiculous.'

She only smiled more.

Victor had estimated close to forty people when he had passed through earlier, and walking through again at a slower, more relaxed pace as part of a couple in no rush, he counted thirty-eight.

He noticed his estimate should have been closer to the actual count, except the thirty-ninth person was no longer present. The young woman with short brown hair had departed.

In something of a hurry too, he saw. Her mint tea was left untouched on the coffee table where she had been sitting, thin wisps of steam still rising from the glass mug.

'What is it?' Raven asked in a quiet voice, knowing him well enough to read the otherwise imperceptible changes in his body language.

He didn't answer for a moment since there were a hundred reasons why the young woman might have left without drinking her tea, and ninety-nine of them were innocent.

'I think we may have a problem.'

With her trademark flippancy he had never appreciated, Raven leaned closer and said, 'Don't we always?'

# TWENTY-SIX

In the heart of the Old Town, in a neighbourhood known as Little Paris, they had lunch – or breakfast, given Victor's sleeping schedule – at Cafeneaua Veche 9. An apt name given it was the oldest café in Bucharest, dating back to the eighteenth century, when it was a hotspot for artists, poets and prominent figures of the time. It had been about five years since Victor had dined here, which he considered an appropriate interval to ensure he remained unremembered.

As he had expected, Raven loved it, and he found himself appreciating the rare pleasure of spending time with someone with whom he did not have to unceasingly lie. The relief from the unburdening of constant deception was another rare pleasure.

'Do you think the bodies have been discovered yet?'

The background noise of the busy café meant they could speak freely with their voices hushed.

Victor shook his head. 'They'll be found in the morning

when housekeeping knocks on the door. We'll be long gone by then.'

His attention to cleanliness throughout his time in the rented apartment across from the hotel, especially with the silicone coating his hands that ensured he left behind no fingerprints, meant all he had had to do was collect the grenade launcher. It now lay as many separate components in different sections of the Danube.

Raven said, 'I was initially annoyed when Schulz switched the rooms. But a face full of shrapnel would have stung.'

'For a fraction of a second only.'

'Would you have been sad if you found out you'd blown me to smithereens? Maybe even shed a tear as you raised a glass of bourbon to my memory?'

'I find hypotheticals to be entirely pointless.'

'That's a yes if ever I heard one.'

He ignored the validity of her point by asking, 'Why wasn't Schulz already dead before I arrived, since he was your target too?'

'Because I wanted information from him first. Besides, he changed rooms at the last minute, had two competent security guys, and the three former Mossad goons didn't know I wasn't Ysiv and were not going to be happy when they found that out.'

'How is that possible?'

'Because they were hired for this gig,' Raven explained. 'Ysiv is known to favour ex-members of Israeli intelligence, but it's not like she walks around with the same ones each time. I studied her for a good while before I killed her precisely so I could pretend to be her afterwards.'

'You went to a lot of trouble to get to Schulz,' Victor

began. 'Which makes me think he's another pawn on your chessboard.'

'If you're asking me if he was working for the Consensus, then the answer is obviously yes. I don't go around hunting Germans just for the fun of it. I even like some of them.'

The Consensus was the name she gave to her enemies, enemies she had once worked for, unwittingly, a long time ago. She called them the Consensus because they had no structure, no members and no concrete presence at all. They were an amalgamation of government officials and private enterprises, the intelligence community, and the super-rich pursuing evermore wealth and power, using their resources and influence to both further their goals and maintain the status quo that enabled them to do just that. They were the Consensus because they all had the same aims and the same willingness to do whatever it took to achieve them.

Like Raven, Victor had ended up working for them without his knowledge. They had wanted both for him to kill Raven, to stop her relentless interference in their schemes, and to use Victor as a patsy in a terrorist attack on American soil. That he had not died back then or ended up in a super-max could be accredited to Raven's assistance. He may even have thanked her.

Victor had been content to walk away with his life and his freedom, but the whole affair only strengthened Raven's resolve to keep fighting them wherever and however she could. He had never been sure whether her crusade against the Consensus was waged in the pursuit of justice that they would never otherwise have to face or to avenge a former colleague, a lover they tricked her into killing. He would have asked her, only whatever answer she gave would change nothing. She would stop only when she'd put a bullet in every last one of them, which was all but impossible, or when they put a bullet in her first, which was infinitely more likely.

When that day came, he hoped Raven had caused enough damage to them that she could finally be at peace as her eyes closed for the last time.

'And Ysiv?' he asked.

'She never knew the Consensus existed, but that didn't stop her from performing their dirty work whenever they came knocking on her door. In an ideal world, I would move on to Schulz's contact in the Consensus, only Schulz didn't know who he was working for. He was trading in stolen plans for the UK's new HEL system, passing it on to his paymaster while selling copies to me on the side for a bit of extra cash. I don't know why the Consensus wants to know how to build lasers to shoot missiles and drones out of the sky, but I can guess it's not because they're interested in protecting civilians. Likewise, I don't want the plans either. What I want, however, is to put a bullet in whoever is trying to acquire them. I don't suppose you know who that person is, do you?'

'No idea,' he answered. 'But if you find out, let me know. It's my client's plans that has been stolen, which is why I was hired to kill Schulz and his buyer. Only you're not the buyer, that will be whoever his contact in the Consensus is.'

'Identifying who these guys are is becoming harder and harder. More and more, not only do they stick to their own, but those operating for the Consensus almost always do so anonymously these days, so they can't give one another up.'

'Maybe that has something to do with you killing so many of them.'

'Too efficient for my own good. I've long suspected it.

'Schulz had a business partner, however,' Raven continued. 'Another German, in Hamburg, named Ido Albrecht. He's my next port of call. Maybe he knows something Schulz did not.'

'It might be wise to keep your head down for a while given that once those bodies in the hotel room are discovered, Mossad is going to realise pretty quickly about Marion Ysiv not being quite as alive as she seemed.'

'Ysiv was former Mossad.'

'And she was with them for a long time. If you think they won't care she's dead, you don't know them at all.'

'If you say so. What makes you such an expert regarding Israeli intelligence?'

'Let's just say I've had a first-hand glimpse into Mossad's version of Old Testament righteousness.'

'Yes, I went to Sunday school . . . an eye for an eye and all that. But you still have both of your beautiful dark orbs.'

Thinking back to a night in Sofia, Bulgaria, when some of his eyelashes brushed the tip of a broken shard of glass destined to skewer him and wielded by a ferocious Mossad assassin, he said, 'Barely.'

# TWENTY-SEVEN

Lambert liked the phone. Although not impossible to fake someone's voice in real time, he trusted emails and the like even less. Nothing digital could ever be safe. At least, that was how he explained it to Victor, who did not doubt the man's sincerity on these points and yet knew Lambert was keeping a little back too. He figured himself to be a personable man and wanted to maintain a rapport with Victor. The more they talked, the closer their relationship, the more trust they built. Lambert wanted Victor to like him. The more he liked him, the less chance he would betray him. The logic was simple, yet flawed. If Victor deemed it necessary to betray Lambert, it would be either a business decision or one born of self-preservation. In both eventualities, it would not matter how much he liked Lambert. Still, Lambert didn't need to understand that.

The other side to the coin of Lambert's thinking was that the more Victor liked him, the more he trusted him, the easier it would be to betray Victor when the time came. Not that Victor expected that time was imminent. Lambert was planning ahead for the day when Victor made a mistake, like the trio of assassins in Belgium, and put his broker at risk, or the day when a client approached Lambert with a contract on Victor's head, else when the nagging sense of dread built to unbearable levels and the simplest way to stop startling at shadows was to have Victor killed.

He had not worked for Lambert long enough to know which of the three was more likely, although Lambert was in a unique position. He had recruited Victor after their paths had crossed on opposing sides some time before, albeit indirectly, so he had a better idea of the man with whom he was dealing.

When Lambert rang, Victor had no good excuse for failing to call in after the contract was complete.

'I thought you were dead,' Lambert told him. 'I thought you'd fu— I thought you'd messed up.'

'Why does it sound like there's disappointment in your tone?'

'Because you enjoy pushing my blood pressure medication to its limits.'

'Diet and exercise could be your best friends if only you'd let them.'

'Yeah, yeah, the kind of self-righteous friend who doesn't get invited to parties. Anyway, stop changing the subject. Why didn't you call?'

'There was a complication,' Victor said, looking at Raven, who, although sitting across from him, gave a mock curtsy in response.

Lambert asked, 'How complicated is this complication?'

'Nothing for you to worry about,' Victor assured him. 'I'm in the middle of resolving it right now.'

*You wish*, Raven mouthed.

'Okay, I'll trust your expertise on that,' Lambert said. 'I'll speak to the client later, so I'll pass on their thanks in due course.'

'Utterly unnecessary,' Victor told him. 'But there is something you need to be aware of before you speak to them that may affect their appreciation.'

'You just told me I had nothing to worry about.'

'You don't. Only one of the customers did not receive the pitch.'

Despite the ambient noise of the café being enough to muffle their voices from the other diners, a waiter, nearby, might overhear, so Victor took to choosing his words with more care.

'What does that mean? One is still alive? Ysiv or Schulz?'

'The former wasn't present for the pitch at all,' Victor explained. 'The woman the other customer was meeting was a charlatan in the most literal of definitions.'

'Are you telling me she was pretending to be Marion Ysiv?'

'That is correct,' Victor answered. 'The true customer has been out of the game for a long time. Your client's information was out of date.'

'Ysiv was already dead?'

'Yes,' Victor said. 'Not only that but she wasn't the true buyer at all, only an unrelated recipient. The client needs to go back to the drawing board if they want to know who the ultimate buyer actually is.'

'Any idea how I explain that to the client without sounding like I'm trying to pull a fast one?'

'I believe that's your job, not mine.'

'Some partnership this is turning out to be.'

Victor said, 'If you'd like to transfer fifty per cent of your stock in the company to me, I'll be in a position to offer you some advice.'

'You really are a sarcastic mother ... *fluffer*, has anyone ever told you that?'

'In those exact words?'

He heard Lambert's heavy exhalation and imagined him rubbing the back of his neck. 'I guess we can't change what happened ... I'll speak with my guy in the Ministry of Defence, see if I can work my world-famous charm and try to stop us from ending up on the kind of list no one wants to be on. In the meantime, you need to pay Ken Harvey a visit. Afterwards, I think it would make sense for you to come see me so you can fill me in properly on what just happened, or didn't happen, in that hotel suite.'

Victor said, 'Okay.'

'Before I go to the Ministry of Defence with my tail between my legs,' Lambert began in a wary tone. 'I take it the imposter is dead in Ysiv's place?'

Looking at Raven once more, Victor said, 'Not exactly.'

She guessed what was being discussed on the phone and, forming a gun with two fingers, pushed them against her temple.

'It's ... complicated.'

As she slumped forward on the table, face first, and mimed post-death muscle spasms, Victor shook his head, while Lambert added, 'Do you know what? I don't want to know any more, but if I tell these people Ysiv is dead, and she's not, then—'

'She is,' Victor said and hung up.

Raven continued to spasm on the tabletop.

141

'You can stop now,' he told her with a sigh.

Her face still pressed into the tabletop, she said, 'Don't pretend to be irritated. I know you want to laugh.'

'Keep dreaming.'

She leaned back up to see him raising an eyebrow of derision and said, 'I'll take that as a win.'

'You have a low threshold for victory.'

'Luckily, when dealing with you, I have a very high threshold for scorn.'

'Why are you even here? Schulz's dead, so your task is complete ... how come you haven't moved on to the next target of your continued crusade? What did you say his name is? Albrecht?'

'For the same reason you're not already on a flight to someplace far away,' she answered with a wry smile. 'It's always fun to catch up.'

'Fun,' Victor echoed without inflection.

'Your robot impression never worked on me, I'm afraid, so you may as well drop it. I know you have a personality in there somewhere. Buried deep down beyond all those barriers you think are so very impenetrable, you're as human as I am. The only difference between you and I is you don't want to be one.'

'I do so love these moments of armchair psychoanalysis from you.'

The wry smile stretched into one of smug satisfaction. 'Exactly, you made a joke. Thank you for proving my point so emphatically.'

'Now I remember why we keep trying to kill each other.'

She laughed. 'Told you it's fun to catch up.'

# TWENTY-EIGHT

The café sat opposite Saint Anton Square, so after finishing their meal Victor and Raven strolled through the large, open space to begin their countersurveillance.

'What did you mean earlier,' she began, 'when you said we might have a problem?'

His gaze sweeping back and forth for shadows, Victor said, 'On my way through the lobby, I saw a young woman looking my way. She tried to hide it, but I know what I saw. On our way out, she was gone. She left her drink untouched.'

'Maybe she went to the little girls' room.'

'Not impossible,' he said. 'Although I trust my instincts. Something wasn't right. She couldn't have been a shadow because seventy seconds beforehand even I didn't know I was about to walk into that hotel.'

'Then she looked your way because she thought you were cute,' Raven said. 'You are ... kinda. And then she did go to the restroom afterwards. Don't overthink it.'

'Which means she was there for you.'

'Give me more credit than that, will you? I wasn't followed. I know how to watch my six as well as you. Better even.'

'Doubtful, but if true, then they were there for Schulz in all likelihood,' he said, thinking out loud. 'He had the booking, after all, so it makes sense. Unless they had found out who he was meeting, which *would* mean they were there for you. Well, Ysiv.'

'Or both,' she said. 'Maybe it wasn't either of them, it was both together. A meeting between private spies would make many people curious, would it not?'

'None of which explains why whoever was curious about the meeting was looking at me.'

'Say they left,' Raven began, 'why did they? If they knew you in some way, why go? Why not wait and see when you leave? She was worried you would recognise her in return?'

'I've never seen her before.'

Raven said, 'Then we're back to the beginning: you're overthinking it. You're being paranoid. Because you haven't seen her since, have you?'

His gaze alternating between pedestrians crossing the square like them, he answered, 'No. I would see her a mile away now. But if she is part of a team, then there's nothing to say she didn't just rotate out and get replaced by someone else.'

'I've not seen any signs of surveillance. Have you?'

'No.'

'And we've been careful,' she continued. 'We've done everything right so far. Between us, we'd know if something wasn't right.'

'I suppose,' he admitted.

'It was Schulz's deal at a place and a time of his choosing.

If she is part of any team, they're interested in him, me or both of us. They didn't know you were going to be there, did they? They didn't follow you; they followed him. They've been watching him; they were already watching him, and that's why they were interested in who he was meeting. Who cares about Schulz in the first place? If you think someone recognised you, that's where your focus should be, but the best thing you can do – we both can do – is get out of Dodge and stay away for a long time.'

'Agreed,' he said, then, 'What's your plan?'

'As I said before, Schulz wasn't working alone,' Raven explained. 'I need to find out if his business partner in Hamburg is also on the wrong side of history. Therefore, that's where I'm going on the next flight out, so I can ask Albrecht if he also happens to be one of the Consensus's cockroaches.'

'Cockroaches?' Victor asked.

She pulled a face. 'Exactly, and just as disgusting scurrying around at the behest of their masters. I'm going to crush every one of them beneath my heel. Want to help me?'

'Why would I do that?'

'Because you're looking for the buyer also and because we make a good team,' she answered, as though it had been obvious. 'Sooner or later, you're going to realise that your skill set is wasted as a hired gun, and you could better serve humanity by doing the right thing.'

'Why would I do that?' he asked again.

She groaned, then said, 'If for no other reasons than to help a gal out. I'm a bit thin on the ground for resources in Germany right now since my last hardware guy got pinched over something else.' She shrugged. 'But, whatever, I'm not expecting trouble, and even if there is, I can just beat him to death with a bratwurst if it comes to it.'

He considered for a moment, weighing up the pros and cons, then decided there was no real downside to sharing. 'Georg,' he said.

'Excuse me?'

'I have a supplier in Hamburg as it happens,' Victor explained. 'I know her only as Georg. She's a fixer, a good one, whose path I crossed well before you and I met. I source weapons from her from time to time, and even though she acts like I'm forcing her to crawl across broken glass to do so, she always delivers. Let's exchange contact details and let her know you'll be passing through. Maybe she can help you out.'

'You'd do that for me? I don't know what to say.'

'She's a supplier, Constance. It's not a big deal.'

'It wouldn't be a big deal for anyone else,' she retorted. 'But this is you we're talking about here. This is like something out of Dickens. Old Ebenezer Scrooge has learned the true value of Christmas.'

'You always find a way to make me regret any favour I do for you.'

'Are you sure I can't tempt you to accompany me on my cockroach-squishing expedition? It'll be just like old times.'

'Even if I had a sudden change in personality, I need to finish another contract, and then an inevitable debrief with my broker to explain fully why only one of today's two targets has been executed.'

'Tell him you've fallen in love with the second,' Raven suggested. 'People always excuse mistakes of the heart.'

'If I'm going to lie,' Victor said with a raise of one eyebrow, 'I need to make it sound at least vaguely plausible.'

'Show him my picture,' she said with a cocky smile. 'He'll understand.'

'Or I'll just try telling the truth for once,' he said, shaking his head. 'That the real Marion Ysiv died months ago and an old ally of mine has been pretending to be her ever since, and I made the mistake of sparing her life.'

'Awwh.' Raven placed a palm to her chest. 'You called me an ally. I've never been so touched.'

'So,' Victor said, not humouring her with any kind of counter. 'I suppose this is where we part ways once again.'

'I guess. Makes a pleasant change to end things on a friendly note this time around. Unless you're planning on shooting me in the back just as soon as I turn away?'

'It didn't occur to me,' Victor answered. 'But since you've suggested it ...'

'Funny,' Raven said. 'Very funny.'

She stepped forward, placing her hands on his shoulders and moving in to bring her cheek to his to kiss him goodbye.

For the smallest of instances he found himself turning his face into her own, but he managed to halt the movement before it went too far.

'What was that?' she asked, withdrawing a little to regain eye contact.

'What was what?' he said in return because he could think of nothing else to say in its place.

Her eyes narrowed as she searched his own. 'Do you want to try that again?' she asked. 'But with a little more conviction this time.'

'I don't know what you're talking about.'

'Your loss,' she said, stepping away with her lips pursed and her head slowly shaking. 'Seeya round, Jonathan.'

# PART THREE

# TWENTY-NINE

The man Zahm met was barely a man at all any more. He existed only because of the many tubes going into and coming out of his body, because of the oxygen mask, the heart monitor, and the multiple daily injections of antibiotics, opioids, blood thinners, steroids, sedatives and insulin.

'He's still in there,' the doctor told Zahm, 'but maybe he shouldn't be.'

Father had once been so overweight he had seemed almost spherical, and shuffled more than walked. At least an entire foot shorter than Zahm, it had been a struggle to keep pace with the man, for Zahm to rein in his long legs and athleticism when they walked and talked together. The diminutive could never understand how difficult it could be for the tall to walk slowly, Zahm had found many times in his life. Despite his age and infirmity, Father never liked to remain in one place for too long. Lying in the hospital bed hid the hump that had only exaggerated Father's stooped posture and snail-like pace.

If once Father had been like a ball, now that ball had been punctured and all the air forced out to leave a crumpled shell, distorted and folded in on itself.

Although Zahm had no squeamishness when it came to violence, the sight of frailty and decay twisted his stomach and quickened his pulse.

'How long does he have?'

'A few weeks,' the doctor said with a shake of her head, 'a few hours. I wish I could be more precise, but at this point, it comes down to how hard they want to hold on. Only last week, I had a ninety-nine-year-old woman, who we didn't think would survive the night after suffering several mini-strokes in rapid succession, pull herself out of bed two days later after the family she hadn't seen in for ever rallied around her to say goodbye. They brought her back. She felt their love and decided not to go just yet.'

'Thank you,' Zahm said, because he did not know what else to say.

There were flowers everywhere. A vase or bouquet rested on every spare inch of space. So many had been sent that some had been placed on the floor when every other po-tential spot had been filled. Cards from all over the world offered their condolences, their respect and admiration. Handwritten notes from movie stars, politicians, CEOs, generals, dignitaries and survivors.

A grateful nation, a proud diaspora.

What did they call him, Zahm wondered. Was he Father to them, too, or was that moniker reserved for those he re-cruited and trained, those he sent to kill and be killed? Was he Father because he loved his children, or was he only their father so they would do the unspeakable without hesitation in the hope of earning his love in return? It was too late to ask such questions so close to the end and so far from Zahm's beginning, when he'd doubted no order and his singular desire was to be a good operative.

He approached the bed, feeling the twinge of horror in the pit of his stomach intensify as he neared Father's rotten form and saw up close the translucent yellow skin ridged with blue veins, the open sores and skeletal hands. The man he called Father had always been old. Yet, he had seemed timeless, immortal almost, a survivor with numbers tattooed on his arm, a veteran of the Six Day War and Yom Kippur, a spy, an assassin, a leader, a hero who had taught Zahm everything he knew, had moulded him from simple soldier into an instrument of pure destruction.

Zahm had no pity for him because so many early lessons of Father's had been in how to regulate his compassion for other people, to distance himself from empathy and to see his enemies as less than human. And not only had he learned to dehumanise his enemies but civilians too, because, at times, innocents would need to be sacrificed for the greater cause. Eager to please his mentor, Zahm had pushed his innate humanity so far away that he could no longer grasp it if he tried, let alone draw it back to fill the void its absence had left behind. Father had taught him so well that Zahm now felt no warmth for the man who lay before him, and yet he was concerned for what it meant for his nation and his people that Father's death was near.

He still remembered what it meant to feel, and so could mimic emotion now. He forced his face into a mask of sadness.

'I'll give you a moment,' the doctor said. 'Just be prepared that he won't know you're there.'

Zahm nodded.

He pulled a chair closer and lowered himself into it as best he could. Built for the comfort of a regular-sized person, he found his enormous thighs so pressed together he would have pushed himself straight back out again, only Father stirred.

Zahm leaned closer, the chair low to the floor so his face was now at the same level as the prostrate old man in the bed.

'It's David,' he said in a voice as quiet and soft as he could manage.

Zahm detected a change in the frequency of the beeping on the heart rate monitor.

'If you can hear me,' Zahm continued, 'I'm so very sorry for disobeying your order. We were all informed that you were to have no visitors, but I had to see you, Father. I know you'd want to know before the end.'

The thin chest rose and fell at a slow, strained rhythm.

Father's eyes were closed, the lids so thin every blood vessel could be seen, and if a bright light was shone, Zahm was sure the eyeballs beneath would be visible through them.

'Father,' Zahm said, leaning even closer and, despite the revulsion he felt, laying a palm over one of the tiny, skeletal hands. 'We've found him.'

From Father's closest, closed eye, a single tear welled and broke.

# THIRTY

A native of Perth, Australia, Ken Harvey had been in London for almost sixteen years, working in the financial industry. As a relationship manager at the start of his career, Harvey's job had been to be the first port of call for investors. When they picked up the phone in response to the latest somersault the FTSE was doing or when the pound decided to take a nosedive, he was on the other end of the line. He had sometimes thought of himself as an emotional masseur, easing the hard knots from panic, stretching out the shortened fibres of stress, and providing a soothing caress to melt away every worry.

He had been the friendly face of the firm for prospective clients, greeting them with a big, white smile and his innate Aussie amiability. He didn't quite understand what made Australians so well liked, figuring at first that Poms could be so uptight that anyone else seemed chilled and friendly in comparison. It wasn't a phenomenon restricted to the United Kingdom, however, which frustrated Harvey. As a cinema lover, he was keenly aware that there were almost no Australian villains in Hollywood films.

*We're just too damn likeable.*

Now, he was going solo with his own firm; he needed to keep smiling despite the initial setbacks and the mounting costs. The office was the most significant initial outlay because it had to be the business. Feng shui experts had designed the layout of the entire interior of the investment firm's two floors in its business-park setting. As soon as a visitor stepped through the front doors, they were bombarded with subliminal signals telling their brain they were in a calm, safe place. Harvey didn't quite buy into such things himself – furniture was furniture, decorations were decorations – but perhaps it helped a little with a certain kind of sucker.

Due to open formally next month, there was still a lot to be done. Bills were rising, investors were getting restless and creditors were piling on the pressure. So, when a venture capitalist with money to burn requested a meeting, Harvey sensed a solution to his problems.

As an emotional masseur, Harvey prided himself on his ability to understand his clients and their wants so he could service their actual needs. Everyone wanted to make money; sure, that was a given. The skill was in learning why. Did they grow up surviving on their overdraft, so now they could only feel secure with an ever larger bank balance? Were they born into money and wanted for nothing, hence tradition dictated they amass even more of a fortune to leave behind? Or was life so insufferably dull because they had achieved tremendous success already, and now only risking their wealth made them feel alive?

The venture capitalist had an easy confidence that

suggested he was from old money. Someone who had never had to work hard because everything was taken care of for him. Probably an underachiever at a prestigious public school with grades nowhere near good enough to land him a place at an elite university and yet had ended up there anyway. Scraped a degree by paying for private tutoring, if not outright paying someone else to do his assignments. No employer in their right mind would hire such an obvious flake, so he'd done an unpaid internship at some company that didn't take on interns unless they were the son of the chief VP's polo buddy. Then, he met the right people and got lucky by backing someone else's talent with the comfort of an allowance or trust fund to fall back on. Before long, he was strutting around, thinking he was a self-made man.

'I hope my guy downstairs wasn't too handsy,' Harvey said with a grin. 'But we take security very seriously here. Until the metal detector is up and running, he has to do things old school.'

'You expect clients to carry weapons?'

Harvey forced a laugh. 'Not exactly, but why risk it? Crime is rocketing in this city, and I want everyone who works here and trusts us with their money to be safe. Look, I'm ambitious. This building is empty now, but all this space will be full to bursting with hungry young brokers, sales-people and the best hustlers. It's going to be a melting pot of ideas and ambition and everyone who works for me will end up wearing watches worth twenty grand a pop. One day street criminals will realise they don't need to risk a smash-and-grab on a jewellery store when they can stroll into any financial institution and bag themselves some real money.'

There was a little small talk, a little easy back and forth

about their respective mornings, the news, the markets and the weather. No chit-chat in the UK could ever be complete without a lengthy discussion on the weather. How rainy it was, or how cold it was, or how windy. It didn't even stop when it was a nice day. Then the Brits couldn't shut up about how sunny it was or the blueness of the sky. Still, when in Rome.

Harvey made a few notes on his computer as they chatted. When he deemed the time for small talk was over, he steered the conversation to financial matters.

The visiting venture capitalist, however, had other ideas: 'Do you know the name Marcus Lambert?'

Harvey found the sudden need to adjust his seating position. 'Yeah, why?'

'He runs a firm of private military contractors. Do you understand what a private military contractor is? In layman's terms.'

'Mercs,' Harvey answered.

'That's right,' the visitor agreed. 'Mercenaries who guard embassies and charity endeavours in all sorts of danger spots. They also protect lithium mines, and form protective details for sheikhs and oligarchs. They fight private wars.'

'I ... I do understand what a mercenary is. I'm involved in the arms industry in several ways, so you don't need to give me a lesson on the subject.'

Fixing him with a stare that made the Australian's skin crawl, the venture capitalist said, 'I'm afraid, Mister Harvey, that the exact reason for my presence here now is to teach you a lesson. I'm here to teach you the error of your ways.'

Harvey stared, then laughed. 'Is this a wind-up? Did Gregg put you up to this?'

'I don't know any Gregg, but he sounds like a fun guy to

know if this is the kind of joke he's likely to play. However, this is deadly serious. You used to handle a lot of the financial matters for Lambert's firm.'

A nod from Harvey: 'That's what they say. A long time ago ... I don't work in that world any more.'

'That's not entirely accurate, is it?' the visitor said. 'You recently gave a briefcase full of stolen documents to a German named Jan Schulz. Not only that, but you hired some of Lambert's contractors to fulfil a contract in Belgium. They shot up a café, remember?'

'I think it's best if you leave now,' Harvey said.

The venture capitalist remained seated.

'Are you really going to make me call security?'

'You mean the guy who gave me the world's most perfunctory pat-down in the lobby? About your height but maybe twenty years older. A bored, dispassionate expression on his face? Counting down the minutes until his break so he can take a nap.'

Harvey reached for the phone to call security.

'I used the elevator today,' the man said. 'In my line of work, I generally avoid them. However, I wanted to time how long it would take to reach your office from the lobby. I don't suppose you've ever timed yourself, but it's just over two minutes from pressing the call button to stepping through your door. And that's without the time it's going to take you to explain to the security guard you need him to come to your office and escort me out, and then the time to process that uncommon request and move from his position at the barriers to the elevator to start that two-minute process. Shall we say three minutes from when you start that call until security is here?'

Harvey hesitated, finger over the button.

The venture capitalist, who by now Harvey was sure was not a venture capitalist, continued, 'Three minutes with just the two of us here alone.'

He rose from the chair, no old-money flake who had recently taken up jogging, but someone else entirely. Someone that Harvey, usually so good at reading people, could not comprehend.

He did, however, understand the dampness of his armpits and the short, shallow breaths he was taking.

'Get out,' Harvey said, standing taller. 'Get out right now ...'

The man stayed in the exact same place.

'You wanted to add an "or" at the end of that sentence, didn't you? But you couldn't quite commit. Don't feel bad about that. It's your lizard brain stopping you from making the wrong call. It doesn't make you less of a man. It just means you're a man who works behind a desk and who encounters a person like me only once in their lifetime, after they've made a terrible decision. This, I'm afraid, is that singularity.'

Harvey said nothing.

'Well,' the man began, 'what's it going to be?'

The Australian had prepared for a day like this, so instead of calling security or shoving the man out of his office, Harvey opened up the top drawer of his desk and pulled forth a shotgun.

# THIRTY-ONE

It was a double-barrelled shotgun, twelve-bore, with the barrel sawn down to maybe thirty centimetres in length. Only two cartridges meant it would never be Victor's first choice of firearm, even with the full-length barrels. Sawing it down for concealability gave it almost no effective range. The cloud of pellets would begin expanding the instant they cleared the muzzle. Within a few metres, that cloud would be so big most of the pellets would miss the target altogether. Those few that did hit would still have more than enough energy to do considerable damage, although three pellets hitting three different parts of the body did little compared to all twelve striking in the exact same place.

In the close confines of an office, however, that drawback became a big problem to solve.

Action was always faster than reaction, so it was possible to jerk clear of a gun's barrel before an enemy could squeeze a trigger when only a single tiny bullet was involved. Victor could not anticipate clearing an expanding cloud of pellets, let alone two clouds fired almost simultaneously.

So, he did nothing for now except rise and take a few steps to put the visitor's chair in front of him.

Harvey was not going to squeeze one or both of the shotgun's triggers. He had done his best to impress Victor, talking himself up, saying that his new offices were due to open soon. He wasn't going to murder someone inside them.

The Australian rounded the desk but was smart enough not to get too close.

'Who gave you the files you passed to Schulz?', Victor said, 'Who stole them in the first place? My client is willing to offer you the deal of a lifetime. They recognise you are just a middleman, so if you give me the name of the thief, I walk away and you'll never see me again.'

Harvey, clutching the shotgun in a tight grip with both hands, shook his head. 'I don't know who the thief is.'

'I don't believe you.'

'I'm telling the truth,' Harvey insisted. 'It was all anonymous, I swear it. I just needed the money to help build all of this. They reached out to me, not the other way around. They needed a buffer. A simple pickup and even simpler handoff. I delivered the files to Schulz, but I picked them up from a dead drop.'

'If I think you're lying to me,' Victor told him, 'I'll have to hurt you.'

'You don't need to do anything. I have no personal stake in any of this beyond the seed money I needed to set up my business. I would tell you more if I knew more.'

'Tell me about Belgium. Why did you hire Lambert's guys to gun down civilians in that café?'

'No, no, no. That's not what I hired anyone to do. That's what they wanted.'

'Who is they?' Victor asked.

'The people who wanted me to pass the files to Schulz also wanted a hit arranged. No one was supposed to fill some eatery full of lead.'

'Then what happened? Who were they supposed to kill?'

'I don't know. Again, I swear. I wasn't involved in the planning, only in gathering the bodies. They needed assets and I provided them and no one told me why. I'm in so over my head. I didn't think it would come to this . . . I just wanted some quick cash, you know.' He blew out a long, heavy sigh of defeat. 'Would it help to say I'm sorry?'

'Everyone's sorry when they're staring down the barrel of a gun.'

Harvey glanced down at the shotgun he held, then back up to Victor. 'But you're the one staring down the barrel of my gun.'

'Only because I'm allowing you to point it at me,' Victor told him. 'I only have so much patience, Mister Harvey, so either you need to decide to use it or put it back in the drawer.'

Harvey followed the instructions, trying to weigh up what to do, and in doing so he looked down at the shotgun in his hands as Victor had expected him to, providing the perfect opportunity to—

Kick the chair into him.

On rollers, it slid straight into Harvey's legs, causing no damage but enough surprise and alarm for Victor to dart to the side as he sprang forward, simultaneously sweeping Harvey's feet out from under him as Victor ripped the shotgun from his hands.

Harvey cowered.

'Like I said,' Victor continued, sitting behind Harvey's desk in the man's own chair, 'my client is willing to give you a chance to make amends. Even if you don't know who the thief is who supplied you with the files, you might still be able to help identify them. Is that something you're interested in?'

Harvey had yet to process the fact he was still alive. Slowly, he opened his eyes.

'Get off the floor, you're embarrassing yourself.'

Harvey did so in slow, awkward movements. Then he slumped down on the chair Victor had been sitting on a minute beforehand.

The Australian said, 'If I can help, I will. I just want a way out of this.'

'How did you communicate with the thief? Email, direct message ...?'

'Phone calls,' Harvey answered. 'They told me where and when I could pick up the files.'

'You said "they"; male or female?'

'I don't know. They disguised their voice with one of those modulator apps or whatever else, so they sounded robotic. I couldn't tell you if the voice I heard belonged to a woman or a man.'

'They called you on your own phone or the office?'

Harvey shook his head. 'Neither. I received a handset in the mail one day. It rang the next.'

'Tell me you still have that phone.'

'Of course,' he said as he nodded. 'Until you showed up at my door I thought they might need me again.'

'You might have just saved your life,' Victor said. 'Give it to me.'

'I don't have it on me right now.'

'Don't play games with me, Mister Harvey.'

The Australian held up both palms. 'I'm not, I swear. I keep it in the company safe. I didn't want to risk carrying it around, you know?'

'If you tell me there's a time lock and it'll only open in the morning, I'm going to be displeased.'

'I can open it any time I want,' Harvey said. 'It's state of the art. Not to brag, but it cost more than a Bentley.'

Victor rotated his head. 'I don't see any safe in your office, so where is it?'

'Downstairs. It's a walk-in. Like a mini bank vault.'

'What's the code?'

'There's two. One six-digit number to gain access to the room itself, then a sixteen-digit alphanumeric code in order to open the vault. Before you ask again, there's no point in me telling you the codes because the vault also needs my palm print to open. I paid extra to get the version that has an electrical impulse sensor too.' The Australian forced a nervous laugh. 'That way no one can chop off my hand to get into it.'

Victor said, 'Perish the thought.'

# THIRTY-TWO

The woman had a tall, shapely figure. She had long, dark hair and wore a smart trouser suit. She looked every inch the professional, as did her companion. Tall too, he had a lean, athletic physique. Just like the woman, he also wore a suit. They were paused, midstride, frozen in time as they walked along a pavement in downtown Bucharest.

The photograph had been taken with a state-of-the-art camera with a long lens, allowing the photographer to snap the picture from a considerable distance without being noticed. More photographs appeared on the wall-mounted screen, showing the man and the woman walking together at different times. Even having lunch. Although, because they had sat inside the café, with other people and furniture shielding them, those shots were not as clear.

Finally, one showed them embracing.

'This is where they part ways,' Karmia Elkayam explained. 'At this point, the team on the ground decided to stick with the killer and let the woman go. Of course, all of this happened unplanned and in a short space of time, the team taking the decision on the ground to reassign themselves in real time, which I think we can all agree is a testament to their adaptability and critical thinking. Since then, we have exploited various local systems in Bucharest, including the CCTV network, transport and commercial services, to extract as much useful footage and digital intelligence as possible. Thankfully, our team had already created a backdoor into many such systems to facilitate their mission so it was possible to keep track of their new targets without being seen.'

Once an operative in Zahm's own kidon unit, Elkayam now outranked him several times over. Whereas he had never had any ambitions beyond serving Father to kill Israel's enemies, Elkayam would be director of Mossad one day, no doubt prime minister in twenty years. She was as skilled at advancing her career as she had been with a blade or gun.

Like the select few others present in the briefing room, Zahm listened to her presentation with great interest. He had already been informed of the basics, of course, but this was the first official meeting of the newly created action group assembled to respond to the unexpected sighting of the killer in Bucharest. Given Elkayam was standing in for what otherwise would have been Father's role, she was overseeing the action group's activities. The infamous assassination arm of Israeli intelligence operated with a high degree of independence from the rest of the organisation, and yet many people from the wider Mossad hierarchy were present.

Zahm felt their gazes and their judgement. Much taller and broader than anyone else in the room, he had never felt so small.

'How is it that we don't have any recordings from inside the hotel? There must be CCTV in a place like that.'

Re'em Herzog was the most senior Mossad officer present for the briefing. Higher up than even Father, Herzog was the Director of European Operations. Approaching sixty, only a horseshoe of hair remained. Although dark, he kept it short enough for as much skin to be visible as strands. His scalp bunched into distinct rolls at the back of his skull as he raised his head. When he smiled, which was rare, or frowned, which was often, his eyes crinkled, and the dimples in his cheeks deepened into vertical lines.

Elkayam said, 'They have numerous cameras, yes, and of high quality too. However, their server suffered a cyber-attack at the same time that wiped all the footage from their cloud. It's not recorded locally to save disk space, so it's all gone.'

'So this assassin is an expert hacker as well?'

'I very much doubt that he has that skill set along with all of his others,' she answered. 'I think it's far more likely he had some help.'

'Is it possible for us to find out who hacked the hotel server?'

'The chain that owns the hotel has hired an online security firm to investigate the hack. Because they use software developed by companies that are friendly to us, we were able to pore through all the data ourselves in conjunction with the firm's own investigation. Cybercriminals leave digital fingerprints just like regular crooks and it seems they were either sloppy or rushed because they left their prints all over this attack.'

Herzog said, 'Don't keep us waiting. Who was the hacker?'

'Although the identity of the actual hacker is unknown, we know the attack originated from the offices of a private military company based in Gibraltar and owned by a man named Marcus Lambert. He supplies mercenaries to clients all over the globe and, rumour has it, he is very friendly with the British Ministry of Defence.'

'Friendly, how?'

'He tidies up the kind of messes that they have to keep at arm's length.'

Herzog asked, 'Who was the assassin in Bucharest to kill?'

'The target was a German national by the name of Jan Schulz,' Elkayam explained, 'who was a private security expert, aka rent-a-spy, in the city to meet a former operative of Mossad, Marion Ysiv. A woman matching her description was seen by our people arriving at the hotel shortly after Schulz. They greeted one another in the hotel lobby and all looked well between them. Her entire entourage was killed in the hotel room along with Schulz, but Ysiv was seen leaving the hotel in the company of the assassin.' She showed several photographs on the screen. 'These were taken by a CCTV camera across the street from the hotel. As you can see, she seems extremely cosy with the assassin. We lose them seconds later as they leave the camera's field of view. Thankfully, by then, our operative who made the initial identification of the assassin had withdrawn as a precautionary measure in case she had failed to hide her surprise at seeing him in the flesh. The team was present to track the activities of a terrorist financier who happened to be staying at the same hotel and took it upon themselves to switch assignments. A difficult decision given the financier's importance but we can all agree it was the correct call.'

'Bring up the second image,' Herzog said, pointing to the screen. 'When we see them from the front, side by side.'

A couple of clicks of the laptop's keyboard and the corresponding still was displayed.

'That is *not* Marion Ysiv,' he said. 'I know her. I used to work with her. This woman dresses like her, but her face is different.'

Zahm looked his way in confusion, but Elkayam did not.

'Exactly,' she said. 'The real Marion Ysiv was found dead in her home in Austria this morning.' Another set of photographs appeared on the screen. These showed a corpse in a state of decay. 'Ysiv was killed some months before Schulz's assassination in Bucharest and buried in her basement.'

'Then who is she?' Herzog asked.

'Her name is Constance Stone, also known by the handle Raven. She is an American national and former CIA, now rogue. Officially, her last assignment was in Yemen almost seven years ago, and she's been a wanted woman ever since. How she came to be working with the assassin is anyone's guess, but whereas we know next to nothing about him, we know a great deal about her thanks to our friends in the US. We didn't know in advance that Constance Stone had been impersonating her for some time.'

Herzog said, 'Please tell me you didn't inform the Americans of this.'

'Of course not,' Elkayam said with a smirk. 'We don't want their great big boots stomping all over this. And we don't need their help either. We already know one of the assassin's legends rented the apartment across the street overlooking the hotel. We know under which passport he entered the country and under which one he left. Because we have such a clear image of his face, we have been able to utilise our own facial recognition technology, combined with the raw data extracted from multiple sources, to build up the kind of profile on him that was impossible six years ago. So far, we have a total of five separate legends used by this one individual. We already know many of the places he has been in over the last twelve months.'

Zahm's gaze was glued to the screen, which showed a photograph of the killer's face. There had been other images over the years, of course. From CCTV cameras, most often, or the occasional passport scan. Almost always long after the fact when it was too late to respond, each missed opportunity a fresh stab of pain through Zahm who had felt so much literal pain at the killer's hand.

These new photographs were not only recent, they showed his face in clear detail in a way Zahm had not seen in all the years since the night they had duelled in Sofia, Bulgaria, when Zahm had been mere millimetres away from driving a shard of glass through the killer's eyeball.

Father had taught Zahm to relinquish so many emotions – empathy, compassion, love – that Zahm felt so little on a day-to-day basis, but he still felt anger.

He could still hate.

Zahm, who had remained quiet until now, could not restrain himself any longer. 'Where is he now?'

Elkayam told him, 'We'll know soon enough.'

# THIRTY-THREE

Victor told Harvey, 'I'm going to put this shotgun down and you're going to maintain your composure and leave it alone, okay?'

A nod from the Australian. Victor opened the breach and withdrew the two shells. He stood them up by their brass strike plates on the desk and laid the shotgun down next to them.

'You're going to take me downstairs to your vault and you're going to give me that phone.'

'Of course,' Harvey agreed.

'I take it the door behind your desk leads to a bathroom,' Victor began. 'But do you have a closet too?'

'Yeah, the works. Why?'

'Because you look like you've been in a sauna,' Victor said.

The Australian looked down at his shirt. A pale blue, it was dark with sweat patches in the centre of the chest, the belly and the armpits.

'We don't want your security guy to get the wrong impression of me, do we?'

'Oh yeah,' Harvey said. 'I'll get cleaned up.'

'Attaboy.'

Not that he expected the man to try anything, but it was too egregious to Victor's professional sensibilities to let Harvey out of his sight, so he stood in the open doorway while the Australian stripped off his stained shirt, washed, and dressed in a fresh shirt.

'You're not going to kill me, are you? After I've given you the phone, I mean.'

'Like I said: the client is granting you mercy. Because I'm of a cynical mindset, I imagine they think you can be of use to them and so will be expecting a lot of you in return further down the line.'

'It never ends, does it? Once you dirty yourself in this business you can never get clean again.'

'Something like that,' Victor agreed. 'But remember: giving me that phone is only solving half of your problems.'

'Why only half?'

'You hired contractors from Marcus Lambert's PMC, remember? The phone gets my client off your back, not Lambert himself. Once we've resolved our business we're going to give him a call. When we do, you had better be ready to give the apology of your life.'

'I will,' Harvey said. 'I didn't even know the men I hired worked for him. I wouldn't do that.'

'They were quick to tell me you had hired them,' Victor said. 'So that's hard to believe. Just think, had you paid them what they were due then maybe you would never have had the pleasure of my acquaintance. It's funny how greed so often proves to be one's undoing.'

'I did pay them,' Harvey insisted. 'They just wanted more. They tried to blackmail me.'

'That's not what they told me,' Victor said in return. 'But the specifics of your arrangement with them are irrelevant to my goals. Whether you paid them or not, they all worked for Lambert, so you had better hope your cooperation now quells his wrath.'

'All of them worked for him ...? How is that possible? I did my background checks.'

'Then your eye for detail is not as accurate as you think, because all three were on Lambert's books as contractors.'

'All *three*?'

'That's what I said.'

Harvey looked away, thinking.

'What is it?'

The Australian said, 'I hired five. A local team.'

'Not American?'

He shook his head. 'They told me they would take extra bodies for backup ... I didn't know the details. Like I said, I just recruited the shooters.'

'Who told you?'

Still following his own train of thought, Harvey added, 'I only did the background checks on the original five ... not the extra bodies, which must have been the three you dealt with.' He sighed, shaking his head. 'This is all my fault. I'm sorry, okay? I screwed up, I know. But out of incompetence, not malice. Please, you have to believe me. I didn't know they were bringing extra guys who worked for Lambert. I assumed they meant guys like them.'

'Like who?'

'The crew that I hired,' Lambert explained. 'At least, they did work for me ... before they tried to stiff me. You don't agree on a fee and then ask for more once you've got the job, do you? That's not how this business works. That's not how any business works.' He snapped his fingers. 'That must be why the others told you they hadn't been paid. My crew kept all the money and didn't want to share it with Lambert's men. That's even worse than stiffing me; they stiffed them too.'

Victor approached the window of Harvey's office. 'Tell me about this crew. Everything you know. Don't leave anything out.'

'Why?'

'Because I told you to,' Victor said.

'They're shooters,' Harvey replied. 'What else is there to say? They were good while it lasted, but they got greedy. Thought they were worth more than I was paying them and played a hand they couldn't back up.'

'How did you leave it with them?'

'I told them to take a hike,' Harvey said with something like a smile. 'Let's see how they get on without me in their corner.'

'Would I be correct in saying that, of the five, two are white, one is black, and two, I'm guessing, are Southeast Asian?'

'British Indians, I think,' Harvey said with a nod. 'Not that I checked. Why? Wait, how did you know all of that?'

'Because they've decided they don't want you in their corner or in the corner of anyone else either.'

'What does that mean?'

Victor said, 'They were waiting outside when I arrived. Five of them in a car: two Southeast Asians, one black, two white. They stood out to me as potential threats, but they had no interest in me at all. I can tell when people mean me

175

harm, and these guys didn't even know I existed. I found that curious, but I had no explanation for why until now.'

Harvey, buttoning his shirt cuffs, approached and followed Victor's gaze.

Below them was a parking area in front of the office building that opened onto the road, snaking through the business park. On the far side of that road, a brown Volkswagen Passat was parked against the kerb.

'See?' he told Harvey. 'There they are.'

# THIRTY-FOUR

'What's taking so long?'

Although the guy in the passenger seat of the stolen Passat was not the youngest of the five-man crew, he was the most impatient. He took a swig of his energy drink and belched out the excess carbon dioxide.

'Easy, hothead,' answered the driver, calmer, a more laid-back kind of guy. 'This takes as long as it takes, okay? Just be chilled.'

Another swig. 'The boat isn't going to wait for us.'

The vessel in question was moored and ready to take them overseas as soon as they had completed this piece of unfinished business. The only issue was the timing of it. The boat was set to leave at midnight. Including driving time, they were cutting it fine to begin with because they didn't want to be in the same country when Harvey's body was found.

'We didn't account for any visitors,' the driver said. 'Which, in retrospect, was a silly mistake. We should have been smarter.'

'I don't see what difference it makes,' the impatient guy countered, fingers tapping the lid of his energy drink. 'Alone or at a birthday party, so what?'

'Either we wait it out so the visitor leaves, or we abandon this mission.'

'That's not an option,' one of the three guys squeezed into the back added. He was not necessarily the leader, because they had no leader, but he was the eldest and most respected. Born in Mumbai but raised in the East End of London, he sounded more Cockney than Indian. 'We told the Aussie what would happen if he didn't pay us what we were worth, so we have to follow through. This business is all about rep. We burn ours if word gets out we're pushovers. You don't come back from something like that.'

'Then let's get this done,' the impatient guy in the passenger seat insisted, crushing the empty energy drink can and tossing it into the footwell. 'The visitor is nothing more than collateral damage. Wrong time, wrong place, blud. No hard feelings.'

'We're professionals,' the most senior guy reminded everyone in the vehicle. 'Let's act like it. We don't kill people for no reason.'

The driver said, 'What happens if we miss the boat?'

'Then we charter another one.'

'What about the Finland job?'

The boat was to take them across the North Sea and through the Baltic Sea before mooring in Helsinki in the morning. A Finnish drug baron had hired the five-man crew to wipe out the leadership of his rivals, an Albanian gang, by ambushing them at the site of a supposed trade later in the day.

'Depends on how long it takes to charter a different boat.

If there's minimal delay, then nothing changes. Might miss a few hours of kip.'

'And if we can't get one until the morning?'

'Then we won't be in Helsinki in time, and we'll have to tell the client we're unable to complete.'

The passenger groaned. 'I need that money.'

The driver said, 'We all need that money.'

The second Asian in the back, a cousin of the more senior man, who hadn't added his thoughts until now, said, 'It might work in our favour to have another corpse.'

His cousin told him to, 'Explain.'

'The visitor could be anyone, right? Maybe when the police find his corpse alongside Harvey, the visitor's presence muddies the waters of the investigation. Maybe they theorise he was the target; maybe they think he's involved with Harvey somehow, and that somehow is the reason they were killed. The visitor could have enemies or even a jealous wife. Who's to say why they were killed together?'

'Interesting.'

'The more questions the cops have to ask, the less likely the answer is us.'

The driver said, 'That's really not a bad idea.'

To no one's surprise, the impatient passenger agreed. 'Then we go in now and fill them both full of lead?'

The most senior of the crew stroked his beard. 'Let me think a moment.' He leaned to one side to peer between the seats to see the dashboard's clock. 'We give the visitor a few more minutes. If he doesn't walk out the door by quarter past, then he gets to hold Harvey's hand as we give them both a gentle nudge off their mortal coils.'

\*

Harvey, who had a strong, even tan, paled. 'What do they want?'

'Was I not explicit enough?' Victor said in return. 'They mean someone harm and that someone isn't me. They're going to kill you.'

Harvey went even paler. 'What do we do?'

'*We* do nothing,' Victor answered. 'I'm not involved. You were the one who told them to take a hike when they asked for more money. Maybe they overvalued themselves, maybe you short-changed them. I don't really care. Once you've given me that phone, it's none of my business. But, just in case ...'

He took the shotgun from the desk and reloaded the two shells. As he did so, the Australian stared at the weapon as if seeing it for the first time. He was scared and overwhelmed. A banker out of his depth.

Victor told him, 'Fetch me the spare shells. I assume you keep them in your desk.'

'I don't have any spare shells.'

'Of course you don't,' Victor replied as he headed for the door. 'Come on. Let's get that phone.'

'If he doesn't leave, are we equipped to deal with a third party?' the driver asked.

They all had suppressed pistols, and a couple had knives as standard. They didn't know for sure if Harvey carried a firearm, but he probably had one within reach. The security was likely to be the same. The strict gun laws in the UK ensured none of the firearms would be legal, but that didn't stop people in the know from having them anyway. Given Harvey's foray into the world of professional killing, it made sense he would protect himself.

'Why do you say that?' the more senior guy in the back asked. 'Why wouldn't we be equipped to deal with an extra body?'

The driver shrugged. 'Harvey's connected, right?' He gestured to the other four men. 'We're living proof of that, aren't we? The visitor could be a player too.'

The guy in the passenger seat scoffed at the driver's cautionary tone. 'Are you actually kidding me right now? We're five savages, five stone-cold pros who drop fools for a living. That guy that we watched walk in? He's Harvey's golfing buddy.' He scoffed harder. 'He's probably a lawyer.' He scoffed even harder. 'No, he's not even a brief; he's an accountant.'

The three guys in the back chuckled along with their impatient colleague. Even the driver, almost always stone-faced, cracked a smile.

'What's the accountant going to do?' the passenger asked, continuing his joke. 'Bore us to death?'

# THIRTY-FIVE

Reaching the foyer of the first floor, Victor headed to the stairs with Harvey following behind him.

'If we're quick,' Victor said, 'we can get to the vault before they enter.'

'What happens then?'

'Then I walk out of here.'

'What about me?'

'If you walk out the front door,' Victor told him, 'they're just going to gun you down. But you could try hiding somewhere. Maybe call the police if you'd prefer prison to death.'

Victor elected not to add that any competent crew could clear the building within a few short minutes, and there was next to no chance of a police response arriving before then. Even if a car did arrive in time, they would not be armed and so could do nothing to actually prevent Harvey's imminent demise.

'I'd rather go down shooting, personally. But that's just me.'

Once they arrived on the ground floor, Victor kept the shotgun beneath his jacket so it was hidden from the security guard's view as he looked over from his desk in response to the sound of Victor and Harvey's footsteps.

'Good evening, Mister Harvey.'

The Australian, panicking at the thought of the imminent threat outside, said nothing in response.

The security guard stood up. 'Is everything okay?'

'Tell him you're giving me a tour,' Victor whispered.

Harvey cleared his throat. 'Ugh, oh, yes ... sorry, how's it going tonight, Franklin? I'm just giving our visitor here a little tour of the premises.'

Although his voice was strained and stilted, the Australian presented a wide smile that put the security guard at ease. He wasn't about to challenge his boss.

'Good job,' Victor told him as they crossed the foyer. 'You're doing great.'

It was a satisfactory job, at best, but he wanted to give Harvey a little boost of confidence. Victor didn't want the man so stressed he forgot one of the two codes required to access the vault.

The building's ground floor consisted of many offices and corridors surrounding the central foyer, with the main entrance at one end of it and the elevators and stairs at the other. Harvey took Victor into the area where the vault was located, leading him through several hallways and rooms.

'Here we are,' Harvey said as they stopped before a door that was identical to the many others in the building except that it had an electronic keypad set into the wall alongside it.

Victor watched as Harvey used an index finger to tap in the code.

The whirring of an electronic locking mechanism sounded and Harvey pushed down the door handle. The door did not open when he tried to push it.

'Ah,' he said with an embarrassed smile. 'It has a regular lock too.'

Victor remained silent as Harvey reached into a trouser pocket to fetch his keys, although from the man's resulting expression, he knew what he was going to say before the Australian admitted: 'I left my keys upstairs.'

'Of course you did.'

'Do we have enough time to go get them? Before the men outside enter?'

'Only one way to find out.'

*'Bore us to death,'* the driver repeated, breaking into an uncommon chuckle. 'That's a good one.'

'Settle down, settle down,' the most senior of the five said as the others all laughed together, loud and mirthful, slapping thighs, rocking in their seats. 'Accountant or not, I want us to keep our game faces on with this, okay? We don't have eyes in there, do we? We take this one for granted, and we're going to find Mister Bore-us-to-Death has dialled 999 from a broom closet before we get to him, and this whole area will be swarming with feds by the time we walk out again.' He leaned to look at the clock once more. 'Okay, looks like it's showtime.'

In an instant, the laughter stopped, and smiles faded to expressions of absolute concentration and grim determination. They fished out balaclavas from pockets or rolled down those already perched waiting. Anyone not already wearing black nitrile gloves fitted them in place. All five checked their handguns were loaded, and bullets were waiting in chambers to be fired. Those who hadn't previously screwed on suppressors did so now. They had two small Makarov PMs, bought cheap, and three Glock 17s, modified with auto sears that turned them from semi-automatic pistols to fully automatic. Subsonic ammunition for both types of weapon meant no one happening to be in the neighbourhood would overhear Harvey's execution.

The most senior guy reached into a pocket for a burner phone and thumbed in the number that matched another phone rigged up to a small explosive device. 'Let's teach this Aussie prick how much we're really worth.'

Harvey uttered apologies as they backtracked through the rooms and hallways of the ground floor.

'This is all a lot for me to take in.'

'You're forgiven,' Victor told him. 'Just be quiet from now on. I want to be able to hear if they—'

An explosion.

A dull thud from a small charge either somewhere in the building or close by outside.

The lights went out.

Before Harvey could unleash a cry of terror, Victor slapped a palm over the man's mouth.

'Ah,' Victor said. 'It seems we've reached the limits of their patience.'

The offices had no generator of their own, so there was no emergency lighting beyond the glow given out by the fluorescent markings above the doors to guide employees in case of a fire or power cut. The five-man crew must have used a remotely detonated explosive device to take out the electricity supply. Probably not for any tactical advantage but purely to avoid being recorded on CCTV, given they had been expecting to find just Harvey and the unarmed security guard inside. Which dealt with one of Victor's future problems for him.

'Nod if you can keep control of yourself.'

The Australian did so and Victor removed his hand.

'What do we do?' Harvey whispered.

'At this point, it depends on them.'

The five-man crew rushed from their car and across the parking area in front of the building, breaching the doors with a sledgehammer carried by the driver, who discarded it the instant after the plate glass doors were smashed open.

Inside the foyer, the lone security guy – who had relaxed back into his chair after Harvey and the visitor had continued on their way – startled by the small detonation that had blown the power, failed to see the dark figures on the far side of the entrance.

As glass shattered, he almost fell out of his chair as he sprung to his feet, startled once again.

Enough ambient light from the exterior streetlamps reached inside the building through its many windows for him to clearly see five silhouetted figures hurry through the smashed-out doors, soles of shoes crunching on broken glass.

They all had guns.

'What . . . is this?' the security guard uttered.

'Harvey's office,' one of them demanded. 'Where is it?'

Hands rising as they jogged across the foyer towards him, the security guard told them, 'Upstairs corner office . . . left out of the elevators . . . end of the corridor. You can't miss it.'

'Do they have weapons?'

'I gave the visitor a pat-down, so he's clean,' the security guard answered. 'But Mister Harvey has a shotgun in his office.'

'Good to know,' the same one told him. 'You've been very helpful.'

Another man shot the security guard twice in the head.

'*Idiot*,' the senior guy chastised. 'We don't know if they're still in there.'

'The light was on.'

'We'll check,' the senior guy told the driver and the impatient guy, pointing at them both. 'You two, cover our six and make sure neither of them can slip away without us knowing. No one walks out of here alive.'

Victor and Harvey had made it as far as the foyer, but failed to reach the stairwell before the five-man crew breached the entrance. Having heard the exchange with the security guard, they backed out before they were seen, Victor ushering Harvey through the closest available door, easing it open and then shut behind him. There were no windows in this corridor, so it was even darker. Only the fluorescent signage provided any illumination.

*No one walks out of here alive.*

Victor revised his earlier assessment of the situation.

He asked Harvey, 'Does the security guard have a set of keys?'

The Australian's breaths were shallow and rapid. His face glimmered with sweat, and his eyes were wide and staring at a point far behind Victor.

'The security guard,' he said again, grabbing a fistful of

Harvey's shirt to focus his attention. 'Does he have a key to the vault room?'

'He has keys for every room ... but not that one.'

'I had a sneaking suspicion you were going to say that.'

Even though Victor was no threat to them, the five-man crew were not going to let him retrieve the phone and walk out of here.

At least, that was their intention.

He would need to explain in inarguable terms that it was not up to them whether he left or not.

Victor rocked his head from side to side to crack his neck.

# THIRTY-SIX

For a moment, Victor stood still behind the door leading to the foyer and listened to hurrying footsteps draw closer. Although he could not decipher how many pairs of feet due to the way the footsteps overlapped, he worked out that it was three of them when he heard one whisper, 'I'll go up the stairs first, you two follow.'

Victor heard the suck of a door opening and only a single set of footsteps for a few more seconds before a second two sets followed. This was the worst-case scenario. One left behind to guard the exit could be caught by surprise. Two, however, was a much more difficult prospect.

In a whisper, he told Harvey, 'You do everything I say and nothing I don't.'

A meek nod of agreement, but a nod all the same.

'You have a toilet on this floor, I'm sure. Does it have cubicles?'

'Two in the men's, four in the ladies.'

'Do you know the way in the dark?'

'Yes,' Harvey whispered.

'Take me there.'

Stairs were always perilous; they were always a choke point. But, with numbers, that danger could be mitigated. As the more senior guy went up backwards, looking upwards to potential threats that might emerge and otherwise shoot him in the back had he been facing the other way around, the second two men could cover the flanks and stop an enemy sneaking up behind.

That wasn't necessary here, given they presumed Harvey and the visitor were upstairs, but they did it anyway.

After all, they were pros.

The Australian did as he was told, leading Victor along the dark corridor, taking a left turn at one intersection and a right at another. Both sets of toilets were on the same stretch of hallway. Victor led Harvey into the ladies.

With no light at all in this room, Victor used the illumination from his burner phone's screen to show the way to the furthest cubicle, guiding Harvey inside and knocking the toilet lid down over the seat.

'Climb up on there and sit down in a squat.' As Harvey did just that, Victor added, 'Do not under any circumstances put your feet on the floor. Do you understand?'

'Yes' was the answer.

The Australian looked awkward and uncomfortable when in position. However, he did not complain.

Victor said, 'Use your left hand to brace if you need to', and handed him the shotgun. 'But you keep this in your right hand at all times. I'll leave the cubicle door unlocked, but pulled to.'

'Okay.'

'If you hear anyone enter the bathroom, it's them. Maybe they'll bend down and shine a torch under the cubicles and back out when they see no feet.'

It had taken about a minute to reach the bathroom and get Harvey in position. Victor imagined it would take the three guys about the same amount of time to find Harvey's office and see that it was empty. Maybe they would search the upper floor. Maybe they would head straight back down to rejoin the other two.

In the first scenario, he might have four minutes.

In the second, less than two.

'What if they don't back out again?'

'You wait until the cubicle door opens and you squeeze the trigger.'

'*God*,' Harvey muttered.

'He won't save you,' Victor told him. 'So you'd better pray to me instead.'


Guard duty was no kind of fun. They were here to dig holes into Harvey, and now whoever the visitor was, not stand by the door.

'Could have sat this one out,' the crew's most impatient member said as he patrolled the foyer, gun up and aiming where he was looking, disciplined despite his frustration.

The driver, covering the other half of the space, said back. 'This is such an anticlimax.'

'Who put him in charge anyway? Not me, that's for sure. I thought this was a team effort.'

'We'll hash it out on the boat,' the driver said. 'We make sure we're running vanguard for the Helsinki job, okay?'

'You and me need to back each other up. Make sure he can't just tell us what to do.'

The driver told him, 'That's it for now. Just keep your eyes peeled.'

The impatient guy said, 'No one's getting past me.'

The foyer was a big, open space with multiple ways in and out, many blind spots and areas of cover. Still, Victor had no way of knowing exactly where the two guys guarding it would be located. At any point he entered it, that could be the exact position one of them could be looking towards.

Or, if he caught one off guard from behind, there was no telling if the second would then do the same to him.

He couldn't go to them.

Victor had to make them come to him.

The more senior of the team reached the first floor, with the other two trailing out of the stairwell seconds later, fast and smooth. All three followed the directions given by the security guard. They headed left along the adjoining hallway towards the corner office. There was no missing it.

They slowed their pace as they approached, but when they heard no sounds emanating from within, they abandoned stealth and charged in.

Empty.

'He's hiding somewhere,' the senior guy said to the others as they checked the adjoining closet and bathroom. 'But we'll find him. We'll find them both.'

The fluorescent safety signs provided helpful directions for Victor to follow. They enabled him to navigate the ground floor to this side of the foyer, which had a central corridor that threaded from where he had entered next to the elevators and stairwell and ended up joining the foyer again near the main entrance. Many rooms led off from this corridor, but they were not of any interest to Victor apart from a wheeled office chair he took from one.

Where a hallway opened out into the foyer, Victor positioned himself out of sight and shoved the chair so it rolled out fast into the foyer.

As the chair appeared in the open space, its solid plastic wheels scraping on the hard flooring – and therefore drew the attention of the two guys stationed there – Victor used an elbow to smash the glass of a fire alarm and exploited the resulting blaring to mask the sound of him sprinting back the way he had come.

The chair rolled into the driver's field of vision first, and he had just enough time to say, 'What the hell is this?' before the fire alarm sounded.

The impatient guy back-pedalled closer. He had to shout to be heard above the alarm. 'Harvey and the visitor?'

'Must be,' the driver shouted back, snapping his gun up to point in the direction of the mouth of the connecting hallway from where the chair had rolled out.

The impatient guy, also aiming in the same direction, hurried over, pressing himself to one side of the opening. The driver followed once the first guy was in position, and took up a mirror-image placement.

Sweeping out, the impatient guy went first, seeing nothing but alternate areas of darkness and light where ambient illumination came through the windows.

'Clear,' he shouted. 'Let's get these dickheads.'

'No,' the driver said, urging caution. 'They want to pull us away from the foyer.' He gestured to the exit. 'They want to make a break for it.'

The other man smiled. 'And it almost worked too. You stay here and wait for him. I'll loop around and come up on their six.'

They used a fist bump to seal their plan.

'Looks like we'll get some fun after all.'

# THIRTY-SEVEN

Victor couldn't be sure exactly how the two guys in the foyer would react to the chair and the fire alarm, but he didn't need to be certain. There were only so many possibilities, after all, and they had already told him enough for him to predict their response. They were positioned in the foyer to stop anyone else leaving, so that was their priority. They could not leave the entrance unguarded. Given there were two of them, one would stay behind and the other would act. Because they knew the direction from which the chair had come, that responder would circle round to flank.

So, Victor waited around the first ninety-degree corner of the central corridor at the opposite end where it joined the foyer near the elevators. He pressed himself against a wall, his right shoulder at the corner. With the only illumination source being the ambient light from outside shining through exterior windows, he projected no shadow onto the floor, but anyone coming along the perpendicular corridor would cast their own shadow in front of them.

*

The three guys upstairs recognised the fire alarm for what it was: a diversion. Harvey and the visitor hadn't made it to the exit with the two other guys downstairs covering it – there had been no telltale gunshots – so they were trying to create a distraction and cause confusion. There was a simple solution for that. Having done their homework, they knew where the fire alarm control panel was, in a closet off the main foyer.

'*Quickly*,' the senior guy shouted, directing the other two down the stairs. 'Harvey isn't this smart so the visitor has some moves.'

The impatient guy of the team liked flying solo because he understood their vulnerability as a single unit in such tight spaces. Together, they would make more noise, create a larger target and search less efficiently than each operating solo.

Trigger control at such moments was paramount. At any point, he could cross paths with either Harvey and the visitor, or his teammates who had gone upstairs. As much as the impatient guy wanted to put many bullets into the visitor for the sheer fun of it, he did not want to put even a single round in any of his teammates by accident. So, he kept his index finger outside the trigger guard. Even the most practised shooters, the most experienced in combat, could squeeze the trigger upon the sudden appearance of a figure emerging out of the darkness only to realise a split second later it was a friend and not an enemy.

He had his pistol out before him, held in both hands and with both arms at full extension. It was the kind of stance that improved shooting accuracy at a distance, but in the close confines of a building interior, the outstretched arms put the gun in a vulnerable position . . .

. . . which Victor was happy to exploit as the weapon appeared in his field of view before the wielder even knew he was waiting around the corner.

He snapped his right palm atop the gun-holding hand and wrist as he used his left palm to punch up at the muzzle from below, levering the weapon back and out of the gunman's grip.

Victor caught the pistol as soon as it left his enemy's hand, and whipped it into his face, crushing his nose and knocking him from his feet before he could react.

Switching the position of the gun in his hand, Victor put one bullet between the wide eyes of the guy on the floor, whose look of abject disbelief became fixed on his face in death.

It should have been two bullets, only the pistol made no other sound save a *click* on the second squeeze of the trigger. A Soviet-era Makarov PM, maybe twice as old as Victor. Whether jammed with the guy's blood or poorly maintained, the result was a misfire. He pulled back the slide to clear the round in the chamber and wiped the weapon on the corpse's clothing to clear off some of the blood.

No spare magazines, he discovered. These guys had not been expecting Harvey to put up any kind of fight. Still, six bullets were better than no bullets.

The timer in Victor's head reached zero. The three from upstairs would be down here by now. No way of knowing if they would come after him together or split up, and equally no chance of pulling off the same trick twice.

If their roles were reversed, Victor would keep one guarding the exit, with strict instructions not to move under any circumstances. At the same time, the other three would sweep the building.

The fire alarm had hidden the suppressed report of the single gunshot, but it then fell silent.

He pictured one or more of the others finding the control panel, and either knowing how to disable it or merely ripping out the batteries.

Either way, the office fell quiet once more.

That suited Victor just fine.

In the darkness, in the silence, was where he belonged.

They were hunting him, but now he was hunting them in return.

# THIRTY-EIGHT

When three of the remaining four gunmen found the corpse of their impatient teammate, they were not surprised. After reconvening in the foyer and leaving the fourth to watch the exit, there had been a feeling of expectation and dread when the fifth guy had not returned from his flanking manoeuvre.

'No way Harvey did this,' the driver said.

'This visitor is a pro,' the senior guy told the others. 'Stay sharp or you'll end up the same.'

On paper, they weren't supposed to know one another – the cousins aside – outside work and beyond the role each of them performed. Personal information was not shared, so if something went wrong, such as one of them getting pinched, it wouldn't come back to haunt the others.

They referred to it as company policy.

Life was too inherently dangerous for people to know who you were in this line of work. They all agreed it was better if you were to them as they were to you, and that should be no one.

Except policy was not reality.

On surveillance, they broke the boredom by talking about sports or girlfriends, or by cracking jokes at one another's expense. After long nights out completing jobs, they sometimes had a beer to unwind – often many beers. Sometimes, there were many beers and then some shots, and, during such excess, the boundaries they were usually careful to maintain faltered.

Every now and again, someone's real name might be said by mistake when telling an anecdote or recounting a poignant moment. Hugs were even exchanged. There were smiles, jokes, fist bumps and slaps on the back, and those small moments of commonality formed deeper bonds.

They were paid murderers, but they were human.

The impatient, dead guy on the floor was more than simply a deceased colleague.

He had been one of their tribe.

'Let's get this arsehole,' the driver said in a whisper.

The other two nodded their agreement. They were all on the same page with this. They were all equally invested in killing this killer.

They had come here to settle their score with Harvey.

Now, they had a new score to settle.

Victor heard their quiet footsteps, having dropped their previous speed to a cautious, careful gait; now they knew he was dangerous. The acoustics of the building, with its empty interconnecting hallways and rooms, meant he could not get an accurate idea of their location from sound alone. The only thing he knew for sure was that they were close.

He heard them as they swept the ground floor for him.

They were slow and methodical, their footsteps light but their breathing hard. Which was reassuring. Their heart rates would still be high, and with that, their ability to aim, to keep their weapons steady and on target, would be compromised.

Three against one put the odds solidly in their favour. If all three split up, they were certain to find him and would do so much faster, although at the risk of facing him one-on-one.

If he were part of their team, he would want to stick together to avoid blue-on-blue accidents in the dimly lit building. He was no physical doppelganger for any of them, and yet, in the darkness, his silhouette would look much the same as any of their own. Victor had the advantage of not needing to confirm the identity of any target before opening fire since any other human shape he saw was an enemy. If they had even the remotest sense of camaraderie, they would take a split second to be sure they weren't shooting at one of their own.

In life-and-death situations, a split-second delay in taking the first shot could mean never getting to shoot at all.

The dead guy's Makarov held eight .380 Auto rounds with a full magazine. Now, six bullets were left. That was technically enough to kill the remaining four. However, subsonic 9mm rounds were not known for their stopping power. There were not enough rounds in the mag to double-tap each one, and anything less than a headshot would not be sufficient. He was destined to lose against all of them in a straight gunfight at close quarters.

He had to split them up.

The three gunmen directed one another with little nods, gestures, quick hand movements and signals. They were no military team with a regimented silent communication system, however they had intuitively developed a rough sign language that they used in circumstances like this, when verbal communication was impossible or unwise.

They knew which half of the floor Harvey and the visitor had to be hiding within.

They had no night vision equipment, no torches on their pistols, but they knew that the visitor didn't either. They were unprepared for this specific battlefield, and he was no more prepared.

They maintained their discipline while they searched, sweeping the building. With a methodical, room-by-room clearance, they eliminated possible positions. As they gradually narrowed down where Harvey and the visitor could be hiding, they systematically increased their chances of finding them at any moment.

Knowing they had to be close now, knowing they would inevitably find the dangerous visitor, meant even higher heart rates and even more sweat. The driver used his left hand, removing it from cradling the gun in his right, to wipe away the rivulets of perspiration running down his face from his shaved scalp. One of the Indians, seeing this, shook his head and gave him a little knowing smile. The driver was known for his excessive sweating.

'Concentrate,' the more senior team member whispered.

In moments like this, thinking could be overthinking. The human imagination had almost no limits. With enough time, the brain and mind could construct something out of nothing. Stalking in the darkness, hunting a deadly enemy, each room became a death trap, each corner a point of ambush, every shadow hiding a monster. In this way, fear was merely

imagination taken to a negative extreme. People said ignorance was bliss, but only those incapable or unwilling to
think. Fear was rational thought let loose. Courage was
often nothing more than failing to properly understand one's
circumstance.

They understood, however. Their dead teammate was a
testament to what the visitor was capable of, and what he
would do to them if they gave him the opportunity. A tiger
behind bars, caged and controlled, was a colourful curiosity,
beautiful and majestic. However, being in the cage with that
tiger was to be lunch.

But fear kept you sharp. It kept you aware. If you were
afraid, you could not be lazy. You could still make mistakes,
but those mistakes you made could not be avoided. Bravery
in this business was complacency, and complacency was
vulnerability.

In the dark, they crept, searched and edged forward with
caution, checking corners and their flanks before committing to any movement that might put them into the line
of fire of their hidden target. They peered along hallways.
They checked behind doors, under tables, always expecting
attack, in constant awareness that he could be anywhere, but
anywhere was getting smaller all the time. At any moment,
he could burst out of the many dark places and shadowed
corners.

The whole time, they listened as they searched because if
their two targets were smart, they would be trying to escape.
They should be trying to find a way out that they could
take without making the noise that would give away their
position.

The crew moved in and out of shadows, stepping into

darkness, stepping out of it. Always looking. Always listening. In constant awareness that the prey they were stalking could be anywhere. And even those places they had searched and cleared, they could not be one hundred per cent sure.

Life and combat did not work like that. It was a given that mistakes would be made.

Here, nothing could be taken for granted.

Frustration was building.

They were running out of time. By now Harvey must have called 999, and even if the Metropolitan Police were not known for their speedy response to emergency calls, they had to be coming.

The three gunmen were running out of space too. They had cleared through so much of the ground floor it seemed impossible they had yet to find either Harvey or the visitor.

'Where the hell are they?' the driver whispered.

# THIRTY-NINE

In the darkness, Victor followed them.

Although the building had many rooms, hallways, cubicles, closets and hiding places, they would eventually find him as a team. Against three, he didn't like those odds. The only way for him to split them up was if they split themselves up. They would only do that when they ran out of options and failed to find him together.

So, he shadowed them as they searched together, staying on their six, following through areas they had already cleared.

He paid little attention to what he could see because he could see so little. He heard the sounds of the building, the ticking of pipes, the flexing of wood and the gentle rattle of wind on windows. Recognising the ambient sounds was crucial when sight was so impeded. The more aware he was of the noises around him, the faster he would notice anything to interrupt that ambience.

Such as their footsteps.

They knew how to be quiet, but three men in conventional footwear could never be silent. Given he was operating solo, making the noise of one man instead of three, they had no hope of hearing him in return.

Because of his positioning behind them, they had to reverse direction to find him. All they had to do was make a little more noise, and he would know when they were coming closer.

As the seconds became minutes they made more noise, as their frustration built to unbearable levels.

Now they had only two choices: withdraw or split up.

Victor was good with either.

The driver, the one who was sweating, slipped off his jacket as he walked. Overheating was no joke. All clothes impeded movement, however light, however fitted, so there was no tactical reason to keep the garment on. Without it, fatigue's nagging, constant, suffocating drag was pushed back, if only for a moment.

'We don't have time for this,' he whispered.

'Co-sign,' another agreed.

'Okay, we split up and clear this place,' the more senior guy told the other two. 'They have to be here somewhere. If we hear sirens, withdraw.'

They all agreed it was a risk to leave the safety of the team but a necessity. Each of them wanted to be the one to kill their targets, and yet all of them wanted to walk away afterwards. No one wanted to die in the pursuit of vengeance.

They had three chances to spot them first. And, whenever the firing started, whichever one of them was the first to shoot or be shot, the others would come running. There was nothing to say one of them had to tackle the visitor the instant they saw him. They could alert their teammates with gunshots or shouts, directing them to join the fray, attacking from multiple sides at once.

Now, as three individuals, the gunmen crept forward, sticking close to the walls, not exposing themselves in the centre of corridors and rooms. The closer they were to solid cover, the fewer lines of attack their prey could utilise against them.

Success in close-quarters battle was all about limiting the enemy's ability to fight back. At such extreme short range, actual accuracy and target acquisition were less crucial because almost anyone could point and shoot and hit a man-sized target when it was standing right in front of them.

Instead, it came down to who saw their enemy before that enemy saw them – who shot first – and although reaction and speed played a significant role in that contest, it was more often down to positioning. Who placed themselves in a more beneficial position, had more cover and gave themselves the most advantages, so that they emerged victorious when they came face to face with the opposing shooter. And in such confrontations, victory meant life and defeat inevitably meant death.

The driver backtracked the way they had come, keen to end this himself, not realising that, in doing so, he was only ensuring he would die first.

Hearing footsteps grow louder as someone approached along the adjacent hallway, Victor raised the Makarov in readiness to put a bullet through the side of the man's skull as he passed.

No convenient shadows were cast here, so Victor used the footsteps to gauge distance and increased the pressure on the trigger in readiness, only squeezing when a gunman stepped into view.

*Click.*

Another jam.

# FORTY

Victor had a soft spot for Soviet-era weapons because they
almost never malfunctioned. Unlike last time, there was no
blood on the gun to possibly interfere with the mechanism,
so this pistol had been neglected, or the magazine had been
filled with cheap, substandard bullets.

Regardless, he had picked his moment to attack, so he
attacked.

As crucial as Victor considered speed, surprise and aggression, momentum was as vital. In combat, under pressure,
nothing went as planned. An enemy was rarely static. They
fought back. They could be unpredictable. But the momentum could not be compromised. If every unpredictable factor
interrupted the course of action to the point speed was lost,
it was over.

When Victor emerged from his hiding place and committed to the attack, there was nothing else in his mind, nothing
else as a priority.

At that moment, he was pure violence.

He launched himself at the driver, barrelling into him from the side. At the same time, his lead hand gripped the man's gun, his off-hand thrusting out as a ram to strike at his enemy's pistol-wielding arm, both as a defensive manoeuvre – ensuring that the weapon could not be swivelled around to point in Victor's direction – and also as an attack unto itself, targeting the elbow and the inherent weakness of a joint.

The driver took it well. Although surprised by the sudden assault upon him, he did not relinquish his whole position. He dodged, adjusted his footing, and manoeuvred with his hips to maintain his robust and balanced stance.

Directing him by pulling on the wrist and, therefore, on the arm, dragging the man's entire torso forward and down, off balance, Victor resisted the urge to deliver a clubbing blow at the exposed head until the moment was just right. Landing at the top of the skull, such a strike would do little more than interrupt the attacker's balance. However, as the driver lurched by, Victor hit the man's exposed brainstem with the grip of the pistol.

He collapsed straight down to the floor, rolling on his side, foetal.

Another gunman nearby was slow to react, his focus elsewhere, and when he did understand the noises behind him and twisted around on the spot, Victor had already closed the distance . . .

. . . so that when this second guy tried to aim his weapon, his target was already too close and within arm's reach.

Holding the Makarov PM by the barrel housing, Victor bludgeoned him with the pistol's grip, bloodying his face as the impacts split the skin of his forehead and cheek before knocking the Glock from his grip.

Dazed and overwhelmed, it required no effort to sweep both legs out from under him.

A third gunman came dashing around the corner in response to the commotion. He hesitated, unsure of what he was seeing and who he was aiming at in the dark, so Victor used the Makarov as a missile by hurling it his way.

The gunman flinched to avoid the thrown weapon hitting him in the side of the head, and instead, it clipped the crown of his scalp.

A glancing hit only, but one that halted his turning arc and ruined his aim, so as he squeezed the trigger, he fired a burst of rounds from his automatic pistol into the ceiling, creating a shower of plaster dust and flakes.

As Victor went to charge the newcomer while he was vulnerable, he felt the hands of the guy with the bloody face grip his trailing leg, and then the sudden, intense pressure of a bite to the back of his calf muscle.

With the pressure came pain, but it failed to become the intended level of agony and bore no significant injury. His attacker made the common mistake of believing more teeth meant more damage done. However, wrapping more of his jaw around Victor's leg meant the force of the bite was dispersed over a wider area.

Although painful, the bite failed to pierce the fabric of Victor's trousers and the skin of his calf. A more experienced or tactically shrewd biter would have used as few teeth as possible. The most effective bites were those in which only the upper and lower incisors were employed. In that way, all the force travelled through those sharp-bladed, and therefore most penetrating, teeth, cutting through fabric and sinking into flesh. Those were the bites Victor favoured and had used to devastating effect a few times. The masseter muscles could produce the most force of all the muscles in the human body, but the teeth had to be employed in the correct way to make the most of that power.

Yet it still slowed him down, making it impossible for Victor to reach the guy with the automatic Glock before he brought his gun back to bear to shoot again.

Instead, Victor threw himself down to the floor, grabbing the guy trying to bite him, and rolling onto his back to use the biter as a human shield.

Victor heard the muted gunshots and felt the man on top of him shudder and spasm with the multiple impacts – but the subsonic nine mils couldn't make it through and through – before the shooter ran out of bullets.

The Glock held seventeen rounds, which, fired at full automatic, were gone in two squeezes of the trigger.

Sliding out from under the dead guy, Victor flipped to his feet.

He saw the dazed driver pulling himself to his feet and the newcomer performing a hurried yet skilled reload of his weapon; the fourth gunman left to guard the exit would be inevitably arriving within a few seconds.

So, Victor retreated.

# FORTY-ONE

Victor dashed through a doorway and into an adjoining open-plan office before the newcomer could line up any shot. Then, out of sight, Victor stood still and stamped his feet on the floor to mimic fleeing footsteps, which the gunman fell for, rushing after Victor and straight into a flurry of punches and elbow strikes his enemy had no time to defend against.

Grabbing the automatic pistol to prevent his opponent from angling it his way, Victor shoved the weakened man backwards. He stumbled into a desk, folding over it and losing the Glock, which hit the floor and bounced twice, first as its grip hit the flooring, then from the muzzle as it cartwheeled over itself.

The man pushed himself off the desk and charged at Victor ...

... who ducked beneath the attack and dived for the gun, scooping it up as he dropped into a forward roll. Then, as he returned to his feet, he spun around and squeezed off a snapshot at his enemy, now redirecting his charge.

Unbraced, the recoil of the thousand-rounds-per-minute rate of fire made the pistol almost uncontrollable. Still, at point-blank range, Victor could not miss.

The burst hit the guy in the torso. Even though none found the heart, and the poor penetrating power of subsonic 9mm ammunition meant no bullets reached his spine, the cumulative damage of the multiple overlapping waves of hydrostatic shock took him straight from his feet.

Knowing his two remaining enemies would be racing towards the sound of gunfire, Victor dropped to the floor and rolled beneath the desk.

As expected, the driver rushed through the doorway but came to an abrupt stop, confused by the sight of his dead teammate and yet no sign of the man responsible.

Victor rolled back out from under the desk and shot him with a controlled burst to the neck.

Pressurised arterial blood spurted out in fast, long arcs as the man convulsed, stumbling, panicking, hands snapping to his neck in a vain attempt to stop the flow, resulting only in the postponement of his imminent death by a few short seconds.

Victor hopped to his feet, Glock up and sweeping the space for the final gunman. Only a few bullets left in the magazine and no time to search the dead for spares.

Here, visibility was better, one wall of this open-plan office being floor-to-ceiling windows letting in enough ambient light from outside to make out the many cubicles filling the space.

Still, he failed to see his enemy's position, only hearing a burst of automatic fire that blasted holes in a nearby cubicle, pinged off a filing cabinet and cracked one of the plate-glass windows.

Victor threw himself out of the line of fire and through a doorway left open by the team's prior searching, slamming the door closed behind him as more bullets punched through it and the intervening partition wall.

He heard footsteps hurrying closer, and the noise of a spent magazine hit the floor outside before a fresh one was reloaded.

The room Victor found himself inside was a cube-shaped office a little bigger than a closet. A stack of box files against the far wall were the only occupants. No furniture. No cover. The door opened to ninety degrees before reaching the perpendicular wall. No window either.

Not ideal.

Victor lay down on the floor, his feet facing the doorway, his arms positioned along his torso and his chin tucked to his chest so the Glock was aiming over his feet at the closed door.

He waited, motionless.

He pictured the remaining gunman on the other side of the wall and door in the open-place office. Holes in the wall and door proved that neither was any defence against even subsonic nine mils. They would neither slow down a bullet nor change its trajectory to any meaningful degree. If the gunman guessed Victor's positioning on the floor, then there was a good chance that, from a long burst of rounds, at least one would find him.

But if the gunman guessed wrong, then the odds reversed, and chances were the bullets would miss.

In either case, the bullet holes through the wall or door would reveal the shooter's own location to Victor, who, unlike his enemy, didn't have the rounds to spare blind-firing.

Would the remaining gunman understand this and risk giving himself away? It wasn't a problem if he shot Victor in the process. But it was a death sentence if the gunman missed.

Had their roles been reversed and it was Victor outside the room, he would kick in the door and charge in fast, trusting to speed and the inarguable fact that reaction was always slower than action. With an advantage in firepower on top, it was a no-brainer move.

Which the gunman realised for himself.

What he'd failed to account for were the windows in the open-plan office, the incoming ambient light visible through the gap beneath the door and the holes through it.

When he stood in front of the door in readiness to kick it in – in doing so blocking the ambient light – Victor squeezed the Glock's trigger.

A burst of rounds spat out through the suppressor, and the pistol clicked empty.

Victor found the gunman prostrate on the other side of the door. Of the five rounds fired, one had hit the man in the left shoulder and another just above the left eyebrow. The first, a flesh wound, the second, fatal.

Considering he had been shooting blind, Victor was pretty happy with his accuracy. He ignored the fact three bullets of the burst had missed entirely.

Since the gunman was dead, two out of five was more than good enough.

As Victor pushed open the door to the ladies' bathroom, he called out to Harvey to identify himself and ensured the Australian dropped the shotgun before he stepped any closer.

Reluctant to leave the perceived safety of the cubicle, Harvey asked, 'But ... what about ... the crew?'

'If Lambert accepts your apology I expect he will send people who can clean up the mess,' Victor answered. 'Otherwise, before I leave, I'll be setting the building on fire with you still inside it.'

Both the electronic keypad locking the door to the vault room and the vault itself had a separate, dedicated power so could still be operated without the mains supply. Harvey entered the first code and then the second, pressing his palm to the reader and leaving behind a print of sweat on the screen.

The door opened automatically and Harvey stepped inside. Lined with shelves, it was almost empty except for a few stacks of banknotes in various currencies, some vintage pornographic magazines – 'I'm a collector ... like with comic books,' Harvey hurriedly explained – and a mobile phone.

'Unlock it,' Victor told him.

The Australian did so, thumbing the code 1-2-3-4 and handing it over.

'Seriously?' Victor asked.

Harvey responded with a meek shrug. 'What happens now?'

'We call Lambert and find out how good you are at grovelling.'

# FORTY-TWO

Zahm had little patience for meetings and the endless discussions therein. Father had trained him to be an instrument of violence, and yet Father's long, slow descent into infirmity had meant the inevitable mirrored ascent of Karmia Elkayam. In the past, Father would make a request to Zahm and he would act upon it. Karmia had a more measured approach. She did not 'do things by the book' because there was no book when it came to the assassination arm of Israeli intelligence. However, Zahm was under the impression that Karmia was intending to author one.

'For those of you who were not with us six years ago,' Elkayam said as she continued her presentation, the images on the screen changing to show a crime scene and several corpses. 'We lost four surveillance operators on assignment in Minsk, Belarus, to this assassin. They were watching a Lebanese man named Gabir Yamout, the business partner of the most notorious arms dealer in the Middle East at that time, Baraa Ariff, also Lebanese. We had identified

Ariff years before the incident in Minsk and taken the decision not to make a move against him despite the fact he
was supplying many of our enemies with rifles, grenades
and other small arms. Instead, in one of the first operations
of its kind, we put his organisation under constant watch
but never interfered with their operations. In doing so, we
not only learned more and more about how the network
conducted business in the region but we also were able to
track many of its customers, a large percentage of which
we might never have otherwise known existed until those
weapons were used against us. It is incalculable how much
intelligence we gathered in this way, how many terrorists
and terrorist cells we identified, how many attacks we were
able to prevent, and how many of our enemies we were able
to kill before they had a chance to kill us first. The operation on Ariff's network was one of our longest-running
and most successful intelligence-gathering operations of
all time.

'Yamout was in Minsk to do a deal with a local gangster, Danil Petrenko. We were not privy to the specifics of
the deal beforehand. Still, our team set up hidden cameras
and microphones in the hotel suite where they would meet.
The day before that meeting, a man claiming to be a staff
member entered the suite and looked around, as you can see
on these stills from our cameras. This man was the assassin
scouting the location prior to his attack the following night.
He killed several members of Petrenko's entourage as well as
Yamout's own, although failed to reach his ultimate target,
which turned out to be Yamout. The only reason he did not
achieve his goal was because of the heroic intervention of
our surveillance team, which had become suspicious of the

assassin and had already reported back with their observations. Understanding the incredible value of the operation on Ariff's network and how it would be interrupted by the death of Yamout, our people took it upon themselves to stop the assassin. Sadly, three of the four were killed in the process. Their sacrifice, however, was not in vain. Yamout lived and returned to Lebanon. Of course, by now, you have all seen the footage of the assassin's attack on that suite.'

'I think half of Mossad has seen it by now,' Herzog said.

Elkayam nodded. 'Such things have a habit of being shared when they should not.'

'I thought Yamout and Ariff were both killed back then,' Herzog said. 'Is that correct?'

She nodded. 'Not long after the incident in Minsk, both men and their families were killed by persons unknown, although Ariff's broken and mutilated body was not found until some weeks later. And, with his death, his network fragmented, and a hundred or more smaller arms dealers sprang up in the void. We've never come even close to identifying them all or their customers. So, not only was this assassin guilty of killing our people, but he was pivotal in sabotaging an operation of incredible value to our nation.'

'Where has he been since the disaster in Sofia?'

Zahm stiffened at the question, at the reminder of the mission he led back then that not only failed in its objective but also lost more precious, irreplaceable lives in the process.

'That was the last we saw of him,' she explained. 'Albeit directly. He vanished, never using the alias again that we tracked to Bulgaria. We doubled our surveillance efforts on the remaining lieutenants in Ariff's network, in case the assassin had been hired to kill any more of them, to no avail.

He vanished, and over the years, we have gathered hints of his presence and activities but have never managed to catch up to him again. He's good. He's too good.'

Herzog turned his attention to Zahm. 'You led the failed mission to apprehend this assassin in order to discover who sent him to Minsk in the first place, yes?'

Zahm, whose strength was immense, found the simple act of nodding to be a physical challenge almost impossible to overcome.

Herzog said, 'I think it would be appropriate to remind us all what happened that night . . .'

# FORTY-THREE

*Six years ago*

It had been Father himself who had asked Zahm to hunt down the man who killed three of his precious children.

'My son, I want your unit to avenge them.'

Zahm, most devoted of sons, had not hesitated to make his parent proud. And Father, already wounded with grief, had warned Zahm not to agree too easily given the danger the killer posed. Afraid of no one and desperate for his father's approval, Zahm could not be swayed. He wanted to avenge his people almost as much as he needed Father's love.

'We will be honoured to kill this killer.'

Without a name and knowing whatever passport he was travelling under would be an alias, they had to call him something. Unusually for Mossad, with its vast resources and friends in the US intelligence community, they had yet to identify the man who had killed all but one of their surveillance team in Minsk. Because the first watcher to note his presence as suspicious had described his appearance as 'man in a suit, dark hair, thirties', he had initially been referred to as 'the man in the suit'.

By the time Zahm had been tasked with leading the mission to exact vengeance, the man they hunted was simply referred to as *helyeph*, the Hebrew word for suit.

In Spain, they interrogated a gangster who had met Helyeph in Minsk the day after the massacre, gaining more insights into his manner, his skills and the sound of his voice. Utilising numerous assets and contacts had told them their target had left Belarus and not shown up again until a hotel south-east of Bologna had scanned his passport. They figured he had travelled by train or car, or maybe even bus, going south and exploiting Europe's Schengen agreement to avoid having his passport registered as he crossed borders. Zahm had been a little surprised that he had used the same passport in Italy as he had in Minsk until he had tracked his movements in Bologna and discovered Helyeph had met up with a known forger who supplied him with a new identity. The forger was a young, talented artist whose paintings didn't sell for enough to pay the rent but whose exceptional counterfeit documents did.

The young forger had not given up the killer willingly, so advanced interrogation techniques had needed to be implemented, and though a friend of their target, who had supplied him with a new set of documents to aid his escape, Zahm had spared the forger's life. Not because of any sense of mercy but because, at that point, they could not guarantee they would catch up to Helyeph before he switched passports once more. Zahm had reported back to his commanders, and separate surveillance had been dispatched to Bologna to watch the young forger should his friend return.

It turned out to be an unnecessary move when the new identity Helyeph was travelling under showed up in Sofia, Bulgaria. The killer had met up with an escort who was to be his companion for what appeared to be a sightseeing trip.

Zahm and his kidon had followed Helyeph and his date to a restaurant and waited.

A curious thing happened. A while after Helyeph and his date entered the restaurant, he went to the bathroom and did not come back. They watched through the windows, checking their watches every few moments as the two or three minutes they figured he would take turned into five, then ten.

The fear of failure, of leaving their dead unavenged, burned hot inside Zahm. He had not placed any of his people in other positions to guard against their target slipping out of the back because of his date. Zahm had wanted everyone ready to scoop both people off the streets in one decisive action. When Helyeph did not return, the burning inside him became an inferno of anger at himself.

He sent Noam inside the restaurant on the off-chance their prey was taking longer than expected in the bathroom, perhaps suffering an embarrassing stomach upset in a cubicle. However, Zahm knew – felt – the truth. Helyeph had made them and escaped.

Zahm sent some of his operatives racing back to the hotel.

'If he made us,' Karmia – at that point under Zahm's command and not the other way around – said, 'he won't have gone back there.'

'Agreed.'

'The woman might know how to find him. And if not, perhaps he cares about her enough to return.'

'Good idea.'

They watched through the windows as Noam entered in jeans and a nylon jacket and headed straight for the bathroom. He returned in less than a minute and took out his phone to call in, but there was no need. Karmia took the call while Zahm burned alive with rage from the inside out.

In his self-loathing, Zahm was slow to give out orders to redirect his people to scour the streets surrounding the restaurant, to race to the airport and nearby railway stations, and to look out for a lone man in the back of a taxi.

What would he tell Father?

'I don't believe it,' Karmia said, her voice quiet, yet the words were delivered with a power that snapped Zahm out of his introspection.

He didn't believe it either, but Helyeph had returned.

They watched him enter the restaurant by the front door and retake the same seat at the table where his date still waited. She was as surprised to see him again as Zahm.

Then she went to the bathroom after a short conversation with Helyeph, and he exited alone.

Zahm said to Karmia, 'Tell the others to get back here right now.'

Despite the confusion at the restaurant, the subsequent snatch could not have been any smoother. Helyeph stayed on foot, maybe hoping to use the metro system to get away, but it gave Zahm enough time to get his team in place to come at him from all sides. Some on foot, the others in two vehicles.

Knowing how deadly this man could be, Zahm ensured he was one of those on foot when they made their move. If Helyeph tried to fight his way out of the ambush, Zahm wanted it to be he who was there to stop him.

With Karmia ahead of Helyeph on a quiet street and Zahm following him, it was time.

One vehicle came at him from behind while the other approached from the front, using the glare of its headlights to blind him.

He tried to shoot, but it did him no good.

In seconds, he was surrounded.

'Hands,' Zahm demanded, fastening plasticuffs in place and trying to resist the urge to crush Helyeph's skull between the pavement and his heel.

They bundled him into the back of one of the vehicles. One of the team had found a quiet location in an industrial neighbourhood to take him. A short drive to the outskirts of the city. Fifteen minutes at most.

They never reached their destination.

'Something's wrong,' Karmia said, driving the first vehicle.

Zahm followed her glance to look in the rear-view mirror at the second car. It veered and swerved behind them. In the dark and rain, it was hard to see specifics, but there was a commotion inside.

By the time Zahm's vehicle had pulled over, Helyeph was already out of the second car, which had crashed into another vehicle, and was fleeing on foot. Zahm sent one of his team to check on the occupants of the second car before taking the others to give chase on foot.

They had all watched the tape. They all knew what kind of man this killer was, but even still, they had been surprised by his ingenuity, his ruthlessness and his will to survive.

Battling him in an abandoned warehouse, other members of the kidon were wounded or killed before, finally, Zahm had him.

Much larger, much stronger, and no less fast, no less experienced, Zahm threw the killer around like a ragdoll and, pinning him to the ground, would have driven a shard of glass through his eye and into his skull had the savage not torn away half of Zahm's nose with his teeth.

In the resulting pain and horror, Helyeph had escaped into the night, and Zahm had never forgiven himself for his failure, for allowing more of his people to be slain.

When Zahm had returned to Israel, his face mummified in bandages and what was left of his nose entombed in dressings, Father had wept.

'My perfect boy, what has this monster done to you?'

Zahm had wept too. Not from the pain, which was the purest of agonies, or the horrible disfigurement, but for failing his father and for the deaths of his teammates. He refused every drug they offered him to ease his suffering. He deserved the pain for making his father cry. He deserved worse than any pain. He deserved to die.

Father never blamed him. At least, he never said the words. In the debriefings, Zahm had detailed every aspect of his mission, how they had tracked the killer down, how they had cornered him, capturing him without a single shot needing to be fired. Then, they had driven him away so they could interrogate him to discover who had sent him, and then the disaster.

'You let your anger control you,' Father explained. 'You were so close to being victorious, and yet you let emotion steal that victory from your very hand. You forgot that a wild animal will do absolutely anything to survive, that it has fangs as well as claws. But you shall never forget this lesson.'

227

'I will not, Father.'

'In time, when you have healed, you must then learn to control your disappointment and harness your rage. This I could not teach you until you first endured such a defeat. And if you listen to me as you listened before, if you master this lesson as you did all of the others, you will understand how to master all of that negativity and make it work for you because, like the civilian mother who can summon impossible strength to save her child from an upturned car, we all have a sealed well of resolve. And that seal can be broken only when we have suffered enough so we can channel our negative emotions into an irresistible force. When, my son, you have learned all I know, then we shall break that seal for good, and that resolve will be yours whenever you choose. You will have more focus, more energy, and most of all, your will to succeed shall make you even more deadly than you ever thought possible.'

Zahm waited.

'Then you will discover you are, in fact, grateful to the man who caused so much harm.' Father rested a palm on his son's cheek. 'In time, you will wish to thank your enemy for making you so much stronger.'

# FORTY-FOUR

The sky was grey. Raven felt specks of rain on her cheek-bones, on her forehead. The address she was looking for proved to be in a bad neighbourhood of west Hamburg. She saw drug dealers hanging around in shadowed doorways and tents pitched by the homeless on every street. Graffiti stained most walls. Most rubbish bins were overflowing. Sirens seemed to be the most common background noise. Not a bad location for a safe house, she thought. In these kinds of areas, no one looked out for one another. No one cared what went on behind closed doors. Here, people did not know their neighbours. Here, pedestrians never ambled when passing along the pavements. Here, everyone was forgotten.

But in neighbourhoods like this, residents were always on the lookout for those who did not belong, creating an alarm system of sorts to ward against other outsiders. When no one looked out for anyone else, everyone looked out for themselves. Such continued wariness, such unrelenting distrustfulness, could prove to be of benefit to an outsider looking to keep their head down. Once integrated, an outsider might find themselves forgotten as well. Once behind closed doors, no one cared about them. The residents, however, did not stop looking out for themselves, ever watchful for the police, immigration officers, debt collectors and rival dealers. Those outsiders did not have the kind of skill set that Raven had. She knew how to blend in in all manner of hostile environments in which she did not belong. Those environments were far more unforgiving than this one.

To blend in here, Raven didn't shower for a few days. She swapped her typical attire for trainers, sportswear and a baseball cap. A pushchair completed the disguise, although she did not go so far as to include a child within it. Instead, she loaded the pushchair with plastic bags containing cheap groceries from a budget supermarket.

When she performed her reconnaissance of the safe house, no one so much as looked at her twice. The building was the last in a row of terraced houses, all concrete and grime, on a side street that snaked behind a line of commercial properties: off-licence, betting shop, laundrette and kebab house. On the opposite side of the street, a blue tent was hitched against the wall of a closed-down grocery store. A man sat outside the tent. He wore a tattered greatcoat, colourful patterned trousers, mismatched shoes and a woollen hat. Super-strength lager cans lay scattered around him. As Raven passed, the man glanced up from rolling a cigarette and snarled her way.

She avoided eye contact and continued pushing the pushchair.

Raven did this preparatory work during the afternoon to

gather as much information about the area while the sun was still out. Aside from the location, there seemed to be no further defences Ido Albrecht had employed. Maybe he believed this was enough. She had already found his home empty and the office he shared with Schulz unused. Thankfully, she already knew from her investigation into Schulz that, between them, they owned a few properties through a shell corporation. Two were currently being rented out after renovations, and the third's planned facelift had been put on hold until it could be rewired.

Such a property made for an effective and convenient place to lie low.

Albrecht had gone into hiding now Schulz was dead, confirming to Raven that Albrecht was in bed with the Consensus. He hadn't left the city. This suggested to Raven that he expected to return to his old life before too long. Maybe he thought lying low for a few days or weeks would cause the trail to grow cold. Or, perhaps someone higher up in the Consensus had assured him that Schulz's death was a temporary setback to their operation, whether a deliberate lie or a good-faith fallacy. Her main concern was they would either discover she was involved with Schulz or suspect it enough to seek to eliminate Albrecht before she could get to him, sending a killer or killers to cut away the infected limb before the disease could spread further.

It was the way they worked, the way they had always worked.

They had no loyalty to one another because each element used a separate component to conduct its mission. One element received orders from its anonymous higher-up and passed them on to another anonymous element below it. If they ever employed a team to conduct an activity, that team worked in isolation, receiving orders from its anonymous superior.

Although their superiors would have done everything possible to isolate themselves, mistakes were made. Albrecht might have known something that threatened their schemes, or he could have guessed enough to compromise his superior in some way.

Why take that risk?

She saw no reason they would change that mindset now, so Raven knew she had to work fast. She hoped that the same line of thinking that had sent Albrecht into hiding here had also given him the good sense not to tell his paymasters where he had gone, whatever their assurances.

Through painful experience, she knew that the reach of the Consensus was limitless. There was no one they could not get to and nowhere that was safe from them. Even with her talents, Raven had been forced to remain on the move for years now, never staying in one place for long, constantly aware that as she was hunting them, they were hunting her in return. Whoever came after her would have the backing and resources of what amounted to a global shadow government. She, on the other hand, was the sum total of her own resources.

They could afford to lose the occasional limb to her efforts. She did not have that same luxury. She was fully aware, every time she made a play like this, it was a play they could anticipate and prepare for to ensure it would be her last. And, although each time she disrupted their plans, she disrupted only one set of their plans, severed just one limb or many, and that limb could be replaced.

But she also knew that, one day, it would not be an arm or a leg she cut off; it would be an eye she poked out that could not be regrown or replaced.

Once, in New York City, with the assistance of the man she called Jonathan – reluctant assistance born out of self-preservation though it may have been – she had believed the wound she had caused them had proved, or at least would prove, to be a fatal one.

Driven by the need for revenge, she had allowed herself to be fooled into believing she was capable of causing that much harm. Now, she knew better. She knew that, alone, she could never do that much damage to them.

She knew that she had to keep severing limbs until she reached an eye. Then, maybe, she would draw enough blood, draw enough attention to them, that someone with the power to do real damage would notice and join her fight. Because, although the burning desire for revenge had never gone away, there was more to her crusade, as Jonathan called it, than pure retribution. Until others joined the fight, she was the only one fighting against their machinations, and she could not sit back and let them get away with it. That was not how she was raised, that was not what led her into the intelligence services, and that was not what gave her the willpower to keep going against insurmountable odds.

She refused to accept it was a losing battle.

Until her last breath, she would fight for what was right.

# FORTY-FIVE

Lambert had been a heavyset guy from the first time Victor met the man, and had been the same in all the photographs and videos Victor had tracked down. From brochures and other marketing materials to trade articles, features in the military press, and even a couple of talking-head pieces he had done for television news items, Victor had been a little surprised by how much material about his employer was out there in the world. Lambert liked having his picture taken, and he liked the sound of his own voice. It wasn't all ego. He was a personable man, comfortable in front of the camera, posing behind his desk inside his headquarters in Gibraltar, and a fine orator when waxing lyrical in promotional pieces about the services his company could provide. Finding information about his military career was more difficult. Still, Victor had a few contacts who, between them, had managed to rustle up enough to fill in the gaps. A veteran of the Parachute Regiment, Lambert retired as a Captain, having served in both Basra, Iraq, and Helmand Province in Afghanistan. How he had gone from Army officer to head of a private security contractor in just a handful of years remained unclear, although there were hints that some events in Helmand had given him the means or connections to launch his next career. In Victor's experience, such meteoric rises in success were never clean. Given his own nefarious profession, however, it would be hypocritical to judge how anyone else conducted themselves.

Meeting Lambert was no simple task. Given he was a direct link to Victor, the broker was a severe chink in his armour. Although Lambert primarily operated out of the headquarters for his private military contractor firm in Gibraltar, he had offices in many other countries. The last time they met in person was at a private airfield in Tunisia at the start of Victor's employment. Since then, there had never been any need for another face to face, but then again, Victor had not failed to fulfil any of his contracts before. It had been a long time since he had not killed a target he had been hired to assassinate. Even longer since he had voluntarily elected not to do so.

Welcoming him into his office near the Gdański Bridge in central Warsaw, Lambert gestured for Victor to sit down.

'Look, it's really very simple why the client is unsatisfied with the outcome of the contract. They not only paid for you to remove both Jan Schulz and Marion Ysiv from this fair Earth of ours, but they wanted to send a message to the intelligence community, both government and the private sector. Steal from us, trade in our secrets, and we will get you. They didn't receive either, did they?' He pulled up an online news article on a tablet. The headline read 'Six Dead in Hotel

Shooting'. 'I'm not going to read out the whole thing, but there's no mention of any woman among the corpses.'

'You know very well that Ysiv was not present in that hotel room, so how exactly was I meant to kill her when she's already dead?'

'You're missing the point,' Lambert began. 'It's not about what I know, it's what the client believes, and the strength of the message they wanted to be sent.'

'There's nothing I could do about that then, and there's even less I can do about it now.'

'Therein lies the stickiness of the situation we've found ourselves in.'

'What are you asking?'

'Beg your pardon.'

Victor said, 'You're not laying out what I already know for the fun of it, and you must know by now that I have no personal stake in my contracts, and neither do I have any direct relations with the client. If there is a sticky situation due to what happened in Bucharest, then it's only you that is stuck. Thus, the only possible reason you're saying any of this is because you're building up to asking me for a favour.'

'I hate to break it to you, Roman, but you can't read me that easily. You're half right, so don't feel too bad about the miss. It's a favour, but it's not for me, and I'm not asking for it; I'm ordering.'

'I'm not a soldier, and you're not an officer,' Victor said. 'You cannot order me, Marcus.'

'Whatever,' Lambert responded. 'I'm not ordering you, fine, I'm *telling* you. Not asking, telling, because I don't have a choice, which means neither do you.'

'The client wants us to make amends.'

'Close. The client is *allowing* us to make amends.'

'You offered me out pro bono.'

Lambert nodded. 'When I explained the Bucharest contract wasn't about the money but about maintaining friendships and building new ones, the failure to complete it satisfactorily means losing those friendships and denying the chance to make new ones. That simply won't do in this business. Losing lucrative deals from one client is bad enough; losing the opportunity to make new clients on top of it is disastrous, but when the word spreads as to why I'm blackballed by the Ministry of Defence, a lot of our other existing clients are going to think twice about whether they want to continue to risk working with us. I didn't come from money, I came from a council estate and left school with a whole four GCSEs. I had to build this business brick by sodding brick. I won't let the failure of one of those bricks bring the whole house crashing down.'

'I'm hearing a lot about how this affects you,' Victor said.

'You work for me,' Lambert explained. 'If my company doesn't have clients, then you will get no contracts, capeesh?'

'You're not the first broker I've had.'

'What does that mean? You think you'll just find another? Put your CV out there and see who headhunts you?'

'Pretty much.'

'I think you're forgetting just how much I've done to keep your past indiscretions from coming back to bite you on the ...' He paused, then almost smiled, but in a bitter way. 'You know what? I was about to censor myself then, but given I'm feeling a distinct lack of parity in this relationship, I don't think I'll continue to bother.' Another pause, this time for emphasis. 'Arse. That's what I was going to censor to spare your delicate *fucking* sensibilities.'

'I appreciate you're upset,' Victor said in an even tone. 'That doesn't mean I'll give you a pass regarding vulgarity. When we agreed to work together, I made it very clear that you would need to humour my *delicate sensibilities*.'

'I don't respond well to threat, direct or obtuse.'

He scratched at his forearm, at his elbow.

Victor said, 'That's good to know because I'm not in the habit of making threats. I state facts only. How you respond to those facts is not my concern. However, I very much recommend they should be your sole concern.'

The fear Lambert felt only made him angrier. Victor saw it in the man's jaw, in his fists. However, the Brit kept his cool and didn't attempt to provoke further. Still scratching at his arm, he jerked open a drawer and pulled out a tub of cocoa butter. He smoothed some into his elbow and the surrounding area while his chest heaved, and each furious breath was audible.

Finally he said, 'You know, I was really, *really* hoping that you would be a team player here. I was hoping that you would understand the difficult position I'm in and think to yourself that it's no real skin off your nose to do me a solid since your actions, or lack thereof, directly contributed to the mess I'm in. I didn't want to mention that I went out of my way to add conditions to the terms of the Bucharest contract. I insisted on those two terms to ensure your problems with the Russian mob wouldn't follow you around like a bad smell. I didn't have to get them added, but I did.'

'I appreciate that,' Victor said, and meant it. 'I did not ask for you to do so, however. You chose to do me a favour, so

I'm under no obligation to return it. I stand my round, as the Irish would say, although only for debts I willingly take on, not for debts imposed upon me.'

'No, you're not under any obligation to repay it, obviously. It would have been nice though, wouldn't it? Reciprocity isn't suddenly a dirty word, is it?' He did not wait for Victor to answer. 'But you're failing to see the bigger picture. Those terms I fought for, for you, are not now going to be fulfilled by the client.'

'I don't blame them.'

'Don't be so naïve,' Lambert said. 'You're exposed now. They might not know who you are, but now they know all that mess involving the Russian mafia was your doing, and now they also know you work for me. Even if you have nothing to fear directly from the client, how long do you think it will be before someone you do fear hears about all of this?'

Victor remained silent.

'I already told you how word of this kind of failure spreads, and other clients will start questioning how they conduct business with me, yeah? Well, some of those clients are going to ask what went wrong, why it went wrong, and who messed it up. I don't know much about you, yet I know a man like you makes enemies just by punching his timesheet. I can insulate you from those enemies as long as I'm CEO of a multinational private military contractor. I have been insulating you ever since you agreed to work for me. All that ends if I'm standing in line at the jobcentre. So, if you won't do it to be a team player, if you won't do it to repay a favour, then I know for a fact you'll do it for self-preservation.'

To release some of his rage, Lambert hurled the tub of

cocoa butter at the far wall, where it thumped off and dropped, clattering to the floor.

'I'm not often wrong,' Lambert said, now calmer. 'So, am I wrong here?'

Victor said, 'What do they want me to do?'

# FORTY-SIX

When Raven returned in the early hours of the morning, she left the pushchair behind. She wore form-fitting sportswear to double as tactical clothing and to provide a plausible disguise as a late-night jogger. Her black hair was bunched up at the back of her head in braids and covered in a beanie hat. She wore black leggings and a black long-sleeved top, with a thin body warmer over the top. The stretchy synthetic material of the workout gear provided her with complete, unimpeded movement in a way regular women's clothing could not. The body warmer provided a little modesty since the workout gear left almost nothing to the imagination. A belt with zipped pouches, meant to hold a phone and other items when running, let her carry the small pistol and spare magazines that the workout gear could not conceal. Thanks to Jonathan, she was armed with a Glock G43 subcompact by way of his fixer, Georg. In a zipped pocket of her body warmer, she had a fluorescent yellow armband reflector she could slip on to strengthen the jogger disguise if she deemed it necessary.

She approached the safe house in a spiral, circling the neighbourhood on the lookout for threats before circling closer, seeing only drug dealers and their customers and a dim light glowing from inside the tent opposite. Raven imagined the snarling man enjoying a nightcap of high-strength lager.

Lights were on inside the safe house too.

From the first floor, which suggested Albrecht was upstairs, but there was only one way to find out for sure.

Raven vaulted over the wall behind the property, picking the section in the most darkness and landing on the other side of the fence in an area of deep shadows, where the lights from the upstairs window did not reach. The backyard was filled with old building materials, piles of bricks and timber, and a hardened sack of cement from good intentions long past. Before leaving the shadows, she listened. She heard no sounds drifting in the air from the other properties nearby. Aside from the breeze, she heard only cats fighting. Maybe the quiet sound of a television playing inside Albrecht's safe house.

The lights on at this time of night suggested either Albrecht couldn't sleep or was choosing not to do so, maybe preferring to sleep during the day. Either way, this was the most opportune time for her, when the night disguised her actions from outside observers.

Using an improvised pick and torsion wrench, she worked the tumblers of the back door's lock until it clicked open.

With slow, careful movements, Raven eased the door open only enough for her to slip inside. There was no telling how much noise the hinges might make, so it was best not to chance it.

She eased the door closed behind her.

Standing still inside a run-down kitchen space, she listened to the darkness. Aside from the sound of her own breathing and the quiet ambience of a city after midnight, she heard nothing.

Dark high-tops kept her footsteps close to silent as she edged inside.

G43 now out of the belt pocket, she had it raised to follow the movements of her head as she looked around, searching for any organic shape amid the hard edges of countertops and furniture.

A TV next to the refrigerator played an old animated movie, the light from which cast the otherwise unlit kitchen in shades of red and gold. A closed door would lead down to a basement but, with the lights on upstairs, she cleared the kitchen and stepped into a hallway.

She took her time, peering through open or half-open doorways and into deserted rooms on the ground floor, almost all stripped bare of life down to threadbare carpet.

A desk lamp in the centre of one room illuminated needles, aluminium foil, a lighter and a bent teaspoon. In another room, a ripped and stained sleeping bag lay open with a crumpled pizza box on top of it. She wasn't sure if such trappings were Albrecht's own or belonged to whoever had been making use of the building while it sat empty. She thought of the snarling homeless guy in the tent opposite. Maybe he had been removed when Albrecht arrived. An unpleasant scent in the air wrinkled her nose.

The wooden flooring of the hallway seemed well-polished and new, no doubt laid down before the refurbishment was put on pause. Still, she kept as close to one wall as possible, where the floorboards were strongest and had least chance of giving her away by creaking.

Her arms were bent at the elbows, which were tucked against her ribs to keep the handgun close to her person. She gazed along the iron sights as she approached the foot of the staircase.

Upstairs, Albrecht was waiting for her.

Except, she was wrong.

He came at her from behind, bare feet silent on the flooring, her only warning a hint of cologne scenting the air, which had been fetid seconds beforehand.

She spun around, the Glock moving in an inevitably wider circle, trailing an instant behind, too slow to angle a shot as he threw himself at her.

A little taller but almost thirty kilograms heavier, it was all Raven could do to remain standing as Albrecht barrelled into her, knocking her back and grabbing her gun-holding hand in both of his own.

She hung on as long as she could, pushed and pulled with his attempts to take the weapon as she jostled for footing, trying to position a leg between his own, to sweep one away and send him to the floor.

Sheer strength wrenched the gun from her grip, but in doing so, he had first to plant his feet, and she stamped a heel over the exposed toes.

The high-tops helped cushion the impact, sparing him broken bones, if not the pain that made him roar.

Exploiting his momentary weakness, she punched his inner wrist with one hand as she used the other to bat the gun from his loosened grip.

She heard it rebound off one of the hallway walls and skit and skirt along the flooring.

244

Using mass alone, he heaved her away and into a closed door that shook and rattled from the impact.

Raven ducked a fist meant for her face, scooting under his arm as the punch collided with the door.

He roared again, more in rage than pain, spinning around to follow her movements and into a high roundhouse kick she whipped into the side of his head.

The German staggered away, the door once more shaking from the impact. Dazed, he still had the wherewithal to raise a guard to block the second kick Raven aimed at the same point.

He tried to snatch her leg as she withdrew it and almost did, catching hold of her ankle for a split second until she jerked it away before he could solidify his grip.

Her balance momentarily compromised, he barged into her, shoulder leading and connecting with her chest, powering her back into the opposite wall.

She grunted, air knocked from her lungs, ducking on instinct, anticipating another punch at her head.

He had learned his lesson with the door, however. He was already going low himself, throwing uppercuts and hooks into her torso before she could drop to the floor and slither out from between his legs.

Spinning around on the spot once more, he stamped down with his bare feet at her skull.

Faster, she caught the incoming foot, catching hold of the arch with one hand and his ankle with the other, then wrenching them towards her to pull him off his feet.

Albrecht hit the floor on his coccyx, crying out in pain, as Raven scrambled to stand.

Tired and hurt, Albrecht was much slower to stand and

much slower when he attacked. Nowhere near as fatigued and much faster, Raven dodged and slipped the clumsy punches and shoves, and avoided his attempts to grab and wrestle. Even tired and slow, with his strength, the last thing she wanted was for him to get hold of her again.

However, the lack of shoes that had aided his silent footsteps up behind her now worked against him. He struggled for secure footings, the soles of his feet slipping on a floor that gleamed with glossy varnish. In his desperate attempts to grab her, he lost his balance, falling down to his haunches.

Before he could rise again, Raven exploded forward, leaping into him with her right knee leading.

He tried to turn away from it, only he was nowhere near fast enough.

Raven's flying knee collided with his cheekbone, fracturing it in three separate places and sending a shockwave of energy that shook his brain inside his skull. He still did not drop somehow, even standing again to throw wild, looping punches with both fists as he staggered for balance.

They were simple to avoid, lacking power or accuracy, so Raven dodged between them, drove another knee into him, striking his abdomen this time and doubling him over into yet another knee that caught him under the jaw.

His hands grabbed her then, but without any strength, so she swept his load-bearing leg out from under him.

Albrecht landed hard on his back, head rising for an instant in an effort to climb back to his feet until a single kick to the face sent him back down again, the back of his skull banging on the floorboards.

Finally, he stopped moving, aside from a rapid flickering of closed eyelids.

Raven touched the back of her hand to her forehead and frowned. 'You made me sweat,' she said to the unconscious man. 'Not cool.'

# FORTY-SEVEN

Lambert had an aloe vera plant on his desk that was too big for its pot. Victor could see where another smaller plant, a pup, was growing too. Lambert saw him looking.

'It's insane,' he said. 'Sodding thing won't stop getting bigger, and now it's having babies too.'

'The pups will have pups of their own eventually.'

'You're kidding me?'

'I would never joke about horticulture.'

Lambert smiled and shook his head. 'Moving on,' he began. 'Since you passed on Harvey's phone, the client has been able to close in on the true buyer of the HEL plans and although they don't yet know their identity, they know where they're going to be. Given that we didn't manage to send their don't-mess-with-us message as loud and proud as they wanted, I've convinced them we can send a more explicit one this time.'

'I didn't like the idea of deliberately going loud last time out. I still don't.'

'Then you're in luck.'

'I don't believe in luck.'

'Figure of speech,' Lambert said. 'You have no need to go against your heightened sense of discretion for this job. Since you're deleting the true buyer this time, that's going to send a strong enough message.'

'Killing,' Victor said.

'Beg your pardon?'

'You said "deleting",' Victor explained. 'I'm not completing the contract by hitting backspace, but I'm happy to try that approach if you like.'

Lambert took a moment to process this and, in doing so, reminded Victor of a woman who had once used 'iced' in a similar fashion. For as long as he had been in this business, the people he worked with seemed to go out of their way to avoid the word 'kill'. He had not understood it at first because he found no reason to sanitise what he did for a living. Even in the military, terms like 'neutralise' were commonplace. He had never been sent out to kill all the enemy combatants in a village; he had been sent out to secure the location. He had never gone to war; he had been on peacekeeping missions. He had never been part of invading a sovereign nation; he had only been part of liberating a populace.

When human beings had been killing one another for thousands of years, it seemed way past time to be honest about it.

Human beings, Victor had learned, were not the same as him.

Lambert regarded Victor with the kind of quizzical gaze Victor never liked.

'I'll figure you out one day,' the Brit told him.

'It's good to be ambitious,' Victor said.

The other man showed a brief, wry smile before his expression became serious again. 'There's a conference in Scotland in a couple of weeks. The buyer is going to be there to collect the plans, so that's where you need to be too.'

'The United Kingdom is not an ideal location for me to return to just yet given the Harvey job so I'll need to tread with care. And talking of Harvey, what happens next given you decided to forgive his past indiscretions?'

'I thought you didn't care about the *why*.'

'I don't care why I'm performing a contract,' Victor said, 'but when I need to kill a whole bunch of people I'm not being paid to kill, I like for that to make sense.'

'Harvey works for me now,' Lambert explained. 'Keep your friends close and your enemies even closer, as they say. But, going back to your concerns, it's taken care of.'

'Tell me about the contract.'

'As I've said, the client doesn't know who the buyer is ... yet. This is where you and your valuable skill set come in. Another exchange like the one in Bucharest is going to be made. The client managed to hack one of the thief's burner phones and intercepted a communication with the person purchasing the intel. The buyer is going to be collecting the HEL plans in person and the client would very much like it if that buyer never left again – and they would also like you to ensure there is no ambiguity about their death. No accident, no suicide, no death by misadventure. They want it known the buyer was murdered, and they want them to be found with enough incriminating evidence that it's not long before everyone knows exactly why.'

'Tell me about this thief.'

Lambert said, 'I can't do that. At least right now. This contract is being put together in real time, so we have to accept a certain piecemeal approach to the information being passed on to us. Regardless, I need you to be at that conference and find out who the thief is meeting. That person is your target. They thought that person was Marion Ysiv, but we now know she wasn't the ultimate buyer. The thief is the traitor who stole secrets, but the buyer is the one benefiting – and is therefore the target the client wants you to make an example of.'

'That won't necessarily be the buyer. It could be a subordinate or someone utterly clueless about what they're collecting.'

'Not according to the client,' Lambert countered. 'Their information is solid: the thief and their buyer are making this exchange in person. They don't trust anyone else after what happened to Schulz. Once you've identified the buyer, execute them in any way you deem fit so long as it cannot be ruled an accident or suicide. The client needs this message to be heard, okay?'

'I remember the earlier part of this conversation, yes.'

'As your employer, it reassures me to know you're paying attention,' Lambert said. 'But do you have anything else to add aside from sarcasm?'

'What about the thief?'

'Irrelevant to the mission,' Lambert answered. 'As long as they've completed the exchange and the buyer is in possession of the plans when you strike, it doesn't matter what happens to the thief. The client will know by then who they are and will take care of them however they see fit at a time of their choosing. I imagine they'll arrest them for espionage or treason when it's politically advantageous to do so.'

'And if this thief gets in my way?'

'You have full discretion here,' his broker stressed. 'Kill them if you need to, or let them walk away; it's your call. The client appreciates the difficulties you'll be facing and is giving you appropriate breathing room to get the job done.'

'How very thoughtful,' Victor said. 'You told me it's confirmed that the buyer will be at the conference to make the exchange, yes?' He did not wait for an answer. 'But how am I supposed to have any idea who they are? The thief might talk with dozens of people throughout that weekend. Even if I never let them out of my sight, I can't possibly know if a microSD card is passed between them or if the thief is given a key to a safety deposit box or the password to a file-hosting service. And there's no way I can shadow them completely without giving myself away in that kind of environment.'

'I hear your concerns and may have said similar to the client when I spoke with them earlier. Don't worry, I'm—'

'I don't worry.'

'I'm told,' Lambert began again, 'the data will be transferred the same way as with Schulz. It'll be hard copies. That's how they work. Nothing digital that can be traced, only printouts. And before you say anything else, just know it will be a substantial number of documents again. We're talking a briefcase full of hundreds of pages of data, so you don't have to pay attention to every Post-it and receipt that might exchange hands. These will be designated top secret so there won't be any doubt about what they are; you'll know when you see them.'

'This is not how I work,' Victor said. 'I work with certainties, not probabilities, and right now, I'll be arriving without even knowing who my target is, let alone where and when I can execute or extract. No professional worth his salt would agree to this contract.'

'For this, you're not a professional, remember? We're not being paid. This isn't a contract. This, my friend, is tidying up our mess.'

Victor remained silent.

'But if you won't do it, then we part ways right now,' Lambert added. 'I'll lose an ally in the Ministry of Defence and plenty of big-money deals going forward. You'll lose your anonymity and your ability to work in the UK, and you'll have to keep looking over your shoulder for the Russian mafia for the foreseeable future. So, Roman my boy, what's it going to be?'

# FORTY-EIGHT

Zahm had nine separate surgeries in the first year alone. In nasal reconstruction, cartilage was most often taken from ears – from the auricular – but Zahm's nose had been so damaged more cartilage had to be harvested from the costal of the ribs. With the lower half of the nose, the nasal tip and the septum all requiring extensive work, it had to be done in stages, waiting for one section to heal enough for the next to be rebuilt. Skin was grafted from his lower back and the back of his thighs. He wore a splint and dressings over his face for the first thirteen months, removing them only for the surgeries and for regular cleaning and re-dressing. He could not train or exercise with any true intensity and lost almost twenty kilograms of lean mass that first year. Unable to be sent on assignments, he was reduced to a desk job, collating and analysing data, and occasionally participating in the training of new operatives, which felt as though he was teaching them how to replace him.

'How do you like your new role?' Father had asked him.

'I hate it.'

'Good,' Father said. 'Because you are a dog bred for the hunt that is now muzzled and chained to a post. Do not let go of that hatred, my son. Keep it tight in your fist. Squeeze it until that fist is ready to explode, and then, when you are finally unmuzzled and set loose, you will terrify all those who see your new fangs.'

'Yes, Father.'

When Zahm had healed from his final surgery, it was nowhere near over.

'You were unmissable before,' Father told him, examining the results of all the procedures, 'and now none who look upon you will ever forget what they see.'

Zahm, who had no vanity, was content to be able to breathe naturally again, but he never missed an appointment and did not once complain through the numerous cosmetic procedures that followed. They were not for his benefit. His disfigurement was an accepted price of his failure, and yet Father would never again send him on assignments until none could tell he had ever been so injured.

Zahm needed to be sent out on missions as much as others needed food to eat.

He could not survive otherwise.

From specialists in rhinoplasty, Zahm now visited dermatologic surgeons whose expertise lay in scar revision. He had procedures to remove excess scar tissue. He sat through laser therapies to flatten and soften the keloids, to lighten and blend the scars with the rest of his skin tone. He had further chemical peels, skin bleaching and dermabrasion. Injections of silicone and hyaluronic acid were used to fill in the skin where weaknesses in the cartilage grafts had caused the surface to become concave. He was sent far and wide across Europe and to the United States to see the very best doctors in the world. In Istanbul, leading hair transplant specialists took follicles from his inner ears and implanted them into his reconstructed nostrils where the nasal hairs, the vibrissae, would no longer grow.

In sparring, they always used four-ounce mixed martial arts gloves, head protectors, gum shields and groin guards. Zahm had not been allowed to train with any intensity, and therefore not with a sparring partner, until not only his nose was reconstructed but all cosmetic procedures healed.

After two years of only watching, of keeping hold of his hatred so tightly that his very sanity was tested to the extreme, there were no volunteers when Zahm was given the all-clear to step onto the mat once again.

Even so out of practice, and at a fraction of his former strength and size, all could see the intensity of the fury that had been caged within him for so long, and no one desired to be the recipient on which that fury was unleashed.

So, it was the new recruits who were brought in and ordered to spar with him.

The head of the Mossad Krav Maga school organised sixteen trainee operatives so they stood in a line in order of size. Though fresh meat in terms of Mossad, all were exceptional physical specimens and combat veterans, and were not only younger than Zahm but in prime condition in readiness for their training.

'You,' he said to the first, the largest, who was bigger than even Zahm prior to his muzzling. 'Get on the mat and stay on your feet for sixty seconds. If you end up on your back, tap or retreat, you hit the track for an hour.'

Outside, the running track baked in the forty-centigrade Levantine sun.

As the first recruit stepped onto the mat and extended a gloved fist to touch with Zahm's own, the instructor told the second, third and fourth biggest to, 'Put in your gum shields.'

The second biggest managed to utter 'Why?' and nothing more before he had his answer as Zahm, barrelling through the strikes of the first recruit, heaved him from his feet and body slammed him into the mat so hard the resulting vibrations rattled the ice inside Father's glass of soda on the periphery of the training hall.

Within ten minutes, thirteen of the sixteen new recruits were sweating and panting on the track, with sunburn and heat exhaustion in their immediate future.

The three others were stretchered to the infirmary.

Zahm, sat on his haunches at the edge of the mat, blood welling on his cut lower lip, every atrophied muscle aching, every weakened joint throbbing, had never felt better.

He looked up to see Father approaching.

He pinched Zahm's shoulder. 'You are soft now, you are weaker than you were, and yet still you are as mighty as ever.'

Zahm nodded.

'I told you your strength is the least of your weapons.'

'You did.'

He took Zahm's huge right hand in both of his own and it looked not as a parent holding his son's hand but a child holding the hand of his father.

'Did you keep hold of your hatred as I told you?'

'For every second of every day.'

'Do you see now the power of the resolve that hatred has gifted you?'

Again, Zahm nodded.

'Then,' Father began, 'I have nothing more to teach you.'

Before his injury, Zahm had been a little over one hundred kilograms in weight at about twelve per cent body fat. By the time he was able to train with full intensity again, he was closer to twenty per cent body fat and at least ten kilograms too heavy. Within three months, however, he had lost the excessive bulk thanks to a regime of morning sprints, afternoon weightlifting and evening training in Krav Maga. His strength took longer to rebuild, and Zahm's patience was tested to the extreme waiting for his lifts to improve and his shoulders to fill out. A life-long devotee to fitness, Zahm understood the detrimental effect of overtraining and the importance of proper recovery, and forced himself to take his time to allow his body the rest it needed to rebuild and avoid injury. Almost two years of sedentary life took six months to repair, but his new-found resolve fuelled him through this rebirth and he emerged stronger, faster and with more endurance than ever before. At his next biannual physical the technician recorded his weight at one hundred and nine kilograms at ten per cent body fat.

The only downside to his rebirth was that now Zahm's reputation worked against him.

'I've been asked to have a word,' Karmia Elkayam told him and Father. 'The recruiting department is livid. Every new class has fewer trainees signing up than the last. Word has spread beyond this facility.'

Zahm was confused and yet Father had a wry smile that Elkayam did not appreciate.

'They all hear they will need to survive the *ogre* if they want to be part of Mossad. Everyone is terrified of you,' she said. Karmia Elkayam was not angry, but she was inflexible. 'This has to stop or this agency will be nothing except old men and women.' She told them both, 'This needs to ends right now.'

'Then it ends,' Father told her.

'Finally,' Elkayam said.

To Zahm, Father added, 'You are too eager to prove yourself, my son. That is not your hatred working for you but your ego working against you. No one doubts you except yourself. There is a solution, however.'

Zahm waited.

'It is time for you to go back on assignment.'

'Thank you,' Zahm said, and the relief he felt was the sweetest of joys.

'It is time for our enemies to bear witness to your new fangs.'

Two and a half years after Zahm had been wounded, Father finally removed his muzzle.

# FORTY-NINE

'Tell me about the conference,' Victor said.

'It's an event held at a big old baronial estate on the shores of Loch Lomond,' Lambert explained. 'Hosted by a non-profit, with a mouthful of a title that I won't bother trying to reiterate here. The salient point is that it concerns global security, international relationships, diplomacy and trade. There will be talks and discussions with various boffins, intellectuals and experts from the aforementioned fields.'

'That is a broad church.'

'Isn't it just? Like any conference it's mostly an excuse for delegates to escape the other half for a few days, meet up with distant colleagues and maybe get their leg over if a cute cultural attaché has one too many Martinis.'

'Sounds charming.'

'There will be representatives of most EU and G7 countries, including diplomats, ambassadors and the odd politician.'

'Along with their respective security details.'

A slow nod from Lambert. 'Who will have their hands full babysitting their respective VIPs, which will not include the thief and the buyer, so you can forget all about them.'

'I won't.'

'Figure of speech. Anyway, what else can I tell you? Oh, yeah, that's right. Last but not least, the private sector will naturally try to flog its wares and bully or bribe – I mean lobby – their public-sector counterparts.'

'Then I'm surprised you're not attending.'

'Ha ha,' Lambert said, 'I'll have you know that I don't need to pimp myself out. Ninety-nine per cent of my business comes to me directly from friends and former colleagues.'

'Including my current client?'

'I've already told you your client represents the interests of the British Government, specifically the Ministry of Defence.'

'Then I wonder who works there who also went to the University of Durham, or who was in the Parachute Regiment at the same time as you.'

'You really don't want to be wondering anything of the sort.'

'While I jest, you need to be careful about working with anyone who knows you and whom you know in return. Things go wrong in this business all the time. Toes get stepped on even when you watch where you put your feet. Suppose the client decides that the work you do for them puts them in a difficult position. In that case, they know exactly how to insulate themselves from any blowback.'

'I appreciate the concern, but there's no need,' Lambert said. 'I know my value. Everyone I deal with knows it too. I make a lot of people's lives a lot easier just by virtue of the fact I'm in their contacts list.'

'I'm talking about me too.'

'You're my guy, so everything I've just said also applies to you.'

Victor remained silent.

'You think I'll throw you under the bus on behalf of a client? No chance. Once you're my guy, you're my guy all the way.'

'I seem to recall three assassins in a Belgium bakery used to be of that impression.'

'Listen,' Lambert said in a careful tone. 'They were moonlighting, right? To start with, that is a violation of the agreement they have with my company and me. You work for me; you only work for me. That's not purely about protecting my interests; it's for the long-term benefit of both parties because I can't protect anyone if they work for whoever comes knocking. All of my contractors know that, including those three. And not only did they break the code and betray my trust but they also royally screwed up in the process. I didn't throw them under a bus; they threw themselves off the kerb and dived head first in front of a double-decker all on their own. You play fair with me, I play fair with you, okay? If you don't believe that, then you're dead wrong, my man.'

'I'd prefer to be wrong than dead if that's all the same to you.'

'And I'm going to prove you wrong time and time again, you'll see. All you have to do is work for me and no one else, and I will have your back until the bitter end. That's who I am, who I've always been. Just don't do what those three bozos did and keep things from me that can bite me on my huge, hairy arse. Had they come to me to hold their hands up and admit their mistakes, I could have put things right. Fired them, sure, but they would still be north of the worms. Instead, they kept me in the dark until it was far too late, and I can't protect either of us if you do the same.'

'Seems reasonable,' Victor said, thinking about Raven, the Consensus, and the young brown-haired woman in the hotel lobby for a brief moment before remembering Raven's counterpoints. 'I'm going to need a pass to the conference, obviously. Weapons. Burner phones. Some tech, too: a magnetic card copier. Maybe some other things.'

'Whatever you need,' Lambert assured. 'I can have a care package waiting for you to pick up when you arrive in Scotland. So ... you are agreeing to the job?'

'You told me specifically it wasn't a job.'

'You know what I mean.'

'It doesn't seem like I have much choice,' Victor said. 'Therefore, the answer is yes.'

'Thank you,' Lambert breathed. 'And, look, anything you don't like when you're on the ground, withdraw. It doesn't look right or feel right, get out of there. But we have to try, okay? We have to show willingness. We have to at least show up before we quit.'

Victor listened.

'You'll have all the resources of my company at your disposal. We will have an exfil team on standby, ready at the drop of a hat, to whisk you away if it goes south. And they're going to get a big, fat overtime bonus for doing exactly squat, aren't they? Because you can do this standing on your head. All you have to do is see who the thief passes a stack of paperwork to, execute that buyer while he's in possession of the paperwork, and be on your merry way. Piece of cake, given your track record.'

'Appeals to my sense of vanity are both transparent and ineffective,' Victor told him. 'But I'll try. I don't want the British Government turning its attention my way any more than you do.'

'That's my boy.'

Victor neglected to tell Lambert that while his statement about the British Government was true, more than that, Victor did not want the British to inform their friends in America and elsewhere about him. Lambert did not know Victor's entire history over the last several years and did not need to hear about it now. The more Victor shared about his history, exploits, enemies and associates, the easier he made Lambert's task of killing him when the time came that Victor's usefulness to his broker was superseded by the threat he posed.

Likewise, Lambert did not need to know about Raven. She was a complication as it was, without intensifying that complication by sharing it with a potential future foe.

'Aren't you going to mention it?' Lambert asked.

'Mention what?' Victor asked.

Using a closed fist, Lambert hit his abdomen several times in rapid succession. 'I'm down almost a stone.'

'Congratulations,' Victor said, although he felt Lambert's weight loss was nowhere near the six-kilogram level.

'I still have a couple more to lose before I'm back at my fighting weight. Used to box at light-heavy in the Paras. Even won a few fights if you can believe it.'

'I believe it,' Victor told him.

'Let me know if you ever want to lace them up and go a few rounds. Although I won't be offended if you're too chicken.'

Victor raised an eyebrow.

# FIFTY

Albrecht woke up to find himself secured to a vertical stretch of exposed pipework in one of the empty rooms of the ground floor. Raven had used duct tape to tie his wrists together behind his back and had looped the tape around the pipe many times. Given enough time and patience, she knew it was possible that its hold could be loosened and even escaped from. However, she had no intention of keeping him like this long enough for him to have the time to work himself free.

'We have a real problem here, Alby,' she told him, 'because you don't want to be here, and I don't want to be here either. But I won't leave until you tell me what I want to know. And don't tell me to "go to hell" or any of that nonsense, since neither of us has time to play that out. Just accept that you'll tell me anyway and, when you do, I'll let you go. You're just a soldier, not a general, so there's no comeback to me if I set you loose. However, when I let you go, you want to be released as you are now. Granted, you're bruised and bloody, but you'll be fine in a few days. You can carry on living your life as if none of this had ever happened. If we have to play out the alternative, in which you don't want to tell me anything, and I have to convince you, then it won't take a few days to get over it. It's going to take weeks before you can work a zipper again, it's going to be months before you can walk, and it'll be years before you sleep through the night without being tormented by nightmares.'

He said, 'Who are you?'

'I'm the angel of death,' Raven answered in words that were more a proclamation of absolute will than mere sounds. 'To the people you work for, I'm vengeance personified.'

Albrecht stared.

'But to you,' she said, 'I'm just a girl standing in front of a boy, asking him not to make her torture him until he soils himself.'

'I work for no one.'

'That's inaccurate, and we both know that, so let's remember everything I just said, shall we? I know who you are, that you worked with Jan Schulz to obtain classified information regarding the United Kingdom's new high-energy laser technology. I know this because I liaised with Schulz; I'm the one who bought those documents from him. Schulz was not what I would call a top-tier operative, okay? He let things slip. He liked to flex his muscles, so to speak. He wanted to impress me. And, yes, maybe I flirted with him and stroked his ego to encourage that, and some might say that's taking advantage, but I've done worse, and I'm sure I'll do far worse before the end.'

'I don't understand what you want from me.'

'You hid out here for a reason, yes? Pretty smart to hide

out in the basement and yet leave the upstairs lights on to trick anyone who came after you. You did that for a reason, because you knew if Schulz had been killed, you could be next?'

'Yeah.'

'Why? Who did you think was going to come after you? Why did you have to go into hiding?'

'Because Jan sold their intel to you,' Albrecht said. 'He said if they ever found out, we would be dead men.'

'And he was right. Schulz may not have been smart, but he had quite the pair of *cojones* to rip off the Consensus.'

'The ... Con ... what?'

'Consensus,' Raven said. 'That's what I call them. They protect the vested interests of the elite of the elite. They're not an organisation; they're a *consensus* to keep the wheels of capitalism turning the way they've been for the last century. Namely with war, because war equals money. No surprise then that they want to take a look at a new weapons system. I just wish I knew why. Given these things are going to be used by the Royal Navy to shoot down incoming missiles, I can't imagine the Consensus are looking to pick a fight with the UK. That's not really their style.'

'I ... don't know anything about that or about them. We just knew that they were dangerous and powerful. But Jan always thought three steps ahead. He knew they were using us to shield themselves from any blowback.'

'So?' she asked.

'So,' he repeated, 'you don't build a wall if you have nothing worth protecting.'

'Schulz was gathering information on them,' Raven said, her heart rate quickening. 'To use against them.'

'From the very start,' Albrecht told her. 'I told him not to do it. I told him they would find out. And they did.'

The way he stared at Raven told her, 'You think I was sent by them.'

'Well,' he said. 'Weren't you?'

'Oh, you sweet summer child. I'm not working for your employers; I'm working against them. I'm on a one-woman mission to be the splinter in their heel they can never dig out. As such, when you tell me that Schulz himself was gathering information that can hurt them, I'm extremely interested in hearing more about that. What did he find out? What did he learn?'

'Who the guy is.'

'Which guy? There's a lot of guys out there. Something like four billion of them.'

'*The* guy,' Albrecht said. 'The one who set this whole thing up in the first place, the one who recruited us to collect the plans from the other person in the chain and then deliver it to him. It was all supposed to be anonymous, of course. Phone calls and emails and dead drops, but Jan went off script and caught the guy in the act of collecting one of the packages. The man didn't realise Jan was watching, but they'd been rotating through a series of dead drop sites, and Jan used some of his friends in the business to stake them out. Once we knew what he looked like, it was only a matter of time before we identified him.'

'Don't leave me hanging.'

'His name is Fabien Gallier. He's a Frenchman, but that's all I know about him. Jan was the one who compiled the information on him, not me.'

'He sounds like an interesting individual, but I suppose

269

you're telling me since Schulz is dead, then the information on Gallier has gone the way of the dodo?'

Albrecht shook his head. 'I'm sure I can find it.'

Raven was unconvinced. 'How?'

'We worked together for a long time and have been friends even longer. Give me the chance to access his computer and go through his things. He'll have it hidden, disguised or in code, but I can find it. I know I can.'

'Okay,' she said. 'For some reason, I believe your sincerity. But I don't understand it. Why are you being so cooperative with me?'

'I never wanted to work for these people,' Albrecht explained. 'I knew there was something ... wrong ... about them, that we were getting ourselves into the kind of trouble we wouldn't be able to get out of again. Jan saw sense eventually, so he started building up insurance against Gallier, but it was too late, wasn't it? You were already on to him by then.'

'Don't ask me to feel sorry for either of you.'

'I'm not. I made my bed. Now I'm lying in it.'

'You understand that even though I will stick to my word and let you live, they won't. They'll come for you, and you'll need a much better place to hide than this dump. You need to disappear. You need to drop right off the surface of the Earth if you can. Take the first passenger shuttle to Mars, and then – maybe – you'll be safe.'

Albrecht looked away, defeated. Scared. Overwhelmed.

'You have supplies in that kitchen?'

'Say again?'

'I want to make some coffee. I could use a pick-me-up, and you sure as shit look like you need a strong one.'

'I stocked it with enough supplies to last me the whole week and more if necessary.'

'It won't be,' she said. 'Because as soon as we're done here, we're going to your and Schulz's offices and getting that insurance policy on Gallier. After that, you're going to start your new life, if you still want a life at all. But, until then, I have some more questions.' She headed to the door. 'Cream and sugar?'

He stared at her, confused.

'How do you take your coffee?' she said in a slow, deliberate cadence.

He finally realised there was no trick. 'Black, please.'

She snapped her fingers in approval. 'This is why we get on so well.'

After checking Albrecht was still secure and there was no chance of him escaping the bonds, Raven searched through the kitchen cupboards to find cups and coffee.

'Ugh,' she groaned as she realised the coffee Albrecht had talked about was a glass jar of instant granules.

Since he wanted it black too, there was little to do except add some water to the kettle, switch it on and try not to think about how the boiling water would encourage the kettle's plastic shell to leach out all manner of endocrine-disrupting petrochemicals into the water.

Taking some charcoal in the morning would help suck out the poison the multinationals wanted her to ingest, she thought, as she stood away from the kitchen window out of habit as the kettle boiled, listening to the night.

The cats were still fighting somewhere outside. Intermittent hisses and wails. Then, a clattering of what she guessed to be the lid of a garbage can.

As the screech of the kettle grew louder and sharper, she heard something else too. Not the cats, not the garbage can lid. This sound was lower in pitch. Not quite a thud. Something with more bass, but also rougher around the edges.

A clack.

Then another one followed, a split second later.

*Clack–clack.*

Even disguised by the kettle's screech, she knew that sound. There was no other sound quite like it.

The sound of two subsonic bullets shot through a suppressor, a double-tap.

With the hallway behind her, she threw herself to the floor, landing into a roll as holes appeared in the refrigerator door. Glass shattered inside.

Coming out of her roll and drawing the G43, she whipped around to face the entrance of the hallway from a forty-five-degree angle, seeing a slice of it just before the frame and picturing a gunman further along, having just put two bullets into Albrecht from the doorway to that room before twisting to face Raven.

She darted across the kitchen, stopping with her left shoulder tight against the doorjamb.

The kettle hadn't quite reached the crescendo of its screech, now so loud she could hear nothing to indicate if the assassin in the hallway had held position or was hurrying closer.

If they had held position and were covering the open doorway, she would be shot as soon as she appeared through it if they were any good. And they were, because they had entered the building a different way, and she hadn't heard them.

Not a team, however, because a team would have entered

from the back as well as the front, covering escape routes as they surrounded their target.

Or targets, of course. Maybe the Consensus had figured out it was their old enemy, Raven, who was behind Schulz's death and had been waiting for her to show.

As steam billowed from the kettle's spout, Raven waited for the click of the switch as the temperature reached boiling point.

*Click.*

At that instant – when the screech changed within a split second from loud, piercing shrill to low rumble, when that sudden change in ambient soundscape would impede the re-action time of the gunman in the hallway – she pivoted out and into the doorway.

And found the assassin, too, had been waiting for that exact same moment.

# FIFTY-ONE

A dark figure, tall and powerful.

The snarling homeless man – the man *pretending* to be homeless, at least – she saw. A good trick, she had to give him that. Hiding in plain sight. Drawing attention to himself with the tent, with the snarl, and in doing so causing her to dismiss him as any kind of threat.

She should know better than that.

She *did* know better than that.

Colliding into one another, there was no room for either to shoot.

Faster, she used her pistol as a lever to twist his own gun out of his fingers.

Stronger, he punched down at her forearm with so much power that the Glock flew out of her grip.

His suppressed Heckler & Koch P7 clattered on the polished floorboards as her own handgun skidded into the kitchen across the tiles.

He moved at a frightening speed, aggressive and yet

controlled, driving her backwards, slamming her into cupboards, into the countertops, dragging her away and tossing her over the kitchen table.

He located her gun, scooped it up off the floor and swung it around to aim where he had thrown her . . .

. . . and found himself confused, pointing the G43 into clear, open space.

Because Raven had already scrambled away, going under the table as he reached for her gun, momentarily disappearing out of his field of vision.

A second's confusion only before he realised, bending over and ducking to peer beneath the table as Raven was coming out again from the opposite side.

Smaller, quicker, she pushed both palms against the table's edge and drove it backwards into him, its legs scraping along the floor tiles.

With his head away from his hips, his stability compromised despite his strength, the impact knocked him off his balance, slowing his reaction. Unable to resist, he was pinned and bent over between the kitchen sink and table as Raven continued to drive the table into his body.

He fired at her from under the table in unaimed, ineffective shots that put holes in the floor and low cabinets.

Her enemy was trapped in one place, but only temporarily. Raven grabbed at anything and everything from the countertop next to her.

She hurled mugs from a wooden stand; the stand itself, once she had thrown all the mugs; nearby salt and pepper shakers followed.

Some of the missiles hit their target, others missed. Enough struck him or landed close enough for him to protect his head and face instead of angling up the gun as he pushed the table clear to rise.

When she had run out of things to hurl at him, Raven vaulted onto the kitchen table and slid across it, using the momentum of a leap to power a kick aimed at the side of his jaw.

It never landed.

Not yet fully clear of the table, he used his strength to heave it up, lifting the closest two legs from the floor and sending Raven toppling off as the table flipped over.

She hit the floor, a sharp jolt of pain shooting up from her butt and ascending her spine. However, the flipping table shielded her in that moment, so when the assassin squeezed the trigger, he was shooting blind.

Bullet holes exploded through the wood, sending a cluster of splinters into her back. She was happy to take pine instead of lead any day.

By the time the table had hit the floor and stopped on one edge, legs pointing back toward the assassin, Raven was through the entranceway and into the hallway, seeking his disarmed P7.

Located at the far end of the hallway, she saw she would never reach it in time.

He pursued her, rounding the tipped-over table in a dash across the kitchen before darting through the doorway, gun up and ready to shoot at Raven's fleeing form further along the hallway.

Only she was not running as expected but ducked down low on the other side of the doorway, so when he appeared through it, she was throwing herself low into his legs and hips, taking him down to the kitchen floor.

She reached for his gun-holding hand, finding it empty because that hand had whipped against one of the upturned table legs as he fell, the shock of the impact sending the pistol flying out of his grip.

A tinny rattle of metal on metal told her it had landed in the washbasin, out of sight and out of reach.

Even on his back, the assassin could use his strength to impede her skills at groundwork, kicking out with his heels into her hips as she tried to scramble on top of him, his raw might propelling her away, giving him room to roll backwards over his head, creating more space in which to get back to his feet.

Although agile, he was still tall and had long limbs that required more room to manoeuvre than Raven.

So, she was first back to her feet and attacking him with punches and kicks.

Fast and skilled, he blocked some and dodged others but could not stop her from landing some of her attacks, and Raven, aiming for vulnerable and vital areas, hurt him with the strikes that landed.

With his size advantage, however, she could not cause enough damage to stop him from fighting back. Which he did, his own punches landing with much more force, doing much more harm than she could do to him in return. In such a battle of attrition, she would always lose, yet with her edge in speed and agility, for the moment she overwhelmed him with her relentless, unceasing ferocity.

He had left the greatcoat behind for increased mobility, opting instead for a long-sleeved T-shirt. Otherwise, he looked the same: unwashed, unkempt. An effective disguise. She'd had no idea he was a professional, let alone one who was so strong. She made the height, the reach and the breadth work against him here. Bigger meant slower and less agile than Raven, who slipped and dodged his looping attacks, sidestepped his attempts to grab and grapple, and repositioned before he could adjust and adapt.

But when he did adapt, all her advantages would disappear.

# FIFTY-TWO

As she rounded the tipped-over kitchen table to create distance to kick, he heaved it up and tossed it into her. Far too big to avoid, it knocked her back and into the refrigerator, pinning her in place for a dangerous second while he rushed closer.

She pushed it away enough to slither out before his punches could find her face, ducking clear and grabbing the kettle as she rose back up to hurl it at him.

He blocked it with a raised forearm, sparing his face from the impact, but the collision caused the top of the kettle to fly off and unleashed a spray of boiling water and a cloud of scalding steam.

The assassin roared, the water and steam engulfing his defending arm and finding its way over and under it to turn one side of his face a bright, livid red.

Invigorated by pain and rage, he grabbed the back of Raven's body warmer as she tried to get her gun from the washbasin, heaving her backwards and throwing her into the closest wall.

The bare bulb hanging from the ceiling cast a harsh downward light on his scalded face, making him appear gaunt and more intense. The light cast deep, defined shadows that showed the chaos of their confrontation as a dance of silhouettes on the walls.

Still holding onto her by the body warmer, he slammed her against the refrigerator, trying to knock the wind out of her or knock her out. Nearby cabinet doors shook with each impact, and kitchenware inside rattled.

Attempts to trip and sweep his legs failed, the strength of his stance too solid and her own leverage too weak.

Instead, she kicked with her heel in stomping attacks at his ankles, at his kneecap, until the pain made him release her to back away.

When he attacked again, he tried to choke her, wrapping both hands around her neck and squeezing. He was strong, and the focal points of pressure were accurate enough to shut off her windpipe, but he gave up the ability to block and defend with his hands and arms. A trade he soon found worked against him as she punched with closed fists, hammer fists and edges of her palms at his elbows, static and unprotected.

She would have gone for his face, where he was already hurt, if only she had the reach. As the damage to his elbows built and the pain rose, he was forced to release her.

The woollen hat came off in the struggle to reveal short, blond hair combed forwards or pressed flat from the hat. He was much younger than she had realised beforehand, the guise of the dirty homeless man making him seem old, more downtrodden, almost wizened; beaten down by life and bad choices.

Now, in contrast, he seemed almost fresh-faced despite the scalded red skin. A new recruit almost. She could imagine him trying to suppress a smile, beaming with pride as he passed out on his first parade. It was almost a shock for her to realise how much older she was in comparison to the man who had been sent to kill her. Not old enough to be his mother, granted, but as good as a whole generation's difference between them. At such a young age, his experience had to be limited.

Yet, the vitality of youth could never be underestimated. Raven had not yet fully recovered from her fight with Albrecht. Brief, yet intense. Her energy levels had not yet been replenished. He was tired, but she was more fatigued. Her limbs were heavy, and her muscles were weighed down with metabolites.

Still, she had the edge in experience, and any desire of his to do a good job, to complete his mission, could never be commensurate with the will to survive. She had that will, and beyond that, she had to endure to keep fighting his employers beyond this night.

The young man trying to kill her now was a no one. A soldier at most. Maybe he'd been told she was a bad guy, a terrorist, an enemy of liberty and democracy, to convince this idealistic patriot to do something unthinkable. Or maybe she was giving him too much credit. Perhaps he was just punching his timesheet.

Raven coughed, spluttered and gasped, but within seconds, she was back to fighting strength again. He, meanwhile, had aching and inflamed elbows that slowed his subsequent strikes, making them easier to parry – and as she responded with counter-attacks too fast for his weakened arms, too sluggish to defend against.

With speed now impeded and fatigue rising, he focused on raw aggression, using his size and strength to bully through her attacks. He slammed her into the table, into the cabinets, into the walls.

Such tactics, however, required more energy. Although far smaller and lighter than he was, Raven was still one hundred and fifty pounds of uncooperative mass that burnt up his precious remaining energy to lift and throw about. Tired, his mouth hung open, and his chest heaved. He could not cope with the pace he had set for himself.

Despite his aggression, he had an earnest look about him. No hatred. No malice. When he took a deep breath and attacked her once again, when he grabbed her clothes and swung her into the wall, there was nothing in his expression except concentration.

They fell to the floor as they grappled, each rolling away from the other, and she could see the exhaustion in the set of his jaw and the flare of his nostrils as he stood again, slower to his feet than she – but still there was nothing, no feeling.

Except now when her strikes landed, he grimaced. He howled when she kicked him between the legs. He did not complain or scream obscenities when she clawed his cheek, trying to impale his eyeball with her fingernails. And in his faultless professionalism, she found she could not hate him. She could not feel anything towards him beyond pity.

Because he was going to die here.

Fifteen years her junior, maybe even more, he had a whole life to live beyond this night, but his life would not extend that far.

Although he had expressed nothing to her – no anger, no

hatred, not even aggressiveness beyond the aggression of his own actions – she could not return the favour.

As she slipped and dodged his slowing attacks, as she leapt up on his back with her thighs on either side of his hips and her lower legs pressed down between his thighs, her own face showed her sorrow, her regret.

Her eyes welled with tears as she wrapped one arm beneath his chin, the pit of her elbow pinching at the front of his neck.

As he collapsed to his knees and tipped forward, she was still on his back, chokehold still closing his carotids and cutting off the oxygen supply to his brain; tears ran down her cheeks.

At that moment, he ceased to fight back, understanding the futility of his attempts. Instead of trying to escape her grip, she felt the gentle begging tap of his hand on her shoulder.

So much said in so little a gesture: a surrender, a plea, a cry of terror and, more than that, a promise, a silent commitment to respect any mercy she showed him and to repent the decisions that had brought him here.

Raven heard all of this and believed the sincerity of the surrender, yet she did not let go. The sincerity was only temporary. He meant it all, but only here, only now.

His next victim, the Consensus's next problem they sent him to solve, would not receive the same consideration.

He tapped again, stronger this time. Believing she had missed the original plea, he re-sent the message louder and with more urgency.

And then, when that message had been delivered and could not be misinterpreted, he tapped more in desperation, and Raven's tears dripped from her face and onto him.

Then the taps stopped, and she felt the slackness of his arms and entire body.

Raven, weeping, maintained the choke until she knew for certain he was dead.

# PART FOUR

# FIFTY-THREE

An announcement over the station's public address system apologised for the late running of the train. Maybe, Victor thought, the audible groans of exasperation from the many waiting travellers could have been tempered if that apology had been via a real person and not an automated voice.

He bought a ready-made sandwich baguette from a kiosk on the concourse. Victor liked buying food-to-go from such vendors because, when there were so many in close proximity, there was no chance of any tampering with his meal. He decided what he was going to eat only mere seconds before ordering it. In a sit-down restaurant, where he could not see the food being prepared, there was always the chance of interference. He chose cheese and tomato for his baguette because he changed the main components each time: a vegetarian option here, as he'd previously had meat and, before that, fish.

A pleasant day outside. Bright, uninterrupted sunshine and a gentle breeze. A comfortable temperature. No one needed to wear gloves or a scarf. No one in shorts either. As he walked about, he heard Glaswegians mention to one another what an uncommonly nice day it was for the time of year. A low bar perhaps, but people reacted in proportion to their environment, he had found. If they found happiness in a spell of nice weather then they would behave better to one another. At least for that day.

Although people's behaviour to one another was not of Victor's concern, it made his life easier. When most people were walking around happy, smiling, it was much easier to spot surveillance; even the best of pavement artists could not necessarily fake that inherent, natural sense of wellbeing and gratefulness while at the same time maintaining their focus shadowing him.

By the time Lambert called, Victor had seen no one that met his criteria as a shadow or more overt threat.

Lambert told him, 'Dossier will be with you shortly, but I thought I'd give you some highlights on the thief. His name is Hereward Woodcroft, and I'll admit he sounds like some portly aristocrat in tweed. But do not underestimate this guy. Although technically retired, he was a field operative for his entire MI6 career, is a former Para like yours truly, and that's not even the half of it.'

'Regiment?'

Lambert made a whistling sound. 'Exactly. Our boy Woodcroft left as a major after a glittering career in Her Majesty's 22nd Special Double-Hard-*Barsteward* Service, including leading just about the most missions of anyone in Task Force Black back in Baghdad when they were mopping up high-value targets alongside the SEALs and Delta.'

'Impressive résumé.'

'His collection of medals makes my own look like I sat behind a desk for my entire tour in Helmand. And now he's a traitor selling out his country.'

'Maybe he doesn't see it like that.'

There was a quizzical tone to Lambert's voice. 'Do I detect a sense of comradeship by any chance?'

'I trust the dossier on Woodcroft will be thorough. You'll appreciate that such a customer will require special consideration on my part.'

Lambert said, 'I have every faith in you.'

Victor stripped down the burner phone and disposed of the parts on his way to George Square, which formed the cultural heart of the city, with its many statues of nineteenth-century influential political figures, military leaders, great writers and pioneers of industry. Victor liked to spend time in such areas, both to satisfy his curiosity as to a city's history, while at the same time exploiting the open area to look out for shadows.

On the areas of grass, tourists ate packed lunches, students read textbooks, and young children played. Pigeons were everywhere, of course, although there seemed to be fewer here than would be found in a similar square in a city such as London. He paused for a while to sit on one of the many wooden benches, doing nothing more than killing time. From his position, he could not see behind himself, but in such a public place almost no professional of any worth would consider this to be an appropriate strike point. Far too many witnesses, far too many cameras, far too many ways to get caught. But because the flow of people here was slow and meandering, with many sitting down, it gave him more opportunities to see if anyone stood out.

When he rose from the bench, he headed back the way he had come so he now faced anyone who had been following him from behind previously. His gaze passed over those sitting on the grass or looking at statues, ignoring anyone with children, any teenagers, anyone sixty or above. He sought out single men or women as a priority, then couples.

A few potentials but no definite shadows, unless he saw any one of them again.

The one person he did recognise was impossible to miss.

As he approached her, he said, 'Thank you for meeting me.'

Raven responded with a wide smile. 'How could I possibly say no to the man of my dreams?'

'I didn't ask you here for a date, Constance.'

'I know you didn't,' she said, 'but I'm still treating this like one and there's nothing you can do to stop me.'

'Given you were able to meet me, I take it everything is resolved with the current chapter of your ongoing vendetta?'

'Not exactly.'

'Then what happened in Germany with Schulz's partner, Albrecht?'

'Dead end,' she replied. 'I came close to finding out who they were dealing with, but the Consensus sent a hitman to kill Albrecht before I could learn anything more. All I got from him is the guy who hired Schulz to pass on the plans was someone named Fabien Gallier. He's French, apparently, but that's all I know because there is nothing out there in the ether about him. Schulz had compiled information on him, only there's no way for me to access it now both he and Albrecht are dead. I was so close ... If I'd have got to Albrecht a little faster, he might still be alive and I would be one step closer to another Consensus scalp. Instead, it's back to the drawing board.' She sighed and for a moment it seemed as though she was going to tell him something else, something that caused her to hesitate. Instead, she shook her head and said, 'Anyway, enough of my woes. Why am I here?'

'I'll tell you, but you have to promise not to hug me.'

Confused, she hesitated. 'Okay . . .'

'I'm here to kill the person who has been buying the stolen plans,' Victor said. 'Until this moment, I had no name for that person.'

'Hold on,' Raven began. 'You're here to kill . . . Gallier?'

Victor nodded.

For all his reaction speed, he was not fast enough to stop Raven leaping into his arms, her legs wrapping around his waist and her hands gripping his shoulders. Her eyes were large with joy and her lips stretched into a wide smile.

'I said no hugs.'

'*He's here?*' she asked, ignoring his attempts to wriggle out of her embrace. 'Gallier is actually here?'

'Not exactly,' Victor told her, 'but he will be, to collect the last of the plans in person from the person who stole it.' He explained about making amends for the uncompleted Bucharest job, about needing to kill Woodcroft's previously anonymous buyer at the conference after the exchange was made. 'It would be useful if you knew what Gallier looked like but at least I now know I'm trying to identify a Frenchman. Will you get down now?'

She did so, saying, 'Although I'm over the moon you invited me along, it sounds like a bit of a shitshow,' immediately holding up a finger of self-chastisement. 'I'm sorry, it was a slip.'

Victor nodded to say it was fine.

'What I mean is,' Raven began, 'this job is wrong on just about every level. I'm just surprised someone like you would agree to it at all?'

'In part because of you,' he answered. 'You not being Ysiv like the client thought, and therefore messing up my work in Bucharest. The client is angry they didn't get to send the message for which they paid. Even though you weren't the buyer, you were a buyer. In their minds the distinction doesn't matter, so I need to make amends for not putting a bullet in your skull.'

'You were supposed to say my "pretty little skull".'

'Why?'

'Because it would have been cute,' she said. 'It would have been fun. I'm sure you used to be more fun than this. Regardless, I'd be delighted to wingman you.'

'Don't you mean wingwoman?'

'No, because I said wingman, so that's what I meant. Wingwoman doesn't roll off the tongue in the slightest. It's a terrible word. I'm your wingman.'

Victor asked, 'So, you're aware of the fact Gallier is going to be dead within a couple of days?'

She responded with a slow nod. 'You think this is where we fall out again, don't you? You think that because he's a representative of the Consensus I need to interrogate him, while you need to kill him, and I won't let you kill him until I've had time with him first.'

'I am going to kill him, Constance,' Victor told her. 'I've come too far and put myself on the line too many times to let anyone or anything stop me.'

She held up her hands, passive. 'Don't start throwing

punches, okay? We don't have to repeat Helsinki. Whoever the Frenchman is, he's the head of this particular snake, I'm sure. I want to put a bullet in him just as much as you do. For once, thank God, we're on the same page.'

'Blasphemy, Constance.'

'It's not, I swear.' Her raised palms fell to her chest. 'I am literally thanking God that there's nothing putting us on opposite sides. And, more than that, we can actually work together for the exact same goal because we have the same target: Fabien Gallier. We're a team again. I've got your back.'

'It's going to be difficult and dangerous. I can't ask you to do this.'

'You don't need to ask me, do you? Because I've already said I'll do it and I want to get to Gallier even more than you do, so asking would be beyond redundant. That said, I'm actually really proud of you for asking, and I'm glad you've grown so much as a human being. The old you wouldn't have had the humility, the inner courage, to admit you can't do this alone.'

'And the new me regrets it already.'

# FIFTY-FOUR

When they had first met, Zahm had been fooled by the kind face and the white smile, which – combined with the diminutive stature – made Father seem like some harmless papa. Only later did Zahm learn that this was precisely how Father wanted people to see him.

'We must use our gifts, whatever they are,' he had said. 'I was never so tall and powerful like you, but when I was your age I had already taken more lives than you might ever take in all your years from this point onwards, because no one ever saw me as a threat until it was far, far too late. You will never have this advantage, my boy. No one will ever underestimate you as they did me.'

Father was no longer going out into the field at that point but sending his children to do what he had once done. Even though he had left a life of violence behind, violence did not feel the same way. He had survived one assassination attempt from old enemies by then and would go on to survive two more.

So, Zahm thought as he looked down on the emaciated old man in the hospital bed, it made sense that the only person who could kill Father was Father himself, his own body turning against him.

From corporal in the IDF's elite Golani Brigade, Zahm had entered selection for the Sayeret Matkal, finishing first in his class by some margin. For five years, he had participated in the most critical special forces operations endeavours in Lebanon, Syria, Jordan and Iraq. He was seconded to the States to work with the US 1st Special Forces Operational Detachment-Delta, once more finding himself west of the Euphrates in Baghdad and beyond. Upon returning to Israel, his unit joined Mossad operatives on their secretive activities at home and abroad. During this time, he was introduced to a tiny, wizened man whom the Mossad agents all called Father.

Even among the committed and dedicated, Zahm's passion had stood out to Father, who looked for zeal as the primary characteristic in candidates for his kidon teams. For only the dedicated, the true believers, could be trusted with the most critical assignments that were also the most dangerous.

Father never offered anyone a position in his deadliest units.

A true believer did not need to be asked. True believers volunteered.

A special forces soldier of an impeccable record, a combat veteran of numerous operations, a war hero by anyone's measure, Zahm had expected Father to be thrilled when he stepped forward and requested to join Father's infamous kidon training. Surely no one else was better qualified?

Zahm had been perplexed by Father's lack of enthusiasm.

'I have no need of a battering ram,' he had told Zahm, shaking his head as his gaze passed over the young man's immense physique. 'I require only scalpels.'

'That will be me,' Zahm, truest of true believers, had responded.

Father had been unconvinced. 'We shall see.' He tutted. 'Can these monstrous hands of yours even hold a scalpel without snapping it like a toothpick?'

When the paperwork arrived, Zahm was thrilled to have been accepted to begin his new education, but that joy was short-lived.

'Follow this person around Tel Aviv,' Father told him on his very first morning. 'If you lose them, you're out. At nightfall, I will show them your photograph. If they recognise you, you're out.'

Zahm's mouth opened.

'No questions. No more information. I have told you all you need to know. Now be the blade you promised me you could become.'

For a man of Zahm's size, the task had seemed all but impossible. He had tracked targets in the military, although always as part of a team and never as primary surveillance. Without the support of a unit, he had to get close and remain close. Then, realising he could not stay at such a distance indefinitely without being noticed, he began anticipating the target's movements. Zahm recognised that he must not only watch but also learn. To predict what the target would do and where he would go next, Zahm needed to first study the target. His gait, his mannerisms, his posture.

As the hours passed and the target went from one street to

the next, caught buses and entered buildings, Zahm began to understand his quarry and to draw conclusions about who he was and what he was doing. For the entire morning and afternoon, Zahm never stopped thinking, analysing and concluding. The target stopped for lunch, for coffee and for snacks. On a scorching day at the height of summer, Zahm took no such breaks. He began his task without time for water and dared not pause to acquire refreshment in case diverting his eyes for mere seconds cost him the place in a kidon unit he so desperately wanted.

After the target had returned home to his apartment in the Ramat Gan district, Father, waiting nearby, notified Zahm the training was over.

Dehydrated to the point his tongue was as rough as Sinai sand, and with his hands cramping, Zahm did his best to hide his discomfort as he fought to maintain his faltering balance.

'Well done,' Father said, 'you stayed with your target the entire day, and he led you to his front door. Who is he?'

'He's a doctor,' Zahm answered, vocal cords more gravel than flesh, 'making house calls.'

Father did not react to this. 'Did he see you?'

'He did not.'

Father carried a canvas shopping bag, from which he pulled several sheets of paper. They were printouts, which he showed to Zahm.

With a crushing sense of disappointment and failure, Zahm looked upon photographs of himself from various points in the day. They were from different angles, but almost all were taken from above, inside a building, as Zahm waited outside the street.

'The *doctor* took these while on his *house calls*. What did I tell you at the start of the day?'

'If he sees me, I'm out.'

Father nodded. 'You're out.'

He turned around and walked away, leaving Zahm standing crestfallen on the pavement as he used all of his will and strength to avoid collapsing out of sheer exhaustion.

He watched the small, ancient man hobble down the street. He hated Father for embarrassing him, for humiliating him, for making Zahm experience his first taste of professional failure in many years.

More than that, he hated Father for denying him the chance to be where he belonged as one of Father's kidon operatives.

'No,' Zahm said.

Father, too far away to hear Zahm's strained, quiet protestation, kept walking.

'No,' Zahm said again.

The tiny figure of Father grew even smaller, blending with the heat haze.

'NO,' Zahm roared, his voice weakened with dehydration but his fury unyielding.

Father, a blurry figure in the distance, stopped.

Zahm staggered after him, fighting the urge to collapse with every step until he came to a stumbling stop before the old man.

'What do you mean, *no*?'

'I'm not ... going anywhere. I'm not out ... I want to learn.'

'You're a battering ram. I need a scalpel, don't forget. A scalpel no one sees until it is too late.'

'The man I followed took these pictures ... because he knew I was following him from the start ... I had no chance to remain unseen.'

'What concessions do you expect from your enemies? Do you think they will play fair? That they will oblige you? Willingly tilt back their heads to give you their throats? Don't be so naïve. Go back to the military where you belong so you waste no more of my time.'

Too weak to be angry, his throat so hoarse every word he uttered meant pain, Zahm said, 'He's one of your operatives ... No one has ever followed him around all day without him noticing.'

'How can you be so sure?' Father asked.

'Because you're old ... you don't have enough life left to waste it setting up raw recruits for failure without good reason.'

Father said, 'You're wrong. One person succeeded in following my man without him noticing. But otherwise, you are correct. This is a test, not to see if you can remain unseen. It is to test whether you will fight to keep your place when you fail.'

'I want this,' Zahm insisted. 'I want *only* this.'

'And now I believe you.' Father looked him up and down, evaluating him with a cold, clinical gaze. 'You are an exceptional specimen, my son. Samson returned. But you are all jagged rock, crudely formed. We must shape you as Michelangelo sculpted *David*, and smooth that stone into something just as worthy of admiration. And yet, unlike Michelangelo's great work, the only people who will ever get to look upon the beauty we shall make of you are those dying by your hand. From now on, I will know you as David.'

'Yes, Father.'

'You must know this will be no easy task,' the short old man told him. 'Although you can break down doors with raw might alone, you must be agile enough to scale any wall and dextrous enough to open windows so you leave no broken door behind to tell of your presence. Your strength is but a single weapon. You already know how to use all weapons, naturally, but I shall teach you to use your mind so that you will always know how to identify the optimal weapon for a given task. In time, you will understand that your strength is the least of your weapons, only to be implemented when all others fail.' Father gestured for him to follow. 'Let us get you some fluids before you pass out.'

'Who succeeded?' Zahm asked, even more desperate to know than he was desperate for water. 'Who remained ... unseen?'

'You will meet Karmia in time.'

For an entire year, Father had put Zahm through training that made his Sayeret Matkal selection seem like a holiday, taxing his awareness, problem solving, ability to learn and adapt, so much so that he had never been as endlessly tired.

Zahm, so eager to please his surrogate parent, never complained and never doubted his instructions. He did everything he was told, absorbing every lesson until, finally, Father saw him not as a battering ram but as a scalpel.

Looking down at Father's emaciated, dying body and thinking about that intense first year of training, Zahm almost missed the click of the door latch. The safest place for him in the world right now was in Father's hospital room in central

Tel Aviv, with armed security outside the door, and a lobby full of soldiers and Mossad operatives paying their respects from a distance.

But Father had taught him well, and Zahm's awareness never dropped, not even when lost in thought, not even when he was so well protected.

'Sir,' the baby-faced IDF corporal said as he opened the door, 'the briefing has been brought forward. Commander Elkayam requests your presence. The target has been spotted in Scotland.'

Zahm waited until the corporal had left the room before placing a palm over Father's withered hand. 'Soon, I will make you proud of me once again.'

# FIFTY-FIVE

The conference was being held on the shores of Loch Lomond in a luxury lodge at the heart of a fourteenth-century baronial estate north of the town of Alexandria. A forty-minute drive from Glasgow, Victor insisted on a circuitous route that took several hours and Raven insisted she hire a car through one of her shell companies instead of stealing one, as Victor suggested.

'Really, Jonathan,' she said, 'are you so strapped for cash?'

They took turns behind the wheel. Raven did not enjoy being a passenger – 'It's so boring' – while Victor was not used to having someone else in a vehicle while he drove. Even though he did not believe Raven would suddenly turn on him when his hands were on the wheel and there was nothing he could do about it, such protocol was so ingrained in his being that it was impossible to enjoy the scenery. As a passenger, however, knowing Raven was now in the vulnerable position meant Victor could appreciate the rugged countryside and views across the loch. He

302

had forgotten what it was like to experience such simple pleasures.

'You're making me anxious,' Raven said, glancing across to him.

'Why? I'm not doing anything.'

'Exactly,' she said. 'You look relaxed. It's freaking me out.'

The estate covered four hundred acres along the west side of the loch, and included an eighteen-hole golf course, a marina for forty boats and an eighty-room hotel with three bars, two restaurants, indoor swimming pool and spa, and a dozen individual holiday cottages and villas. The conference was being held in the main hotel with its several function rooms, but talks and demonstrations would be held at various points around the grounds, utilising some of the estate's many other buildings.

Although most of the guests for the weekend were attendees and delegates to the conference, almost half were regular holidaymakers. Albeit wealthy ones.

'I've never seen so many Bentleys and Range Rovers in one place before,' Raven said as they drove at a slow speed along the lane leading to the estate and the magnificent baronial home loomed ever larger and more impressive. 'You know, for our first romantic weekend away, you did good.'

'First and last,' Victor replied.

'I'll pretend I didn't hear that.'

Victor had been in numerous luxury hotels, experienced countless grand and impressive lobbies, and this one was no exception. Brass fixtures shone in the light from glittering chandeliers hanging from a vaulted ceiling high above. Many lush plants rising from ornate pots decorated with colourful, swirling patterns were stationed near armchairs with thick padding and high backs. The concierge's station and the front desk were both dark-stained walnut with leather and brass detailing. The soles of Victor's shoes tapped against marble tiles.

At check-in, he said the name Lambert had provided him with, and waited while the clerk typed on a keyboard and checked a screen shielded by the desk.

She recited the particulars of the booking and handed over the key cards. He ignored the frown Raven wore while she listened, only commenting when they were walking away towards the elevators.

'Two rooms?' she asked, incredulous.

'Yes.'

'Two rooms?' she repeated.

'Was I ambiguous with my first answer?'

'What is this? Some kind of joke?'

'What this is,' he began, 'is protocol.'

She huffed.

'I haven't slept in the same room as anyone else in a very long time and I'm not starting again now when we have a job to do. And, naturally, I think it's best for us to maintain a little professional distance, don't you?'

'Distance,' she repeated, sarcastic.

'To avoid any misunderstandings.'

'You're misunderstanding me right now,' she said. 'You think I'm going to jump your bones without permission? That I couldn't possibly keep my hands to myself if we shared the same room? Oh, please, Jonathan. I haven't survived this long by having an uncontrollable lady-boner.'

He did his best not to smile.

Seeing this, she added, 'Given you have no other discernible personality traits, your arrogance is quite telling.'

'I'm glad to hear we're on the same page with this. Take an hour to unpack and recharge and then let's go find this thief.'

# FIFTY-SIX

Downtown Tel Aviv had once been too busy and too noisy for Zahm. He had never been one for crowds, for masses of people, whether at home or abroad. But Father had taught him the value of a crowd. Even someone as large and imposing as Zahm could blend in with enough other people around him.

He sat in the outdoor area of a café, a parasol shielding him from the brute force of the Mediterranean sun. He wore lightweight cotton cargo trousers, a triple-XL short-sleeved linen shirt – that might as well have been a tent around his midriff, yet was almost glued to his shoulders and across his back – and robust walking shoes not made for this kind of heat, but Zahm never wore anything on his feet that would impede his movement or cushion kicks or stomps. He wasn't expecting to need to do either here, yet as Father had taught him: chance favoured the prepared mind. Need was something that had a habit of catching people off guard at the worst possible time, a fact he had used against his enemies several times himself. 'You never want to find out that which you need, you do not already possess,' Father had once said.

'Is it confirmed? Zahm asked. 'Is the killer attending the conference as we thought?'

Sitting opposite him, Karmia Elkayam finished chewing and said, 'Representatives from Lambert's PMC acquired two passes for the weekend and booked two rooms, one of which for an identity confirmed via facial recognition to belong to Helyeph himself.'

Such was Zahm's excitement he failed to notice the reluctant way in which Karmia had spoken, as though the news she was giving him was bad, not good.

'When do we leave?' Zahm asked.

'That's what we need to talk about.'

Between them was a selection of dishes: labneh, hummus and falafel for them to share. Zahm had eaten a little, to be polite, but he wanted to get to the point of the meeting.

'The feeling in-house has changed regarding the conference since how we last left it.'

'I understand the window of time is tight and I imagine there have been many discussions about any action taking place at the conference, which is why I propose close surveillance only until it's over. I've already been studying the terrain. There are limited roads and transport links, so we will be able to follow him easily and trap him with the entire kidon at the same time. Bury his body in the Highlands.'

Elkayam said, 'Mossad is not sending you to Scotland.'

Zahm's worst fear had been realised, but he was ready. 'I don't ask to lead, only to follow. I will drive the car and nothing else if that's what it takes.'

'We're not sending anyone to Scotland,' she explained.

'The direct action against Helyeph has been withdrawn and we no longer consider him an enemy combatant.'

From his worst fear to utter shock, Zahm was speechless. Nothing could have prepared him for what he was hearing.

'Remember,' Elkayam began, 'this enemy is only one by chance. We are no hated foe of his, are we? He's not looking to annihilate us off the face of the Earth in the name of his god, his land or historic grievances. He's a mercenary, a killer for hire, and that's it. We need to think of him in these terms and these terms only. We are only even talking about him today because our paths unfortunately crossed and put us into an inevitable confrontation. Let us not forget that he, unknowingly, interrupted a long-running operation of our own that only a select few personnel were aware of in this organisation. And it was our boys who intervened in his own mission – a deliberate intervention this time, not accidental, as with his stepping on our toes. Our surveillance team were brave and heroic, naturally – that is without question – and yet their intervention was an unsanctioned one, wasn't it? No one ordered them to try to kill the assassin, did they? Their decision on the ground in the heat of battle led to a cascade of unfortunate events. Because of that decision, lives were lost. And those lives led us to an equally unwise path of retribution that resulted only in yet more pain, more suffering. All of those deaths attributed to this man were entirely avoidable.'

'You're saying that our dead mean nothing to you?'

'Do not dare put words into my mouth.' She leant forward to face him down. 'I feel every loss.' She thumped a fist against her chest. 'I grieve each time one of our own dies and I hold that grief inside me always. So, never tell me otherwise. What I'm *quite plainly* saying is, let's not get any more of our people killed.'

'You want to let him get away with it?'

'Get away with what? Self-defence? We attacked him both times. All he is guilty of is hitting us back harder than we hit him in return. We send more people after him and what will happen?'

'We will kill him.'

'Do you guarantee to me here and now, do you swear on your life and the lives of your loved ones, that no one else will lose their life in the pursuit of taking his?'

'You know very well it's not that . . .'

'It's a yes or no question.'

He was silent.

'Exactly,' she said. 'I will not sanction any action that puts my people at risk.'

'Every fight is a risk,' he countered.

'And this is a fight that serves no purpose.'

Zahm, aghast, struggled to find words to accurately convey his disgust.

'No strategic purpose,' she continued. 'Revenge was always Father's way, but that's not my way . . . Unless there is some as yet undisclosed intelligence to show me otherwise?'

She gave Zahm plenty of time to provide that intel, but there was none. She knew it. He knew it.

'Exactly,' she said again. 'The only purpose of this operation would be to exact vengeance on someone who never sought to hurt us.'

'He did hurt us.'

'And pain fades. Wounds heal, do they not? Unless we refuse to let them. If we keep picking at the scab it continues to bleed. This is a wound that is already healed and that already has a scar. We're not gaining another wound.'

'I will gladly die to avenge our dead.'

'That's the problem,' she said. 'I don't want you to die. I don't want anyone else to die.'

'No one will,' he insisted. 'This time will be different. This time—'

'This is not a discussion,' she said, interrupting. 'The decision has been made and I've made it. Mossad will observe the killer only. We will gather intelligence from a distance, but there will be no direct action made against him. It's over.'

Zahm said, realisation hitting him at last, 'This is like an unexpected break-up, isn't it?' He didn't wait for an answer from Elkayam. 'You're giving me this news in a public setting so I won't make a scene. I have to hand it to you, Karmia, you really do think of everything.'

Stone-faced, she said, 'I don't give a damn if you make a scene. Scream if you feel like it. Shout. Tell me how much of a bitch I am.'

'Because you have people surrounding me ... behind you, red cap and blue jacket; behind me, mirrored sunglasses ... the beige Toyota SUV across the street.' He kept his gaze on her as he spoke. 'But that still makes no sense. It's not as though I'm going to attack you, is it?'

'Do you think I would need their help if you did? And that's not all you're wrong about,' Elkayam said, shaking her head at him. 'I knew you would make a scene and I didn't want the higher-ups to witness it. That's why we're doing it here. I'm protecting you from yourself. However much Father shielded you from the mess in Bulgaria, that stain has never gone away. And since he can no longer help you, it's up to me now. I don't expect a thank you.'

'Good.'

She said, 'We've decided it's best if you step back from operational planning for a while. Let's say until your frustrations fade and you understand the value of a more considered approach.'

'Who is "we"? You're in charge now.'

'I don't want to order you, Ari,' Elkayam said. 'I want you to agree with me.'

'Would you like me to begin calling you Mother?'

There had been no change in Elkayam's expression. Like Zahm, she had absorbed all of Father's lessons, to dull her empathy, to make her a better assassin. Unlike Zahm, however, she had also learned to master her other emotions too. None of his words, his anger, had any effect on her.

She said, 'I've decided it would be best for you to run a training exercise for the next few days.'

All Zahm could say was, 'Why?'

'It's just a few days.'

'You mean until the conference in Scotland is over?'

'A week at most,' she said.

'To keep me occupied, to keep me under observation until I no longer know where to find him.'

Each of the words that passed Zahm's lips tasted like poison.

'I think it's for the best, don't you?'

He looked to the Toyota SUV across the street, to the man in the red cap sitting behind Elkayam, then peered back over his shoulder to look at the woman in the mirrored sunglasses.

'Now it makes sense why you brought the extra bodies,' he said, turning his gaze back to her. 'In case I refuse to go on this *training* exercise. I'm guessing it will just so happen to be run in the centre of a military installation with round-the-clock security.'

'You're a good man, you're loyal,' Elkayam began, 'you've served Mossad well, you've served your people well. I know you won't refuse an order, but the higher-ups don't know you like I do.'

'I'm afraid you don't know me at all.'

'Do not do anything you will regret. Ari, you need to let this go.'

Zahm stared down at his open palm, at the hatred he had held there for so long.

'Our ultimate revenge is our continued existence,' she said as she looked around at the other people in the café, in the street, enjoying their lives. 'Never forget that.'

Zahm didn't hear. He stood.

On cue, the man in the red cap did the same and the doors of the Toyota across the street opened and two men climbed out. Zahm didn't need to look over his shoulder to know the woman in the mirrored sunglasses had risen too.

'Just a few days?'

Elkayam nodded. 'That's right. It's for the best.'

Zahm nodded too. 'Okay. If that's what will put your mind at ease.'

'I appreciate your understanding. I know this is hard for you. I know how close you are with Father.'

As Zahm left the boundaries of the café, with the man in the red cap and the woman in mirrored sunglasses trailing behind him, he thought about Father lying on his deathbed, unable to speak, unable to even open his eyes, and yet he had shed a single tear when Zahm had told him the news that they had found Helyeph.

As Zahm crossed the street and approached the Toyota that was parked adjacent to a restaurant with diners eating at tables on the wide pavement, he thought about a time in Switzerland when Father had requested his presence. Father had cried then too as he told Zahm about the deaths of his surrogate children in Minsk.

*My son, I want your unit to avenge them.*

'Tough break,' one of the Mossad operatives standing outside the SUV said as Zahm neared.

'Yeah,' the guy in the red cap, the team leader, said. 'This is bullshit. We're all with you, man. We have to take you to the base at Barkan. We don't want to, but orders are orders.'

'I appreciate that,' Zahm said. 'I know you're only doing as you're told.'

The lead operative said, 'Thanks. No hard feelings, yeah?'

'None at all,' he agreed. 'Which is why I swear I'm not going to hurt any of you any more than is necessary.'

A confused expression, then, 'Wait ... what?'

# FIFTY-SEVEN

Zahm shot out a kick to the team leader's closer leg, sweeping it out from under him and dropping him to the pavement, where a second kick caught him in the face.

The other three operatives were slow to react, fully convinced that any confrontation had been avoided. Their arms had fallen back to their sides, their defences lowered.

Zahm had landed a couple of punches on the next-closest operative before the other two could respond.

Not only were they Mossad trained, experts in Krav Maga like Zahm, they had been selected for this task because they were strong and they were tough. They could take a shot.

Against multiple opponents in an open space, aggression and positioning were everything. Each time Zahm landed a strike on one of the operatives, he immediately moved position; attacking another; never staying still, never letting them surround him as they tried to do so several times.

Throwing one over the bonnet of the Toyota, he grabbed

a chair by its legs and swung it in a one-hundred-and-eighty-degree semicircle because even without seeing, he knew the woman he had just knocked to the floor via a leg sweep would be back on her feet and rushing up behind him.

He was right, the woman charging headfirst into the swinging arc of the chair that sent her straight back down to the pavement.

The lead guy had stood back up by then, taking a few steps to steady himself as his sensibilities began to return.

For now, Zahm ignored him because the one on the other side of the Toyota was up again and rounding it to attack so Zahm ditched the chair – too unwieldy to be of any use against someone who could see it coming – and met the operative head on, delivering a low stomp kick aiming at the lead knee but catching him a little higher on the thigh.

A miss or not, it buckled his charge, forcing him to stagger in an uncontrolled manner into the elbow strikes that Zahm was throwing in readiness. The inertia of his charge too great to stop now, he slammed straight into Zahm and sent them both as one flailing mass that tripped over the woman on the ground recovering from the chair to the face.

The lead operative had picked that exact moment to throw himself back into the fight. This, although honourable, made the situation worse for all of them as he charged only to immediately trip over in the melee.

Zahm's athleticism was greater – and he had taken no punishment compared to the others – and so was much quicker to adapt. However, with three of them now as overlapping and interlocking obstacles on top and below him, he was not the first back one up to his feet.

The one who was reached into a pocket and withdrew a baton that he whipped to full length with a flick of his wrist.

Spitting out blood, he growled, 'I didn't want it to come to this.'

The baton came at Zahm from a high angle, the operative pushing out his offhand to keep Zahm at distance, so Zahm backed away, opting to dodge the weapon instead of trying to parry or disarm it and risk a broken arm or worse.

The dazed operatives on the ground formed an obstacle by default, almost tripping Zahm without trying before he stepped backwards over the squirming limbs, his attacker having a better view of the hazard around over his teammates without trouble.

Continuing to dodge, Zahm backtracked until he reached where the chair he'd discarded had ended up. Lifting it in both hands, he held it by the back with the legs out in front of him, and stabbed with them at the baton-wielding operative, out-ranging his own weapon.

Zahm thrust the chair legs at the man's lead hand until the weapon had been knocked aside, before switching his hold on the chair so he could batter the operative with the back of it and knocked him into the side of the vehicle, winded. The baton flew from his grip as he used his arms to interrupt the path of Zahm's next attack, preventing the chair connecting with his face, but Zahm kept attacking with the piece of furniture until the wood was cracked and the backing splintered.

With his diaphragm paralysed, no air in his lungs, and his arms numbed from the chair, the operative had few options to mount an effective counter-offensive.

So, he backed away.

Zahm would have let him retreat – he didn't want to hurt

him in the first place – but he could not risk the operative rejoining the fight when the other three had managed to untangle themselves and were back on their feet. Therefore, Zahm threw the chair at the fleeing man.

Although the chair's aerodynamic capabilities were almost non-existent, the dazed operative could not move with any speed and the chair impacted him between the shoulder blades, knocking him off his feet mid-stride and sending him straight down.

He hit the pavement face-first.

A civilian, watching from nearby, winced. 'Ouch.'

The lead operative was next to his feet to attack Zahm from behind, who managed to turn around in time to counter but could do nothing to prevent taking the full force of the man slamming into him at hip height.

His balance compromised, Zahm shot out his feet to widen his stance and avoid being taken to the ground, but the inertia of the charge drove him backwards until his back collided with the Toyota. The metal bodywork warped and dented.

Bent over, and with his arms wrapped around Zahm's hips in an attempt to take him down, the lead guy could do nothing to prevent the hammer fists and heel palms thrown at the back of his head. Even with their power limited due to Zahm's poor positioning and leverage, the brainstem was an extremely vulnerable part of the skull. Zahm only did enough damage to put the man out of the fight, stopping when he felt the grip around him weaken.

Tossing him aside, Zahm sent a punting kick to the face of the woman in the process of pushing herself back to her feet.

The last remaining man wore the expression of someone

who wanted to back out of a bad decision but knew they had come too far. He took a deep breath and stepped forward to throw fast, accurate punches that Zahm intercepted with his arms and shoulders, happy to barrel through the attack so he could land a single, devastating punch of his own.

With all four operatives squirming in pain or unconscious, Zahm took the car keys from the pocket of the lead operative and climbed behind the wheel of the Toyota.

On the far side of the road, Karmia Elkayam stood watching, her sidearm in hand and pointed his way.

They both knew she wasn't going to shoot him, so he nodded his goodbye and started the engine.

# FIFTY-EIGHT

The thief was easy to find. The conference literature had a schedule of all events and the participants therein. With Woodcroft listed as a participant in several, they knew for certain where and when to find him. Lambert had arranged guest passes for Victor and Raven, although the broker did not know for whom the second pass would be, beyond their gender.

'It's cover,' Victor had explained. 'I'll blend in better if I'm one half of a couple instead of a singular whole.'

In one of the main lodge's three main conference halls, Woodcroft was on a panel discussing the training of insurgent forces in Africa and the Middle East, and how such endeavours more often than not backfired on Western governments. They were broad, inconclusive talking points, but the audience seemed receptive.

'They knew all this from the eighties,' Raven whispered to Victor. 'Fast forward a few decades everyone refused to listen because it didn't suit their agendas.'

When Woodcroft spoke, he did so in a confident, relaxed voice. Unlike the other delegates, he'd had first-hand experience of such training operations in his days with the Special Air Service.

After the event had concluded – without any actionable strategies – Woodcroft spent time in the hotel hallways and lobby chatting with guests and delegates. Throughout the lodge and its grounds were clusters of men and women in business attire who were attending the conference. Some had lanyards with laminated passes hanging in front of their sternums; others had name badges pinned to their lapels.

Woodcroft cut an impressive figure. He had a tall, solid physique, straight-backed, and yet gave off an easy-going demeanour. He wore a tailored stone-brown suit and brown brogues, no tie, the collar of his charcoal buttoned-down shirt open. He had a short, neat beard and greying hair only a little longer than Victor's own. Although he walked with a leisurely gait, as though he was in no rush and had no troubles, his head rotated back and forth, his eyes in constant motion. He may have dressed like a wealthy gentleman, but Victor saw a soldier on patrol in hostile territory.

With his jacket buttoned and the cut of his suit a flattering, close-fitting style, it was simple to deduce Woodcroft was unarmed. No surprise in the UK, of course, although Victor had encountered enough firearms in the British Isles to know that just because they were illegal didn't mean they were unobtainable.

'He's hot,' Raven said as she and Victor pretended to chat.

'If you say so.'

'Don't be jealous.'

On paper, Woodcroft was present for the weekend on

behalf of a munitions manufacturer, Zeus Industries, which produced training ammunition and other non-lethal military hardware. He had a pin of the company's logo on his lapel: a fist holding a thunderbolt. Woodcroft was an ambassador who offered an accredited expert validation of the product during the firm's presentations. He was also to hold a demonstration of the ammunition the following day.

Raven rubbed at her ribs and said, 'I'm going to go back to my room and take some painkillers. Are you good on your own?'

Victor nodded. 'Are you okay?'

'The hitter the Consensus sent after Albrecht, and maybe me, was no walk in the park.'

'Are you sure you're operational?'

'That depends.'

'On what?'

'Whether you're asking if I'm okay to be put on an operating table and for you to cut me open to see what's inside, or if I'm capable of completing our objective?'

'I mean the latter, but now I'm wondering if maybe slicing you up with a scalpel is not the better use of both our times.'

Her eyes narrowed, and he felt both evaluated and judged. 'A man quips when the truth is too uncomfortable to admit.'

'The only truth I'm comfortable to admit is that I didn't use a strong enough dose when I poisoned you back in Canada.'

'Thank you for proving my point,' she said, looking smug. 'It's comforting to know I'm always right.'

'Go and take your pills,' Victor said.

Lambert's dossier put Woodcroft at forty-six, six-three and eighty-five kilograms. The dossier was wrong, Victor saw. He didn't doubt the age and the height were accurate, but the weight was a good five kilos too light. Woodcroft was solid and strong, with a narrow waist tapering in a notable V shape to his shoulders. Even had Victor not known anything about his history in the 22nd Special Air Service, everything about Woodcroft told him the man was a threat.

Then he became a problem.

Victor's practised gaze analysed people in seconds, in fractions of a second sometimes. He had been doing it hundreds of times a day for many years. So, he only looked at Woodcroft for a moment and only then under the guise of a more sweeping, natural glance around the room.

Although Victor diverted his gaze, he kept Woodcroft in his peripheral vision and saw that Woodcroft analysed him in return.

A soldier on patrol in a hostile environment, not a professional assassin, Woodcroft's searching glance was not as efficient as Victor's own. That gaze paused on him for no more than two seconds, which was pretty fast for someone who was no professional. Victor was impressed.

And again, because he was no professional, Woodcroft's reaction was not invisible.

The short pause was enough to tell Victor that Woodcroft saw through his veneer of normalcy. Maybe the man didn't quite know why just yet, although it didn't matter because the next time he saw Victor he would pay him far more attention.

The care package Lambert had arranged that Victor had collected prior to leaving Glasgow consisted of several cheap burner phones, first aid supplies, surveillance equipment, two Taurus G2C handguns along with magazines, ammunition and suppressors, and a card-cloning device. About the size of an external hard drive, the device had a narrow slot for the cards, a couple of buttons, a port for charging, and nothing else. All of the controls were applied remotely, via an app. Simple to use, it required no more skill than the ability to insert a magnetic card into a slot, which typically would be a credit card, and use the app to copy the data stored, before removing the card, inserting a blank card, and again using the app to paste the information and transform the previously blank card into a clone of the one copied.

After Raven had finished taking her painkillers, they found a housekeeper in one of the bedroom-lined hallways. Victor engaged the woman in conversation, distracting her with questions about sheets and turning over the room. He extended the discussion with a long-running diatribe about the various cleaning and cosmetic products provided by the lodge, giving Raven the opportunity to use her sleight-of-hand skills to take the master key card from the maid's belt, where it was attached with a bungee cord, and insert it into the card-cloning device.

The cloning of the information from the card took Raven no more than seven seconds and she returned the card without the housekeeper noticing.

An extra-observant security guard monitoring the CCTV might wonder what Raven was doing so close to the maid. However, careful and deliberate positioning meant the specifics of her actions would go unseen, with the security guard seeing only her back.

'Admit it,' Raven said when they were out of earshot.

'Admit what?' Victor asked.

'That this life of yours is easier when you have a partner. Don't try to deny it. You know I'm right. All you have to do is say what is obvious to both of us.'

'What would be the point?' Victor asked. 'If I deny it and offer a counterpoint, you will just say I'm lying. And if I agree, it changes nothing.'

She smirked at him. 'Then it changes nothing.'

# FIFTY-NINE

There were no broken bones, at least. Possible hairline fractures to jawbones, cheekbones and orbital bones not-withstanding. Plenty of bruising, nosebleeds and lots of swelling. Some of the operatives were going to need stitches. By the time Karmia Elkayam had been able to get up and try to intervene, Zahm was already behind the wheel of the Toyota and speeding off down the road.

She unlocked her phone to call it in.

'Four of you,' she said to the sorry collection of Mossad's "finest" while she waited for the line to connect, 'and you still failed to restrain him.'

'It happened so fast,' one protested.

'Did you expect he would attack you slowly?'

No one offered a response.

When Herzog answered the phone, she explained what had happened in as few words as possible. 'Zahm refused and your heavies failed to stop him stealing their vehicle.'

'I won't say I told you so,' Herzog said, 'but I told you so. Is he going to do what I think he's going to do?'

Elkayam said, 'Yes.'

'We'll have people at the airport.'

'He won't use the airport.'

'We'll notify every border checkpoint. It's not as though he's difficult to spot.'

'Which is why Father trained him so well,' she said. 'If you think he won't be out of the country before nightfall then you have no idea how good your assassins really are.'

'I told you to do this at headquarters,' Herzog said again. 'Now we have one of our own going rogue on a revenge mission to the United Kingdom. Whatever happens, we're not coming out of this looking good. I had better start working on our cover story. Have our assets in the UK head to Scotland and let's hope we can intercept him before he arrives at the conference.'

'No,' she said. 'If we do that we make things worse, not better. And there's simply no need. This will resolve itself.'

'Explain.'

'Either Zahm succeeds or he fails,' Elkayam began. 'Neither creates any problems for us to fix.'

'Then tell me why. What happens if he fails to kill this killer?'

'I will grieve for him.'

'That's not what I meant.'

'I know it's not what you meant,' she said. 'If Zahm fails, it will be because he was killed in the process. No one aside from us will know why. However he gets to Scotland, it will be using identification that labels him as anything but Israeli. His corpse will be that of a Syrian, Jordanian, Iraqi ...

maybe Egyptian. If his corpse is discovered, then MI5 will waste their time trying to solve an impossible mystery before moving on to more important matters of national security.'

'And if he should succeed?'

She answered, 'If he succeeds, he won't make a mess and yet he won't get caught. It's not as though the killer has anyone who will miss him, is it? And Zahm will come straight back home, I assure you. He will gladly, proudly, accept any punishment we deem appropriate for disobeying orders.'

'If you're wrong,' Herzog began, 'then your career in Mossad is going to become very difficult.'

Before she hung up, Elkayam said, 'I'm never wrong.'

# SIXTY

The next morning, Woodcroft was up bright and early to take a run around the estate. It would be impossible to follow him while he exercised and have any hope of remaining unseen, so Victor did not attempt it. He witnessed the start of the run and the warm-up that preceded it, which consisted of some light stretching. Woodcroft wore tatty old joggers and a sweatshirt, his trainers equally well used. He took no water with him and did not have any headphones or earbuds to play music. Whether these were tactical decisions to ensure he had his hands unencumbered at all times and his senses sharp, Victor could not be sure. There was just as much chance this was just the way the man preferred to go for a jog.

Woodcroft had a long stride, moving with the athleticism of someone with a high level of endurance. He set a quick pace for himself, no idle jog but a swift run that would rapidly elevate his heart rate.

No case, no backpack in which to hold many documents, so Victor left him to it.

While he waited for Woodcroft to return, he ordered a couple of coffees from the lounge bar and took a seat outside on the patio overlooking the loch.

By the time Raven joined him, a waiter had already brought the coffees over and Victor passed one across to her.

'Sugar in your coffee?' he asked.

'No, thank you.' She paused, then added, 'That's when you're supposed to say "you're sweet enough as it is".'

'Since when?'

'Since always. It's a nice thing people say to one another from time to time.'

'I cannot tell if you are being serious here or not.'

'Of course I'm serious.' Her tone was curt. 'What's the big deal about being nice? It costs you nothing and I know you don't mean it, so where's the harm?'

'I prefer honesty. Everything is simpler when we only say what we mean.'

'So you tell people you're a hired killer when they ask what you do for a living?'

Thinking of the drink he'd shared with Emilie in Rotterdam, he said, 'Sometimes.'

'And you've never even told me your name,' she added. 'After all this time, after all we've been through together, you can't possibly think I would do anything with it. I mean, do you?'

'A man I once knew … a former friend … he used to say, "people like us don't change, we adapt". I adapt when I need to, but I don't change. If you think one day you'll see a whole new side of me, Constance, then you're deluding yourself.

There is no other side to me. This is the best it's ever going to get.'

Woodcroft was gone for forty minutes. When he reappeared in Victor's field of view, his pace was only a little slower than at the start of the run. He was not going to win any elite cross-country races, but Woodcroft's fitness level was impressive nonetheless for a man in his mid-forties. Certainly, he would be in the fifth percentile or higher for a man of any age when it came to cardiovascular fitness. And his morning's exercise did not end with the run. Sweaty and dishevelled, Woodcroft performed a series of strength and mobility exercises. He used the branches of trees to do pull-ups and then chin-ups. An efficient order, Victor noted, since the change in hand positioning enabled the biceps to assist the back muscles to a greater extent in the second exercise, which meant Woodcroft was able to perform more total repetitions. He followed with press-ups, star jumps, burpees; he did crunches, and variations of hip bridges, curtsy squats and finally a number of yoga poses.

Raven said, 'Must be nice.'

'What must be nice?'

'Exercising because you want to,' she explained, 'not because you need to.'

'Everyone needs to exercise.'

'I dream of being a couch potato,' she said in a wistful tone. 'Some people want to grow old with someone. I just want to get fat with someone. Waddaya say?'

He did not answer. Instead, asking, 'How is your brother, Ben, doing?'

'He doesn't talk to me any more,' she answered with a

sigh. 'Which I understand, I guess. I mean ... Well, I put him in danger, I put his family in danger. I totally get why he wants nothing to do with me, but it still hurts. It really hurts, you know?'

Victor was silent.

'No, of course you don't understand actual human connection.'

'I can imagine it,' he said.

'I suppose after all this I could stop by his farm. Assuming he still has the farm, I mean. Maybe he sold up and became a jazz musician.'

'He likes jazz?'

'No, he doesn't like jazz. No one likes jazz. It's like nails on a blackboard only there's a whole band performing it on a stage, each with their own blackboard all scraping their nails without the common decency to do so in harmony.'

'I see,' Victor said. 'Why don't you tell me how you really feel?'

'My dad loved jazz,' she explained. 'He'd play it in the car on every trip, even though he knew we hated it.'

'His car, his rules.'

'My ears, my rules. Anyway, why are we even talking about jazz?'

'You were saying Ben might have moved and taken up a new line of work.'

'Oh yeah,' she began. 'Or he's still there, still growing corn or ... do they grow corn in Scotland or is that just the Midwest?'

'I seem to remember cows.'

Raven stood. 'I'm going to take a nap.'

*

By the time Woodcroft had finished his callisthenics and yoga, the grey sweatshirt was almost as dark as Victor's charcoal suit. Still, Woodcroft wasn't done, heading to the lodge's fitness suite. Victor did not know what he still had left to exercise, but perhaps at this point he was more interested in a sauna than further exertion.

Again, Victor did not follow him inside. The information provided by the client was inflexible in the instruction that Woodcroft would deliver to his contact by handing over hard copies of the stolen plans. A briefcase's worth. Until Victor saw Woodcroft in possession of such a case or bag then there was no need to shadow him that closely. So long as he knew where the man was, it was enough.

Still, Victor did not like the questions that remained unanswered. Did Woodcroft know the identity of his buyer, or would he be meeting Gallier for the first time when the exchange was made? Would the Frenchman arrive at the estate only for the time of collection, or was he already here? Was Gallier one of the many people Woodcroft had exchanged words with so far during the conference? Had the buyer sat in attendance at his company's presentation?

The intensity and thoroughness of Woodcroft's routine had been inspiring, even to a man of Victor's physicality. It even gave him some interesting ideas of how he might mix up his own fitness regime. What was also interesting was the fact that Woodcroft conducted this workout at all. Despite the dangerous activities he was involved in, he felt no need to preserve his strength and energy in the same way Victor did, who saved the most demanding exercising for when he wasn't working. Had he performed an equally intensive workout himself, then should he need to be at his physical best either later today or even the next morning, that best would be impeded. The body took time to recover and the more intensive the exercise, the longer the recovery.

More interesting, however, than both Woodcroft feeling no need to conserve his strength and the ideas he gave Victor for his own training, was the fact that Victor was not the only person paying Woodcroft so much attention.

At first, Victor had mistaken the woman as a colleague or partner of Woodcroft's. Seeing how interested she had been in what the man was doing, it seemed that perhaps she had been waiting for an opportunity to converse with him, maybe to discuss the trade that was to take place later on, but no, Victor decided.

She had made no move to engage him despite ample opportunity. Similarly, this woman had not followed Woodcroft to the fitness suite where, almost certainly, there would be a degree of privacy either in the changing rooms or sauna.

Given the man was a delegate at the conference, a speaker and representative of Zeus Industries whose presence had been listed for weeks in advance, and whose photograph and profile appeared in the conference brochure and on various signs, there had been no need to watch Woodcroft from afar to learn who he was or what he was doing. Certainly, no intelligence operative would have needed to watch him like that. She would know in which cottage he was staying and could retrieve the stolen information at almost any time, if that was her goal.

Unless, like Victor, she was trying to locate Gallier . . . but the odds there was anyone else aside from himself, Lambert and Lambert's client knowing of Woodcroft's illicit activities had to be astronomical.

Which left only one reason to watch Woodcroft like Victor was doing: this woman was like Victor.

But unlike Victor, who meant Woodcroft no harm because his target was the buyer, she intended to kill Woodcroft.

When Victor synced back up with Raven after her nap, he told her, 'We have a complication.'

# SIXTY-ONE

There had been a look the woman gave Woodcroft, the kind of gaze usually reserved for observing the object of one's affections. There was no affection in this look, of course, but she had that same longing to be close to him. A certain excitement and anticipation.

Victor knew she enjoyed her work.

A mistake to have let this show, although understandable. She was too focused on her target and not her surroundings. Because she was intending to kill him, she watched him closely. She was trying to learn his habits, his routines, his strengths and, most importantly, his weaknesses. To determine when best to strike and how to strike required a significant degree of preparation and understanding of the target. In comparison, Victor had only to watch out for a case or bag capable of carrying hundreds of pages of raw data.

She was still in her twenties, so maybe she had yet to learn the value of blending into the background. Being noticed at all was never a good thing because even if there was nothing to notice in that moment, being noticed now meant closer attention paid next time. The more times that Victor was seen, the more chances that someone would begin to ask questions about him. Who was he? What was he doing? The more questions asked, the more chance of coming up with the correct answers.

The ebb and flow of people through the lodge, the conference and the estate let Victor follow the woman from a close distance without giving himself away. Like Victor, her cover as a guest allowed her to access the various panels, talks and demonstrations.

At breakfast, she took a seat at the far end of the dining room in one corner, her back protected by the wall and her field of view over the rest of the space unobstructed. She favoured a light meal: fruit, eggs and lots of coffee. She had a sweet tooth too, he noticed, but a high degree of willpower. A chocolate muffin sat almost untouched on a plate, only a few small bites taken from it.

The only notable times she kept her distance from Woodcroft throughout the day were when he was scheduled to appear at a talk or demonstration. That made sense. She wasn't going to learn much about the man himself or how best to kill him when he was sitting on a stage talking into a microphone. Clearly, she was not planning a public execution. In these breaks, she ate more food or exercised. She enjoyed swimming lengths in the lodge's indoor pool, he found. While she was doing so, Victor took a step back. Even if her attention was more focused on her mission than external threats, it would not have taken long for her to notice a lone man watching her swim.

But Raven could do what he could not.

'Her name is Madeline Belford,' she told him as they had afternoon tea at a table in a corner of the lodge's expansive lobby. She spoke in a matter-of-fact tone that veered almost into boredom, as if finding this out had not only been a simple process for her but one that was a complete waste of her skill set. 'I timed it so I was in the changing rooms when she arrived, so I could see which locker she used. I began my own swim before she had finished changing so it appeared natural when I got out of the pool while she was still doing lengths. Each locker comes with a key already inserted, which is attached to a rubber wristband. The locks are decent enough, but no effort to pick either. I went through her things and her ID seems genuine, so it's either her real name or her legend is rock solid.'

'Now we just need to find out which room she's staying in,' Victor said. Then we can—'

'She's in room 331,' Raven said. 'You have to sign in at the spa's reception desk to use the pool or the sauna. I had to do so and so did Madeline. On the way out, I took a glance and saw where she had signed in, along with her room number.'

'Good work,' Victor said.

'Oh, please,' Raven replied. 'A child could do it. Do you want me to have a snoop around her room, see what I can find out about her?'

'No,' Victor answered. 'You can keep eyes on Madeline while I do so. I think I have about exhausted the limits of my anonymity with her at this point. Even with all of her attentions directed at Woodcroft, she still strikes me as a competent professional. She will notice me eventually, especially if I don't leave her alone.'

'Your call,' Raven said. 'Don't go rifling around through her underwear.'

'Don't be disgusting, Constance.'

'What's disgusting about it?' Raven asked. 'She is kind of cute. Aren't you curious to know if she wears a thong or not?'

'I know you make these kind of remarks purely to get a rise out of me,' Victor told her. 'So you may as well give up trying.'

'I will never give up. One day I'm going to break through this icy façade of yours to reach something approaching a personality beneath it. I'm sure you had one at some point long ago. No one is born this dull. While I do appreciate that you put a lot of work into being boring, since it's a learned behaviour, it means it can also be unlearned.'

'You're already fighting one impossible-to-win battle against the Consensus,' Victor reminded her. 'Do you really need to wage another war in which there can be no victory?'

She didn't answer that. 'Any idea who else is interested in Woodcroft? Who would want him dead?'

'I don't think we know enough about the man to speculate as to what enemies he might have or guess who might profit from his death.'

'But what we do know is that Woodcroft is in bed with the Consensus whether he understands who he's dealing with or not. So he's a threat to them by default. Which to me sounds like a pretty good reason for removing the last link in the chain.'

'Then surely they would be after you too? They would have to know by now you were playing Ysiv, and that you killed their man in Hamburg. If Madeline was after you too

338

then I think we would have noticed her before now.'

'I agree,' she said, 'which leads me to believe that this hit was arranged before my trip to Hamburg and is not in response to my actions there. Once Woodcroft has delivered the HEL plans he's just a liability, a gap in their defences that needs to be filled.'

'Then why don't they simply kill him and take the plans?'

'Then he still is of some use – only not in the way it appears. They didn't ask him here to make the exchange, they lured him here to die. They want to remove Woodcroft as a liability, and tell a story with his death and the information that he has this time around. No doubt with the blame deliberately pointing away from them but somewhere else that can be of benefit . . . Maybe they're not even after these plans and they never were. They could be trying to bring someone down with its theft. They might have an enemy they don't want to kill, they want to hurt.' She paused to process her words, her thoughts, and what they meant. She said, 'Whatever they're doing, we have to stop them.'

'I fully intend to stop them, Constance,' Victor told her, 'because the only way of keeping this client onside is to kill Woodcroft's buyer, the Frenchman named Gallier, if you're right. And to do that Woodcroft has to make contact with Gallier and, quite naturally, he needs to be alive to do so. But that's it as far as I'm concerned. This guerrilla war of yours is yours and yours alone. I am glad that, unlike in Helsinki, our interests have continued to align, but I don't want you to take that as our motives also lining up. I need to put things right with this client and that's it. I don't want you going rogue with this and taking matters into your own hands. We handle this my way, in a manner of my choosing. If a corpse turns up in this place before the conference is over, the lie of the land will change completely. Woodcroft might get cold feet, or Gallier decides to change the place of the exchange or call if off entirely.'

Raven said, 'Then how do you want to do this?'

'So far we only really know her name,' Victor began. 'If we're going to deal with her without turning the whole conference into a crime scene then we need to know a lot more about her. Woodcroft has a two-hour presentation scheduled for later this afternoon. During which, you keep an eye on Madeline and I'll check out her room.'

'Told you,' Raven said.

'I know I'm going to regret asking, but what did you tell me?'

'That these things are easier when you're not operating alone. Or, as I like to say, teamwork makes the dream work.'

He raised an eyebrow.

'You should stop doing that,' she said with a playful grin. 'You're developing a wrinkle.'

# SIXTY-TWO

Woodcroft's demonstration was set to take place over a two-hour time slot with a short interval at the halfway point, and given Madeline was apt not to keep tabs on her target during his scheduled events, Raven was curious what she would get up to during the time period of the event. Given she had already eaten not long before and had already taken a swim, two hours seemed a lot of time to kill. Maybe she would get her nails done in the spa, maybe she would read a book, Raven wasn't sure.

But she wanted to find out.

As the man she called Jonathan stayed close to Woodcroft for the demonstration, Raven shadowed Madeline to her room. Raven did not follow close enough to see her enter it, instead witnessing only Madeline enter the elevator and then, a few minutes later, following and pausing outside her door to listen for sounds of Madeline's presence, which were the radio playing and the shower running.

Raven returned to the lobby to wait there, figuring if

Madeline left her room, she would come out this way. Although there were multiple ways in and out of the main lodge, there were few reasons to use them unless heading to very specific parts of the estate, none of which were relevant for the conference.

Maybe after her shower, Madeline would take that nap or otherwise relax and unwind in the room, in which case Raven would remain in the lobby passing the time reading the complimentary newspapers and sipping the occasional coffee.

However, about twenty minutes after Raven had listened to the shower running in Madeline's room, her mark stepped out of the elevator. Previously, she had been dressed in smart, professional attire, consisting of trousers, blouse and blazer, and shoes with a modest two-inch heel. Now, she wore a baggy jumper, jeans and knee-high boots. Her blonde hair was pulled back into a ponytail.

She headed straight through the lobby to the exit at a swift pace. Not in a rush and yet eager to get on. She was clearly not going for a simple stroll; Madeline had somewhere to go and was keen to get there in good time. The change of clothes suggested she was leaving the estate. Or, at least, going somewhere within it that was not the main lodge and accompanying buildings.

Raven waited until Madeline was out of sight and then stood up herself. She had paid for her drink when it was served so there was nothing stopping her leaving when necessary. By the time she had stepped outside the lodge and onto the parking area in front of the building, Madeline had crossed the space and was walking along the driveway.

Raven sent a message to her partner using one of the burner phones his broker had supplied: *The coast is clear.*

Following, Raven walked at a similar, if slower, pace. She wanted the distance to build as much as possible given the driveway was relatively straight and almost devoid of foot traffic. If Madeline turned around then Raven wanted to be seen only as a shape in the distance, shapeless and indistinct.

From her preparatory works, Raven knew the layout of the estate and knew that the only place of any relevance along the driveway within the grounds was the grounds-keeper's cottage near the main entrance.

The driveway was long but still only a five-minute walk from the entrance to the lodge. Because there were no bends or curves of any note it was easy to keep a couple of hundred metres behind Madeline and still have her visible ahead. At that kind of distance, Raven could only tell it was her because she already knew. She was little more than a tiny, blurry figure – as Raven would be in return should Madeline check her six.

As she closed in on the groundskeeper's cottage, however, Raven decreased the distance between them. If she was going to go inside or meet her partner nearby, Raven needed to be closer to witness the specifics. This increased the risk of being spotted, of course, but so far Madeline did not seem concerned about being followed at all. That could be a sign of overconfidence or a simple ignorance to the realities of the profession. She might not feel at risk. Every contract she had ever fulfilled could have been a walk in the park so far. She might never once have been a target herself.

Sometimes, the only way of understanding the need to take more precautions was to find out the hard way you weren't taking enough, Raven knew.

Trees flanking the driveway provided nearby cover for Raven to utilise as she closed the distance. Doing so was a double-edged sword because, although she could duck behind a thick tree trunk to ensure Madeline did not see her should she turn around, Raven also had to then emerge from behind that tree trunk not knowing if Madeline was still looking her way to catch her in the act. That kind of appearance would seem conspicuous even from a distance. Therefore, Raven started to use the trees only when she wanted to get much closer as Madeline reached the cottage.

The building was a small, handsome two-storey structure set back from the driveway and surrounded by a low stone wall. To Raven's surprise, Madeline did not approach the cottage after all. She walked by it without slowing and exited the estate through the main gate.

She took a left turn, disappearing out of sight beyond the hedgerows but heading south. A village lay in that direction, maybe a mile away. Given Madeline liked to be near to her target, Raven did not imagine Madeline would be walking any further than the village. A rough twenty minutes there at Madeline's pace, including the walk along the long driveway to the lodge, and another twenty minutes back didn't leave much room in which to manoeuvre. She had already burnt up another twenty minutes showering and getting changed, so whatever she was doing, she had only about an hour to finish it. Although, she may have already done enough shadowing of Woodcroft that she no longer felt the need to keep close to him until it was time to strike.

From her own research, Raven knew the village consisted of about thirty buildings in all, which were mostly residential but also included a post office, a grocer's and a pub. There were large towns with more resources a short drive away, but Madeline was not driving, unless she had a vehicle stashed somewhere in the village. Raven considered it far more likely that the village was Madeline's ultimate destination.

Maybe she had something to post, maybe she wanted to buy some cigarettes, or maybe she wanted a drink in the pub. All innocent enough, although Raven didn't believe in any of those explanations.

Madeline may have been carrying a small purse that could hold a letter or letter-sized object, except she was here to fulfil a contract not catch up with a pen pal. Similarly, at no point during the day had Raven seen Madeline smoking. Which left the pub.

A drink seemed unlikely given the lodge had three bars of its own, unless Madeline was not merely going to have a beverage but to meet someone there away from the lodge and the prying eyes of those inside.

But the question was, who was that someone?

# SIXTY-THREE

*The coast is clear.*

Victor would have preferred Raven to use purely factual information instead of idioms in her messages, but that conversation could wait for another time because he did not know how long he had before the *coast* became *unclear.* While Woodcroft was participating in the demonstration run by his employer, Madeline was elsewhere. He didn't need to know those specifics, just that Raven was watching her while she was doing so and that Victor therefore had the perfect opportunity to take a look inside Madeline's room.

Like a regular hotel, there were several entrances and exits and ways to ascend and descend through the various floors. Victor elected to use the stairs because that was his preferred manner, although he remembered Raven's words in Bucharest about it looking more natural to use the elevator. She was probably correct in this. No, she *was* correct. But Victor decided he would prefer to look unnatural and be alive than natural and dead. There were always compromises with such things.

Echoing footsteps in the stairwell told him he was not the only one using them. Five guys in dark suits were descending as he ascended: two wore navy, two charcoal and one a black pinstripe. They had the solid, square look of security personnel but not employees of the hotel. He took them to be part of a VIP's retinue, although whoever their client was, they must not require direct protection right now.

They were good too, because as Victor threaded between them on his way up, he felt their prying gazes, assessing him as he assessed them in return. They weren't at the level where they could hide it, but as he left their cluster he caught one glancing back over his shoulder. Whatever they thought of Victor, he warranted a second look.

No words were spoken and as he opened up the stairwell door on Madeline's floor he listened hard for any change in their pace that might suggest their interest in him had gestated into suspicion.

When he heard none, he continued on his way.

There was an inverse relationship between the quality of a hotel and the brightness of its hallway lighting. Cheap hotels tended to be as bright as daylight, while high-end establishments like this one had more muted, atmospheric illumination. Rich people did not want every year of their lives to be displayed in full on their faces under glaring fluorescent bulbs, Victor assumed. The thick carpeting meant he could walk with speed without making noise, which was useful since little sound escaped from the adjacent rooms and none from the wider hotel reached here.

He paused in front of the door to Madeline's room.

Maybe she had employed some measure to let her know if somebody trespassed in her space, but probably not. She had not displayed the professional paranoia elsewhere to indicate it would present here in her room. Even if she did, it was a hotel room, ultimately; a maid or someone from maintenance or management could access the room at any point they chose.

Using the cloned master magnetic card, he unlocked the door.

Her room was little different from Victor's own. Not a junior suite but one of the larger rooms that the lodge designated an executive double. The layout was the same, with only the smaller size and the absence of a sofa making up the differences.

Like his own room, Madeline's was so clean and neat and organised it did not seem lived in. He checked the wardrobe, he checked the drawers, finding clothes hung on coat hangers or folded neatly.

He was not surprised to discover there was no helpful itinerary or schedule to tell him how or when she planned to kill Woodcroft.

The wardrobe contained a small safe large enough to secure a compact laptop but not much else. Mostly used by guests to put jewellery, wallets and passports inside, it could also fit handguns or other small weapons. Given he found no other weapons inside the room, either they were in the safe or she had them on her person. Unless, of course, her specialties lay in accidents or suicides.

The bathroom was much the same as the rest of the space, clean and neat. Like the bathroom in Victor's junior suite, this one contained a washbasin with a shelf above it and above that a mirror. Next to the washbasin was a toilet and beyond that a walk-in shower cubicle with a sliding glass door.

She had a cosmetic bag on the shelf above the sink that contained make-up and skincare products, a hairbrush and medication: the contraceptive pill and some prescription hay fever tablets.

There was one notable fact about the bathroom, however, which told Victor a lot while also asking more questions.

The toilet seat had been left in the upright position.

Madeline Belford was not here as a lone operator.

She had a partner.

A man ...

... who then entered her hotel room.

# SIXTY-FOUR

Raven paused at the entrance to the estate. It was a risk to step out because she could not see Madeline's current position. For all she knew, Madeline had walked a few metres along the road then stopped and turned around to wait to see if anyone followed after her. If this were the case and Raven stepped out, then she would have fallen for the most basic countersurveillance technique in the book.

How long to wait? The longer Raven lingered, the longer Madeline was out of her sight, which was a fail by any definition of surveillance. She reminded herself that losing sight of her quarry was not necessarily a problem now, however. Given the village was the only walkable location, Raven already knew where Madeline was going. It was the professional inside her telling her not to lose a visual, but that professional had been trained and schooled in the arts of surveillance, countersurveillance and the associated skills. All invaluable, yet one of the most important lessons any professional learned could not be taught, only acquired by experience, a talent that had no name to describe it because it was a combination of knowledge, instinct and adaptability. It was knowing when rules needed to be broken. Even the best spymasters in the world could not teach it.

So, Raven waited.

She provided Madeline plenty of time in which to wait to see if she was being followed. Of course, Raven realised, Madeline had not needed to check her six while walking along the driveway from the lodge to the estate's entrance because all she had to do was leave and, shielded by the hedgerow, wait.

An achingly simple technique that also happened to be the perfect ruse.

Raven took a seat on one of the posts that lined the driveway at the entrance, between the hedgerow and the line of trees. She took out her phone and played with it like anyone else would do while waiting for someone or something. If Madeline reappeared, unconvinced that waiting behind the hedgerow was enough to expose a shadow, she would emerge only to see Raven doing nothing at all, not even looking her way.

The solution to a perfectly simple ruse was equally simple.

Raven was not necessarily the most patient of operatives, whether working for herself now against the Consensus or back when she'd performed black-bag jobs for Uncle Sam, but her nameless partner taught her the value of sometimes doing nothing at all.

When, after ten minutes' waiting – ten agonising, stressful, intense minutes of waiting – had passed, he was proved to be correct.

Raven exited the estate and rounded the hedgerow to find

Madeline was not there waiting to confront her. Instead, she was tiny in the distance. Raven couldn't help but smile. Because, had Madeline left the estate ten minutes ago and kept on walking, she would be so far along the road to the village that the changes in elevation would mean Raven should not be able to see her at all.

So, it had been worth the wait.

By Raven's calculations, Madeline had waited something like six or seven minutes before walking, assuming her pace now was the same as her pace had been previously. Of course, Raven would elect not to tell her nameless partner what he had taught her.

That man required no further validation to the benefits of his methods.

# SIXTY-FIVE

Before Madeline's partner entered the room, Victor first heard the *buzz-click* of the door's magnetic reader being activated by a key card and the immediate withdrawing of the deadbolt. Already in the bathroom, Victor stayed put. Given the dimensions of the bedroom, this was the best – and only – place in which he had any chance of remaining hidden.

Victor was unable to close the bathroom door completely without it making a telltale sound of its own. He took hold of the handle and pulled it towards him so the door was open to about sixty degrees, and pressed himself against the perpendicular wall in the resulting gap.

He figured it was better to have the door open so the bathroom was visibly empty to the person entering the bedroom instead of it being almost closed, which might invite suspicion; it had been open when Victor arrived and Madeline's partner might have been the last one inside the room.

The minuscule gap between door and frame provided no

real visibility for Victor to see through, so he caught only a nondescript blur of a figure entering Madeline's bedroom.

A man's height and width, as expected, dark garments.

The bedroom door closed with a clunk.

For a moment, nothing happened. The man stood still. He might be checking his phone or watch, or perhaps sniffing the air for any change in scent. Victor wore no fragrances to leave behind in his wake, and although the hotel shampoo he had used while bathing had been strongly fragranced, it would take a canine's nose to notice at any distance beyond a few millimetres.

From the man's position, the bathroom lay off to his right, the doorway of which lay a metre along that interior wall.

Footsteps on carpet as the man stepped away from the door and passed the bathroom to enter the bedroom proper.

The footsteps came to a stop. The sound of a wardrobe door opening followed. Then a quiet series of four beeps preceding a mechanical whirr.

The safe.

Victor heard nothing for a few seconds and he pictured the man taking something out or placing something inside.

A clunk of metal as the safe closed before another four quiet beeps as the man inputted a four-digit code and a new whirr as the safe locked itself once more.

The wardrobe closed and more footsteps signalled the man nearing.

He stopped in the space directly in front of both the bedroom door and the entrance to the bathroom. He was less than half a metre from Victor, who could hear the man's breathing. There was a slight raspy quality to it that suggested the man's sinuses were a little congested. Seasonal allergies maybe. The prescription pills in the cosmetic bag on the shelf above the washbasin could be for him.

Another footstep.

Then two more.

But not the dull sounds of shoes on carpet. These were the sharper taps of shoes on tiled flooring.

Madeline's partner had entered the bathroom.

# SIXTY-SIX

The walk to the village was pleasant enough, the scenery green and rolling from what Raven could see, although the tall hedgerows flanking the road restricted her view of the countryside. The temperature was a little too chilly for her personal tastes – the temperature of Britain was *always* too chilly for her tastes – but the wind was nothing more than a light breeze. The road itself curved only a little this way and that, although it rose and fell and rose again with the undulations of the Scottish topography.

Now she knew that Madeline was in fact taking care to make sure she was not followed, Raven kept even further behind. By the time she reached the village herself she had not even seen Madeline enter its boundaries.

A quick look in the windows of the post office and the grocer's confirmed that Madeline's only conceivable destination had to be the pub. It was named the Highlander's Targe, which meant nothing to Raven until she stepped inside and saw several round shields hanging from the walls or on posts on the inside. They were the same design as the one held by the Highlander on the pub's sign, so she put two and two together. The targe was clearly a small, round shield that had a colourful fabric covering and a rough cross-shaped pattern of metal studs. Even though she was no fan of the weather in this part of the world, each time she set foot in the British Isles, she found herself learning something new.

Every day's a school day, she thought.

Because the pub was hundreds of years old it had low ceilings that made Raven feel claustrophobic. She didn't have to duck, but she was acutely aware that there was little clearance between the top of her skull and the thick, dark beams that ran the length of the ceiling. Not the kind of place to visit in heels.

Hard to know how busy it was since she had no frame of reference, but it had maybe one person for every two tables. A young barmaid was bored behind the bar, and it seemed as though she had no one else helping her so this must be an expected amount of patrons for the day, for the time.

It was a warm and homely space, people smiling and chatting and laughing but at a respectful volume. Not the kind of bar where everybody had to shout just to be heard over everyone else shouting. The chairs and tables were all dark-stained wood. The floor was carpeted. The interior was shaped like a U with the bar occupying the space between. It had a beer garden out back with wooden benches under parasols, which Raven had seen as she walked by it to check out the other two potential destinations.

Upon entering, Raven could not see Madeline at first

and she was careful not to do too obvious a sweep in case Madeline was watching the door or turning to see who entered upon hearing it open.

To act like she belonged, Raven approached the bar and caught the attention of the young barmaid. A quick perusal of the whiskies behind the bar and Raven asked for a Glenfiddich and a packet of crisps, although at first she said *chips*, much to the confusion of the barmaid, before realising that quirk of a shared language.

The barmaid was quick to pour her Scotch and fetch the chips, which was a problem because Raven had not yet identified whereabouts Madeline was sitting. Given the U shape of the premises, Raven could either sit down in the correct side of the U or the wrong side, and only know when it was too late to make a change.

Instead, after paying for her order, she asked where the ladies' room was located and headed in that direction, using it as an excuse to extend her sweep of the pub. Because the entrance to the restrooms was on the right-hand side of the U she was able to scan the patrons in that half of the pub with what looked like perfectly natural curiosity. And since she would be walking both ways through the space, she did not need to get a good look at every nook and cranny on the first pass. Upon exiting the ladies' room, she passed through the right hand of the U shape a second time from the opposite direction, performing a second sweep.

No Madeline.

Raven picked up her whisky and her chips from the bar and went into the left-hand side of the pub's U-shaped interior. In between the short walk to an empty table along the far wall, sitting down and getting comfortable, she was able to perform a complete sweep of this side of the space without it looking like one.

Still no Madeline.

Raven tore open her packet and wondered what she had done wrong, which of her assumptions and deductions about Madeline's behaviour and intentions was incorrect. Had she bought a packet of cigarettes? Had she in fact gone to the post office to send something ... or pick something up? Or could whoever she was meeting have a place to stay in the village, like a rented cottage?

The latter point had not occurred to Raven before now, and as she munched on the salt and vinegar-flavoured chips it seemed an unforgivable mistake.

So lost in thought, she barely tasted the snacks. What should she do? The answer was unfortunately there was very little she could do at this point. If she left the pub and her whisky and snacks behind it would be the kind of action that people would notice. And although that was not necessarily a problem by itself, it could come back to haunt her later on depending on how the rest of her actions played out at the lodge. But the primary concern was if she did leave not knowing where Madeline was currently, she could inadvertently run into her and in doing so tip Madeline off to the interest Raven had in her. Therefore, it was better to just stay put and accept defeat. She had lost her target. It happened. Let it go, she told herself. Don't make it worse.

At least, she thought, she was now free to drink the whisky and eat her snacks. Both of which seemed to taste a lot better now she could relax and enjoy them.

She wondered if this was once again the influence of her

nameless partner, who always preached patience. Would the Raven of a few years ago have rushed out of the door to try to regain a visual on her target? Maybe.

Regardless, that young Raven would not have been able to control her surprise as effectively when Madeline suddenly reappeared. As well as the door that led to the restrooms on the right-hand side of the pub's U shape, on the left-hand side was a door that led to the beer garden.

It opened and Madeline entered through it, a man following in behind her.

# SIXTY-SEVEN

Victor stood motionless as Madeline's partner entered the en-suite bathroom. Three steps took him over the threshold but he did not pass the opened door.

Instead, he stopped on the other side of it with Victor mere centimetres away.

Because it was a luxury establishment, the doorway was wide enough for the man to step through it into the bathroom without needing to open the door further. Had that been necessary, he would have found it immovable as it met with the resistance of Victor standing behind it.

So close, the man smelled of cheap deodorant. Something with hints of mint and citrus and altogether synthetic and sharp instead of fresh. Maybe he always wore too much, or it could be the seasonal allergies affecting his ability to recognise how strong he smelled.

Victor had angled his toes outwards to reduce the amount of space his feet took up. Breathing in was pointless since

Victor's chest extended beyond his abdomen, but he relaxed his shoulder and lowered his sternum to reduce the natural curvature of his spine and flatten himself further.

He kept still as he mentally rehearsed what he would do if the man took any more steps into the bathroom, whether to use the toilet or to satisfy what might be a primeval instinct that something was wrong. Even if the man was not consciously aware of Victor's presence, the brain might have picked up on minuscule signs of danger that had put the man at unease.

That was not the case Victor discovered a moment later when he heard the light rustle of fingers passing through hair and realised the man was looking at himself in the mirror to do a little grooming.

Then noises Victor could not interpret until he heard the man clear his throat and say, 'It's me.'

He was making a call.

'Yes, I have it,' he said. 'What time are you returning?' A pause. 'Okay, I'll keep my head down until tomorrow night. One question, however . . .'

As the man said this, he edged backwards a little, nudging the door with the back of his foot.

Because the other side of the door met the tips of Victor's shoes, it did not move.

For an instant it seemed as if the man had not noticed this, but then he cut off what he was saying and said, 'I'll call you back.'

Victor needed no other invitation.

He thrust the door forward to slam into the man – only the man did the exact same thing in reverse, throwing his weight backwards.

He had the advantage in leverage and so instead of Victor slamming the door into him and sending him off balance, the door slammed into Victor.

He took the impact on his hands and arms, which he'd raised to shove the door.

The man's phone clattered on the flooring, discarded, unnecessary for what would follow.

Victor heard the brush of a hand on fabric as the man went to draw his gun; at the same time he was stepping forward to create space as he spun around, all of which took time and coordination.

During which, Victor shoved the door again, knowing it would not meet the same resistance as before since the man was in the process of moving away, out of range of the swinging arc.

Now Victor could throw himself into the man on the other side, who was one of the groundskeepers judging by his attire of dark green overall and thick-soled boots.

Catching him mid-draw, Victor collided with the man, pinning a Walther Q5 pistol between them and knocking him backwards into the washbasin.

The collision stunned and disorientated the man for a second, letting Victor grab his lead wrist in one hand and hold it in place between them while he threw elbows with his free arm.

The first few strikes hit the groundskeeper in his unprotected face before he managed to bring up his own free arm to block further impacts.

It was what Victor wanted. He ceased the elbow strikes to grab his enemy's overalls and turn him around on the spot so he could sweep his legs out from under him.

With limited space, the groundskeeper didn't go all the way down, the bathroom door blocking his fall.

Victor kept hold of the arm so he could disarm the gun, but the groundskeeper adapted fast and released the weapon before Victor could take it for himself.

It clattered and skidded on the floor tiles.

Twisting as he impacted the door, the groundskeeper was able to rebound and transfer some of the energy that had thrown him into escaping Victor's grip and launching a counter-attack of his own.

The groundskeeper was young and strong. Maybe eighty-five kilos at six feet tall, he moved well, nimble on his feet and quick with his positioning, always turning with Victor's attempts to grapple instead of fighting them, always keeping his legs spread apart to distribute his weight evenly and provide a stable base from which to strike and wrestle. He twisted out and slipped free of Victor's attempts to trap and lock his arms, blocked and parried the elbows and palm-heels aimed for his face, sprawled his hips back to render futile Victor's attempts to perform a takedown.

While the groundskeeper had the advantage in youth and therefore stamina, and was no less fluid and skilled with his hand-to-hand combat technique, he lacked experience. The younger man knew how to strike and grapple, and how to defend against similar attacks via endless hours of training and sparring, and yet such practice could not simulate a genuine life-and-death confrontation and the nuances of facing an enemy as ferocious and savage as Victor.

When they were close enough and the entirety of the enemy's focus was on striking, Victor grabbed the man's groin and squeezed and twisted with all of his considerable grip strength.

The groundskeeper sucked in a sharp breath and his eyes widened, the intensity of the pain so overwhelming that all his attacks faltered, all his defences failed.

Enabling Victor to sink his teeth into his enemy's face and rip out a chunk of flesh from his cheek ...

... which Victor spat back out into his opponent's face, blinding him with his own blood, further overloading his senses, adding horror to the pain and desperation.

Releasing the man's reproductive organs, Victor pushed him backwards to create space, then put a stomp-kick into his abdomen to double him over, at which point Victor snapped a guillotine choke around the man's neck.

Bracing his core, Victor forced the groundskeeper's head against his abdomen to increase the pressure on his enemy's carotids, ignoring the ineffective punches the man threw in response. Bent over and with no leverage, there was little power in the hits and then even less once the lack of oxygen supply to the brain began to shut down neural pathways.

When the groundskeeper stopped fighting back, Victor broke his neck.

# SIXTY-EIGHT

Raven had jokingly thought that maybe Madeline was coming to the village to buy a pack of cigarettes to have an illicit smoke, but she now saw it was the person she was meeting who had the habit. As he entered the pub behind Madeline, the man tucked a packet of cigarettes and a lighter into an exterior pocket of his jacket.

He was a handsome man of about forty, with brushed-back black hair and a short, neat beard. Too tanned for a native Scot, he seemed more Mediterranean in heritage. She had not seen him previously at the lodge or on the estate during her stay so it appeared that, whoever he was, he was not directly involved in the operational fulfilment of Madeline's mission. Maybe a client, maybe a handler, depending on who she was working for and whether she was a lone operator or part of some organisation. The Consensus could very well have used their power and influence to direct someone at an intelligence agency to do their dirty work for them.

Madeline and the handsome man took a seat close to Raven but sadly not so close that she would be able to over-hear the ensuing conversation. They already had a couple of drinks waiting for them and Raven gave herself a mental ad-monishment for not noticing the ice cubes in a glass of soda were still of a large, defined cube shape. Was she getting rusty? Had she spent too long on her own? Sometimes it was necessary to have a team or partner to bounce ideas off or to point out oversights in technique that could be corrected before they became outright flaws.

Although operating alone came with many drawbacks, one of the advantages was the ability to gaze around a room without it looking too suspicious. People with nothing else to do could be expected to idly watch those around them. In a group, in a couple, such actions stood out more. Both Madeline's gaze and that of the man she was sitting with almost never left the other and when they did, it was for only the briefest of moments.

Out of earshot, Raven could only observe, and had to do so from her peripheral vision to maintain discretion. Still, there was an interesting energy to their body language. There was a power dynamic, Raven realised, with Madeline listening more than speaking, which made her think the man had a position of power. An authority figure, it seemed, Madeline's client or handler. But such a dynamic also could be observed in a romantic couple where one partner was more dominant, the other more submissive. And though either dynamic could be mistaken for the other since there was much crossover, Raven detected each here. But both were stilted. They were trying to disguise a professional rendezvous under the simple pretence of two people sharing a drink in a pub, and they were also attempting to hide their attraction for each other. Madeline was struggling more with this, finding herself leaning closer towards the man as he spoke before realising what she was doing and then overcompensating by creating distance. Raven could see the desire to touch him. When he laid one hand on the tabletop Madeline immediately went to put her hand on his before snapping it back.

They had the look of two people having an affair; Raven guessed that affair had ended and yet Madeline had not moved on. She wondered if the man was using Madeline's attraction to him to manipulate her into doing something to which she might not otherwise have agreed. Although she could not hear what they were saying to each other, Raven learned a lot about their relationship nonetheless. But why had they met here? She could imagine Madeline wanting to meet him just to spend time in his company, but given the affair was over, the man had no personal reason to do so from his own perspective. This was a professional inter-action, albeit between two people who had had far more personal relations.

Given they had spent enough time together for an affair to manifest, Raven put him as her handler. A client simply wouldn't operate that closely with an operative for them to develop feelings and act upon them.

Her phone rang.

'Hello Jonathan,' she said. 'To what do I owe this pleasure?'

'How long until Madeline returns?'

'She's currently having a drink with a handsome stranger.'

They were too far away to hear her, but she spoke in a quiet voice so patrons sitting closer could not overhear.

'That's not answering my question. I need to know.'

'They're about halfway through their drinks so I'd guess about an hour.'

'Okay,' he said and hung up.

'Always a delight to chat,' Raven said to no one but herself.

After thirty minutes, Madeline checked her watch, and although Raven was no lip-reader it was clear enough to see Madeline then say to the man that it was time she left.

As they were making a slow exit, continuing their conversation while standing up but not actually making any move to leave just yet, Raven exploited the delay to stand up herself to get another drink. She did so from the same point of the bar she had ordered from previously because from there she could see through the windows at the front of the building to the small parking lot outside. No doubt Madeline was going to walk back to the lodge, but where was the man going? Wherever it was, he would be driving there. Seven vehicles parked outside the pub. Raven wanted to see which one was his.

Yet the man did not leave right away as he and Madeline approached the door. Instead, he headed to the restroom.

As he did so, Madeline waited for him, which further confirmed to Raven that she still harboured romantic interests in the man. She did not want to leave first while he was still here and she still had a chance to spend more time in his company, however brief, however fleeting.

After Raven had ordered another whisky, she kept her gaze in the direction of the young barmaid because Madeline was now standing within five feet of her near to the entrance to the pub. This was far from ideal as, without the man to distract her, Madeline would begin to spend more time checking out her surroundings. She could not fail to miss Raven standing so close to her.

Raven felt Madeline's eyes examining her from behind and she knew it was coming at least eight seconds before Madeline asked, 'I know you, don't I?'

# SIXTY-NINE

Victor took a moment to regain his breath. The grounds-keeper had been a formidable adversary, tireless and skilled. And yet they had not been enemies in any conventional sense. Both assassins, yes, except neither was the other's target. Nothing more than the accident of bad timing had led them to fight to the death. Only now the man was a corpse on the floor of Madeline's bathroom could Victor see the pointlessness of it all. Did it occur to the groundskeeper to question why he was fighting, and then why he was dying?

Spitting out the man's blood and cheek flesh into the sink, Victor set about washing out his mouth and using a thumb-nail to pick the remnants of skin from between his teeth.

After which, he called Raven, who said, 'Hello Jonathan. To what do I owe this pleasure?'

'How long until Madeline returns?'

'She's currently having a drink with a handsome stranger.'

'That's not answering my question,' Victor said. 'I need to know.'

'They're about halfway through their drinks so I'd guess about an hour.'

He said, 'Okay,' and hung up, then called Lambert.

'Roman, how goes it?'

'You have backup nearby, correct?' Victor asked his broker.

'Of course. They're in a holiday rental further up the loch. I told you I would have a team on standby to get you out of the country or clean up your mess if it would help.'

'It will,' he said. 'The second part.'

'It's done already?'

'Not exactly,' Victor answered. 'There is another party involved who is at odds with our objective. I'm currently in someone else's bathroom and there's a corpse on the floor. Can your people handle that?'

'I'm not paying them for their personalities.'

'It needs to be done immediately. There's about an hour's window of time.'

'They can be there in fifteen minutes. What are the particulars?'

Victor provided the room number and an overview of what to expect. 'Are you certain they can gain access and get a body out of here without anyone noticing?'

'Again, they're in a holiday rental, but they're not there for the fresh air and stunning views,' Lambert answered. 'They all have site clearance as part of one of the many third-party firms who handles renovations and maintenance. No one is going to get in their way and no one is going to bat an eye at people in overalls carrying out waterproof sacks. Have a little faith, okay?'

'Sure,' Victor answered and hung up.

He took the dead groundskeeper's handgun and phone for himself, and then searched through his pockets. He had a big set of keys that no doubt opened various sheds, outbuildings and such around the grounds. A set of car keys with a Ford fob. His wallet had a driver's licence, single credit card and some cash. Almost certainly the credit card and driver's licence were part of his cover instead of in his real name.

The groundskeeper's phone was locked and this did not change when Victor held it up to the man's face. However, pressing's the man's thumb to the screen unlocked it. A burner, it contained nothing except the default apps and had only been used to send messages and make calls. The log showed only one number but several calls over the last couple of days with the contact name as a single letter: M. In the messages, again there was one exchange with a different contact designated with the letter G. So far there had been one message sent by the groundskeeper and one received:

*M + W present.*
*Await details.*

Victor changed the settings on the phone so it unlocked with a code instead of a thumbprint, pocketed it, along with the man's wallet and both sets of keys.

Because of the size of the lodge there were several parking areas filled with hundreds of vehicles, all of which Victor ignored. Behind the main building there were dedicated spaces for the staff and less than a minute of walking while thumbing the key fob meant he found the groundskeeper's vehicle. A white Ford Kuga.

Before climbing inside, Victor checked the boot and found

it empty. The interior of the car was clean and uncluttered. The glovebox, however, contained two identical manila envelopes.

As he went to open the first, Victor noticed a van pull into the same car park. He watched as three men and two women disembarked. They wore maintenance uniforms and took a large cleaning trolley from the back of the van before heading to the hotel.

Glancing at his watch, Victor was impressed to see it had been fourteen minutes since his call with Lambert.

Inside the first envelope was a dossier on Woodcroft consisting mostly of photographs of the man along with pertinent details such as his age, height, weight, hair and eye colours, and dominant hand. A short biography included a summary of his military career and civilian consultancy roles for many different employers, the latest being Zeus Industries.

The second envelope also contained a dossier. This one for Madeline Belford.

The groundskeeper had not only been her partner, Victor saw, but her future murderer too.

As with the dossier on Woodcroft, this one comprised many photographs of Madeline, her relevant characteristics, and a biography. Victor read through the details, which were few given her far younger age than Woodcroft's. She had no military background and only a single, and current, employer.

The British Secret Intelligence Service, more commonly known as MI6.

# SEVENTY

In such instances it was always useful to feign ignorance and delay responding because sometimes such problems resolved themselves. Here, the man might reappear all of a sudden or the pub might receive another customer coming through the door and disrupting the discourse.

So, Raven did not respond, pretending either not to hear for a moment or believing the question had been asked of someone else. A perfectly natural-seeming reaction. In such a public place conversations were happening all the time, questions asked back and forth within earshot but not necessarily directed at the listener.

However, Madeline was quick to follow up with a more pointed, 'Excuse me.'

Now, it was less tactically prudent to continue the façade of ignorance without it seeming like a deliberate attempt to ignore the question, so she turned around on the spot with a bemused expression to meet Madeline's gaze.

'Are you talking to me?' Raven asked.

'You're staying at the lodge up the road, aren't you?' Madeline asked in return.

A few inches shorter even with the boots, her head was angled upwards to meet Raven's eyes. Up close, Raven put her somewhere in her late twenties. She was about five foot four and one hundred and thirty pounds. She didn't have the kind of athleticism of Raven's physique, but Madeline was slim and fit regardless. Nothing about her physicality suggested she was any kind of combatant, although technique always triumphed over strength.

'Yes,' Raven answered. 'I'm here for the conference. I'm assuming you are too?'

'You're American,' Madeline said.

Raven nodded. 'For my sins, yes. Please don't judge me for it.'

Madeline laughed at this. 'Why would I judge you for being American? Aren't we practically siblings?'

'True, but that doesn't mean that we always see eye to eye, does it?'

'Oh, no,' Madeline said in return. 'I don't think it would be healthy if we did. Anyway, what brings you here? I see you are drinking Scotch. Am I not right in thinking the lounge bar in the hotel has a large selection of whisky?'

'True,' Raven agreed, 'but I have a taste for single malts and I wanted to see what was on offer at a proper local public house instead of a corporate-owned hotel.'

'What's the verdict?' Madeline asked.

'I gotta say, I'm a little disappointed. I was hoping to find something I hadn't come across before, but no dice.'

'Too bad,' the younger woman said. 'How are you finding the conference so far?'

'When you get to my age,' Raven began, 'you've kind of seen it all before.'

'What do you mean, your age?' Madeline asked, eyebrows arching. 'You can't be much older than me.'

'Ohh, you charming girl.' Raven smiled. 'I know you're just being polite, but I appreciate the compliment regardless.'

'There's nothing polite about it,' Madeline insisted. 'I don't know if anybody has ever told you this before, but you are really very pretty. What am I thinking? I bet you hear it all the time.'

'Wow,' Raven said, 'if you keep going on like this then I think you and I are going to be the best of friends.'

'I would like that very much,' Madeline said with a smile of her own. 'I'm at the conference alone and it all feels a little intimidating.'

'Why is that?' Raven asked.

Madeline said, 'I feel very much like a small fish in a big pond. There are all of these captains of industry, government officials, experts in their fields, and then there is me.'

Raven asked, 'What is it that you do?'

'I'm a researcher for an international security consultancy, which means, in layman's terms, I'm a secretary, here to take notes.'

'I'm sure there is a lot more to it than just that and I'm equally sure that you are very good at what you do.'

That last comment caused Madeline's expression to change, and she regarded Raven with a questioning look. 'Why would you think I'm good at what I do?'

In response to this challenge, Raven replied, 'Well you've got me there. I have no idea how good you are and what you do, but I was being polite.'

'When we can be honest instead,' Madeline began, 'isn't being polite a waste of time?'

Raven was unsure how to answer this particular question, but she didn't need to because the man Madeline had been seated with emerged from the door to the restrooms and walked over.

Although his gaze was on Madeline, he recognised the interaction between her and Raven, and so said, 'Hello' to Raven when he reached them. To Madeline, he asked, 'Who's your friend?'

A French accent. Parisian, if she was not mistaken.

Raven fought to hide her reaction.

She thought back to what Albrecht had said about his and Schulz's employer: *His name is Fabien Gallier. He's a Frenchman ...*

Madeline answered, 'We haven't been formally introduced but she is also at the conference.'

Despite the public setting, Raven could not help but feel boxed in as she stood with the Frenchman to her left and Madeline to her right, both of them far enough apart that Raven had to swivel her head back and forth to look at them one at a time but not together.

'Well,' the man who had to be Fabien Gallier said to Raven, 'nice to meet you, but I'm on my way now so I think there is little point exchanging names and ... how do the English say? *Chit-chat.* I'm sure you're a delight, mademoiselle, but I don't suppose we will ever see one another again.'

Raven responded with a polite smile and a nod of agreement.

The Frenchman reached for the pub's door and opened it before stepping through.

Madeline went to follow, and then looked back over

her shoulder and said, 'How is your husband finding the conference?'

For a second, Raven hesitated, unsure how to respond, until Madeline continued by saying, 'Tall guy I've seen you with, dark hair, likes his suits. Although, you're not wearing a ring so I suppose he is a boyfriend. Long term, I'm guessing, seeing how comfortable you are with him.'

She phrased it as a question but it seemed like a statement nonetheless.

Raven said, 'I think he would rather be playing golf.'

Madeline responded with a polite smile. 'I can imagine,' she said. 'I keep seeing him around. He seems bored.'

'He does have that look about him, doesn't he?' Raven said, keeping her tone light.

'Maybe we could all have dinner together?' Madeline suggested. 'Or at least a drink? I'm Madeline, by the way.'

'Marion,' Raven said in response. 'And yes, that would be nice.'

'Will you be about this evening?'

'I expect so.'

'Great,' Madeline said as she stepped through the exit. 'I hope to see you both later then.'

Raven adjusted her position so she could see out of the window as Madeline approached the Frenchman, who was standing outside a black Range Rover. They exchanged a few words and Madeline gave him a hug he was slow to reciprocate before she continued on her way.

Before Gallier climbed into his vehicle, he looked in the pub's direction, and although Raven was sure, given it was bright outside, he would not be able to see her, it still felt as though he was staring right at her.

*I don't suppose we will ever see one another again*, Gallier had said to her.

*Oh*, Raven hadn't said back, *I don't know about that.*

# SEVENTY-ONE

The lounge bar had sumptuous armchairs, low to the ground and bulging with padding. There was no uniformity to them. Some were plain earth tones, others with a velvety texture, others still in multicoloured tartan. There were leather sofas too, which glistened in the dim light of the chandeliers above. The walls were painted with a pale green that was broken at intervals by glass-fronted cabinets that contained all sorts of decorative plates, crockery and glassware. Atop one cabinet stood a stuffed deer: a doe, with eyes that seemed to follow him around the room. Two tall mirrors stood above it and to either side, so high up the walls that no one seated or standing in the lounge would be able to see themselves looking back in return. Instead, Victor could see reflections of the chandeliers and the upper portions of the opposite walls, including the windows and their drapes.

A lone young man tended the bar. In many countries he would not be old enough to drink, but in the UK, at eighteen or nineteen, he was employed selling alcohol. Despite his age, he seemed quick and competent, mixing whisky cocktails and recommending various brands and ages to curious travellers and seasoned Scotch drinkers alike.

Outside, the sun was setting and the waters of the loch were shades of red and orange.

Knowing that yesterday the groundskeeper had told Madeline he would keep his head down until the next evening – when the exchange must be taking place – meant it had not been necessary to shadow Woodcroft or Madeline closely during the daytime. And, given Raven's encounter with her in the pub the previous afternoon, maintaining distance was necessary to avoid giving themselves away. To stay in character, both Victor and Raven had attended various panels and demonstrations, sometimes together, sometimes apart. Rain all day meant the lodge had been busier with few people going outside unless they had no choice.

Without knowing where Woodcroft would meet Gallier, waiting in the lounge bar was as good a place as any as far as Victor was concerned. Every table had a glass tumbler in which a small flame burned to provide a homely and romantic light. Victor liked these kinds of details. A regular bar would not have such elaborate adornments. And although he was not expecting to suddenly need an improvised weapon, it helped him to relax knowing a compact Molotov cocktail was ready and waiting should he need one.

Raven arrived wearing a three-quarter-length red dress with a slash on one thigh. It was a bright, fire red. Her dark hair was combed back and crested on her shoulders.

Sleeveless, her lean muscle tone was on full display, as was every curve. There was a sheen to her olive skin that made her seem to glow in the dim light of the bar. Gold earrings glittered. As did bracelets and rings. Careful make-up accentuated her eyes with hints of copper and bronze. Her lips glistened with a coating of glossy mahogany.

Approaching Victor, who rose to greet her, she said, 'You really should know better than to stare.'

'If I didn't,' he countered, 'I'd be the only one here.'

'Is that flattery?'

'It's a more of a question.'

'I'm not hearing one.'

'What are you doing, Constance? What is this?'

'This?' she said, gesturing at the dress, at her appearance. 'Is me.'

'Perhaps you're forgetting that we're supposed to be undercover.'

'Don't pretend this dress isn't making you want to be under my covers right now.'

He rolled his eyes. 'This is my point.'

She acted ignorant, blowing on her nails, which were black as the pits of Hades. 'How so?'

'Could you at least sit down?'

'Does it intimidate you that in these heels we're at eye level?'

'It exasperates me you would dress this way.'

'In what *way*?'

'Cut the act,' he said. 'You know what I mean.'

'Pretend I'm an imbecile,' she began. 'Spell it out to me.'

'Are you joking?'

Her expression hardened. 'Do I look like a joke to you?'

Before he could stop himself, he said, 'You look a million dollars and that isn't something—'

'Finally,' she interrupted. 'I knew you could do it.'

'Do what?'

'Pay me a compliment.'

'I'll pay you a hundred compliments if you sit down right now.'

She beamed, 'Deal', and took a seat.

'That's a little better.'

'I can't wait,' she said, eyes gleaming in the flattering light of the table's candle.

'For what?'

'Are you a goldfish? The compliments, silly. The hundred compliments in fact. Well, I suppose you already paid me one so let's say a mere ninety-nine to go.'

'It was a figure of speech.'

'Spoilsport.'

'You still haven't told me what you're doing dressing like that.'

'Why would I? I can dress however I like. We're not exactly a married couple, are we? And even if we were hubby and wife you wouldn't get to decide how I dress. I always knew you were old-fashioned, but I didn't know you were a chauvinist at the same time.'

'You know exactly what I mean,' Victor said in return. 'You've dressed up. You look amazing so that—'

'Ninety-eight to go.' She grinned when he rolled his eyes again. 'They're going to roll right out of your skull if you're not careful.'

'The way you look,' he said, choosing his words with care, 'is only going to draw more attention our way.'

'Don't flatter yourself,' she said, dismissive. 'No one is going to be looking at you. And before you tell me for the eleventh-millionth time that I know what you mean ... yes, I do know what you mean. But that's kind of the point. People are going to look at me and the last thing they're going to see is who I really am. They're not going to see Raven on the hunt for the latest Consensus cell. I'm hiding in plain sight.'

'And where does that leave me if we're operating together?'

'You could smarten up yourself,' she suggested. 'Have a shave. Wear clothes that fit well. Do something with your hair that isn't so ... *practical.* I picture you with a quiff and faded sides, a patterned shirt, and a blazer with shiny brass buttons. And some trousers that show off your toosh.'

'No chance.'

'An entirely predictable answer. In which case people who see us side by side are going to assume the only reason I'm with you is because you're filthy rich or you have an enormous—'

'*Constance.*'

'Stop being so boring, Jonathan,' she said. Then, after a pause, 'Do you?'

'This conversation is over.'

'I'll find out anyway,' she said with a grin. 'Mark my words, once this mission of ours is complete, you're mine.'

Victor remained silent.

'Returning to that mission,' she said, 'any further messages today on the groundskeeper's phone?'

'Not so far.'

'W for Woodcroft, M for Madeline and G for Gallier.' Raven shook her head. 'The guy was no spymaster.'

'Given he didn't expect to die, he wasn't thinking what might happen after the fact.'

'Woodcroft is technically a traitor,' Raven said, thinking out loud, 'so I suppose it makes sense the British intelligence community wants him dead, only Scotland is not foreign soil so this is not the remit of MI6. But just because she's an intelligence operative doesn't mean she's not also one of them, or, at least, one of the people they use. I was just like her once upon a time, don't forget. Maybe she knows where she's taking orders from, maybe she doesn't. I could tell they have a history, so he could be manipulating her, of course.'

'It would help to know if the groundskeeper was SIS as well, but I don't think I would like this additional problem any better.'

'No plan survives first contact with the enemy and all that,' she told him. 'And given the Consensus set her up with a partner who was planning on killing her, we shouldn't overthink it. No doubt the groundskeeper was going to dispose of Madeline just as soon as she had killed Woodcroft. That's their style, all right. They like to sever the connections just as soon as they're no longer needed.'

'As you know more about these people and how they operate, what will Madeline do given her partner hasn't been answering her calls and won't show up where they're meant to meet?'

'I noticed no difference in her behaviour so far. If she has even the remotest idea about who she is working for, then she'll have no choice but to stick to her objective if she values her life. But she'll be on her guard, that's for sure. She won't think he's changed his mind and quit on her. She'll know something has happened to him and therefore she is under threat herself. Of course, she doesn't know we can't risk touching her just yet without scaring away Gallier.'

'The flip side to that coin is that she knows with absolute certainty that you had nothing to do with it since you were with her the last time she spoke with her partner. In a bizarre twist of fate her number-one enemy in this place is the one person she will trust.'

Raven said, 'I don't know about that. She seemed pretty savvy to me when we spoke in the pub after her meeting with Gallier.'

Victor said, 'I'm frankly a little relieved you didn't kill Gallier there and then.'

'The thought never even crossed my mind. We're a team, remember? I know the requirements of your contract. I would never do anything to jeopardise that.'

'Thank you,' he said.

'Maybe the reason Gallier hasn't messaged the groundskeeper is because Madeline has passed on that he's missing.'

'I don't think so, because Gallier would have reached out to him separately and the last message from G was to await details. I imagine that will be once the specifics have been confirmed with Woodcroft. Once the groundskeeper gets the word, so will we.'

Raven smiled. 'Gallier is going to get one hell of a surprise when we show up instead of his assassins.'

# SEVENTY-TWO

The sound system played a low-volume musical mix that varied between upbeat soft-rock hits and more melancholy ballads. Victor couldn't help but wonder which songs would persuade patrons to drink more. Would the latter convince them to drown their inevitably many sorrows or would the former encourage them to let loose and have a good time? No doubt some marketing firm had conducted a survey on this very topic and the seesaw in the tone of musical ambience could be a direct result of their research, which had concluded that upbeat and melancholy songs had equally persuasive effects.

A group of women in glamorous dresses gradually grew larger and larger as more arrived to join the cluster. Each new arrival announced their name as they did. This indicated to Victor that they did not know one another already. Perhaps, at an event earlier in the day they had arranged to meet up afterwards, with everyone knowing someone but not everyone knowing everyone.

Someone who Victor took to be a manager entered the lounge and opened a cabinet door in one of the walls. Painted green to blend in, it was only noticeable because of the brass knob the manager twisted and pulled. From his position, Victor could not see what she did, but a moment later the lights were dimmed significantly inside the lounge. It took on an even cosier ambience, although an elderly lady looked up from her paperback novel to tut in disapproval.

'How am I meant to read now?' she said to no one but loud enough for everyone to hear.

The manager, quick and efficient, had already left by the time the woman voiced her displeasure.

Although Victor liked the dark from a professional perspective, when not in action and trying to blend in, the dim lighting worked against him here. He could still see everybody in the room and make out their stature, proportions and body language. He could not, however, see facial expressions and eye movements with enough clarity to accurately predict a person's attitude and the focus of their attention. Of course, the opposite was also true. Sitting alone, and far away from anyone else, no one could make any accurate interpretations of his own intentions.

While Raven excused herself to use the bathroom, Victor went to the bar for another drink, he sensed someone had entered and was approaching. He didn't need to look over his shoulder to know who was nearby. He saw the ripple of a reflection in the bottles behind the bar. Just a blur, but enough to know who it was without turning.

'Brutal day,' Hereward Woodcroft said after asking the bartender for a large Scotch.

'Isn't it just?'

'People think the Romans couldn't conquer Scotland,' Woodcroft said, shaking his hands to flick off some rainwater. 'The truth is, they decided they didn't want to drown.'

'Does that make Hadrian's Wall a dam?'

'Very good,' Woodcroft replied. 'I'm Harry, by the way. Hereward really, but if I introduce myself with that then I have to suffer through the exact same small talk every time.'

'I met a clever woman in a hotel bar once,' Victor said. 'She told me that people with interesting names were always boring because every time they introduced themselves to someone new they had to have the exact same conversation.'

'Agreed,' Woodcraft said, holding out a strong hand. 'I was dull as ditchwater before I started saying my name is Harry.'

'Ken.' Victor shook the hand. 'I like the fact you didn't say dishwater.'

'Most people wouldn't even have noticed,' the man said and Victor regretted making the comment. 'Well played, old boy. I take it you're here for the conference.'

'I'm not here for the weather. You?'

'Oh, yes,' Woodcroft said with a chuckle. 'I'm prostituting myself out on behalf of some upstart Yank company, Zeus Industries.' He shook his head. 'More *realistic* fake bullets. I mean, seriously? Do they understand what an oxymoron is over there? Give me strength.' He paused, composed himself. 'What about you?'

'I'm the founder and majority shareholder in Zeus Industries.'

Woodcroft's smile dropped from his face and the ruddiness of his complexion lost a little of its colour.

Then he roared with laughter.

'*You absolute swine*,' he growled, still laughing. 'You really had me for a second.'

'For two seconds,' Victor corrected.

'You know, you have an impenetrable poker face, has anyone ever told you that?'

'In as many words.'

'So, given you're not the chief moneyman of the company I've just slighted, what are you doing here?'

'A fact-finding mission, we might call it,' Victor answered. 'I work on behalf of a multinational defence conglomerate and we're currently trying to enter the UK market.'

'Isn't everyone?' Woodcroft answered. 'I find these kinds of shindigs little more than a school dance with everyone standing with their backs against the walls, facing the dance floor but too chicken to ask a girl to boogie.'

'Interesting way of looking at it.'

Woodcroft swivelled around and leaned against the bar. 'How about we play a game?'

'That really depends on the game,' Victor answered.

'Cagey, aren't we? Fear not, there's no money at stake, only pride. I like to call it spot the spook.' Woodcroft gave him a conspiratorial look. 'These places are crawling with spies. What do they say about rats in London? You're never more than six feet from one? In one of these conferences, you're never more than six feet from a spy. You have to be careful what you say because you're almost guaranteed to have one in earshot. The problem is they're becoming harder and harder to pick out of a crowd now they don't wear tuxedos any more.'

'Did they ever?'

'Maybe, maybe not. Gone are the days when the only

people who got the tap on the shoulder in this country were the upper-crust Oxbridge types. That made it a little easier to pick them out. These days, however, they're just as likely to have a bindi and a Brummie accent.'

'What are the rules of the game?'

'Spot the spook? Simple. It's all in the name,' Woodcroft explained. 'Take this room. There's that group of women over there who will no doubt be sozzled on gin within a couple of hours. We have a few lone men scattered about. That couple in the corner. What's that? About two dozen people?'

Having already counted twenty-six in all, twenty-seven including the young barman, twenty-nine with himself and Woodcroft, Victor said, 'Give or take.'

'I reckon that's two spies. Not quite one-in-ten but close enough.'

'Are they together or apart?'

'That's the game,' he said. 'We decide if they're flying solo or a double act. So, who's your money on?'

'Two of the group of women,' Victor answered. 'The tall one who is doing all of the talking and the one nodding along a lot.'

'Why? Tell me your thought process. That's the fun part.'

'The tall one talking is doing so to establish her bona fides so everyone else trusts her and opens up more easily.'

Woodcroft leaned his head a little closer and said in a quiet voice, 'Oh, I like that. Then what about Miss Nod-a-lot? Why not one of the others?'

'The over-nodding is a nervous tic,' Victor explained. 'She's not long out of university and so probably new to the business. She doesn't realise she's doing it.'

'I can't fault your reasoning,' Woodcroft said. 'For a first-timer, I'm impressed. I'd say that's two for two.'

'What about you?' Victor asked. 'Who are the two spies in your opinion?'

'Oh, that's easy,' the older man said with a smirk. 'We are.'

# SEVENTY-THREE

The lounge bar was accessible from the lobby via a large, arched entranceway. Restrooms were located on the opposite side of the lobby, so when Raven had finished powdering her nose she strolled back through the space. Out of habit and long experience, she performed a quick threat-assessment sweep as she did so, noting the concierge, the clerks behind the desk, the regular guests and those attending the conference passing through or relaxing on the many comfortable chairs and sofas. None of which required so much as a second glance.

Six people, however, caught her attention.

The first five were a group of guys in suits, who looked like a close protection detail without a client nearby to guard. They had square, military-like builds and postures, standing briefly together as a quintet near the lobby's main entrance before heading out. Perhaps they were now heading to join their VIP, but they had a vibe about them that told Raven they were on the clock and had not simply been chewing the fat.

The sixth was all alone but stood out the most.

Given he was at least six-four and at around two hundred and forty pounds of solid muscle mass, he could hardly have melted into the background.

But there was more to him than just his size. He had dark hair and the skin of someone from the Middle East, and she guessed he was from the Levant, maybe Syrian, Jordanian or Israeli. He had a fuzz of stubble and an air of dishevelment as if he had been on a long, tiring journey. Although he seemed physically fatigued, he was alert, his head and his eyes in constant motion.

When inevitably he looked Raven's way, her gaze was already elsewhere and yet she felt him track her as she passed through the lobby.

'Marion,' she heard a voice call out and she looked back over her shoulder to see Madeline approach. 'Wowza,' the younger woman said. 'You certainly know how to dial it up to eleven.'

'You're too kind,' Raven said in return.

'Are you heading to the bar?'

'I am. Would you like to join me? Well, us?'

A broad smile. 'Absolutely.'

'I can't wait to hear your reasoning,' Victor said to Woodcroft. 'Why are we spies?'

There was a glimmer in the older man's eyes as he sipped his whisky. As he lowered his glass and went to answer, he looked away towards the bar's entranceway as Raven reappeared and instead he uttered, 'My, my, my.'

Madeline walked in alongside her and the two women approached them, Raven smiling at first to Victor and then to Woodcroft before saying, 'Are we interrupting?'

'My dear, you wouldn't be interrupting me if I was midway through my wedding vows,' Woodcroft was quick to reply. 'I'm Harry.'

'Charmed, I'm sure,' Raven said with a genuine smile, 'I'm Marion,' then to Victor, 'This is my new friend Madeline I was telling you about.'

'It's a pleasure to make your acquaintance,' he said.

'Likewise. I've seen you around a few times. And nice to meet you too, Harry.'

Woodcroft said, 'The pleasure is all mine.'

'Well, isn't this nice?' Raven said with a smile. 'The four of us getting to know one another.'

She sent Victor a short, sharp raise of her eyebrows.

'Are you here alone?' Woodcroft asked Madeline.

'I was supposed to have a date, but he's only gone and stood me up.'

'The cad,' Woodcroft said with a tut. 'I expect he must have a damned good reason else deserves a damned good hiding.'

She replied, 'Your guess is as good as mine.'

Raven said to Victor, 'May I have a word?'

'Sure.'

'Don't let me interrupt,' Woodcroft said before checking his watch. 'I need to be somewhere, as it happens. Nice to meet you all.'

Madeline said, 'I should go see where my date is hiding. Hopefully I'll see you all later on.'

Raven said, 'I look forward to it.'

Woodcroft finished his drink and said to Madeline, 'I'll happily accompany you until that dastardly date of yours shows his face.'

'That would be wonderful, thank you.'

He set the empty glass down on the bar and departed with Madeline alongside him.

'This must be it,' Victor said, gaze following them as they left.

'There's a guy in the lobby,' Raven began. 'A big guy, huge in fact. He's just arrived. Something about him is not right. He's not here for the conference, but he's here for something.'

'You're not giving me much to go on here.'

'I know, although it can't be a coincidence, can it? Woodcroft is making his trade with Gallier and someone else shows up at the same time?'

'The Consensus?'

'I'm not sure. They're normally more subtle with their people. There's nothing subtle about this guy. He's a bulldozer.'

Gesturing towards Woodcroft and Madeline as they exited the lounge bar, Victor said, 'He's going to collect the plans and head to his rendezvous and she's going to be there waiting for him. Whoever the new arrival is, we're on the clock now so he's going to have to wait.'

The groundskeeper's phone buzzed in Victor's pocket.

'Gallier,' he said to Raven as he read the message. 'The exchange is taking place at the north lodge in thirty minutes.'

Marion Ysiv. At least, the woman who had been pretending to be her. Constance Stone, also known as Raven. This was the first time Zahm had seen her in person, and he was surprised by her glamorous attire and demeanour that was a stark contrast to the hardened operative he had read so much about. He had expected her to be more blending in than standing out. However, he saw more and more people in their evening wear and realised that she matched the environment, whereas he did not. Dressed in the same clothes he had been wearing for his hurried journey into, and then across, Europe, he was a mess.

He had expected to find a Mossad welcoming committee and had spent half the day sneaking through the estate in an effort to both avoid and identify them. Instead, nothing. Karmia Elkayam had not sent anyone to interfere, he was surprised to learn.

She was going to let nature take its course.

Zahm had no plan beyond the speculative preparations he had done on the way from Israel to Scotland. He knew where Helyeph would be, and that was it. With Mossad pushing him out of the workgroup and no kidon tasked with the mission to assist with intelligence gathering, surveillance and logistics, he had to keep things simple.

Find him.

Kill him.

Knowing Raven was here meant Helyeph had to be close, causing a rush of anticipation that Zahm had to fight to control. Already driven by an unbreakable desire for vengeance, he knew he had to temper his temper. All those long, gruelling lessons from Father paid off now, because a younger, unschooled Zahm would have torn this estate apart in his search.

Instead, he took a seat on one of the lobby sofas – the armchairs being too small for his dimensions – and he waited.

Six years had gone by since he had last seen Helyeph with his own eyes. Six years since the killer had seen him in return. Zahm could picture the man's face with perfect clarity, whether as he was then or his new face from the recent surveillance footage, but would the killer recognise him?

It hardly mattered. Zahm intended to remind Helyeph exactly who he was and why Zahm was killing him.

He watched Raven converse with a younger woman before they crossed the lobby together. Zahm resisted the urge to follow them. Raven would only notice him – how could she not? – and he knew he only had one chance to catch Helyeph off guard. Zahm was not going to waste that unique opportunity.

Besides, he did not need to follow her. Raven's presence alone told him his prey was close. He remembered Father's many early lessons about patience and waiting. Zahm had listened to Father back then, had learned from him as he had learned again during the years of recovery when Father had told him to use his failure, to harness his hatred. Father had been right, as he was always right. Zahm was grateful indeed, grateful to the killer who had inflicted so much suffering, who had caused so much rage.

Soon, Zahm would prove Father right for the last time.

# SEVENTY-FOUR

The north lodge was located at the most northern point of the estate's extensive grounds. The property could sleep eight people in four bedrooms as part of a single expensive booking. Because of its distance from the main lodge, it was not involved in the conference and no attendees were staying here. Fabien Gallier, his representatives or those elsewhere in the Consensus cell from which he operated had booked the north lodge for the entire weekend, Victor assumed. Its isolated location made it an apt place for the handover between Gallier and Woodcroft.

Standing on a spur of land that jutted out into the loch at the other side of the golf course, the building consisted of two halves: the original fifteenth-century gatekeeper's cottage and a modern glass-fronted extension facing the loch itself. Surrounded by woodland on the other three sides, the north lodge was all but invisible from the rest of the estate. Only by traversing the narrow, private road or passing by in a boat would anyone find it. From the north, the lodge could be reached via a large wrought-iron gate that once marked the north entrance to the estate proper but was now locked except on rare occasions.

After Woodcroft had left the lounge bar he had returned to his cottage to collect a large sports bag that he carried in his right hand. Given Victor knew where the man would be heading, he had waited nearby, hidden in the treeline, for Woodcroft to arrive.

The rain had stopped and he walked at a slow, leisurely pace – a man taking a relaxing evening stroll – slowing down to a stop when he reached the mouth of the narrow road that led up to the north lodge because a figure stood sentinel. Even at distance, Victor recognised him as one of the suited men he had passed on the stairs the previous day en route to breaking into Madeline's bedroom. The five men had had the air of close-protection detail and now he understood why they had given him that impression. The sentinel was here now to protect Gallier. Their presence at the conference had been merely as cover.

Too far away to hear the resulting conversation and with only twilight by which to read their lips, Victor did not know what was said between them, but he could guess well enough. Only a brief exchange of words was had before the sentinel stepped aside and gestured for Woodcroft to continue along the narrow road.

Once the former SAS man had gone, the sentinel raised his index and middle fingers to his right ear, where an earpiece was no doubt positioned. Victor saw the man's mouth moving, but again the distance and the semi-darkness meant he could not read his lips, and yet the context was still obvious.

Having shadowed Woodcroft, Victor called Raven to report his observations.

She said, 'I saw those guys myself earlier. They left not long before Gallier messaged the groundskeeper's phone. If there are five of them, then I bet another one will be positioned at the north gate and the remaining three will be with Gallier himself at the lodge.'

'The north gate is usually out of use,' he said in return. 'The other four will be forming a close perimeter around Gallier. But why does he need Madeline at all if he has these five guys on hand? Surely they're not just for show. They could kill Woodcroft for him.'

'Madeline must be part of the narrative he's building. Don't forget, he had the groundskeeper ready to kill her once she had completed her mission. That would mean two corpses at the scene of the exchange: Woodcroft and Madeline, one a current British intelligence officer and the other an ex-spy and former member of the armed forces. That's a lot of egg on someone's face. The only thing I don't understand is why does Gallier need extra security when he believes he has Madeline and the groundskeeper in his pocket?'

'Two reasons,' Victor suggested. 'The security guys are just that: security. They're here to make sure no one else interferes with his plans. Given what happened to Schulz and Albrecht, it makes sense that Gallier would want to be cautious. Plus, they help build a different narrative for Woodcroft's benefit. They tell him that this is a legitimate exchange. Otherwise, he's showing up by himself to meet Gallier at an isolated location. A man of Woodcroft's background and expertise would sense something is amiss like that. The security guys tell him that Gallier feels the need for protection, that he doesn't trust Woodcroft. It's a form of hiding in plain sight. He sees the security and thinks that Gallier is paranoid or nervous, or simply of a tactical mind-set. All of those things also say that this isn't a set-up.'

'Are these security guys any good?'

'Competent so far,' Victor answered.

'We're going to have to take them out first regardless.'

He resisted asking 'To a movie or to dinner?' saying instead, 'What's happening with Madeline?'

From the main lodge, Raven followed her south. The younger woman walked at a quick pace, following the winding path down to the marina where some forty boats were moored along two jetties. At that point, any further attempt to follow Madeline would be doomed to failure given the lack of cover, so Raven hung back. Following closer would have been unnecessary, as she soon discovered when Madeline climbed aboard a small, two-seater motorboat.

Raven watched as she unmoored the vessel and piloted it out of the marina and onto the loch where, away from the ambient lights of the jetty, Madeline and the boat soon disappeared into the rapidly approaching night.

Raven called her nameless companion to summarise what she had witnessed, adding, 'I think she's heading north. At least, that's what it looked like before I lost sight of her.'

'How long will it take you to get up here on foot?'

'I'm fifteen minutes away if I want to maintain any appearance of normalcy.'

'If Madeline is taking a boat up here she'll arrive within mere minutes. I can't afford to wait for you and lose a visual on Woodcroft.'

'Sure thing,' she said. 'But if things turn bad you let me know and I'll start running, okay?'

A suppressed weapon was not silent, Victor knew all too well. Here, where it was so quiet, the distinctive clack of a suppressed gunshot would travel a significant distance. Certainly, it would reach the ears of Woodcroft and anyone outside the nearby lodge, if not those inside the building too.

The terrain was not ideal either. Victor had to stick to the trees as he circled around the sentinel.

Now the main half of that man's job had been done, he was more relaxed. Still on guard duty and yet, inevitably, he was not expecting a person like Victor to sneak up behind him.

A clubbing blow with the grip of the Taurus to the brainstem was enough to transform the otherwise straight-backed man into a collapsing mass of slack limbs that Victor caught before it could reach the wet ground. He dragged the man backwards into the darkness of the woods and dumped him where he would not be seen from the road.

Although not necessary to kill him, Victor had still needed to ensure he was out of action long enough to complete the contract. Maybe the blow to the brainstem would prove fatal by morning, or he might wake up days or even weeks in the future surrounded by overjoyed family members and surprised medical staff.

Either way, he had been given the chance to live.

A chance, Victor knew, no one would give him in return.

# SEVENTY-FIVE

Victor kept to the trees as he approached the north lodge. Aside from the inevitable crunch of his footsteps on the wet ground it was almost silent here so far away from the main lodge. When he paused, he heard the sound of gently lapping waves and a background murmur of traffic in the distance.

The isolated spur of land on which the lodge was nestled restricted the path he could take to reach it. He followed the curve of the narrow road until it opened out in front of the building. As he reached the edge of the treeline, he faced the modern half of the lodge where two bifolding glass walls of floor-to-ceiling windows faced the nearby shoreline. A stone patio area framed this corner of the lodge, on which stood a table and chairs and a hot tub. Orange light glowed from beneath the water of the hot tub and illuminated wisps of steam rising from the heated water into the chill air. Curved steps that followed the contour of the patio descended to a neatly trimmed lawn that encircled the building and separated it from both the loch and the woods.

The glass walls meant Victor could see inside to the large open-plan entertaining space. One of the walls had been folded in on itself and now the security guy standing on the patio pulled it shut. Maybe open only for Woodcroft or merely closed now it was dark. By the time Victor arrived, Woodcroft was already inside with two other men: one, another of the security team; the other had to be Gallier.

The fourth member of the security detail patrolled at a slow, steady pace sticking to the lawn, which was broken up by the occasional isolated tree whose trunk and low-hanging branches were wrapped with strings of fairy lights. They glowed yellow beyond the ambient illumination from inside the lodge.

With the shore to his right and the road to his left restricting his ability to manoeuvre around the property without revealing himself to the security guy on patrol, Victor had to wait until the man came close.

Scooping up a rock from the undergrowth, Victor tossed it at a nearby tree trunk.

It made a distinctive thump as it impacted before ricocheting away out of sight.

Immediately, the security guy spun on the spot and approached the treeline. Backlit by the house, his silhouette was distinct and obvious. In the darkness beneath the trees, Victor was invisible by contrast.

He tossed another stone, but this time at the lawn behind the man.

Again, he spun in response, giving his back to Victor, who sprang out from his hiding place, kicking the back of the man's knees while he snapped on a chokehold that pinched closed the carotids and compressed his windpipe.

His attempt to cry out was a muted, strained croaking nowhere near loud enough to reach across the lawn and into the house.

As he fell to his knees from the kick, Victor wrapped his legs around the man's hips to drag him down backwards into the undergrowth.

Unlike the sentinel, who had complied and dropped without a fight, this security guy was less amiable to Victor's means of persuasion. With a thick, muscular neck, the choke was taking longer than expected to shut off the blood supply to the man's brain. He managed to tuck his chin down so he could flare out those neck muscles to further prolong his consciousness. He fought back too, throwing hard elbows and reaching to claw at Victor's eyes.

In daylight, those inside the lodge might have seen the commotion in the undergrowth, but with a well-lit interior and the darkness outside, no one noticed.

Because of the noise of the security guy croaking and struggling, Victor did not hear the sound of an outboard motor, and only realised when the man had finally begun to weaken and slow in his attacks that a boat had moored at the shore just out of sight of the house.

It took another few seconds for the security guy to fall unconscious and for Victor to rise up from the ground. As with the first sentry, he needed to stay down, so Victor placed a kick to the temple before moving on.

Woodcroft was still conversing with Gallier inside the lodge. Two other security guys were still present as well, the one on the patio and one inside. The fifth was somewhere out of sight.

Victor also saw the dark silhouette of a figure crossing the lawn from the shore.

Madeline.

At this point it made no difference to the specifics of Victor's own contract if she killed Woodcroft, assuming the plans were indeed present inside the sports bag. He could not, however, know that for sure. About thirty metres from Victor's position, she was too far away to take any shot and hope to score a lethal hit before she made it to cover. Even at closer range, he would have stayed his hand. Those inside the lodge and anyone else nearby would hear and respond. If a firefight broke out, Gallier could escape before Victor reached him.

She headed to the far side of the lodge, no doubt to the front door on the north side of the building or maybe a window left open on the ground floor to facilitate her entry.

Victor called Raven and said, 'Get here fast.'

# SEVENTY-SIX

As Victor crossed the lawn, Woodcroft began laying out documents on the long, glass dining room table for Gallier to peruse. The handful of fairy-light-wrapped trees dotted across the lawn provided Victor with a little concealment, so the security guy on the patio did not see him straight away but it was temporary cover only. As soon as Victor emerged to cross the final stretch of grass he would be seen.

He had no choice.

Madeline was entering the building from the opposite side and would be coming up behind Woodcroft at any moment. Whether she killed him or not may have made no difference to Victor's contract, although he could not predict either her or Gallier's subsequent behaviour or that of the remaining security guys. Right now, Victor had an opportunity to complete his mission. He may not have another.

Victor picked his moment and dashed out from behind the last tree, his gun snapping up to draw a bead on the suited security guy on the patio.

The better illumination and difference in elevation meant the guy saw Victor within an instant, which was still far too late.

Two squeezes of the G2C's trigger put a double-tap to the man's forehead.

A spray of exit-wound blood painted a section of the nearby glass wall and the man dropped straight down in a heap next to the hot tub.

Victor hurried up the curved stone steps, gun sweeping fast to find the next threat – the fourth suited security guy – and shot him through the glass wall before the man had finished drawing his own pistol from an underarm holster.

Glass shattered and cracks spread out across the entire three-by-two-metre pane.

Because of the snapshot, the security guy didn't go down straight away. He staggered backwards, managing to draw a handgun – a Beretta G92X – so Victor squeezed the trigger three more times, blowing more holes through the glass wall.

The man was hit twice in the torso as he continued to stagger until he collided with the large kitchen island and tumbled backwards over it.

With the new bullet holes and the resulting spiderwebs of cracks, the massive windowpane collapsed under its own weight.

Huge glass shards rained down and exploded on both the stone patio and the hardwood flooring. Glittering fragments scattered across both.

Both Gallier and Woodcroft had hit the deck by then, the Frenchman out of sight on the far side of the kitchen island and Woodcroft having thrown himself to the shaggy rug that lay between two leather sofas.

'You,' he said, seeing Victor. 'What are you doing here ...? Who are you?'

'I'm your guardian angel.'

The soles of Victor's shoes crunched on the broken glass as he entered the building through the collapsed section of the glass wall.

The two large leather sofas faced each other in the centre of the entertaining space. From one, a huge wall-mounted television could be watched. From the other, the view was of the majestic loch. The long, glass dining table ran perpendicular to the sofas and parallel to the glass wall facing the loch.

As Woodcroft began to rise, Victor told him to, 'Stay down,' then added, 'The documents on the table. Are these the entirety of the plans you stole?'

'That's not exactly how I'd describe it.'

'I don't care how you'd describe it.' He approached the table to check they matched the descriptions supplied by the client. 'Are these the whole of it or not?'

'Why do you want it?'

'I don't. Is this all you stole or is there more to come?'

'It's not what you think,' the Englishman said. 'I'm not a traitor and I'm not a common thief.'

'Believe me when I say I never judge anyone's ethics. But if you don't answer my question right now I'll shoot out your joints one by one until you do.'

'That's everything,' the Englishman sighed.

Dark-stained hardwood flooring covered the entertaining area and extended into the hallway past the kitchen portion of the space. The fourth security guy was unmoving atop the island. Blood dripped in a steady flow from the marble countertop.

'Then, unlike that poor guy, you get to live through this if you keep out of my way and forget what I look like. Do you think you can do that?'

'The gunman wore a balaclava,' Woodcroft said, monotone and robotic. 'He had a Turkish accent.'

'Nice details,' Victor said, turning his attention to the island behind which Gallier cowered out of sight. 'By the way, the blonde woman you met earlier, Madeline, is here to kill you on Gallier's behalf.'

'You traitorous piece of shit,' Woodcroft yelled to the Frenchman.

'Language,' Victor told Woodcroft. 'I imagine Madeline is in earshot and deciding when to make her move, so if you see her, you have my permission to run.'

From behind the island, Gallier said, 'The people I work for are very powerful. You don't want them as your enemy. Trust me on that.'

'I've already been their enemy and here I am anyway,' Victor told him. 'I'm afraid you can't threaten me, you can't bribe me, and you absolutely cannot appeal to my good nature. The best thing you can do is stand up and accept your fate with a little dignity.'

'You were sent by Marcus Lambert, weren't you?'

Victor, beginning to circle the island, stopped.

'I'll take your silence as a yes,' Gallier continued. 'Wouldn't you like to know what kind of mess you're cleaning up? And how by cleaning up someone else's you've dropped yourself right in the middle of one of your own making?'

When Gallier rose up from his hiding place to face his assassin across the island, Victor found he could not squeeze the trigger and put two rounds through the Frenchman's skull as he had intended.

'Congratulations,' Victor said. 'You've bought yourself a stay of execution.'

'Once I've told you what you don't know,' Gallier said, unafraid and confident. 'You won't shoot me. In fact, you'll escort me out of here and wish me a pleasant journey.'

'Let's not get carried away.'

The Frenchman smiled. 'Let's.'

# SEVENTY-SEVEN

Aware the fifth security guy remained unaccounted for, as was Madeline, and Woodcroft was a Special Forces veteran, Victor stayed mobile. He kept his weapon up and his eyes on a continuous sweep. This portion of the building was a single floor, the glass walls rising up all the way to the roof to create a double-height space. A small, inner balcony looked down over the entertaining space, from where it joined the first floor and the second, original half of the lodge. That balcony and the hallway leading to the kitchen were the most obvious entry points, but as Victor had stepped through the destroyed section of glass wall, so could someone else.

'Marcus Lambert is working for the same people as I am,' Gallier explained. 'Only, he doesn't know it. Because I'm your client.'

'You hired me to kill you? I can't help but feel there are cheaper methods of suicide.'

'That part was not me,' he said, 'but Schulz, Harvey, the trio of contractors in Brussels. All those targets came from me. You were removing assets whose usefulness had expired. Did you really believe it was a coincidence Harvey recruited gunmen from Lambert's own company? The people I work for like to keep things neat, simple, so the cleaning up is equally tidy.'

'I don't believe you.'

'Because Lambert told you he was working for the Ministry of Defence? Did he give you a name? Any hint to the client's position in the government?' The Frenchman paused, reading Victor's expression. 'Ah, I see he didn't need to hide it from you because you never even asked, did you? My employees told me you were nothing more than a mercenary, only I didn't quite believe them until this very moment.'

Victor remained silent.

'Of course,' Gallier continued. 'My mistake was not realising my own usefulness had also expired. Naturally, my employers would use you once more because you are so very efficient at solving their problems. If you kill me, you'll continue being their pawn until they decide you too are no longer useful to their goals.'

'I've been doing this job a long time,' Victor told him. 'As I said to one of those contractors in Belgium, it's only ever a matter of time before a professional is turned on by a client or a broker. So, this isn't the sales pitch you think it is because what you're warning me against is my everyday reality. Do you have anything else to offer or shall we skip to the end?'

'They know you were in Ireland recently. They know why you were there.'

Often, Victor chose to remain silent lest he reveal his

thoughts. Now, he was silent because he could find no words. He had no response except a visceral feeling of dread deep inside him the likes of which he had never experienced before. He had known no fear since those first troubling months in the orphanage. Now, realising he had put Mother Maria at risk, a lifetime's worth of terror returned in a single, horrifying moment so intense it paralysed him.

'Lambert recruiting you was no accident,' Gallier continued, 'but he never knew where the orders were coming from because no one who works for us ever really knows. You compromised yourself the moment you agreed to work for him. He might be trustworthy as an employer, but he's never been in charge. Everything you've done for him, they've been watching. They realised a long time ago that it was not only a waste of resources trying to have you killed, it was a waste of your talents too. Now they know even you care about someone, you'll never be rid of them.'

When he had told Mother Maria it was rare to lose his temper he had recalled each of the times it had happened in recent years. He had not expected to lose it again so soon.

Victor found his voice at last.

'Tell me who they are otherwise I will force feed you slices of yourself until either your stomach explodes or you run out of flesh to swallow.'

'Did you not listen to a word I've said? I don't know where my orders come from any more than Lambert knows. But I can help you find out. If you lower your gun and allow me to walk out of here ... If you help me, if they think I'm dead, then there's a chance you can get close to them.'

In his anger, Victor's awareness of his surroundings was compromised.

He saw the fifth security guy emerging onto the inner balcony an instant too late, the man opening fire with a suppressed sub-machine gun before Victor could line up a shot.

# SEVENTY-EIGHT

The Heckler & Koch UMP spat out 9mm rounds at a rate of six hundred per minute that rained down from above in a violent storm as Victor ran for cover, splinters exploding upwards behind him from the hardwood floorboards.

He dived for the cover of the kitchen island at the far side from where the fourth security guy lay dead, sliding on the flooring as subsonic nine mils thumped into the marble countertop, sending debris and dust into the air.

At fully automatic, the UMP emptied an entire magazine in three seconds, Victor knew well, so the instant the storm of bullets ceased, he popped out of the cover of the island to see the suited gunman reloading on the balcony above.

He was fast with his reloading, pulling free the empty mag and discarding it in one smooth motion before slamming back in a fresh, full thirty-round magazine.

Victor could not have reloaded any quicker. However, aiming his gun and squeezing the trigger took a lot less time.

He fired off several bullets in rapid succession because he

saw the telltale bulk of body armour beneath the man's suit jacket.

He flinched with the impacts, although Victor could not see if any of his shots penetrated the vest.

However, the UMP fell from the man's grip as he grimaced and reached out to steady himself on the balustrade.

Whether any of Victor's bullets had reached a vital organ became an irrelevancy as the security guy failed to grab a hold and instead doubled over the balustrade and fell.

He struck the dining table head first and yet more glass shattered into thousands of pieces.

Victor rose out of his position at one end of the island to check the man was indeed dead and found the corpse had come to rest on the floor atop a bed of bloody documents.

Before he could return his attention to Gallier, Victor heard Madeline – emerging from the hallway behind him – say, 'Drop the pistol.'

He did as he was told, releasing the Taurus from his hand. No great loss since he had emptied the magazine into the final security guy. It crunched on the haze of broken glass littering the flooring.

'Turn around,' Madeline told him.

Victor obeyed, facing the woman, who had the familiar shape of an FN Five-seveN pointed his way.

'Good choice,' he told her.

The way Madeline held it suggested a competent familiarity with the weapon. She had her index finger inside the trigger guard so she was intending to shoot and there was nothing he could do to interfere when all it would take was a few pounds of pressure to send a high-velocity round his way.

Stepping further into the kitchen area from where she had been waiting out of sight in the hallway, she maintained enough distance to render any surprise attack an impossibility. In stressful situations, people tended to move too close to a potential threat for fear that, at range, they would miss. Madeline had trust in her abilities as a markswoman.

'Who are you and what the hell are you doing here?'

'I'm looking for my cat,' Victor said. 'She's gone missing. I don't suppose you've seen her, have you?'

Madeline stared with a wide-eyed expression of bemusement.

'What are you doing here, Maddy?' Woodcroft asked, as he rose to his feet. 'I was hoping seeing you at the conference was merely a coincidence.'

They were good, Victor thought, both of them. He had not even suspected they knew one another before now. At the bar earlier, they had pretended to be strangers with impressive and convincing ease.

'You stole top-secret plans,' she reminded him. 'What did you think was going to happen?'

'Why does it feel like I'm the only grown-up in the room?' Woodcroft's voice grew louder with frustration. 'I didn't steal anything that wasn't already stolen. Our own government leaked those plans before I even came across them. Don't you see? I'm trying to draw attention to the fact it's already out there. You think matters of national security are decided in Whitehall? Don't be so naïve. The politicians don't chose when we go to war, they declare war when they're told to do so. They leak our own top-secret intelligence to our enemies to embolden them to start their own conflicts, to annex land or to reignite old grievances. Why? Because then we respond. Because *NATO* responds. All I did was repurpose what was already out there so the powers that be could no longer turn a blind eye. That's why you've been sent, Maddy, because I made sure they had to respond. If they ignored that I have the plans, it's an admission that they want them out there. So, if you have to kill me to stop the next proxy war from escalating into World War 3 then please, for the love God, put a bullet through my skull.'

'Do it,' Gallier told her. 'He's a traitor. He betrayed your country. He deserves to die. You have orders ... follow them.'

Given the Frenchman's employers had sent Victor to kill him, Gallier would no longer care about fulfilling their designs, so this was an interesting play. Gallier saw Woodcroft either as an immediate threat to be removed or else an obstacle to the success of his ad hoc plan to fool his Consensus bosses as to his death.

Woodcroft laughed. 'You see, Maddy? This is exactly what I'm talking about. This man works for the people who want those wars so they can supply the bombs, so they can bid for the rebuilding contracts, so they can loan money to the aggressors and the defenders alike, so they use that money to buy their weapons to use against one another, so that when there are no more lives to end with those weapons, the survivors are left with debts that take generations to repay. You're only obeying orders, Maddy, I know. You were told to work with him and you didn't ask why. But you need to start questioning those orders before you end up in my shoes with the gun of someone you've worked with pointed at you.'

Victor watched as the young woman's gaze alternated between Woodcroft and Gallier, and he was deciding if, in that alternation, he might have time to dash to cover, but Madeline was shrewd. She identified that although the Englishman and the Frenchman, both of whom knew her and she knew in return, vied for her compliance, it was Victor who was the danger.

She fixed her gaze, and pointed her gun, at him alone. 'What is your role in all of this?'

Victor said, 'I'm only here to do a job. In fact, I'm not being paid, but that's by the by. Whatever the differences between the three of you, consider me Switzerland.'

'He's a killer,' Gallier told her. 'You can't trust anything he says.'

'Where's your friend?' Madeline asked Victor. 'The American woman.'

'Late,' Victor said.

He could see the deliberation in her young face. She had her orders but Woodcroft's plea had made an impact. She had been sent to kill, although she was no uncaring mercenary like Victor. As such, he had no idea what she was going to do. The longer she was deliberating, the better, however. She was the only one holding a gun, after all.

'It might be worth noting,' Victor said to her, 'that your groundskeeper partner had two dossiers in his car. One for Woodcroft and one for you.'

'What? How do you . . . ?'

'Once you'd completed your mission,' he continued, 'he would have killed you too on Gallier's orders.'

'You see, Maddy?' Woodcroft added. 'These people are snakes. Everything they do is venomous.'

'Is this true?' she asked the Frenchman.

He said to her, 'They'll say anything to stay alive. You know that.'

'When we were supposed to meet in Brussels and you didn't make it. You said those gunmen who opened fire in the café had been sent to kill you ... were they? Or was that just for show? So I'd do anything you asked of me to keep you safe?'

'Don't let them get into your head.'

'You know how I feel about you.' She paused. 'How I felt.'

She edged further into the room, maintaining a tactical distance from Victor, Gallier and Woodcroft. The three men all faced her from different positions. Where Victor stood, his back was to the glass walls and the lawn outside. Madeline's focus was already on him as the greatest threat, but as she neared, he realised she was no longer looking at him. She was looking past him.

Madeline was still too far away to make any kind of charge, so Victor glanced back over his shoulder, hoping that Raven was approaching, except by his calculations she was still several minutes away.

For a second, Victor was not sure what Madeline was looking at, until a figure passed through the weak yellow glow of one of the fairy-light-wrapped trees.

The silhouette of a man.

A huge man, striding across the lawn.

He picked up his pace as he neared the building and Victor saw the man had a pistol in his hand – a G92X, no doubt taken from one of the security guys. Madeline saw it too, but was too slow to process what she was seeing. Her mission already compromised by Victor's presence, another unaccounted-for person added yet another problem for her to solve.

She asked, 'Who is that?'

Neither Woodcroft nor Gallier was able to answer. At first, neither could Victor.

As the huge man drew closer, the orange light from the hot tub uplit him, and Victor saw him clearly.

A square, plain face. Dense eyebrows that almost met in the middle were one of two distinguishing features. The second was the nose that seemed a little too small for the face surrounding it, and Victor knew that nose had been reconstructed.

In that moment, Victor recognised the man, knew he had met him for the first time in the backstreets of Sofia, Bulgaria, before fighting for his life in a derelict factory on the outskirts of the city. Although Victor did not know the identity of the man, he knew he was an Israeli intelligence operative, an assassin in Mossad's feared kidon units. And while Victor had survived the encounter, he had only done so by the slimmest of margins after this man, this kidon assassin, had overpowered and outfought him. Then, Victor had been able to use his skills and his savagery to nullify the Israeli's size and strength. Now, however, the man was even bigger, even stronger, and there was a look in his eyes that Victor almost never saw because it showed an unbreakable resolve the likes of which had kept him alive several times before when by all rights he should have died.

It was Victor's will to live but in reverse.

This was the will to kill.

# SEVENTY-NINE

A woman and two men stood with Helyeph. Not Raven, this woman was someone else. Zahm recognised her as the woman who had embraced Raven in the lobby, although she did not seem so personable now. It made no difference to him who she was in the same way he did not know the two other men. They were nothing to him. All that mattered was vengeance.

Unlike the other three men, the woman held a gun she kept pointed at the killer. Whoever she was, she was no friend of his. Men like him had no friends.

Following Helyeph from the main lodge had been a test of Zahm's willpower the likes of which he had never experienced before. Upon seeing him for the first time in person in all these years Zahm had almost roared, such was the rage he felt.

But he had not waited all this time to fail. Unable to secure a weapon in the UK from Mossad agents as he would have done on a sanctioned mission, Zahm had needed to pick his moment with care.

Watching from a distance as the killer had dispatched a man in a suit standing at the mouth of a narrow road, Zahm had continued to wait. He had continued to wait until Helyeph had moved on before finding the still form of the suited man in the undergrowth. Zahm had taken the Beretta G92X from an underarm holster.

As Zahm crossed the lawn, the woman saw him and the killer turned to look his way.

For a moment, their gazes locked and Zahm saw that he was recognised.

*Good.*

Zahm needed Helyeph to understand why he was to die.

Understanding the intense violent focus in the Israeli's eyes, Victor was already diving to the floor before the other three people in the room knew what was about to happen. The G92X barked multiple times in rapid succession as the huge man opened fire. More holes blew through the glass walls and glittering shards clouded the air.

Madeline – the only one with a gun and therefore the most immediate threat – was hit three times in the centre of her chest and collapsed straight down, her Five-seveN falling from her grip and skidding along the wooden flooring before disappearing out of sight beneath one of the leather sofas.

Woodcroft, experienced and fast, threw himself down before bullets came his way, but the Israeli was a crack shot and Victor saw blood colour the Englishman's white shirt.

Gallier, furthest away and in proximity to the impenetrable cover of the island, ducked behind it unscathed, the bullets sent in his direction plugging holes in the kitchen cabinets instead of his torso.

Counting rounds and so knowing the Israeli's magazine was empty, Victor jumped up to his feet.

Stepping through the collapsed section of the glass wall, the Israeli said, 'You remember me, don't you?' as he released the spent mag.

With five metres between them, Victor could cover the distance before the kidon assassin had reloaded, but then what? The man was at least twenty-five kilos of solid mass heavier, and although Victor would bet on his own skills over strength alone, he knew from painful experience the Israeli was also a master combatant.

'I do,' Victor answered, and ran.

# EIGHTY

Zahm smiled as the killer turned and fled. Reloading a fresh magazine into the Beretta, Zahm gave chase. He did not want to execute Helyeph so impersonally with a gunshot in the back, but he could not allow his prey to escape either.

Squeezing the trigger, he tracked the killer as he dashed for the hallway that led off from the kitchen, the bullets punching holes in the wall beyond as they missed by mere millimetres, Helyeph as fast a target as he was a cowardly one.

Which was a relief.

Zahm could not bear the thought of his revenge ending too soon.

Heading into the hallway, Victor weaved as he ran from the gunfire. The layout of the lodge was unfamiliar, but there would be a front door, of course. Without a weapon, he was trusting to speed versus the assassin's accuracy with a pistol. Besides, escape was only a temporary respite. This Israeli had tracked him down here and might do so again.

Instead, Victor headed up the stairs as soon as he reached them, picturing the small balcony overlooking the entertainment area and the fifth security guy's dropped UMP.

He heard the thunderous sound of the Israeli's footsteps chasing him.

Reaching the landing, Victor sprinted down the short hallway, with doors to bedrooms and bathrooms leading off from it, to where the balcony lay.

As he reached the end of the hallway and saw the security guy's weapon lying on the floor of the balcony, Victor dropped into a slide to scoop up the SMG as he rolled over onto his stomach to face back and aim in the direction he had fled from to see the huge Israeli emerge at the top of the stairs.

Victor squeezed the trigger and nothing happened.

*Click.*

He squeezed again as the Israeli strode closer.

Again, nothing happened.

Made by Heckler & Koch, the UMP was the successor to the venerable MP5 and its variants, still in use because it was as reliable as sunrise. There was a greater chance of being struck by lightning than one misfiring and the UMP was no different.

But this was no misfire.

As Victor went to clear any jam in the chamber he saw the bullet hole in the weapon's housing and realised one of his many shots had hit the gun as well as the security guy. The SMG was damaged beyond repair, its precision internal engineering ruined.

The kidon assassin stalked closer, so wide he almost filled the hallway from wall to wall.

Victor didn't understand why he hadn't been shot already, but he was grateful he could at least stand up to meet his end instead of dying on the floor.

The Israeli stopped and watched as Victor discarded the ruined UMP and rose to his feet.

He had some dust from the marble countertop on the shoulders of his suit jacket and a few small fragments of glass glittering amid the threads of his trousers.

The kidon assassin seemed content to let Victor swipe the debris away. He watched him do so with the lifeless eyes of a shark.

Death had always been only one mistake away and yet Victor could not decipher what he had done wrong to lead to this moment, which was a frustration he had not anticipated. It had always seemed certain he would know the exact moment he set the wheels in motion that guaranteed his doom.

Now, his mind was blank.

'Why are you smiling?' the Israeli asked him.

'Because this is funny,' Victor answered. 'It's funny only now that I face the final bullet that I understand that nothing I've ever done actually matters.'

He had told Gallier to meet his fate with a little dignity because, when faced with inevitability, that was the only thing left over which there could be any control. Victor, who had spent the entirety of his adult life fighting to master every aspect of it, needed to die with a semblance of autonomy.

He brushed more glass dust from his jacket and straightened his back as his executioner approached.

'You think I'm going to shoot you?' the huge Israeli said as he thumbed the release to let the magazine fall from the

Beretta's grip. He proceeded to pull back the pistol's slide to eject the remaining round from the chamber before tossing the weapon away. 'You wish.'

# EIGHTY-ONE

Victor only had a second in which to be confused before the huge Israeli charged him. With nowhere to go except over the balustrade, Victor had no choice except to meet the charge head-on.

Although it was impossible to know what being hit by a train would feel like, now he had some idea at least.

The initial collision knocked the air from his lungs while simultaneously sending him straight down to the carpeted floor.

Before Victor could regain his breath, the assassin grabbed him with fistfuls of shirt and jacket and heaved him back up to standing – and then beyond – the strength of his enemy so great he had no trouble lifting Victor up off his feet.

The Israeli slammed him into one wall and then the one opposite and back again, the impacts jolting Victor as they shook picture frames from their hooks, which crashed down to the carpet.

Only the tearing of his clothes stopped the assault as Victor fell from the assassin's grip.

Despite the pain of being slammed back and forth, there was little actual damage and it gave Victor the opportunity to suck air back into his lungs as his paralysed diaphragm recovered.

He scrambled after the discarded Beretta. Unloaded, but if he could get to it and then to the magazine . . .

He barely made it a few steps before the Israeli took hold of him from behind, first ramming him sideways into a wall, then wrenching him away and hurling him to the floor.

Victor rolled over shoulder to shoulder to avoid a stamp, then backwards over his head to get out of the way of a follow-up kick.

Coming up to his feet, he slipped the assassin's looping punches, countering with short, rapid hooks of his own to his enemy's abdomen. The fifth hit was a brutal punch to the liver that stayed the Israeli's momentum and he shoved Victor away as he backed off a few steps to create distance and give himself a moment to recover.

Victor, not quite believing that his enemy could take such a shot and stay on his feet, was still glad of a pause in which to get back his breath.

He glanced around for anything that could be used as an improvised weapon. He would have killed for a heavy glass ashtray or candlestick. He would have been content with a broom. A lamp at a pinch.

Broken glass from the smashed picture frames was out of reach.

The hallway was bare and he dared not try any of the

adjoining bedrooms in case doing so only limited his options further. Here, at least, Victor had room to back-track and there were no corners in which the Israeli could trap him.

As the assassin attacked again, Victor whipped up a kick with his left leg, landing below the man's arms held up high to protect his head. Victor's shin slammed into the lower ribs and abdomen beneath the sternum, again right over the liver.

Instead of crumpling as anyone else would after a second such blow to the same vulnerable area, the Israeli merely grimaced, and for a moment wobbled on weakened knees, his elbows instinctively dropping to protect the site of impact, exposing his face in the process.

A second kick, powered by the ricocheting effect of the first foot landing back on the ground and bouncing immediately back, sailed over the assassin's lowered guard, Victor's shin striking across the side of his skull.

He should have toppled over like a felled tree, and yet somehow he remained standing.

Victor repeated the attack, his shin landing on the exact same point of the skull.

This time, the man's whole body slackened, his arms flopping loose at his sides, the strength of his stance melting away as his head was forced into a quick, sharp rotation, blood and sweat flicking away.

As Victor's left foot came down again and he bounced a hop for stability and to regain his balance, the huge Israeli was already shaking off the blow. Even without the disparity in size and strength, the man's rage, his hatred, was more powerful than any of Victor's strikes, no matter how accurately landed.

In a straight fight, there was only ever going to be one outcome.

However, now on the other side of the assassin, Victor turned to dash for the stairs.

The huge Israeli tackled him from behind, throwing himself into the back of Victor's legs, one shoulder colliding with the pits of his knees and his arms wrapping and trapping them together.

Victor tipped straight over, thrusting out his hands to break the fall and spare his face from slamming into the floor.

The assassin scrambled up his trapped legs and onto his back, knees either side of his waist. Victor flipped himself over the moment he felt his legs released, both to prevent the Israeli getting an arm around his throat and to better protect himself from whatever else might come next.

He threw up a guard and lurched his head from side to side as the assassin punched downwards with hammer fists at Victor's face, followed by elbows when the hammers failed to get through his defences.

The Israeli let all of his considerable weight sit across Victor's abdomen, his knees at either side of Victor's waist pressing inwards to both lock him in place and take away little of the crushing load.

The elbows had such incredible force behind them that even though Victor blocked and slipped so only glancing blows found their target, his head rattled from every impact.

If Victor didn't find a way out of this mount soon, he knew he never would.

'Thank you,' the Israeli said.

# EIGHTY-TWO

It was half a mile from the marina to the north lodge, and Raven had sprinted the entire distance. Ditching her hiding-in-plain-sight heels, she had run barefoot along asphalt paths and dirt tracks, and through woodland. Her feet were scuffed and cut in numerous places by the time she reached the lawn surrounding the building.

Exhausted, her face shimmering with sweat, she checked there was a round in the chamber of her pistol and thumbed off the safety catch.

The cool, soft grass of the lawn felt like heaven to the battered soles of her feet as she emerged from the treeline.

Ahead, she saw into the north lodge through its glass walls, one of which had partially collapsed. Moving at a tactical pace with her weapon up, she saw a huge quantity of broken glass, blood, bodies. It was carnage.

She noted three of the corpses were suited security personnel, one on the kitchen island, one in the debris of a smashed glass dining table, and the third on the terrace separating the lodge from the lawn. Woodcroft lay unmoving between two leather sofas. Madeline on the flooring near the kitchen area. Gallier was nowhere to be seen.

Dull thuds emanated from upstairs. Raven heard grunts and the unmistakable sounds of clubbing blows blocked and landed. Something – a vase or decorative plate, maybe – smashed. A door rattled. Heavy footsteps. Heavier stomps.

A large pool of blood surrounded Madeline, but Raven saw the woman was still alive, and hurried closer.

'Jesus,' she breathed, seeing the three bullet holes in the centre of her chest, which may have missed her heart and spared her an instant death but had nonetheless caused massive damage to her thoracic cavity.

Pale, Madeline was still lucid. Her eyes focused on Raven.

'I should ... have asked questions ...' the young woman wheezed. 'I didn't know ... who really ... gave me my orders.'

'Where is my friend?' Raven asked her. 'The man you met earlier tonight.'

'Upstairs ...' Her voice was almost inaudible now. 'My ... boat.'

'What about it?'

'Gallier ...'

'He's still alive? He's using your boat to escape?'

Madeline, eyes still open and her gaze locked on Raven, said nothing further.

She backtracked the way she had come, stepping out onto the terrace and gazing at the nearby shore and the loch beyond. She saw no boat but it had to be nearby, and south along the shoreline the way Madeline would have piloted it from the marina. It had to be close. Gallier was close.

Looking back over her shoulder, her gaze was drawn to the inner balcony overlooking the main entertaining area. From her position, Raven saw a section of the hallway beyond and her nameless partner slammed into a wall by the giant of a man she had seen in the lobby earlier. The dishevelled Levantine, who then threw savage punches that could not be parried, pummelling the man she called Jonathan to the floor and lifting him straight back to his feet to do the same thing all over again.

At this distance and with the limited view, it was impossible to make a shot without an almost equal chance of hitting her partner as his attacker. Although the man was much larger, the hallway was narrow so they were too close together and too much in constant motion to risk it, otherwise she would have taken it before dashing towards the shore.

Raven had a near-overwhelming desire to help her partner, her one ally who might also be the only friend she'd had since she began her crusade against the Consensus. But the Consensus were her enemy and defeating them her life's work. She had already sacrificed her own existence to fight them with everything she had, and she would keep fighting until either she killed them all or died in the process.

Sacrificing a friend was a price she had no choice but to pay.

# EIGHTY-THREE

Despite the huge amount of muscle mass the Israeli carried, his stamina was excellent, his conditioning on a par with that of the best endurance athletes in the world. Still, his fury was unsustainable. Every time a blocked or glancing blow dazed Victor, he recovered in seconds. In comparison, every time the assassin threw yet another strike with every ounce of strength behind it, it drained from a well that could not be replenished.

Inevitably, his pace had to slow.

The delay between one downward elbow and the next extended with every strike.

Despite the man's incredible strength and advantageous position, the drop in pace meant Victor had the time to shake off the jolt of disorientation that each impact created before the next one hit his guarding arms or glanced off his skull.

Then, he was able to time his enemy.

As the next elbow was sent down at Victor's face, he jerked

his head to one side to avoid it, then wrapped an arm around the Israeli's own before he could withdraw it, holding him in place with his balance compromised so that Victor could use his free arm to send a punch through the resulting gap in his attacker's defences.

The position of the assassin's head meant a closed fist was a bad idea, despite the inherent advantages in power and accuracy. The bones of Victor's fingers and hand were no match for a solid jaw that, hit head-on, would only recoil backwards so far before the anatomy of the head and neck prevented further motion. A hook was much kinder on the hand since the jawbone had more range of motion hit from side-on, meaning less rebound energy sent back into the fist. He had no room to hook here, the assassin's arms blocking any meaningful angles of attack. Not wanting to risk cracking knuckles or phalanges on the man's chin, Victor opted for an uppercut with the heel of his palm.

He struck the point of the assassin's chin, snapping his head up and back.

Feeling him weaken, Victor released the trapped arm, freeing up that hand to throw hooks into the man's flank, hitting the same section of the delicate lower ribs in a machine-gun rhythm.

The Israeli threw counter-attacks, made clumsy from the uppercut, which Victor slipped and parried before the Israeli scooted away to avoid more of the stinging hooks.

Victor rolled backwards over his head as soon as he was free, coming onto his knees, then hopping up to his feet.

Drenched in sweat and breathing hard, Victor readied himself.

His enemy grinned in return, showing two rows of pink, bloodstained teeth.

To Victor's surprise, the smile was no crazed, psychopathic grin. Almost impossible to believe, it looked as though the assassin was actually enjoying himself.

Zahm *was* enjoying himself. Despite a few good shots taken, he was feeling good. He had never imagined it would be easy. Helyeph, after all, had triumphed in their previous encounter. Now, that killer was looking hurt and exhausted. But he was not quitting. He was in this to the death, just like Zahm.

Had he not hated the man with such unyielding purity, Zahm would have respected that.

He thought of his dead people, his dead teammates, his dead friends. He could never respect the monster who had taken their lives.

Helyeph backtracked as Zahm stalked closer, trying to create distance in which to use his speed, which Zahm had to grudgingly admit was superior to his own. Not surprising given he outweighed his enemy by maybe as much as thirty kilos.

All that weight required oxygen to function, he knew, so the smaller man would have the better stamina by default. However, the killer was tired and injured, and he was slowing.

Zahm closed the distance as his enemy continued to shuffle backwards, waiting, timing and yet running out of room, the stairwell looming behind him.

To Zahm's surprise, the killer exploded forward, no longer counter-attacking but launching a full-blown assault of his own.

The speed and ferocity forced Zahm back, disorientating

him as kicks and punches slipped through his defences in rapid, relentless stabs of pain.

Such pain, however, was never going to stop him.

Nothing could stop him.

He let punches land, did not bother to check kicks, so he could get inside the man's reach and wrap his arms around the killer's thighs, powering forward as he lifted Helyeph from his feet to drive him into one of the bedroom doors, which shook and rattled with the impact before the killer fell down to the floor at the foot of the door.

So close together with their limbs entwined and the door behind restricting movement, Zahm was unable to engage a chokehold that would have finished his foe.

The upside of the door, however, was that the killer had nowhere to go. Bunched up between Zahm and the door, all Helyeph could do was block and parry the various strikes Zahm threw down at him. But he could not dodge them. He could not escape.

And, inevitably, more and more attacks found their way through the killer's defences, and with each one that landed those defences became weaker. He sank lower as Zahm battered him down.

Turtling to protect his face and head, Helyeph continued to absorb the barrage of punches, elbows, knee strikes and kicks.

Defending without attacking in return was akin to submitting, so perhaps the killer had finally given in to the hopelessness of his predicament, figuring all was lost. Or, perhaps, he was praying that Zahm would tire as he punched himself out.

Whether carefully considered plan or Hail Mary pass, it was not going to work.

Zahm heard Father's words as he exacted his vengeance.

*Do you now see the power of the resolve that hatred has gifted you?*

Yes, Zahm did see.

What he did not see, however, was the killer grabbing a shard of glass from one of the fallen picture frames, until he thrust it into Zahm's neck.

# EIGHTY-FOUR

The relentless attacks of the kidon assassin faltered.

A look in his eyes revealed his surprise, as though he had never considered his mortality was at stake as he tried to end Victor's own. The glass shard was too small to keep hold of after it pierced flesh – only as long as a disposable lighter and as wide as a finger – but the neck was the most vulnerable part of human anatomy for such a weapon.

Attacking with the shard in his right hand, Victor had stabbed the Israeli in the left side of his neck, aiming for the carotid. It had not been severed since no geyser of blood erupted from the wound, although the walls of that artery had been compromised. Victor could see the pulse thumping beneath the split of skin where the shard protruded. Capillary action drew a steady trickle of bright, arterial blood along the edge of the glass, from which it dripped down onto the Israeli's clothes.

In Victor's experience, such wounds, even if not immediately fatal, would pacify the most ferocious of enemies.

Here was no different.

The huge man retreated a step and brought a tentative palm up to the wound.

The difference was the placidity lasted mere seconds.

If the assassin had been determined before, now he was indomitable.

If he was enraged before, now he was berserk.

Victor, already prone and exhausted, was unprepared for the renewed assault.

He tried to scramble away, only for the Israeli to grab his ankles and drag him along the carpeted hallway towards the interior balcony. Victor tried to anchor himself on doorframes, only to find the strength of his grip was nowhere near enough to counter the tremendous power of his foe. There were no weapons to grab either, no other dagger-like shards of glass to utilise. Attempts to kick his way out of the assassin's vice-like grip were equally futile.

When they reached the balcony, the huge Israeli wrenched Victor up by the ankles, lifting him off the floor while at the same time spinning him around to hurl him over the balustrade.

# EIGHTY-FIVE

As Raven had deduced, the boat Madeline had piloted was moored just to the south of the north lodge's short beach. Raven had passed within ten metres of it on her way here, but with the intervening trees it had been as good as invisible. She approached as close to the shore as possible where there was less undergrowth and therefore less chance of making any noise and alerting Gallier to her presence.

Not that it would have made much difference, she realised, as she grew closer.

On the boat, he was clueless. She could see his panic and confusion as he alternated between trying to manually lower the engine into the water at the boat's stern and thumbing buttons at the elevated dashboard in the vessel's centre.

'You've never driven one before, have you?' Raven asked, drawing a bead on the Frenchman.

He froze, head swivelling in her direction.

Then his gaze lowered and she said, 'Nuh, uh,' as she shook her head.

She could not see what he was looking at, but it had to be a weapon set down while he tried to work out how to get the boat started.

'You have to turn on the power first,' she told him. 'There's a battery either just outside the console or in a cupboard beneath it. You need to turn it on before you can use the other controls. Then, you can lower the engine into the water. Then, you can drive it away from here.'

'What do you want?' he asked.

'World peace,' she said. 'And I mean it too. I want you people to stop lighting the fuse of conflicts and throwing gasoline onto the resulting fires.'

'I'm just a middleman.'

'That's what you always say. It's never anyone's fault, is it? The blame is always that of the next guy up the chain. The problem is, I can't get to him because he uses people like you. So, what is a girl to do? I can't cut off the head of the snake because I can't find it.'

'I told your partner, the man in the suit, that I can help him. I can help you too. The people I work for have betrayed me.'

'My heart bleeds.'

Gallier said, 'I have no reason to protect them any more and I'm not as ignorant as they believe. If you want that snake's head, I'm your only chance of getting to it.'

'I had a sneaking suspicion you were going to say something like that. At another time, in another place, I would have taken a gamble that you weren't bullshitting me. But I'm learning to pick my battles and take what victories I can along the way. Because I'm in this for the long haul. If I can't cut off the head of the snake then I'm going to slice and dice every piece of the body I can find.'

Gallier, realising that his fate was sealed, rolled the dice and went for his weapon.

Raven put a single bullet between his eyes.

# EIGHTY-SIX

In an ideal world, Victor would have landed on one of the luxuriously well-padded leather sofas. Failing that, the dead security guy who had smashed the glass dining table would have served as a makeshift cushion.

Instead, Victor struck the hardwood flooring.

Already dazed from the huge Israeli's pummelling blows, that slackness of limbs and slowness to respond saved Victor from greater injury. He hit the floor loose, instinctively rolling on impact to further disperse the energy that otherwise might have snapped bones.

He felt the cuts and stabs of many shards of broken glass as they penetrated his clothes and his flesh before he came to a stop somewhere between the sofas and the kitchen island.

His vision blurred, he saw only the hazy shape of Madeline's corpse nearby on the floor.

He lay on his back, chest heaving, every sensation a combination of pain and fatigue. No thoughts were possible as the room span in maddening, chaotic circles around him.

Nausea threatened to overwhelm him and he fought not to vomit.

Without thought, however, instinct remained.

Honed from a lifetime of violence, Victor required no conscious effort to push himself upright and attempt to stand as the floor shook beneath him, foretelling his enemy's imminent arrival.

Victor's hands seemed to shine as though they had an inner light until his vision began to improve and he saw they were embedded with pieces of glass that reflected the glow of lamps and ceiling fixtures. Unable to grip or brace with his hands, he fell back down to the floor.

After his vision, his wherewithal returned and he realised that Raven should have reached the north lodge by now.

'Where are you?' he whispered.

'Right here,' the Israeli answered.

The trickle of blood from the shard in his neck had worsened with the exertion of dragging, lifting and throwing Victor from the balcony. The Israeli's clothes were now sodden and glistening.

Still undeterred, he hauled Victor to his feet. 'Are you sorry yet?'

'For what?' Victor asked in return.

A headbutt turned his world black and he opened his eyes again to find the kidon assassin dragging him through the collapsed glass wall and onto the stone terrace outside. Victor glimpsed the lawn and the shore of the loch beyond, the dark waters lapping gently against the pebbles.

He saw the hot tub too and understood the Israeli's intentions.

Powerless to stop him, Victor felt himself lifted from the

stone paving of the terrace and had just enough time to suck in a lungful of air before his head was shoved beneath the surface of the hot tub's water.

Zahm thought about the men and women who had died by Helyeph's hand, as he forced the man down into the water. The Israeli had both of his huge hands gripping the back of the killer's head as his body was bent at the waist over the side of the hot tub. Unable to find any kind of purchase with his feet, Helyeph's legs splayed and kicked to no effect.

Far larger, far stronger, Zahm's position was insurmountable.

The killer fought the entire time, refusing to give up even when his doom was assured. All the man did was hasten the depletion of oxygen that could never be replaced.

To Zahm's surprise, there was no sense of triumph as he felt the man weaken. Instead, the Israeli was afraid he would return home only to find Father had already passed before he learned his favourite son had corrected his most grievous error. Or, even worse, as Zahm visited Father in hospital to tell him the news, the old man would no longer be able to comprehend his son's triumph and Father would die ignorant that his dead children had been avenged.

Helyeph continued to weaken, his attempts to fight back slowing, the kicking of his legs reduced to little more than an impotent dance.

Although he could not answer even if Zahm asked again, he knew that the killer was sorry now, finally, as he drowned, the water in the hot tub darkening with both of their blood mixing into a tempest of red.

When the first bullet hit him, Zahm barely felt it.

The second was an unmistakable stab of pain in his upper back akin to a wasp sting that he refused to heed. So focused on his mission to kill Helyeph, no amount of pain would stop him.

The third, however, buckled his legs and made him take notice of what was happening.

Releasing his hold on the killer, Zahm spun around to face back inside the building to see the shooter.

A man.

The one Zahm had shot and who had fallen down between the leather sofas. Dressed in a smart suit, he was almost as tall as Zahm, although with a more slender, athletic build. He was unsteady on his feet, the white shirt beneath the suit jacket was red with blood and his skin was pale. In his hand, he held an FN Five-seveN, the same gun the young woman had been pointing at Helyeph when Zahm had arrived.

The man squeezed the trigger again, this time missing, and Zahm realised for the three bullets that had found their mark in his massive back, others had not. The man was weak with blood loss, his marksmanship skills compromised.

Zahm charged.

He saw muzzle flashes and felt the sting of more bullets entering his flesh, but they did not slow him. The Five-seveN fired a small-calibre, high-velocity round that drilled neat holes deep into Zahm's body and yet, unless they struck a vital organ or critical blood vessel, did not have the stopping power to impede his momentum.

His will could not be broken while his body still functioned.

The last of the man's shots clipped him on the side of Zahm's skull before the pistol clicked empty.

Although not his true enemy, the man had interrupted Zahm's mission, and he enacted his rage at this injustice with brutal punches and elbow strikes that knocked the man to the floor.

Zahm found himself unsteady then and grimacing, the cumulative effect of several tiny bullet wounds robbing him of some of his balance and coordination.

By the time he had regained control of his movements and turned around, the killer had dragged himself out of the hot tub to face him once again. Helyeph, drenched with water, battered and half-drowned by Zahm, with many pieces of broken glass protruding from him, was not finished.

Zahm staggered towards him, expecting the killer to flee once more.

He did not.

He did not even fight back as Zahm grabbed hold of his throat in both hands to crush his windpipe and strangle him.

What Helyeph did do, however, was thrust out his forearm into Zahm's throat, impaling his own limb on the shard of glass sticking out of Zahm's neck that was otherwise too small to grip.

With a twist of his forearm, the killer wrenched out the shard and released the dam of Zahm's carotid artery.

The Israeli fought on, but a severed carotid only ended one way. The shard had plugged the wound and slowed the rate of blood loss down to a constant flow that now became a pressurised burst.

He roared when he saw the dark spread of crimson soak his clothes and understood what it meant. There was no fear in that exclamation, only frustration.

453

Victor prised himself from the man's faltering grip and created distance. The huge Israeli still had time before his inevitable demise to snap his spine or break his neck. Strength was always the last attribute to die, Victor knew well.

The Israeli became less coordinated in his attacks. The punches lost their snap. When he tried to grab hold of Victor, his fingers grasped only air. The blood loss drained the Israeli's stamina more with every passing second.

'*Coward.*'

Still backtracking, Victor said, 'The only thing my mother ever taught me was it's far better to be a live coward than a dead hero.'

Stumbling after him, the Israeli responded, 'I'm no hero.'

'You're no coward either. So, what are you?'

'A failure,' was the answer.

'Why are you even here? What did I do to you that made you so desperate to kill me you abandoned all instincts to protect yourself?'

'You ... know why.'

'I killed some of your people in Minsk a long time ago, I know. Then again in Sofia. I imagine one of them was your wife? Your brother?'

The Israeli seemed to laugh as he shook his head, but only made a croaking sound that coughed up blood. 'They were my people.'

Victor told him, 'They threw the first punch, not me. You threw the second. Now the third. Lesson number one: Don't pick a fight you can't win. If you miss the first then you'd better pay attention to number two: Know when it's time to take the L.'

'Others will follow ... will avenge me.'

'I don't think so. If others cared about me as much as you do then you wouldn't be here alone, would you?'

The Israeli dropped to his knees.

No longer any threat, Victor relocated his gaze to Woodcroft, who lay squirming on the floor, Madeline's empty Five-seveN still clutched in his hand.

'Thank you,' Victor told him. 'You saved my life.'

'An Englishman pays his debts. I'd be dead now had you not shown up earlier.' Woodcroft grunted. 'Although, I imagine death is less painful than this.'

'I'll call you an ambulance once I've left,' Victor said. 'So long as you remember to forget all about me.'

'Who needs a balaclava and a Turkish accent when you have your massive chum here.'

The Israeli, still on his knees and now shivering as blood loss caused his body temperature to plummet, said, 'Go ... to hell.'

'You're not the first person to say that to me in recent times,' Victor admitted. 'And you won't be the last. My fate is set in stone, I know. But right now, I'm alive and you're dying. That's what your hatred for me has done for you. I don't hate you for beating me half to death. I don't hate anyone because hate is worthless in this business. Does the fireman hate the blaze he puts out? Does the decorator think ill of the bare wall? Why would I be any different? Why are you? I should be brickwork to you when you've been paid to paint it. If that's how you'd thought, your friends and family could have been spared their grief.'

The Israeli's skin was as pale as the marble island.

Victor couldn't be sure what the man heard and understood.

The flow of blood from the Israeli's neck had slowed. On his knees, his body trembled as his oxygen-deprived brain continued to shut down essential processes in an effort to live a little longer.

His eyes stared into space.

'Father,' he wheezed. 'Forgive me.'

# PART FIVE

PART FIVE

# EIGHTY-SEVEN

Public transport, always a good tool with which to draw out shadows, was of limited use in Glasgow. Victor took the subway, picking a direction at random, sitting in the train's last car, but there was only a single line that ran in a loop through the city. Getting off at one station only gave him the choice of catching another train going in the exact same direction or heading back the opposite way. He wasn't going to lose any enemies like that, but maybe he could draw them out since his actions would be so unnatural that anyone mimicking them to keep with him would stand out by echoing his abnormal behaviour.

With a black eye, facial bruising and swelling, stitches, and bandages wrapped around both hands, he would be any shadow's easiest assignment whatever he did.

At the next station three other people joined the car: a pair of elderly women arm in arm, and a man who took a seat opposite Victor. This man wore jeans and a blue blazer. He had a leather satchel over one shoulder and held a newspaper folded up in one hand. About fifty, lean and strong. A middle-aged man who cared about his health or liked to look good, perhaps. Except Victor's keen assessing gaze found little discolorations on his ears, on the inner folds of cartilage. A fine job done by a talented surgeon, but there was only so much that could be done to repair cauliflower ears.

A common injury in mixed martial arts; many fighters never sought to have them repaired, proudly keeping them as a badge of honour. Unless, of course, the fighter wished to disguise his combat experience to appear less threatening to his targets when performing a contract.

When Victor left the train at the next station to wait on the platform for the following service, the man with the scarred ears remained on board.

His overland train south was running slow. Intermittent announcements over the public address system suggested signalling problems on the line, the cause of which was indecipherable in the tinny, distorted sound. Passengers who needed some station or other were told to move to one part of the train, the specifics also lost, causing nearby people to frown and shake their heads at one another. Victor did the same to blend in, but tried not to make eye contact with anyone lest they subsequently engage him in conversation.

A group of Italians, whom he took to be two families travelling together, had no idea what the announcement said, and he debated whether to translate for them until he realised he had heard no useful information to pass on.

\*

In London, he had a beer in a run-down bar near Euston

Station while he watched for shadows. At a booth nearby, a pale dog with fluffy hair was strewn across both its owner's lap and the table itself. The owner had fallen asleep after one too many. Perhaps the dog lay across both for comfort or maybe in a stealthy effort to inch closer to the torn-open bag of crisps that lay on the far side, finished except for a few crumbs. The dog's eyes swivelled to look Victor's way and he detected a hint of guilt in them.

'Don't worry,' he told it in a whisper, 'I don't snitch.'

The coffee shop was loud and chaotic even after nightfall. A line of four people stood at a respectful distance before the counter, at which a single guy worked the machine and the tills. Despite the chill drafting through the open door, his face glistened with perspiration. Overworked and underpaid, his expression was one of restrained exasperation. No doubt his co-workers were on their break or hadn't shown up for their shift, and he was dealing with increasingly irate customers who expected their caffeine served in a more timely manner.

Victor, who recognised his patience was beyond the norm, could not share the look the woman in front of him gave him, which said *How long does it take?*

Few things ever frustrated him and frustration wasn't going to summon more staff to the rescue or encourage the lone barista to make coffee faster. He could not make it any faster with a gun to his head.

A man joined the queue behind Victor, standing way too close for Victor's liking. Standing beyond arm's reach from the frustrated woman in front of him, Victor edged forward to create more space behind him.

The man behind him stepped into the resulting gap.

Although it was an invasion into Victor's personal space he found almost intolerable, the man was no threat. Even the most amateurish of professionals would attempt to maintain at least some distance.

After ordering and receiving his black americano, Victor sat down opposite Raven, who had a seat at a table in a far corner of the coffee shop.

She said, 'It's really not that bad. The swelling will be gone in a few days. The black eye will be concealable with make-up by tomorrow if you'd like me to show you how.'

'I'll let nature take its course.'

'I'm sorry,' she said. 'That I wasn't there to help. I'm sorry I went after Gallier instead.'

'You did what you had to do,' Victor said. 'I wish you hadn't done so, but I don't blame you for that.'

'I don't think I would be so forgiving if you had abandoned me in the same way.'

'Then let's say you owe me one if it makes you feel better.'

'It does.'

The first time they had seen one another since the night at the north lodge a week before, he saw a weariness in her gaze as well as concern.

She said, 'Don't you get sick of it?'

'Of what?'

'Of this,' she answered, voice a little hushed to ensure she would not be overheard by any of the other patrons. 'This life. The violence, the pain.'

'I find the latter is considerably reduced if I deliver more of the former to my enemies than they do to me in return.'

'I'm being serious here, you know?'

'I am too,' he said. 'What are you really trying to tell me?'

'I killed a kid,' she answered with a heavy exhalation. 'In Germany, when I went after Albrecht. Not literally a minor, obviously. But some young guy who was ... far too young.'

'I know you well enough to know he came after you and not the other way around. And I imagine whatever you did to him he was planning to do a lot worse if you had let him.'

She described what had happened in the safe house.

'Then I don't see what the problem is.'

'Because you're a computer,' she said. 'Everything is binary to you. Ones and zeroes, yes or no. Someone tries to kill you, you kill them and that's the sum total of your thought process. It's not like that for me. I wonder if he had a sister, if his girlfriend is pregnant. I think about his mom's tears when she finds out he's dead.'

'He should have thought about those tears,' Victor said. 'He caused them, not you. Had he never crossed your path then there would be no need for his mother to weep, would there?'

'I wish I could see it like that. I really do.'

'It's always more personal when it's up close,' he said. 'When you have to use your hands. It's been a while since you used anything but a gun, hasn't it?'

She nodded. 'I suppose it has been, although that's not something I had considered until now.' She paused to consider it more. 'So you're saying it affects you more like that? When it's ... up close and personal? And I mean the literal you as opposed to the collective, because I thought none of this affected you even a little bit.'

He saw the hope in her eyes, in the way she looked up at him. He saw the longing in her expression for him to share this feeling of hers. If he could relate then it would help

Raven get through it. Victor considered lying to her in an effort to provide a little comfort, but for all his ability to deceive, when it came to some topics, he just could not be convincing.

'No,' he said. 'It doesn't affect me more. It doesn't affect me at all. But maybe once it did, a long time ago. I remember back when I still wore a uniform I heard the other guys who had found themselves in such situations talking like you are now. Guys who had only ever seen an enemy drop through an optic at fifty yards who then found themselves jumped in a house they were clearing and suddenly with no other choice except to reach for a blade for the first time. Some of them could handle it, it made no difference to them, but they were the tiny minority. For most, it was hard. Even for the ones who found it easier than the others it had an impact.'

'I choked him out,' she said and he could see in her vacant expression that she was visualising the moment. 'I could have left him unconscious ... but I didn't. Once he was out, it was over. He was no threat at that point, was he?'

'Temporarily,' Victor answered. 'You spare him then and maybe his eyes open thirty seconds later and he snaps a rear naked choke on you from behind when you're not looking. You think he would have quit when you went limp? Of course not. He also wouldn't now be torturing himself about the decisions he made when his life was on the line.'

'He tapped,' she said. 'He couldn't speak with my arm around his throat. Tapping was his way, the only way, of begging for mercy.'

'Which he would not have granted you in return, Constance. You know that.'

'I can't know for sure.'

464

'That way madness lies,' he told her. 'We don't think the same, I know, we don't operate the same. But we both understand how the world we live in operates. Take it from me, hired killers aren't known for their mercy, especially when it comes to their targets. I wouldn't have spared you in that moment and neither would he have done so.'

'You didn't kill me,' she countered. 'In Bucharest. I was your target, wasn't I? Just like Schulz. You didn't put a bullet through my brains, did you? And I was your target. I, however, still killed the kid, who wasn't mine.' She looked away for a moment. 'I always wondered what happened to you to make you so cold and what it would take for me to fall as low. Now I think I'm already falling, that I've been falling for a while and I just didn't realise.'

'Thankfully I'm not so easily insulted when it comes to my humanity or lack thereof,' he said with a raised eyebrow. 'And you weren't my target. Marion Ysiv was my target, and you were simply pretending to be her.'

'That's not true. Yes, I wasn't the real Marion, but the person your client wanted to kill was the Marion Ysiv I was pretending to be. The real version wasn't dealing with Schulz, I was.'

'We have history,' Victor said. 'We haven't always been on the same side, granted, but you helped me when I needed help, and even if we didn't part on the best terms, your prior actions helped save my life. Hence, I find it's not so easy to take yours in return.'

She listened.

'Someone told me recently that even though everything else can be taken from us, our honour cannot be, it can only be given away willingly.' He paused, then said, 'I thought I'd already done that a long time ago. I guess that maybe I have a little left, after all.'

'Likewise, I was wrong to think this time would be any different and I could actually hurt the Consensus. By killing Gallier, I even helped them achieve their goals, didn't I? Back to the drawing board for me then. What about your broker? What are you going to do now you know he was working for the Consensus?'

'He didn't know,' Victor answered. 'And although ignorance is no defence, I think it's better for everyone concerned if the Consensus believe I'm none the wiser. Now Gallier is dead they'll think they've covered their tracks and the Ministry of Defence believe they've sent a message to other would-be thieves and their buyers.'

'Did Woodcroft make it?'

'As far as I'm aware, but I'm not going to swing by the hospital to check.' He stood. 'Besides, I'm flying out in the morning and we have unfinished business. Come on, let's make a move.'

'Where are we going?' she asked.

'My hotel is nearby.'

Raven smiled. 'Finally.'

# EIGHTY-EIGHT

She watched them drink coffee. She watched them leave.

On appearances, they could be any professional couple. They had an obvious chemistry, and yet it was restrained. To anyone else they might have seemed like colleagues embarking on an office romance. Bankers getting frisky, maybe. Given this was the centre of London where every other person worked for a financial institution, it would be an easy mistake to make.

She knew better.

It had been a long time since she had ventured into the field like this and she found that she had missed the exhilaration.

Although the woman had a name, her partner did not. At least, none anyone knew. Constance Stone, otherwise known as Raven, did not enjoy the anonymity of the man with whom she had drank coffee. Who was he? Who was he *really*?

Karmia Elkayam did not know ... yet. It was a frustration, and yet a temporary one. She had seen him before six years ago in Sophia, Bulgaria. He had shot her – although her body armour had saved her – and she had shot at him in return as he fled into the night after ripping the end off Zahm's nose.

Poor Ari, who could not let go of the failures of that night.

He had never understood the theatrics that Father had employed to manipulate his operatives and she had never had the heart to explain to him how he had been nothing more than a tool in Father's eyes. At least, that was how she saw it. She could not conceive that Father's tears had been genuine because she would never send her own children – biological or surrogate – into danger.

She found her eyes filling with tears.

She would sit shiva for both.

Although Helyeph had seen her before, she saw that he did not look at her twice. Six years was a long time for anyone and Elkayam knew how to avoid attention. She had been the only trainee to ever succeed in Father's first-day test to remain undetected when following one of his veterans.

It was not the way she acted, or the way she operated.

It was the way she never showed a reaction.

That was how shadows gave themselves away. They were always so concerned a target would notice them that they could not stop themselves reacting when that target turned their attention the shadow's way. Like tapping a kneecap with a rubber hammer, a reflex occurred. Maybe subtle, maybe not, that reflex was there anyway and an observant target might notice.

Karmia Elkayam never reacted.

On an assignment, should a bomb detonate on the same street, she would not even blink. That had been her talent.

No use in the hallways and briefing rooms of Mossad's headquarters, but it had been invaluable in the field.

When the killer walked passed her so close that she felt the disturbance in the air by her cheek, he had no idea they had once been mortal enemies.

She still had it, she found. Although there had never been any doubt.

Once the killer and Raven had left the coffee shop, she called Herzog.

He asked, 'Are you satisfied now?'

'We have lost an irreplaceable operative,' she answered. 'So, no. I'm not satisfied.'

'And yet, as you predicted, the British have not identified him as one of us. It was quite the mess in Scotland and no doubt it will be a long time, if ever, until they figure out what happened and why.'

She said, 'Ari needs to be returned to Israel. I don't care how you manage it, I don't care what you tell the Brits, but it must happen.'

'I believe you are forgetting you were meant to prevent this very outcome,' Herzog reminded her. 'However, he was one of us so I will ensure he is laid to rest as one of us.'

She said, 'Good.'

'And what of the killer?' he asked. 'What happens now?'

'He shall work for us going forward,' Elkayam said with supreme confidence. 'He simply doesn't know it yet.'

# EIGHTY-NINE

Victor watched the five men huddled behind the rear of the vehicle. Anxious faces. Worried expressions. Short, curt sentences exchanged. Too far away for anyone to hear, they were in too much of a huddle for Victor to read all of their lips, but he only had to read a few words to understand the problem.

To his surprise, he did not hesitate.

'Man down?' he asked, approaching.

All five looked his way.

One said, 'Steve's throwing up behind the chapel.'

'Food poisoning,' another explained. 'He says he can still do it once he's cleaned himself up, only I can't see it happening.'

'I'll step in,' Victor said.

All five looked relieved.

'You legend. Thanks.'

They didn't ask who he was, they simply directed him to where he needed to stand based on height – third row, right-hand side – and the rest was self-explanatory.

They dragged out the casket from the back of the hearse. He followed the instructions so they lifted as one.

Victor matched their pace and followed the directions given to him. It was not something he had ever done before and until moments ago it was something he had never imagined he would ever do.

A break of protocol.

A cardinal sin of his professionalism to allow himself to be so vulnerable.

It was unlikely, if not impossible given recent events, that anyone could have followed him here – he had burned through every last penny of the payments for his recent contracts to pay for more flawless legends composed at speed to be able to attend – so when he had the sensation of being watched, he tried to ignore it. Gallier had claimed the Consensus knew Victor had been to Ireland and why, and at the time he had believed it, but the Frenchman's claims had lacked specifics. Maybe the Consensus had known about the ferry from Liverpool Victor had taken and Gallier used that one fact to make a gamble when his back was against the wall. A clever play that had stayed Victor's hand.

Alternatively, if it had been no play and they had indeed managed to track him to the nursing home, what the Consensus had discovered was of no value to them any longer.

Nature had taken its course.

And, if the new legends were not as flawless as Victor believed, and representatives of the Consensus or other enemies had shadowed him here, then he had to die someday. Maybe a professional drawing a bead on him right now would have the decency to hold their fire for a few minutes. Or, if not, and they took the shot regardless, then at least Victor's final moments would be spent doing something worthy for once.

When they set the casket down on the lowering device over the grave, the other five men were red-faced and breathing hard, so Victor pretended it had been comparably challenging for him too.

'Good on ya,' one of them told him, giving him a pat of gratitude on the arm, and for once Victor did not have to fight the urge to respond with extreme violence to such a harmless moment of physical contact.

He felt watched once more.

A stranger to everyone here, it made sense that some people would wonder about him. Who was he? Who was he to Mother Maria?

When the casket was in the ground and the funeral over, mourners filed out.

The order of service listed the details of the wake, which was being held in a nearby pub. Not every mourner would attend and no one knew him here so he needed no excuses to slip away early and go back to his existence. Still, he couldn't bring himself to leave. He was the last to arrive at the wake because he had made sure to be the last. If he was breaking protocol to such a severe extent he could at least maintain some small sense of tactical behaviour.

One half of the pub had been reserved for the wake, he found. The other half had few patrons and Victor wondered if their dour faces were a direct result of the nearby event. Hard to crack a joke with black-clad mourners nearby.

Victor could not remember the last time he had worn a black suit. He felt uncomfortable inside it, knowing he looked too good, the suit only emphasising his dark hair and eyes, both the leanness and athleticism of his physique. His intention had been to rent one from the cheapest high-street outlet he could find in the hope that the substandard quality, combined with his typical preference for an oversized garment, would lessen his overall appearance. But at the eleventh hour he had realised how disrespectful that was to the person who had done so much for him. Instead, he had paid a Savile Row tailor triple to make him a bespoke two-piece black suit – that fitted him as it should – in a traditional English cut in less than a week. A similarly custom white Egyptian cotton shirt with herringbone weave, black Oxfords and black woven silk tie finished the look.

He could not have looked more like an assassin cliché if he tried.

By the time he had joined the wake, some mourners had removed their ties and Victor resisted the urge to do the same. Another vulnerability, and yet it felt a small sacrifice to pay his proper respects.

Although he had learned how to make small talk and how to converse with strangers, he had no frame of reference for his current situation. He did not want to lie, and yet he could not tell the truth either.

'I knew her when I was very young,' he said, or variations of it, always immediately asking questions to keep the conversation away from himself. Thankfully, people always seemed to prefer talking about themselves than they did others.

Platters of finger food had been positioned on tables before he arrived and many mourners were eating. He saw not everyone did, so it felt appropriate to stick to sparkling water. There were several types of sandwiches, lemon drizzle cake and Black Forest gateau, numerous biscuits, scones and bite-sized sausage rolls.

He decided it would be no disrespect to Mother Maria's memory to take his leave when the number of mourners had fallen by half.

Once more he felt watched, which again was to be expected now he was in such close proximity with the other mourners, but it was different. He was not by himself any longer. He was mingling and conversing, not a stranger in the same sense he had been in the cemetery.

Returning from the bar with a second water, he passed one of the tables with the platters of food. Two hours into the wake, the platters were not going to last much longer. Had they been poisoned, most of the mourners would now be dead or showing the first signs of a slow, painful demise.

Still, there were only so many protocols Victor was prepared to break in a single afternoon.

'You should tuck in while you still can,' a man suggested as he assembled a plate.

Victor said, 'I've eaten already.'

'It's all home-made,' the man said, looking up and presenting one of the small sausage rolls. 'All of it. Not a single thing was bought in a shop.'

The man was in his mid to late thirties. A little shorter, a little rounder. There was nothing immediately threatening about him, despite his assassin's cosplay of white shirt and black suit.

Regardless, Victor felt the compulsion to widen his stance a little.

'How did you know her?' the man asked, popping the sausage roll into his mouth.

Sticking to his vague cover story, Victor answered, 'I knew her a long time ago, when I was a boy.'

Chewing the sausage roll, the man raised a finger until he had swallowed, then said, 'Same.'

The other mourners began to fade from Victor's consciousness.

The pub became quiet around him.

The man continued, saying, 'I noticed you earlier and was wondering if we'd get a chance to talk.'

Now Victor understood why he had felt so watched.

The man asked, 'You're from the orphanage, right?'

No amount of controlled breathing could prevent Victor's heart rate shooting up. The rest of the world ceased to exist as he found himself in a void of nothingness except for the man with whom he was speaking.

'I don't recognise you – I mean, we're grown men now, of course we're going to look different – but I'm sure you were there. We're about the same age, so I bet we were there at the same time.'

'I think you must have me confused with someone else,' Victor managed to say in response.

'I know some of us don't like to talk about that kind of stuff, but we have nothing to be embarrassed about. You don't have to be either. I'm obviously not going to judge you, am I?'

It was all Victor could do to maintain his composure and not flee at speed, and yet he had to retreat – this was one battle for which he had no skills – backing off a step, saying, 'I'm afraid you're mistaken.'

The man shrugged, reaching for another sausage roll. 'If you say so. You do you. I'm not ashamed of growing up in a place like that.' Then, as Victor continued to back away, added, 'Take care.'

Managing to turn around without collapsing, Victor set his water down on the table and headed for the door.

But the man wasn't finished, continuing to speak, saying, 'In fact, I'm the opposite of ashamed. I'm proud of growing up there. And I'm so, *so* grateful for those like Mother Maria, who was there for us when no one else wanted to be ... Aren't you?'

Because he would never disrespect her memory, Victor halted his retreat to admit, 'Yes, I'm incredibly grateful.'

He turned back to see the man nodding to himself.

'I knew I recognised you. We're men now, we've changed a lot in twenty-plus years, but the eyes never change, do they?'

Victor stepped closer. 'I guess not.'

'Nerdy kid who liked trains, yeah?'

'I still like trains.'

'Didn't you use to have an accent?'

'Yes. Didn't you use to beat me up?'

A flush of embarrassment. 'Oh ... I ... well ... yeah ... I guess I did, I ... used to have a lot of anger issues back then. Away from home ... tough childhood, you know? Of course you know. Anyway, I'm really sorry about it.'

'No harm, no foul. It was a long time ago, so don't sweat it.'

'I don't think I'd be so forgiving if it was the other way around. You're a far better man than me.'

Victor said, 'I seriously doubt that.'

'I was such a bully, wasn't I? Man, I'm so disgusted with myself ... I wish I could take it back. Tell you what, do you want to take a free shot to even the score? I won't mind.' He stood square on, raising up his chin like a target. 'I'm not joking, I swear. Hard as you can. If anything, it'd make me feel a whole lot better.'

Again, Victor said, 'I seriously doubt that.'

'Your call.' The man showed his palms to surrender the idea. Then he asked, 'What have you been doing with yourself all these years?'

'Working, mostly. But I'd prefer not to talk about my job right now.'

The man nodded. 'I understand. Our mundane everyday experiences feel so incredibly trivial at a time like this, don't they? I wonder if we need to be adjacent to death, to someone dying, to appreciate we're alive at all.'

'I've often thought the same,' Victor told him.

'I don't have to make a move for a while . . . Fancy getting a drink and sitting down for a chat?' The man glanced around the room. 'I don't know anyone else here and I want to talk about Mother Maria with someone who actually knew her in the same way I did. If you'd be up for it, of course?'

Victor said, 'I'd like that very much.'

# ACKNOWLEDGEMENTS

I've been writing about Victor for well over a decade at this point, and while I know him like the back of my hand, I somehow never seem to know what he will do next. I hope that keeps the books as exciting and unpredictable to read as they are to write, but it also means the challenge of coming up with something new each time that builds upon every story that came before it.

Therefore, it's becoming more and more important to have the help and support of my agent, James Wills, my editor, Ed Wood, and the various talented people who cast their gazes over the manuscript at different stages of its completion, including Nithya Rae, Lynn Brown and Frances Rooney. You all have my heartfelt thanks. Similarly, every friend, relation and random stranger who eases the process by offering suggestions, advice, comments, questions, or even just nodding along as I waffle, has my gratitude. In particular, the help of Bodo Pfündl and Charlie Kawcyzynski has proved invaluable.

And, as always, thank you to every reader who has been kind enough to send this author an email or direct message. Even if sometimes I'm sadly too busy to reply, they are always welcome.

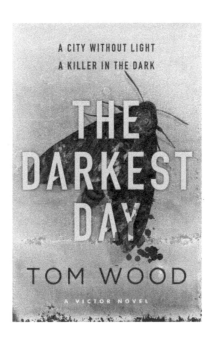

A CITY WITHOUT LIGHT
A KILLER IN THE DARK

THE DARKEST DAY

TOM WOOD

A VICTOR NOVEL

*He is darkness. She wants him dead.*
*In a city starved of light, she might just succeed.*

She moves like a shadow; she kills silently: Raven.
This elegant assassin has been on the run for years.
This time though, she has picked the wrong target.

The hitman known only as 'Victor' is as paranoid as
he is merciless, and is no stranger to being hunted.
He tracks his would-be killer across the globe, aiming
not only to neutralise the threat, but to discover who
wants him dead. The trail leads to New York ...

And then the lights go out.

Over twelve hours of unremitting darkness, Manhattan
dissolves into chaos. Amid looting, conspiracy and
blackout, Victor and Raven play a vicious game of
cat and mouse that the city will never forget.

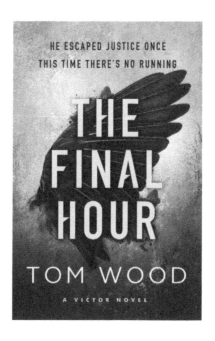

HE ESCAPED JUSTICE ONCE
THIS TIME THERE'S NO RUNNING

# THE FINAL HOUR

## TOM WOOD

A VICTOR NOVEL

Former CIA agent Antonio Alvarez has been
tracking a vicious murderer for years, a nameless
hitman responsible for numerous homicides.

Once, the Agency deflected him away from
his search, but now promotion has given
him a second chance to right the past.

Only problem is, the killer has vanished.

Thousands of miles away, the professional known as
Victor has stopped working – recently he began to care;
he made mistakes. But there's another assassin, Raven,
who needs his help – and she is hard to refuse . . .

# DISCOVER THE MAN BEHIND THE ACTION
# TOM WOOD

© Charlie Hopkinson